Praise for Previous Bc

'A very impressive set of stories. Perfect for dark and cold evenings as we enter the more eerie part of the year. Strongly recommended!'
Runalong The Shelves on *Darkness Beckons*

'*Close to Midnight* illustrates what great shape the genre of horror is in... If you're a reader who enjoys quality fiction of the dark kind, this is a series to be cherished. There isn't a bad story in the entire book.'
Stephen Bacon

'*Close to Midnight* is a very solid collection of horror featuring stories of varied themes and content, and yet they all feel very comfortable inside the spine of one book. Worth a look if you like chills down your spine late at night as you lie in bed reading.'
Horror DNA

'Morris has assembled an especially strong group of stories with dazzling, diverse approaches to horror. Highly recommended.'
Cemetery Dance on *Close to Midnight*

'If you love short and sometimes shocking horror stories, you can't go wrong with this collection!'
On the Shelf Reviews on *Close to Midnight*

'I'm impressed with the imagination and variety coming from the writers. *Beyond the Veil* is another happy clump of ickiness...and I mean that in a good way.'
The Happy Horror Writer

A FLAME TREE
BOOK OF HORROR

ELEMENTAL FORCES

An Anthology of New Short Stories

Edited by Mark Morris

This is a **FLAME TREE PRESS** book

Stories by modern authors are subject to international copyright law, and are licensed for publication in this volume.

FLAME TREE PRESS
6 Melbray Mews, London, SW6 3NS, UK
flametreepress.com

US sales, distribution and warehouse:
Simon & Schuster
simonandschuster.biz

UK distribution and warehouse:
Hachette UK Distribution
hukdcustomerservice@hachette.co.uk

Publisher's Note: This is a work of fiction. Names, characters, places, and incidents are a product of the authors' imaginations. Locales and public names are sometimes used for atmospheric purposes. Any resemblance to actual people, living or dead, or to businesses, companies, events, institutions, or locales is completely coincidental.

Thanks to the Flame Tree Press team.

The cover is created by Flame Tree Studio with elements courtesy of Shutterstock.com and: kittirat roekburi and Peangdao.
The font families used are Avenir and Bembo.

Flame Tree Press is an imprint of Flame Tree Publishing Ltd
flametreepublishing.com

A copy of the CIP data for this book is available from the British Library and the Library of Congress.

1 3 5 7 9 8 6 4 2

HB ISBN: 978-1-78758-867-7
US PB ISBN: 978-1-78758-865-3
UK PB ISBN: 978-1-78758-866-0
ebook ISBN: 978-1-78758-869-1

Printed and bound in Great Britain by Clays Ltd, Elcograf S.p.A.

A FLAME TREE
BOOK OF HORROR

ELEMENTAL
FORCES

An Anthology of New Short Stories

Edited by Mark Morris

FLAME TREE PRESS
London & New York

CONTENTS

INTRODUCTION

Mark Morris

In 1980 my friend Ramsey Campbell, who has been writing horror fiction since before I was born, edited two volumes of an anthology called *New Terrors*, which I first read as a single-volume 650-page Pan paperback in 1985, under the umbrella title *New Terrors Omnibus*.

Prior to writing my own introduction to this latest volume of a series that has become unofficially known as the ABC of Horror (if you're not sure why, the titles of the first five volumes, viewed in order, provide a clue), I decided to reread Ramsey's introduction to the pair of anthologies he edited over forty years ago.

I did this because, at the time of its publication, *New Terrors* was billed as a book containing stories that explored contemporary fears, and I was curious to discover how much, or how little, our fears as a species might have shifted in the intervening decades.

Since 1980, of course, the world has changed a great deal, most notably in terms of technological advancement. Forty years ago, there was no internet and no social media, and mobile phones, or something similar to them, were only to be found in *Star Trek*. As a result, communication was far slower, and the idea of acquiring pretty much whatever you needed or wanted simply by pressing a few buttons from the comfort of your armchair was, similarly, the stuff of science fiction.

Medical innovations, too, have come on in leaps and bounds since 1980, as a result of which people are living longer, healthier lives, and this despite our increasing consumption of 'fast' or processed foods, and our tendency to have far more sedentary lifestyles than our predecessors.

However, everything has a price, and for every positive action there seems to be an equal and opposite reaction. Medical advancement, for instance, has led to massive over-population, which in turn has led to an increasingly greater demand on global resources, ultimately resulting in ecological imbalance and climate crisis. Similarly, while the internet and social media might have increased global knowledge and awareness, and improved certain aspects of communication and socialisation, it has also, conversely, encouraged competitiveness and thus sparked a mental health crisis, fuelled the rise of ignorance through misinformation, and in the worst instances created a climate whereby mob mentality and cyber-bullying can run rife.

None of these 'modern' issues – and you can add further terror-inducing incidents to the mix, such as the horror of 9/11, and the isolating uncertainty of a global pandemic – were around in 1980... so has all of this had an effect on the kinds of stories that modern practitioners of horror tell today?

Well... yes and no. Four decades ago, Ramsey Campbell wrote, "Why do people still read tales of terror? This is probably the hardest question in the field. 'Still' usually means either that the psychologists have exorcised our terrors or that 'reality' (nuclear and post-nuclear warfare, terrorism, and so on) is so disturbing that it makes the tale of terror redundant. I believe this book is an answer in itself, but my own response would be: some of the stories... deal with states of being which are necessarily inexplicable, while the more openly horrific stories deal with fears and obsessions (which have certainly not been cleared away by science – indeed, science has created some of them) in a form sufficiently metaphorical to make them bearable to confront."

What strikes me about that paragraph is that it is just as relevant today as it was forty years ago. Okay, so the genre has expanded and diversified, both in terms of its practitioners, and in the subjects they explore (gender issues, for instance, are central to many of the most important and influential works being produced within the genre today – for examples, check out the work of writers like Alison Rumfitt, Gretchen Felker-Martin, Eric LaRocca, Hailey Piper, and many more), but fundamentally our fears – of death, illness, pain, alienation, victimisation, and that big one (which in fact plays a major part in many of the previously mentioned fears), the *unknown* – are the same as they ever were. In response to an article in the UK newspaper, the *Guardian*, which talks about the surge in popularity of horror fiction, and suggests that this is due to the increasingly political nature of horror, renowned screenwriter and horror author Stephen Volk suggests that "the eternal themes of horror – including, crucially, transgression – that reflect 'real world anxieties' remain the same. It's what horror does and always has."

I agree. The world constantly changes, and horror fiction changes with it – but at its core, our fears as human beings are the same as they ever were. That's why, among these pages, with authors given free rein to indulge their imaginations, you'll find fears a-plenty. Folk horror tales like Paul Finch's 'Jack-a-Lent' and Tim Major's 'The Scarecrow Festival' suggest there is terror and mystery to be found in deeply embedded traditions. Laurel Hightower's 'The Call of the Deep', Kurt Newton's 'The Daughters of Canaan', and Jim Horlock's 'They Eat the Rest' show us that as a race we remain unsettled by the idea that our thousands of years of evolution and 'civilisation' are nothing but a thin veneer that ancient and powerful forces could sweep aside at a moment's notice. Aaron Dries's 'The Wrong Element', Gwendolyn Kiste's 'The Only Face You Ever Knew' and Poppy Z. Brite's 'The Peeler' explore the flimsy nature of our own identities and personalities, to devastating effect. Andy Davidson's 'A House of Woe and Mystery', Paul Tremblay's 'The Note', and Nicholas Royle's 'The Entity' show us just how mentally disabling, and therefore terrifying, the truly unknown and unknowable can be. In Luigi Musolino's 'The Plague', David J. Schow's 'Red Meat Flag', Verity Holloway's 'Eight Days West of Plethora', and Will Maclean's 'The Doppelgänger Ballet', we are subjected to squirm-inducing body horror, and reminded that human beings are often just as terrifying – if not more so – than the monsters that lurk in the shadows. Sarah Langan's 'I Miss You Too Much', and Christina Henry's 'Nobody Wants to Work Here Anymore' are examples of tales that combine various elements of the above. Finally there are a handful of stories here that are wistful, or darkly humorous, such as Annie Knox's 'Mister Reaper', Tim Lebbon's 'Unmarked', and P.C. Verrone's 'A Review of *Slime Tutorial: The Musical*'. Yet, although these tales may be capable of rousing a chuckle, or perhaps even a tear, from the reader, that certainly doesn't mean they are any less adept at shining a harsh light on the human condition, or digging deep into our innermost fears.

Over forty years ago, Ramsey Campbell's *New Terrors Omnibus* showed me how varied and far-reaching the horror genre could be. Hopefully *Elemental Forces* and the earlier volumes in this series are continuing that tradition. However much the subject matter and themes of horror may expand, evolve, and fluctuate, one thing remains constant. Horror is an exploration of human fears and phobias, and as a species we will always be afraid.

Mark Morris

THE PEELER

Poppy Z. Brite

Ecstasy belongs to the past.
– Deborah Landau

Barton left the ship at Harafa on a two-day pass. The wharves of this strange city were dark, a series of great grey warehouses looming over the silent piers, an occasional furtive movement in the shadows. He ignored any signs of life. A quarter-mile inland, he began to see the glow of the red-light district. Soon he was amidst its pandemonium, its narrow streets and glowing windows advertising the pink and black and golden girls within. The air smelled of sewage and food frying in hot oil. He was hungry, but he could afford no more than a drink or two, and he would need it to steady him before the thing he must do tonight.

The bars closest to the wharves were rip-off joints, and so were the bars second-closest. He made it a block further before the thirst overwhelmed him. Choosing a place at random, he let himself into a dark little room where other drinkers huddled in small knots. The place smelled of ancient beer and fish. The man behind the bar looked as if he would smell the same, but his nod was friendly enough.

"Double whiskey. If you please."

"One moment."

The whiskey was before him, more expensive than he had expected. He drank it in three swallows and banged the glass back down on the bartop. Warmth bloomed in his belly, a seed of false courage taking root.

"Another?" said the barkeep.

"I've only enough for the one."

The barkeep nodded and didn't offer a charity drink. Barton didn't want one anyway; it wouldn't do to be drunk tonight.

"You in town long? This is a hard place to be when you're broke."

"I'm headed to the Peeler."

The bartender's eyes widened a bit. "Better have some oysters first. Put the iron in your blood."

"Told you, I'm out of money."

"On the house. Free for anyone going to the Peeler."

He'd had oysters back home, but not since he was a boy. He realised he was hungry. "Well. I'd be obliged."

The barkeep ducked through a low doorway from which a faint cacophony could be heard. A few minutes later he reappeared bearing a large plate. "Dozen oysters. Help you keep up your strength."

The oysters were raw, served in their own half-shells on a bed of rock salt, an oddly fancy presentation for such a hole-in-the-wall place. He picked up the shells and tipped the molluscs into his mouth one by one, along with their liquor. They tasted of the clean deep sea, of night watches on the deck of his ship when the ocean glittered with phosphorescent life. When he had finished them, he did feel stronger. Perhaps the Peeler wouldn't be so bad.

"Want to talk about it?" the bartender said.

No, Barton imagined saying. *No, I don't want to talk about it. No sane person would want to talk about it, and who would want to hear the story? Grow up thinking something's broken inside you, not thinking about girls like you ought to, feeling the wrong way about the other boys. Then – this is a laugh, barkeep – you meet the boy, the right boy, and you realise nothing that feels like this could be wrong. This is what you were made for, this boy, this love. You're happy for the first time in your life. And then you get drafted.*

Even that might have been bearable. He wasn't opposed to serving his country, and he knew Rudy would be safe at home, because Rudy's vision was so bad that he had to wear glasses as thick as the bottoms of Coca-Cola bottles. No branch of the military would take him. Except Rudy wasn't safe at home, wasn't safe at all.

But the bartender had been kind, so Barton just shook his head.

He lingered for another few minutes, but knew he was only postponing the inevitable. He nodded thanks to the barkeep and left the place, getting his bearings before heading further inland. Occasionally he caught sight of his reflection in a window, a big man in fatigues moving silently through noisy streets. Soon he passed from the red-light district into an emptier area, a place where the streets were cobbled and vehicles rushed endlessly over a great viaduct toward God only knew what. Maybe not even God knew; Barton didn't think this part of the city had much truck with Him. The light here felt somehow dead. Glancing up, he realised a full moon had risen, spilling its cold illumination down over the city. He imagined it shining down on Rudy, two different places lit by the same chilly moon.

As he passed under the viaduct, blurred movement overhead made him flinch backward. The falling man might have hit him otherwise, might have knocked him right out of this sorry life. There was a flail of limbs, a sound like a thick steak hitting a marble countertop, but louder, so much louder. Then the man lay broken before him, not six feet away. Blood welled from every part of him, a dark rich flow filling the cracks between the cobblestones, shimmering in the light of that remorseless moon. Barton stared wildly up at the viaduct, from where the man must have jumped or been thrown. There was nothing to see, no other pedestrians craning for a good look at this fellow's misfortune, only the rush of cars. He was still looking up when the man's hand clutched at his shoe.

He screamed, really screamed for the first time since childhood, and stumbled backward. If the viaduct wall hadn't been there, he would have fallen right into the growing puddle of blood. As it was, he banged the back of his skull against the bricks. Silver spangles filled his vision. He blinked them away and stared down at the broken man, the man who was still, impossibly, moving. His body was prone, his head twisted on his neck so that Barton could see his face. His teeth were bloody splinters. One eyeball quivered on his cheek; the other regarded Barton with hellish awareness.

"Heela," said the man.

How could any kind of speech emerge from that bloodhole? Surely it was the last firing of a damaged brain, meaningless noise, no different than the sounds a cow might make in the slaughterhouse.

"Heela!" the bloodhole insisted.

"Christ, pal, don't try to talk. Look, help is on the way, all right?"

Barton had no reason to believe that, but he did hear footsteps approaching, coming fast. The man who appeared from the darkness was taller than Barton, but not as broad through the chest. His skull was lumpy and unevenly shaven, razor-nicked in a few spots, paler than the rest of his curdled-milk complexion. His eyes were bright and somehow ratty, seeming to jitter in their sockets.

"You roll him already?" the man said.

"What?"

"Roll him, you roll him? No? Good, no trouble, we go half and half, what do you say, sailor, half and half, no trouble, good deal, right?"

"You're talking about robbing him."

"Roll him, yeah, he don't need it, not no more, right?"

The skinhead dropped to his knees, dragging his trouser legs through the lake of blood. Barton took a step forward. Slick as a magic trick, a knife appeared in the skinhead's pallid hand. "He don't need it no more! Share or piss off, but don't mess me around!"

Barton moved fast, seized the skinhead by his collar and hauled him up. It wasn't hard; you built up a lot of muscle on the ship. He grabbed the skinhead's wrist and twisted hard. Bones grated against each other. The skinhead screamed. The knife clattered onto the cobblestones and Barton kicked it away.

Tears stood in the skinhead's eyes. "You broke my fuckin' arm! You don't, you don't have to, you don't have to do that, you fuck!"

"You tried to rob a dying man but *I'm* the fuck. Right."

"You broke my—"

Barton feinted towards him. The skinhead stood his ground for a moment longer, clutching his wrist with his good hand, then whirled and ran.

Barton prodded the broken man with his foot, got no response. He used the toe of his boot to turn the man's body over. While Barton and the skinhead had tussled over him like some tawdry carnival prize, the man had finished his dying. A pink-grey coil of intestines trailed from his belly. His good eye stared skyward, sightless.

Sightless.

He thought of the letter he'd received from Rudy last month. The Coke-bottle eyeglasses were no longer doing the job. There was an operation he could have, but without it, the doctors thought he would be blind in a year. The thing was, Rudy painted. Had done so since childhood. He created beautiful canvases in butterfly-wing jewel tones, paintings that filled the jagged spaces in Barton's heart when he looked

THE PEELER • 9

at them. The operation was expensive and his family wouldn't help him. *I don't think I can stand it,* Rudy had written. *There's still so much work I want to get out of me. If I can't make art, I'll go insane. I won't want to live anymore.*

Barton had racked his brain for days trying to figure out a way of making the money. Finally he remembered something he had heard on shipboard, on the night watch. The dog watch, they called it, when the stars unfurled a glittering carpet overhead and strange stories might be passed around. *In Harafa,* a boatswain's mate had told him, *there's a thing called the Peeler. A thing or a place, I don't know exactly, but they buy pain. And they pay well.*

Buy pain. He had envisioned some sort of sex dungeon, a place where you were beaten and burned in front of a live audience. But no, another sailor chipped in, it was worse than that. The Peeler actually *took* something from you, something you could never get back. It was an open secret, the kind of place that could exist on the fringes of a city like Harafa by greasing the right palms.

Barton looked down at the dead man, observed the twisted limbs and smashed face. Had this man just come from the Peeler? Had he sold something he couldn't afford to lose?

"*Rudy* is what I can't afford to lose," he muttered. "Never mind this poor bastard. Remember Rudy."

As soon as he turned the next corner, he stopped thinking about the dead man.

Past the viaduct, his surroundings soon became seedier. Not interestingly seedy like the red-light district; this was just an area of scrubby wasteland and swaybacked industrial buildings, occasional shuttered businesses with names like Cryptid Imports Limited, Wo Fat Noodle Company, Premature Burial Solutions. Some of the signs were written in characters Barton could not read. These streets had a stagnant, swampy smell, though he saw no standing water. He was beginning to wonder if the directions he'd ferreted out of the other sailors were wrong when he saw a green-lit sign ahead. *It ain't an ordinary type of green,* a hick lieutenant had told him. *It looks like poison. Like the sickest you ever felt in your life. It's a green you don't want to look at.*

Barton had dismissed this as melodrama, but there *was* something awful about the sign's verdant hue. MEMORY, it read, aglow in an upper window of an otherwise dark building. There was an appearance of wrongness about the place, some unnatural slump or angle that the eye and the mind could not reconcile. He didn't know what was causing the effect – maybe just apprehension – but he knew he didn't want to go in there.

No, he couldn't think like that. He thought instead of Rudy's eyes, soft blue behind his glasses. That wasn't quite enough to get him going, so he took out his wallet and flipped through it to a photograph of him and Rudy together at the beach. Not touching, not even looking at each other, but something in the arrangement of their bodies spoke of love. He put his wallet away and made himself ring the bell beside the door.

Nothing happened for what felt like several minutes. He began to worry that this place was all rumour and raree show, a story for sailors to tell on the night watch, nothing more. He was about to push the bell again when a buzzer sounded and the door's lock clicked open.

Barton stepped into a tiny foyer where a single electric bulb flickered high overhead. Before him, a narrow staircase led upward into gloom. He didn't want to climb it any more than he had wanted to ring the bell, but climb it he did, his boots loud on the cheap linoleum. At the top was a curtain made of heavy red fabric. He pushed through it, hating its musty smell. And on the other side, everything changed.

He had no real frame of reference for the room he saw. The closest comparison he could make was to a ship's bridge, with its banks of lights and dials and knobs. This place was like that, times a hundred. There seemed to be machines everywhere, all of them whirring and flashing. At the centre of the room sat something that looked like a huge electric dynamo. Barton could not hear it humming, but he thought he could feel it in his teeth and behind his eyes, a subliminal itch. Closed doors stretched away down a long hallway. All this was presided over by a pretty receptionist who looked as if she belonged behind the desk of a five-star hotel. Above her left breast was pinned a nametag that read *Moneta*. He could see no one else in the place. The receptionist smiled at him and said, "Removal or addition?"

"Uh, removal, I think."

The woman's smile grew more dazzling. "Yes, if you were coming in for an addition, you'd know."

Then why did you ask me? Barton thought, but he just nodded.

"Are you familiar with our removal procedure?"

"Not really."

"I'm required to tell you that the services we offer are one hundred per cent legal in this country. I'm also required to tell you that once a procedure has begun, it cannot be stopped. In your case, we would be removing one or more of your assets in exchange for a one-time cash payment. Here's our price list."

She handed him a yellow sheet of paper. Barton scanned it. There was only one item that would provide the sum he needed.

"My mother," he said.

His mother. The lodestar of his childhood, which had been an otherwise lonely time. He had never made friends easily. He was bigger and stronger than most of his schoolmates, but he had no taste for fighting, and bullies quickly learned the taunts that brought shameful tears to his eyes. One day he couldn't stand it anymore and laid into them, giving one a black eye, another a bloody nose. The school suspended him. For the bullies there was no punishment.

"I'm not mad at you," his mother had told him that day. "I'm not disappointed in you either. But I can see you're disappointed in yourself."

He'd shrugged, still too angry and hurt to articulate his feelings.

"You don't want to spend the rest of your school days getting into trouble. You're too smart for that. Know what I used to do when I was a girl? When other kids would pick on me?"

"What?"

"I'd pretend I loved them. No, listen" – she'd seen his scowl – "I know it sounds sappy, but I'd look at them, and I'd try to see the things that made them act mean, the things that hurt them or scared them. And instead of giving back my own meanness, I'd start to feel sorry for them. I wouldn't want to be mean anymore."

"Did it make them stop picking on you?"

She smiled. "Well, it made me stop caring so much when they did. And when they saw I didn't care, they didn't do it as often. So I guess you could say yes, it did."

He hadn't expected it to work. He didn't have her good heart. But the next time a kid said something that angered him, he remembered his mother's words. He looked at the boy currently plaguing him, a rat-faced kid named Lew Mayorkas, and noticed for the first time that Lew had real horrorshow acne. It must be awful to look at that in the mirror every day. The realisation didn't make him love Lew, but it took away some of the sting. The time after that, it was a little easier. And Barton was amazed to see that after a while, the bullies really did seem to get bored with him. He still didn't have a lot of friends, but he no longer had so many enemies.

"Very good," said Moneta, noting something on a paper form. "Is your mother deceased?"

"Yes."

"Fine, that entitles you to an irreplaceability bonus." She beamed at him. "Now please follow me."

Irreplaceability bonus? He thought of the boatswain's mate saying *They buy pain.* Was it possible that they actually bought joy? What was he about to sell away?

The receptionist led him past the banks of lights, past the dynamo, down the hallway. Opening an unmarked door, she ushered him into a claustrophobic little cubicle. In the centre of this room was what looked like a dentist's chair. Except he had never seen a dentist's chair with leather shackles on the arms and footrest. They looked more like something that belonged on an electric chair.

"The restraints are only to keep you from hurting yourself during the procedure. Please have a seat."

He thought again of Rudy's eyes and sat without further hesitation. Moneta fastened the shackles around his wrists, knelt and fastened the shackles around his ankles. Would a metal cap complete the electric chair picture? No, instead she brought a pair of heavy black headphones and clamped them over his ears. Twisting his head, he could see a cable connecting them to a larger cable on the floor. That cable led to an even larger one, and at the spot where they entered the wall, the braided wires were as thick as Barton's wrist.

Moneta stepped over to a bank of machinery on the wall, flipped some switches, typed briefly on a keyboard. Then she stepped in front of him, made sure she had his attention. *"Okay?"* she mouthed with an absurd thumbs-up. He nodded. She twisted a dial, and Barton's world ended.

Had there ever *been* a world? He couldn't conceive of anything outside this world of agony. There was no individual part of him being hurt, no thread of physical pain he could fixate on. It felt as if every atom of him was being turned wrong-side out, as if dirty fingers were rummaging through his brain, seeking to take what was not theirs, tossing some things aside, seizing others with no care at all. He saw his mother at the end of her life, so fragile in the hospital bed. He saw her young and strong, digging in her garden. She smoothed his hair on school picture day; she brought in a cake with his name and ten flaming candles on it; he cried on her bosom over a skinned knee, smelling her hairspray and Shalimar perfume; she pushed him on a swing until he flew higher than the clouds.

Without warning, the memories began to swirl away. He was reminded of a film he'd seen where a flower blossomed, withered, and died in an instant. Like dead petals, his recollections of his mother lost their colour and scattered. He scrabbled after them, grasped for them, but even as he touched them, they were gone. A red wave washed over him, drowning him. He sucked it in. Then it was over. His body felt as limp as a strand of seaweed. It occurred to him that they shouldn't call this the Peeler; a better name would be the Drainer.

"Well done!" said Moneta, taking off his headphones and unfastening his restraints. "That will make a lovely past for some motherless soul."

Barton rubbed his eyes, dazed. What had he done? What had he given away in an instant?

Faint images of some woman, like faded photographs loose in a drawer. He didn't care.

He collected his payment and his bonus, thanked Moneta, ducked back under the musty curtain. Outside, the night air revived him. He took a moment to get his bearings. There was the viaduct. On the other side were the pleasures of the red-light district, and he had a roll of money in his pocket. Had he really been planning to send it to Rudy? Just so Rudy could keep painting *pictures*? He laughed, a harsh impatient sound. Let Rudy pay for his own operation or go blind. It was nothing to Barton.

For a moment, he wondered again exactly what he had given up. He still remembered having a mother, but the image of her face was dim, a dying flame. There was no resonance to it. Likewise, the things she had taught him were now meaningless. Why love anyone, why endure the bother and mess of sharing a life with anyone? Why bother looking out for anyone but yourself? Love was a fool's game, and his mother had been a fool raising a foolish son. The Peeler had done him a tremendous favour.

He set off for the red-light district, the sound of his boots echoing off the pavement in the empty night.

THE ENTITY

Nicholas Royle

They pick me up from the local station and drive me back to their place. The drive takes about fifteen minutes. I'm trying to memorise it in case I need to retrace my steps, on foot, and can't get a phone signal to look at a map. I haven't seen Ruth for about forty years and I've never met her husband Martin, a Francophone Belgian, before today. It feels a little weird to be sitting in the back of their car being driven to their no-doubt enormous house in the middle of nowhere to pet-sit their dog, cat and five tortoises for a week when, really, I barely know them and they hardly know me.

I did know Ruth at university. We nearly had a thing, but then we didn't and instead became good friends, but at the end of four years she moved to Brussels to work as a translator and it was there she met Martin, who people reckoned was a bit of an odd one, but they stayed together and got married and I virtually never heard from Ruth again until three weeks ago when she contacted me out of the blue via social media to offer me the pet-sitting gig. It couldn't have come at a better time, as I had a story to write for an anthology and no ideas and even if I'd had an idea, the truth is I find it increasingly hard, if not actually impossible, to get any writing at all done sitting at home. Nothing suits me more than to be taken out of my home environment, away from all the usual distractions, so that writing can become either my top priority or in this case my second priority after walking the dog.

Don't ask me where we are. Somewhere in the Dordogne. I took a train to Paris and then one to Bordeaux and then a local service east for an hour. I could be anywhere. The key thing is I'm away from home. Don't get me wrong, I love my wife and she is very loving towards me, but if I need to write, I have to get away.

We leave the main road and join a minor road that winds through countryside that's fields of sunflowers one minute, forest-clad hills the next, and end up on a track with grass growing in a line down the middle. When we get to the end of the track, Martin points a device at the windscreen and a gate opens. The car scrunches on to the gravel drive and Martin turns right and stops under a car port. He'll need to reverse out to leave, I can't help noticing. I'm more of a reverse-in-and-drive-out-forwards kind of a guy. Get the hard bit out of the way first.

Their house – I say their house, it's more a collection of buildings set in half an acre of land – is stunning. They show me around. Martin seems okay. Maybe people misjudged him, or maybe all those years married to Ruth have shaved the rough edges off him. Martin asks if I want him to show me the walk he does every day with Luca, the dog. I know I said he seems okay, but do I really want to go off with him for a walk of – he tells me – about two and a half miles? I'd much rather Ruth show me the walk, but I don't really feel I can say that.

Sure, I say.

So we go left out of the gates, up the green lane. Luca is with us and I stop and wait when he starts rooting round in the undergrowth.

I tend to just keep walking, Martin says. He'll follow.

So we walk on up to the top of the rise and finally Luca joins us at the top. Then we plunge into the forest and Martin points out a patch of disturbed earth.

Wild boar, he tells me.

Les sangliers? I say.

Yes, he says.

The path takes us out past a house – it belongs to 'the English people', Martin tells me, but they're never there – and then we have to stop and put Luca on a lead because the French owners of the next house pretty much insist on it.

The walk goes on. Luca is now off the lead and without warning stops to do his business. I'm expecting Martin to produce a little bag and pick it up, but instead he gets a stick and pushes it to the side of the track, which soon becomes a road and then we turn left into another track through the forest and this eventually passes an empty house that's in the process of being done up and then with some twisting and turning and slightly awkward negotiation of a stony path we end up on a narrow road

THE ENTITY • 17

between fields full of reasonably fearsome-looking horned cattle, until we pass a tennis court, which seems slightly incongruous, and the rear entrance to a chateau – the inhabitants of the chateau own most of the land, apparently – and then more fields with more cows, past a house with a dog in the garden that barks at Luca and a sign on the house that says 'Smile, You're on Camera. Dog and Traps'. In French, naturally. There are two elderly Mercedes parked outside, a green estate model and a grey saloon. Once we get Luca away from the dog, we're back in the forest for a while and there's more twisting and turning and all the way along the walk there have been alternative paths to take that we haven't taken and I'm thinking there's no way I'm going to be able to remember this. Finally, however, we're back, having done a circle of two and a half miles.

They show me around the living quarters – a converted barn – and they tell me about the two men who did the conversion, locals who specialise in this sort of thing.

One of them was a water diviner, Ruth says. He went around saying there's a spring here and a spring there.

He also told us the house has an entity, says Martin.

An entity? I say.

Yes, he didn't say much more than that and we didn't ask, says Martin.

Great, I think. An entity.

They show me the cat, who runs away, and the enclosure in the garden that they insist contains five tortoises, although I only see two.

Do I have to walk them too? I ask.

Martin appears to be considering the question, but Ruth gives me a smile that takes me back forty years, when I would sneak her into press shows of films I was reviewing for the college newspaper and then, as I say, we nearly got together, but managed somehow to avoid it. It probably wouldn't have worked.

Where are you going walking? I ask them.

The Basque Country, Ruth reminds me.

Oh yes, I say. I wouldn't like it there. I don't like complicated underwear.

No, I remember, she says, laughing.

I allow myself a sly look at Martin, who's frowning.

And you'll be back on Thursday? I ask.

Yes, at three o'clock, says Martin, and I remember that this is one of the things people used to say about him, that he was obsessive about punctuality, which seems a pretty harmless sort of thing to be obsessive about, but I think it was one of a few things.

Help yourself to the books, Ruth says, pointing to a bookcase next to the French windows, and the DVDs, she adds, pointing to the other end of the living area where there is a large TV.

I kind of wish they'd hurry up and set off and within five minutes they do, avoiding a big goodbye so as not to upset Luca, who I've to keep inside until I hear the gate clang shut after them. I hear the car on the gravel – there's another car, to which they've left me the key – and then the gate and then it's just me and the menagerie.

★ ★ ★

I try to take Luca for another walk, the same walk, while it's fresh in my mind, but he's not having it. He sits down halfway up the green lane, apparently determined not to leave sight of home. I can't really blame him, as he's literally just done this walk, so I give in and we head back, which I suspect is one-nil to Luca and may cause problems down the line, but we will see.

Instead, I feed him and the cat. The tortoises are more or less self-catering. Ruth said I could pick a few dandelion leaves if I were to see any on my walks. Then I feed myself – Ruth left a pasta sauce made with her homegrown tomatoes – and have a local beer, which is not bad at all. I get my laptop out and answer a few emails and create a file called 'Story', which I sit staring at for five minutes before writing a single word, 'Untitled', and then a line of random text that I will later select and replace with my opening line, whatever it happens to be. I sit there for another five minutes in case it should come to me and when it doesn't I open a web browser and look at my social media for a bit until I realise the dog has gone to sleep in his basket and I think I might as well do the same.

★ ★ ★

Monday.

For some reason the title cards for *The Shining* come into my mind.

Ruth told me Luca doesn't have to eat first thing, but he looks pretty keen to get out, so I make a quick coffee and butter some bread. There's homemade jam in the fridge, though I couldn't tell you what sort. I hope it's not fig. Like Ruth, I studied languages and so I'm able to speak to Luca in French, which is the only language he understands, but don't worry, I'm going to translate what I say to him into English, just for you.

Shall we go for a walk? I say to him, picking up the lead from the shelf by the door. He bounds up to me, tail wagging, and when I open the door he darts through the doorway. I lock the door even though, as Martin showed me, the French windows on to the terrace don't lock. We scrunch to the side gate, which doesn't require the zapper, and then we turn left on to the green lane we didn't get very far up last night. This morning he's more in the mood and gets to the top before I do. We pass through the forest and I see the House of the English People coming up through the trees. I can't resist a little nose around. It's clear there's no one at home. They have French windows, too, and maybe they'd be unlocked like Ruth and Martin's, but I don't try them. I content myself with inspecting their living room from outside. It has the look of a stage set. The curtain is up and we're waiting expectantly for someone to walk on stage. But no one does.

Come on, Luca, I say, let's go.

I remember to stick the lead on him before we get to the House of the French People. In the front garden there are two empty deckchairs, turned to face the house. Luca pulls me towards a shed on the other side of the track. Even a dog his size – he's a Tibetan terrier, small to medium size under all that long hair – can generate a considerable amount of traction when he gets his head down. I give him a few moments, wondering what he can smell at the bottom of the wooden door to the shed. I can guess. He can't be the only dog that comes past here.

A little way past the House of the French People, after the track has turned into a road, there's a patch of white stones or chips of stone embedded in the tarmac. Something about it draws my eye, but also drawing my eye is Luca's scampering form rounding the next bend and I can't remember how far it is down there to the next road where there might be actual cars or something, so I run to catch him up.

I would have walked right past the left-turn into the forest if Luca had not stopped there to wait for me. A short way into the forest there's a path on the left. Do we take it or go straight on? Frankly I have no idea and Luca rests on his haunches waiting for me to make my mind up and I understand that at moments like this he won't dictate the route to me, but he might pause if there's a choice to be made. He must have been down most of these paths with Ruth or Martin and presumably none of them leads to a deadly bog or a concealed abandoned mine-shaft. You'll have gathered by now that I don't actually know much about dogs. Indeed, up until a couple of years ago I would have happily included 'dogs' in a list of personal dislikes, had somebody asked me to compile one.

I decide not to take the path on the left and Luca trots along behind me perfectly happily and as soon as there's a downhill section he bounds off in front of me. A year or two ago I was standing outside a fancy bakery waiting for my turn to go in. It's a small place and they seemed to want to keep the one-in-one-out system that had been introduced post-lockdown. For once there was no one else outside waiting, just me and, after a moment, a woman with a dog that was off its lead, and it came up to me, slowly, but very much as if it knew what it was doing. I was at an extremely low point at that time, worrying about a health matter, the possibility of something serious, and there was something going on at work. It's fair to say I was depressed. The dog, a spaniel of some kind, brushed against my leg and sat down looking up at me. It was one of the strangest things that's ever happened to me. I swear it knew how I was feeling and wanted to comfort me. I know it sounds ridiculous, although people with knowledge of dogs might disagree. And then the person who had been in the bakery came out and it was my turn to go in and the dog went back to its owner and I went in and bought a loaf of sourdough bread that would turn out to be more holes than bread. Four quid for a load of holes and a bit of bread and a crust to break your teeth on.

Luca stops and squats right at the edge of the path. I somehow can't tear my eyes away although I remember reading somewhere that dogs don't like to be watched when doing what Luca is doing. It seems to take him a long time but then it is done and he moves away and paws at the ground. I don't know what that's about. I find a stick – there's no shortage of sticks in the forest – and approach the doings and am disappointed to see that it is runny. This isn't the kind of thing I can flick away into the part of the forest where only hunters might step in it. Instead I collect a number of sticks and build a little structure over it. I don't know if this is the right thing to do. I suspect not, but we didn't see anyone walking here yesterday and I haven't seen anyone at all today.

I keep an eye on Luca for the rest of the walk, which is uneventful, and even if I dither over the route once or twice we do actually make it back, and he seems well in himself, but I'm in uncharted territory here. Ruth and Martin said I could call them or message them at any point with any questions no matter how minor, but my feeling is that I should try to ride this one out.

In the afternoon it's too hot to sit on the terrace, so I sit inside at the dining table staring at my laptop. I write an opening sentence and delete it. I look out of the French windows. I write another sentence and delete that. I look at the bookcase to the left of the French windows. I hear a noise in the back kitchen and when I go to explore I almost step on the cat, who has just entered the back kitchen via the cat flap. I sit back down and write another opening sentence. Sitting on top of the bookcase is an antique doll, its head turned towards the dining table. I hear a noise from the main kitchen area. I get up to investigate. The noise appears to be coming from above the range cooker, but all there is above the cooker is an extractor hood and above that a vent going up to the ceiling. As I stand there looking at it, I hear the noise again. There's something up there inside it, or on the roof above it, or *in* the roof, but there's not much of a cavity, as I can see from the setting of the skylight. Anyway, I swear I can hear something moving up and down inside the shaft of the vent. A bird, a squirrel? The squirrels here are red, not grey, and I've only seen one, in the forest. A mouse, a rat? The noise stops. I stand in the kitchen for a while longer but it doesn't start up again.

I sit down and delete my opening sentence and then suddenly I'm watching my hands as they fly over the keyboard and before I know it I've got an opening paragraph. There's nothing more boring than reading about a writer writing, so I'll spare you the details, but after five minutes I save what I've done and close the laptop and sit back with a small feeling of satisfaction.

I feed the animals and myself and then open the laptop again and change what I've written from third person to first person, then save it and close it.

★   ★   ★

I wake several times in the night to the sound of heavy rain and get up on Tuesday morning to find it's rained in through the kitchen skylight. Then I realise it's not rain and that the dog has been unwell. Luca is curled up on the floor in the living area, possibly looking a bit sheepish. I clean up the mess and wash the floor, thinking this is just about preferable to having a leaking skylight to deal with.

I message Ruth and ask how it's going in the Basque Country and she says it's lovely, lots of cliff paths and little coves. I tell her about Luca and she tells me not to worry and to give him mashed rice and squash from the garden until he's back to normal and to make sure he drinks plenty of water. When I take him for a walk, it's not long before it becomes obvious he still has bad guts. We press on. I figure out what it is about the pattern of white stones on the road past the House of the French People that drew my eye: it looks like the distorted human skull in the foreground of Holbein's painting, *The Ambassadors*.

Great. A *memento mori*.

I write in the afternoon. When I say I write, I mean I open up the laptop on the dining table and change what I wrote yesterday from past tense to present tense and add a couple of paragraphs. Then I sit back and look out of the French windows. I look at the bookcase to the left of the French windows. I look at the doll on top of the bookcase.

There's a new noise in the living area coming from the fireplace. When I investigate by sticking my head in the fireplace and looking up the chimney, I hear a frantic twittering or squeaking. Birds or rodents, maybe. While I'm puzzling over that, the noise of something moving about in the extractor vent starts up again, so I head back round to the kitchen area. It stops when I get there and I hear the twittering start up again from the fireplace.

I go into my bedroom to wash my hands and I see that my bed is a mess. I'm sure I remember making it after getting up. I straighten the duvet, wash my hands and sit down at the dining table again, but decide it's not happening and close the laptop and look out of the French windows. I should look around a bit. I step out on to the terrace. The gardens are ahead of me, containing flower beds, vegetable garden, swimming pool, tortoise enclosure, various raised beds, large numbers of trees. There's a workshop and a garage containing a ride-on mower and a BMW. Towards the back of the garden is what Ruth called 'the other house' and I'm going to call the Other House. They are in the process of doing it up as guest accommodation. It's left unlocked, they told me, as there's nothing of value in it, but then they effectively leave the main house unlocked as well. Unlived in and a little bare, the Other House is somewhat cooler and has the feeling of a long-term project. There's a living area, a bedroom and a shower room downstairs. Upstairs are two more rooms that could become bedrooms. I glance into both and walk into a spider's web in one of them and decide I've seen enough.

★   ★   ★

On Wednesday morning I get out of bed and almost step on a lizard. I wonder why it doesn't run away and when I put my glasses on I can see why not. It's missing its tail and left foreleg and won't be running anywhere.

I think I know what *you* got up to last night, I say to the cat as I fill its bowl.

I grab the dog's lead and we head out. Up the green lane, through the forest, past the House of the English People, past the House of the French People, past Holbein's skull, down the road, into the forest, stopping to answer the call of nature (Luca – back to normal, almost), past the Empty House, down the stony path, up the narrow road and as we approach the rear of the Chateau and are about to turn left on to the tree-lined avenue that becomes a track and leads past the House of Cameras and Booby Traps and the two Mercedes, I see that two cows from the field on the right have escaped and are wandering in the road. I call the dog and attach his lead.

I watch the cows from a distance. One is smaller, possibly a calf, with its mother.

It's not worth it, I say to Luca. Too risky. If it were just me, maybe. But with you, I can't take the risk. What do you think?

I kneel down and look into the dog's eyes.

Do you agree? I ask him. Are we agreed? Not worth the risk? Wasn't someone killed just recently? A woman walking a dog? Let's go back.

So we turn around and walk back down the narrow road and now that I've seen the escaped cows, all these other cows in the fields either side of the road, kept in their respective fields by the thinnest of electrified wires, take on a different aspect. I hear a car coming behind us, so I move with Luca to the side of the road and hold him close, my arm around him. He's panting and I can feel his heart beating. It's one of the two Mercedes from the House of Cameras and Booby Traps, the green one. It slows down and the window on the passenger side descends. The driver, a dark-haired man in his forties with an unlit hand-rolled cigarette between his lips, leans towards me. He removes the cigarette and says there are a couple of cows loose – he nods towards the road further up – and we should take care. I thank him and say we've seen them and does he know whose they are and when they might be put back where they belong. He shrugs. I thank him again and he drives on.

We carry on down the narrow road then turn right up the stony path, past the Empty House, into the forest. Walking the route in the opposite direction I notice different things. I see signs saying 'CHASSE GARDEE' nailed to trees telling me the forest is a private hunting ground, which I already knew anyway. I see alternative routes as tempting options when they might be traps or dead ends. On occasion, I fail to see the right path, even though it's right in front of me. I've always felt that going back is not simply the opposite of the way there.

Nevertheless, we do make it back, but not before an outburst of torrential rain. My shirt is stuck to my skin, my glasses sliding off my face. Luca appears completely indifferent to the rain and gives himself a vigorous shake as we enter the house.

I go into my bedroom to change into dry clothes and see that my bed has been messed up again. Just like last time, I remember making it in the morning. I retrieve my laptop from under the pillow – one of my ingenious hiding places in a strange environment – and take it into the main living area, where I give Luca a look intended to tell him I get it about the bed, and bravo, but that's enough, okay? Installing myself at the dining table, I open up the laptop to find that my story has disappeared. I look in Word under File and Open Recent. It's not there. I look in the folder where I saved it. It's not there.

Cheers, Entity, I say, reflecting on how I've always blithely believed there was no need to put a password on my machine. I like being able to open the lid and dive right in. Although I probably don't really believe the Entity has opened my machine and deleted my file, I decide to set up a password. I look at the doll on the bookcase and choose a password I've got a chance of remembering. I practise entering it a couple of times. Then I write some notes to help me get back to where I was in the story, which was not very far, I have to admit, but I manage to lose myself in doing that for a couple of hours.

It's stopped raining, so I close the laptop and after a quick look around I open one of the deep drawers in the kitchen and wedge the machine in there between two stacks of bowls, then I pick up the lead from the shelf by the front door.

Shall we try again, Luca?

As we walk I try to figure out what happened to that file. The House of the English People. Was my machine too full? The House of the French People. Was my machine out of memory? Holbein. Had I accidentally deleted it myself? Empty House. Did I even check in the bin? Forest. Could the file have been called something other than what I thought it was called? Stony path. Did I create it in some other application and not in Word? Narrow road. Was the Entity real? Chateau. Tree-lined avenue. Cows. The cows are in their field. The dog at the House of Cameras and Booby Traps is out in the garden, but we get past without difficulty.

When we get home, I feed both the animals and put a pan on to boil for pasta. I take the laptop out of the kitchen drawer and set it up on the dining table, surprising myself by remembering my password.

The new file that I created filled with notes to remind me where I'd got up to with the story that disappeared has also disappeared. This time I check in the bin. The bin is empty. I try other applications. I look in recent files. I do a universal search for a phrase I know I used in the notes. I put it in double inverted commas. Nothing.

This isn't funny any more, I say, though I don't know who I'm saying it to.

I restart the machine.

The files do not reappear.

My phone vibrates. A message from Ruth. A picture of her and Martin on a cliff top smiling at the camera.

Looks fantastic, I message back. Have a great time.

I close the laptop and sit back in my chair at the dining table staring out through the French windows. As if in mockery of my efforts, the light in the garden is exquisite. The sun is low in the sky and seems to pick out every single flower in Ruth's beds. I see the Other House at the end of the garden and suddenly I remember something. I remember Ruth saying something to me one evening on Hampstead Heath, when the light was similar to now.

Where's the other Tim? she said.

I probably frowned at her.

What other Tim? I said.

You know, she said, the relaxed Tim, the Tim who's not so intense, the Tim I used to have a laugh with.

He's right here, I said.

She gave a sort of sad little smile.

Where's the other Ruth? I said.

Which other Ruth? she said.

The Ruth who seemed to want what I wanted, I said. The Ruth who laughed at my jokes.

She laughed at that, but it was a hollow laugh.

*   *   *

Thursday.

The Entity is upping the ante.

For a moment or two, after I've pulled back the curtains in front of the French windows, I can't make sense of what I'm looking at. It's a confusion of black and red and white, and appears bristly. There's a sense of violence and energy. Slowly the elements come together and I realise I'm looking at the body of a wild boar lying on its side on the terrace. There's blood and its face is damaged and there's some material on the window, all of which leads me to suspect that it ran into the window, killing itself. Presumably not on purpose, although the way this week is going, I wouldn't be surprised.

I reach for my phone to message Ruth or at least take a picture, but then I decide against it. I find a wheelbarrow in the workshop and load the carcass on to it, with some difficulty and not without getting its blood on my hands, and wheel it up to the far end of the garden, where I leave it outside the Other House. Let them deal with it when they get back. Which, I remember, will be in a few hours. Three o'clock, if Martin is as punctual as he was always supposed to be.

What I can't work out is if the creature crashed into the French windows in the night, it surely would have woken Luca, who would probably have woken me in turn.

When I get back to the main house I see Luca standing behind the French windows watching me. I slip in without letting him out that way – I don't want him snuffling round the body of the boar – and then get his lead and offer him outside the front door and we head up the green lane, past the House of the English People, past the House of the French People, past Holbein's skull, down the road, left into the forest, past the Empty House, up the narrow road and as we approach the top of the hill and the rear of the Chateau I am scanning the skyline on the left for the wandering cows. They are indeed wandering. They look like the same two, a cow and a calf. In the field they have escaped from there are normally six cows: four are dark tan in colour and two are light tan. The two I have seen wandering have been dark tan. But why just these two and why are they not *always* wandering, only sometimes? If there's a way out of the field, why don't the other cows escape?

We double-back down the narrow road and cut the corner by the tennis courts, emerging on to the tree-lined avenue nearer to the House of Cameras and Booby Traps. I look back to the right towards the Chateau and there are the two escaped cows right down there, at a safe distance. We walk on.

★   ★   ★

I'm sitting at the dining table, staring at the doll on the bookcase. In front of me, my laptop is open. This time there was no file relating to the story I'm supposed to be writing for whoever or whatever to delete, so instead, whoever or whatever has deleted some other stuff, random files, as far as I can make out. Novels, stories, notes for projects, an unfinished script. All stuff that's backed up at home, but that's not the point.

I think for a moment about upgrading my security to Touch ID. I look at the tip of my right index finger and decide I want to keep it.

I close the lid of the machine and get up from the dining table and wander over to the bookcase. It's a mixture of cookbooks and travel guides – I see one to the Basque Country – and novels in English, Julian Barnes's *Before She Met Me*, Rachel Cusk's *The Temporary*, and detective novels by Fred Vargas and Georges Simenon, in French, and French translations of novels by Len Deighton and Mick Herron. I'm making assumptions about whose books are whose. *War and Peace*? *Dracula*? Those are harder to call.

Seeing *Dracula* reminds me of the film *Martin*, by George A. Romero, often considered a vampire film and probably only once interpreted as a biopic about Ruth's husband Martin, on the occasion when, not long after she met and formed a relationship with him, I sent her a copy of the DVD as a joke – a joke not appreciated by Martin and possibly not by Ruth either, because it was after sending it to her that I didn't hear from her again for over thirty-five years.

I flick through the copy of *Dracula*. There are no clues as to whose copy it is. No bookmark, no name in the front. I put it back and turn away from the bookcase, looking around the room. I see the TV and remember Ruth's offer to browse their DVDs.

The Ipcress File, *A Dandy in Aspic*, *The Conversation*. Again, I'm quick to make assumptions. *Enemy of the State*, *Funeral in Berlin*, *Martin*.

Martin.

I pull out the DVD case and see that it is indeed George A. Romero's *Martin*, the film I sent to Ruth, in a light-hearted reference to her new boyfriend, more than three and a half decades ago, in a different format. I wonder who replaced the VHS with a DVD? I open it and remove the disc. In good condition, no fingerprints. Who bought it? It's among the spy movies. I imagine Martin choosing to internalise his hurt. I open some more of 'his' DVD cases and inspect the discs. They're all in good condition, like *Martin*. Towards the right-hand end of the shelf there's a shift in genre. *Grease*, *Saturday Night Fever*, *The Sound of Music*. I remember Ruth suggesting we go to see *Grease* and me demurring. I open *Grease* – also in good condition, but a few fingerprints. *Saturday Night Fever*, likewise. When I remove the disc of *The Sound of Music* I see there's another DVD underneath. Reading the title of this film produces a confusion of feelings, good and bad. I've only seen the film once, forty years ago, with Ruth – *The Entity*.

Why doesn't it have its own case? Was it lost or thrown away? I remember we saw the film on release, at a public screening, not at a press show, so it was a film we saw in the evening and after the screening, instead of the sandwiches on paper plates that would follow a 10:00 a.m. press show, we found ourselves in the West End and hungry. We went to the Stockpot on Panton Street and then for a drink at the Blue Posts on Rupert Street and then ended up back at my flat. It was the high point of the relationship we didn't quite have.

I sit there on the floor, clutching the case of *The Sound of Music* and the two DVDs, unable either to put them back or to see if I can work out how to operate the DVD player and have another look at *The Entity* and see if it offers any further clues to what is going on, when a sudden twittering issues from the fireplace. I'm certain it's a bird. I imagine it being stuck, unable to get out in either direction, panicking. As I stand in front of the fireplace, asking myself what I can do, not only to help the bird but to put a stop to its noise, which is louder than before and more desperate and becoming unbearable, I hear a commotion from the kitchen area. I walk around there and whatever was trapped in the vent and making a racket the other day is back and making more noise than before. Both noises appear to increase in volume at the same time.

In a bid to control myself, because I can feel anger and frustration rising to the point where I'm visualising myself climbing up on to the cooker and ripping the vent away from the wall, I sit down at the dining table. I'm tempted to open my laptop, but resist. Instead I look at the doll on the bookcase. The vacancy of its expression seems ironic, almost as if it's signalling that it's joining in the campaign of harassment.

As I stare into its eyes, I notice something I haven't noticed before. Its eyes are not identical. I get up and reach for the doll and sit back down, placing it on the dining table. Its right eye looks like how I expect an antique doll's eye to look, but its left eye looks different, less like an imitation eye and more like an optical instrument, more like a lens.

I pick the doll up and bring its head down sharply on the table top. The head breaks into several pieces and among them sits a tiny device, black and shiny like a beetle. I may have never seen a hidden surveillance camera before, but it's clear to me that that's what I'm looking at. I pick it up between finger and thumb and place it lens down on the tabletop.

Now, everything looks suspicious. An empty electric socket in the kitchen. A fly ribbon's hanging empty canister. The microwave oven. The TV and accompanying devices. The car key. The zapper to open the gate.

I go into my bedroom. I look at the light over the mirror and wash basin. The reading lamp. A pottery cat on the window ledge.

The terrace. The bird feeders. The rattan garden furniture.

Luca exits the house via the French windows behind me and curls up on the gravel. I look at him, lying there unsuspecting and trusting, and something passes through my mind, but I shut the thought down. I'm not going there and they know I wouldn't go there. Whatever this is about, I'm not going there.

I look at my watch. It's twenty to three.

I go back into the house and take a large, broad-bladed knife from the knife block. Placing it on the worktop, I hoist myself up until I am standing on the cooker. I kneel down and grab the knife, return to a standing position and insert the blade of the knife between the edge of the vent and the wall and apply leverage. I get the fingers of one hand under it and pull and a section of the stainless-steel structure comes away. I let it fall and look down, worrying for a moment that Luca might have followed me in. He hasn't, but I see him now at the French windows cocking his head at a quizzical angle. I throw the knife into the sink and stick my hand up the remaining part of the vent and root around. I feel something hard and grab it and give it a tug. I withdraw my hand; it's holding a loudspeaker. No doubt there will be a similar sort of device up the chimney. I jump down.

I look at the knife sticking out of the sink.

I'm not going there either.

I leave the house and stand on the terrace looking out into the garden. I see the Other House. I start walking. Luca gets up and follows me.

No, I say to him, you stay here.

I hold him and stroke him.

I get to my feet again.

Sit, I say, and he sits. Wait.

I walk away from him and I don't hear his feet on the gravel behind me. I walk across the grass, past the flower beds and the raised vegetable beds, past the tomato plants and the compost heaps, across another expanse of grass and soon arrive outside the Other House. I open the door and enter and cast only the briefest of glances around the downstairs area as I climb the stairs. Light falls through a large skylight over the staircase. I go into the first bedroom and look around. It's bare and there are no cupboard doors or anything. There is one window. The ceiling is high and steeply sloping; there is no loft.

I turn around and enter the other room. Here again there is one window and light pours through it. There are two doors in the far wall. I step forward and open the one on the left. A small loft space full of boxes and suitcases. I step back out and move across to the other door and open it. A small box room, but this one is empty, apart from a thin tracery of spiders' webs. I go back to the other loft space, the one that's full of boxes and suitcases, and, yes, there's enough light to see cobwebs to the sides of the space and between the boxes and cases, but nothing hanging down from the low, sloping ceiling.

I drag a load of boxes and cases out of the way and in the far wall, low down, previously hidden by a pile of boxes, is a dark vertical line, a break in the wall. I kneel down and get my nails into the gap and a panel no more than three feet by two feet comes away. I discard it.

Within, in a cramped space barely six feet high, three feet deep and as wide as the room behind us, crouched on floor cushions in front of an improvised workstation comprising laptops, screens and other devices, Ruth and Martin turn to look at me. I take in sleeping bags, bottles of water, a camping stove: the paraphernalia of paranoid survivalists. Or, in this case, perhaps, vengeful pranksters.

A lot of things go through my mind while the next few seconds play out. The Basque Country. Complicated underwear. Not just the creature in the vent and the birds up the chimney, but also the messed-up bed, the dead lizard and the body of the wild boar. Not the work of the dog and the cat, then, not an accidental death. The escaped cows? A neglectful farmer? Doubtful. The deleted files. Luca's bad guts. Did they poison their own dog? Or was that just a bonus?

Martin. *Martin.* Was it all Martin? I remember Ruth's photo message supposedly from the Basque Country. Was she in his thrall? Was he coercively controlling her? Was he really that jealous of the night Ruth and I spent together, before he had any idea she existed, after seeing *The Entity*? I remember with scorn the copy of Julian Barnes's *Before She Met Me* in the bookcase in the main house. It's not even one of his good ones. I remember the spy novels and the spy films. Did he want me to see those? Did Ruth want me to find *The Entity*? Did he even know about the copy of *The Entity*? Well, he does now.

They both look braced for something.

The truth is, I don't know what to do. I don't really want to do anything.

I remember Ruth saying, Where's the other Tim? And me saying, Where's the other Ruth?

I think I just want to pack my stuff and go.

But then I hear it. We all hear it. The clang of the gate. The scrunch of the gravel.

I look at my watch. It's just after three.

I look at Ruth and Martin, their eyes wide with fear.

NOBODY WANTS TO WORK HERE ANYMORE

Christina Henry

"There's a rat in the refrigerator."

Jen looked up from the reorder forms she'd been painstakingly filling out based on last week's numbers. She wished, for the ten-thousandth time that day, that Quinn was there to do this. A promotion to manager of this burger franchise had brought a raise but also, in her mind, an amount of aggravation greater than the increased compensation.

"What?"

McKayla stood in the door – seventeen, stringy blonde hair in a stringy ponytail under her hat, acne-splotched chin. McKayla had a little voice, a diffident manner and a conflict allergy. She was constantly in Jen's doorway, asking for help with something – especially fractious customers.

This, Jen thought, *is why it doesn't pay to be the manager.*

Regular employees got to pass off their difficult problems to her. It had been much nicer when she'd been the passer rather than the passee.

Quinn had been a good manager – calm, collected, never ruffled by anything. But he'd disappeared a week ago – really disappeared, like up and vanished into thin air – and now McKayla was Jen's problem.

McKayla took a deep breath, preparatory to raising her little voice, a thing Jen had encouraged her to practise. Just then McKayla's words sank in.

"Wait," Jen said, alarmed. It would not do if customers heard an employee shouting about rats on the premises. "Come in and shut the door."

McKayla entered, uncertainly, the way she did everything. Her red polo had come untucked from her black pants. Jen wanted to point this out but knew from experience that if she did, then McKayla would get derailed from her original mission. It didn't take much with her. She was a pinball caroming off the flippers of life.

The girl shut the door behind her and stood there, twisting her fingers together, looking everywhere except at Jen.

"Tell me what happened," Jen said. There was a good chance there was no rat at all, just a skittering spider she'd seen out of the corner of her eye and turned into a rat.

"Well, um, I, um, went into the refrigerator to get lettuce because we were out up front."

Jen made a mental note that this task probably had not been completed and that Brian, who was on the sandwich-making station, was probably having a fit. Brian had wanted to be manager, unlike Jen, and every day he found some fault and expressed it loudly.

Just as she thought this she heard Brian bellow, "McKayla! The lettuce!"

Brian's voice was the opposite of McKayla's. Even when speaking in what he called "a normal tone" it wasn't what you'd call an inside voice.

McKayla winced. "He needs the stuff."

"All right, don't worry. You went to get the lettuce."

"I w-went to get the lettuce," McKayla said. "And on the shelf where it is, where it's supposed to be, there was a rat. A big one. Eating it. And I kinda screamed a little and it, um, looked at me."

"It looked at you? It didn't run away?" If there *was* a rat, then that was pretty scary. It was either completely acclimatised to humans or it was rabid or something. Jen didn't know what to make of this story, but she still wanted to believe there was no rat at all. "Well, let's go take a look."

She indicated that McKayla should follow her, fervently hoping there was no rodent in the refrigerator. It would be nothing but trouble for her if there were. She'd have to call an exterminator, who'd probably contact a health inspector. The presence of a health inspector would result in fines at best and a temporary closure at worst, and Carl, the franchise owner, would go through the roof.

As she led McKayla down the hall she wondered why a rat couldn't have appeared last week, when Quinn was in charge.

The hallway was redolent with the scent of slightly stale fry oil, a smell that Jen found clung to the inside of her nose even when she left the restaurant.

"McKayla!" Brian yelled from the kitchen. "Where are you?"

The door to the walk-in refrigerator was open. Jen strode in, but McKayla paused, hovering in the doorway.

"What now?" Jen said, glancing back.

"The rat," McKayla said, whispering so low that Jen barely heard the words. "His eyes. He had red eyes."

Jen suppressed a sigh. The girl had probably seen a reflection of her own red uniform – if there was a rat at all, and Jen was still holding out hope that McKayla had been mistaken. The inside of the walk-in refrigerator had several long shelves that ran perpendicular to the door. She went around the first shelf to the left over to the one that held several sealed bags of shredded lettuce. All the bags sat there, neatly stacked, untouched by man or rat.

"Is it there?" McKayla called from the doorway.

"No," Jen said. She took one of the bags down and carried it over. "Bring this to Brian before he has a heart attack."

McKayla just stood there, her dishwater eyes confused, the packet of lettuce limp in her hand. "I don't understand. He was *there*. He spoke to me."

Jen paused in the act of chivvying McKayla out of the doorway. "It spoke to you?"

Maybe the girl was doing drugs, or had a fever.

"Yes," McKayla said, pushing one hand against the side of her head as if she were trying to dislodge something stuck there. "He said my name."

"Oohkay. We'll discuss this later, on your break maybe. In the meantime, get back up front. It's nearly the lunch rush and they'll need you."

McKayla wandered away from Jen, her whole body communicating 'dazed and confused'. Jen flipped off the light and turned to pull the refrigerator door shut behind her.

Something skittered across the floor. Jen paused, staring hard into the shadows. Nothing, she concluded. That gleam of red was nothing but her imagination. She closed the door firmly, her mind already moving back to paperwork.

Quinn, she thought in despair, *how could you just* disappear *like that?*

Quinn had closed up last Tuesday, sent everyone home and said he had some things to finish up in the office. Jen was apparently one of the last people to have seen him. She'd been the lowly assistant manager then, blessedly free of excess responsibility. She'd waved to Quinn from the parking lot as he locked the back door.

The next morning his car was still sitting in its usual place, and according to police he'd not withdrawn any money from his accounts. The security footage from the cameras in and around the store was mysteriously blank. He'd just *poofed*, vanished into thin air.

The office Jen currently occupied still had Quinn's personal items on the wall, his employee of the month awards and snapshots with friends. Jen didn't have the heart to get rid of them. She kept thinking about Quinn waving goodbye, the way he'd seemed perfectly normal.

She picked up the pen, tried to focus on the order forms. Something streaked across her memory and she put the pen down again. Quinn, waving to her as he pulled the back door closed. And just before it shut completely, had something darted inside, close to the ground? *A rat?*

She shook her head. She was imagining things.

McKayla passed by the open door, walking in a strange way – shuffling, her eyes staring like she was in a trance.

"McKayla?" Jen called.

The girl didn't answer, just kept scuffing along in the direction of the refrigerator.

Jen went after her, caught up before McKayla reached the fridge door. She put her hand on McKayla's shoulder.

"He's calling me," McKayla said. "He keeps saying my name."

McKayla's face was pale and covered in sweat. She tried to move forward, to open the refrigerator door, but Jen firmly steered her in the direction of the office. "I'm calling your mother. I think you've got a fever."

McKayla wrenched out of Jen's grasp and put her nose close to

Jen's nose. Her breath smelled like something had died inside her.

"He's... calling... me," she said, flecks of sour spittle landing on Jen's face.

There was a strange light in her eyes, something that made Jen want to curl up and hide, a feeling she had certainly never experienced before with McKayla.

"W-who's calling you?" Jen said, trying to get a grip on herself and the conversation.

"The rat," McKayla said. "He's calling me and I must obey."

The kid's having hallucinations, Jen thought.

McKayla didn't wait for Jen's response. She started for the refrigerator again.

Brian appeared at the other end of the hallway. "Hey, McKayla, what the hell are you doing? You can't just walk away from your station. We're short staffed as it is."

Jen approached him, gesturing for him to lower his voice. "I think she's sick. She's all sweaty and appears to be hallucinating. I'm going to call her mother."

"Great," Brian said. "I'll just handle everything myself, shall I?"

Jen heard the refrigerator door open and shut behind her. "I'll call around, see if anyone wants to pick up an extra shift. Just do your best for now."

Brian stomped off. Jen looked at the refrigerator door, debated if she should call McKayla's mother first, then decided to go after her. McKayla might faint and hit her head or something.

"I really don't want to be in charge," Jen muttered. She didn't feel equipped to deal with this. And for some reason she kept thinking about the movement around Quinn's ankles on that last day, the thing she hadn't registered at the time.

Her hand closed around the door handle and she jerked back, crying out. Across her palm was a bloody streak in the shape of—

"What the fuck? Teeth?" Jen held her palm closer to her face. It sure as hell looked like teeth imprints, deeper at the centre, like two protruding rodent's teeth.

"No," she said. "The door handle did *not* bite me."

But she shook her sweater cuff over her hand anyway before pulling the handle down. The door did not bite this time (*it didn't bite the last time*) but swung open and halted, like an open, welcoming mouth.

Jen hesitated. *Why did I think of it as a mouth? It's just a door. It's not a great gaping maw waiting to swallow me down...*

"Jen!" Brian shouted. "Did you call anyone yet? We're swamped up here."

"Not yet," she called back. "Go back to your station."

The scrape (*bite*) on her hand throbbed. The cheap fibres of her manager sweater caught in the edges of the wound and scratched painfully. And something else was scratching, something inside the refrigerator.

Scritch, scritch, scritch. Pause. *Scritch, scritch, scritch.*

Like something was digging. Methodically digging.

Jen eyed the door, not certain it wouldn't swing closed behind her as soon as she stepped inside. A long, pained moan came from the darkened corner behind the shelves, but it didn't sound like McKayla. It sounded like a man's voice. A familiar man's voice.

"Quinn?" Jen said as she stepped inside the fridge.

*   *   *

Brian was at his wits' fucking end. He was the only one making sandwiches. The drive-thru was backed up "for a mile" according to Tanya, who was a nasty bitch at the best of times.

All she does is put the food in the bag and hand it out the window. What are her panties in a twist for?

Jen was doing a terrible job since she'd taken over from Quinn. Brian had hinted strongly that *he* should be considered for a leadership position but Carl seemed to think that since Jen was the assistant she should be moved up. Now here he was alone, fucking McKayla having disappeared, and Jen wasn't doing a goddamned thing about it.

*   *   *

The door did not slam closed on Jen, but she thought she felt warm breath blow over her face, like a big sigh of contentment. *That's just the cold air blowing around,* she thought. But she realised that the air in the refrigerator was quite warm, much warmer than it should be, and she felt a flash of annoyance. *Another problem for me to solve.*

Then she heard the groan again. It did sound like Quinn, it really did, but Jen didn't understand how he could suddenly be here.

She rushed around the shelves and stopped. A man stood by the back wall. He was tall and thin and wore a manager's sweater over his uniform pants. He scratched at the wall and Jen saw dark streaks running there.

"Quinn?" she asked. "Quinn, is that you? How can you be here? Where have you been?"

He turned around, slowly, and Jen screamed.

The skin of his face was torn away in ragged strips, blood running down to his neck, and the tips of his fingers were worn away.

Quinn groaned again, and took a shuffling step toward Jen. "He took me away, because I wouldn't obey. And now I have to. I have to obey. He's calling me."

Jen staggered back, away from Quinn's seeking hands. The bite on her palm burned now, and the burning spread up to her wrist and forearm.

He sounds like McKayla. And where is McKayla? She went into the refrigerator. I saw her.

But there seemed to be no one but herself and Quinn, and Quinn needed a sedative and an ambulance immediately. Jen held up a hand like a stop sign, backing away from Quinn and around the shelf.

"Just stay here for a minute and I'll call someone to help you."

I'm going to have to shut him in here. I can't have him wandering around the store like that. At least he won't freeze.

The refrigerator was noticeably hotter now. Sweat pooled in the small of her back and trickled down her temples.

Something is really on the fritz, she thought, her brain trying to latch on to anything that was normal and not Quinn's shredded face.

She turned toward the doorway, but every step she took seemed to take the door farther from her instead of closer. *How can that be? It's only a few feet away.*

The doorway stretched away from her like a rubber band being pulled, and it now looked impossibly distant. She began to run, but the harder she tried to get there, the more out of reach it seemed.

I'm hallucinating. This bite on my hand has poisoned me. No, it's not a bite. Door handles don't bite.

"Jen," Quinn said behind her, and his bloodied hand landed on her shoulder. "He's calling you, and you must obey."

His mouth came close to her ear, and his breath was rank, and Jen thought again of McKayla.

"He wants your flesh."

"No," Jen said, but her voice was little, as little as McKayla's, a tiny pathetic squeak.

A mouse, I'm nothing but a mouse, she thought as a shadow seemed to swell before her, a shadow that was sort of shaped like a rat, only much bigger than it ought to be. A rat the size of a raccoon, and its eyes glowed red, and it called her name.

A rat like that could gobble up a little mouse like me.

★ ★ ★

"That's it," Brian said, throwing up his hands in frustration. "Tanya, you make the sandwiches. I'm going to go call in extra help myself."

"It's not my job to make sandwiches. I'm on drive-thru," Tanya said.

"Just do it," Brian snapped, yanking off his gloves and throwing them on the counter.

"Hey," Tanya called after him. "You're not the boss of me!"

"No, but I should be," Brian muttered as he stomped into the back.

Jen wasn't in her office and the refrigerator door was open, which meant she was still dealing with the McKayla situation, whatever that was about. The light was off in the fridge, which was weird, but Brian had bigger problems than whether or not Jen chose to flick a light switch. He went to the phone on Jen's desk and started methodically calling everyone who wasn't on shift at that moment.

★ ★ ★

The rat swelled, grew, became the size of a wolf, the size of a bear. Its mouth was a massive, monstrous thing with flesh clinging to its giant front teeth.

Mine, she thought. *That's my skin, my blood there*, and the bite on her palm seemed to swell in response.

The eyes weren't red. McKayla was wrong about that. They were made of fire, and a whiff of smoke and sulphur reached her. Her body was a creation of stone, impossible to dislodge. Smoke filled her eyes and nose and mouth, pressed into her ears, coated her skin. The bear-rat changed again, its body a pliable thing, pushing and stretching from the inside. But no bones cracked and no blood flowed, and that was somehow more terrible than if they had.

A long forked tail swam out the back of the creature and a long forked tongue uncurled from its mouth and long curved claws reached from unnaturally long fingers. Steam rose from ragged fissures in its body. It was like seeing the innards of the Earth given form and power.

Then Quinn grabbed her under her right arm and his grip was hard and unyielding. Before she could struggle, before she could even think about getting away, McKayla was there, holding her left arm. They pulled her toward the creature, the thing that was not a rat at all. Jen whimpered, dug in her heels, tried to arch back and away, away from the thing, this terrible thing, but Quinn (*Quinn, you were my friend*) and McKayla (*I always looked out for you*) pulled her horribly, inexorably toward its mouth.

The mouth grew and stretched and its teeth were sharper than they had been a moment before and a carrion reek emitted from its throat.

"Quinn," she pleaded. "Help me."

Quinn shook his head, slowly, from side to side.

"He wants your flesh, and you must obey."

*   *   *

Brian slammed down the phone.

"Useless," he muttered, stalking out of the office. Not one person was willing to come in.

"'I have school, I have a kid,'" Brian said in a mocking, singsong voice. "Nobody is committed to their job besides me."

The sounds of a scuffle reached him and he glanced back at the open refrigerator door. It was all darkness, though.

He thought he heard a short, sharp scream that was abruptly cut off. He rolled his eyes. Whatever. McKayla was probably having a meltdown and Jen had had to slap her.

Tanya was sweaty and bitchy when he got back to his station. "Where have you been? I can't keep up."

Brian made an Executive Decision. *I'll prove to Carl that I'm the one who should be in charge here.*

"Let's close the floor. Take everyone off the registers, drive-thru only."

Tanya looked doubtful. "Is that what Jen said to do?"

"Jen's dealing with McKayla. I think she's having a psychotic break or something."

"Jen's having a psychotic break?"

"No, McKayla," he said, shoving her aside so he could start filling orders. "Come on. Put a note on the door that says 'short-staffed, drive-thru only.'"

"I'm gonna get in trouble," Tanya said.

"I'll take responsibility," Brian said.

That manager's job would be his in no time.

★　★　★

McKayla shuffled into the hallway. The sounds of ripping and tearing and crunching and crying were behind her now. A buzz had filled her ears, a low voltage static that chased away any thoughts that tried to form.

He had told her to bring more, to bring the others. Quinn wasn't very good at doing what he wanted, Quinn wasn't a good listener, and so Quinn had followed Jen and now it was all up to McKayla.

Her sneakers scuffed and squeaked on the tile floor.

But if…

The words tried to push up from the back of her mind, but they were drowned out by the buzzing. Tanya appeared in the hallway, headed for the break room.

"I don't give a fuck what he says. He's not in charge and I'm entitled to my fifteen-minute break."

She stopped when she saw McKayla, her eyes widening.

"Hey, kid. You look like shit. I thought Jen was calling your mom."

Jen, McKayla thought, and a scream welled up inside her but the noise in her head smothered it.

"Kid?" Tanya said.

McKayla turned toward the open refrigerator door, pointed.

"Jen," she managed to say. "Jen."

"Is something wrong with her?"

McKayla nodded, and the scream inside her tried to come out again but it seemed to be stuck, lodged there like bile.

Tanya frowned, her gaze following McKayla's trembling fingers. She strode toward the refrigerator. "You go sit down in the break room. I don't know what the hell is going on today."

McKayla waited for Tanya to go inside, waited for the door to swing shut behind her, waited for the smoke in the hallway to curl and dissipate before she went into the kitchen to get someone else.

★   ★   ★

Brian noticed McKayla shuffle by like an actor in a zombie show and wondered what the hell Jen was thinking. There was obviously something wrong with the girl and Jen shouldn't be sending her back out on shift. Then a large order spit out of the machine, and he put his head down and forgot about McKayla.

★   ★   ★

McKayla took Laura next. Laura was always nice to her, even when she messed up, which she did all the time. She didn't want Laura to be afraid, so she held Laura's arm tight as they went down the hall.

Laura patted her hand. "It's all right. If Jen fell down in the refrigerator, I'm sure she'll be fine. Might have got her bell rung."

This story was what He had told her to say. Somehow His voice blasted through the buzzing while her own voice was squashed into a corner.

Laura reached for the door and cried out. She held up a bloodied palm. "Jesus! What the hell? It looks like something bit me."

She crouched down and peered at the handle. "I don't see anything sharp, though. McKayla, get me a bandage, okay?"

McKayla had already turned away, the voice telling her to move on. She would get Ava next. Laura was a goner now that she'd been marked. It was too bad, because Laura was always nice to her.

★   ★   ★

Brian was so busy until 1:30 p.m. that he didn't notice there was no one taking the drive-thru bags he'd filled. He shouldn't have been doing that, either – he was supposed to make the sandwiches and Tanya was supposed to pack the bags and add the fries and onion rings, but Tanya had disappeared after having a total shit fit about her break. Now Laura was gone, too, and he didn't know what that was about because Laura was usually reliable.

He grabbed the drive-thru bags, quickly filled the soda orders and handed out the food to a snippy asshole in a black BMW.

"Took you long enough," the driver said, practically throwing his platinum card at Brian.

Some of us actually work for a living, was what he wanted to reply, but managers were supposed to be above the fray.

"Thank you for your patience," he said, handing back the card along with a 'Buy 1 Get 1 Free' coupon. The man sniffed and gunned his engine as he pulled away.

Brian tended to the next few orders until finally there was a break in traffic. He turned around, ready to bellow at everyone else shirking their duties but there was no one in the kitchen with him.

What the hell? Where did they all go? Are they having a period party or something?

"This is what happens when you make a woman a manager," he muttered, taking off the drive-thru headset and throwing it on the counter. If anyone drove up in the next few minutes, they could either wait or go to the Other Place across the street. It killed him to give up sales but someone had to take this group of layabouts in hand.

He stalked toward the break room, ready to terrify the lot of them back into service. But there was no one in the break room, or in

Jen's office. The door to the walk-in refrigerator was closed, though. *Are those bitches having a secret meeting in there?*

The door opened and out came McKayla, looking more like a zombie than ever.

"Hey, McKayla," Brian said. "What's going on?"

She didn't answer, only kept shuffling toward him with blank dishwater eyes, and for some reason he couldn't understand, he felt afraid.

He found himself shrinking away, backing up to get away from her until he was in the kitchen again. Patties smoked on the grill with no one to tend them, and the persistent, tinny sound of "Hello? Hello?" came through the abandoned headset by the drive-thru window. Brian knew he should do something about all those things, prove his worth, but there was McKayla, and McKayla was not right, and he was all alone.

⋆ ⋆ ⋆

McKayla moved toward Brian. She knew what she was supposed to do, because He wanted all flesh and it was up to her to deliver it. But the buzzing was loud, so loud, and it wasn't just in her head anymore. It crawled under her skin and coated her throat and followed the pathway of blood through her heart.

She didn't want it anymore. She was sick of the buzzing and the noise, sick of the scream stuck inside her, sick of the crunching sounds.

So she went right past Brian and on to the bubbling fryer. The scent of hot oil filled her up, made her whole.

Yes, this will end it.

She plunged her face into the fryer.

⋆ ⋆ ⋆

Brian screamed. He didn't even know he could scream like that. McKayla's body bucked and danced, like she was being electrocuted, but her hands held fast to the hot counter and her head stayed inside the fryer, and into the kitchen billowed the strangely tantalising smell of freshly cooked meat. His gorge rose and Brian ran down the hallway to get Jen, to get somebody, *anybody*, because he was *not* the manager and this was *not* his responsibility.

I'm not paid enough for this shit, he thought as he threw open the door. The words on his tongue dried up.

Something crouched there, just inside the entrance, like a hugely swollen spider drunk on prey. Dark stains and abandoned shoes littered the floor all around it. His brain didn't want to say what the thing was but he knew, he *knew*.

It opened its mouth and Brian thought, for a moment, that he saw the dead screaming faces of his co-workers inside there. Then his own thoughts were gone, stuffed into a box in the corner, and there was only His voice and His voice said, "Bring me flesh."

Brian turned and shuffled away.

★   ★   ★

Sam was in a rush, running late to work as usual, when she pulled up to the drive-thru. There was a sign taped to the speaker.

SPEAKER BROKEN, WALK INS ONLY

She huffed out a sigh, but swung the car around to park. It would take longer to cross the traffic to go to the drive-thru across the street, she reasoned. And she really preferred the cheeseburgers here.

When she reached the glass door she saw another sign.

PLEASE BE PATIENT

WE ARE SHORT STAFFED TODAY

THERE'S A DEMON IN THE REFRIGERATOR

NOBODY WANTS TO WORK HERE ANYMORE

"Haha," she said, smiling at the wage-worker humour.

There was a strange smell in the restaurant when she entered, and a haze of smoke hung by the ceiling. Sam hesitated, then made her way to the counter. She'd committed and she didn't have time to stop anywhere else.

There was one skinny kid behind the register and he was so pale that he looked like a zombie.

"Rough day, huh?" Sam said.

"May I take your order?" he said, his voice slurred with exhaustion.

"Yeah," she said, and dug in her bag for her wallet, which had fallen to the bottom as usual.

She wasn't looking when the shadow rose up to take her.

THE SCARECROW FESTIVAL

Tim Major

"Oh God! Oh Jesus Christ!"

Andy dropped to the ground on his knees before the wicker man, his arms outstretched in supplication.

"Oh my God! Christ! No, no, dear God! Christ!"

He registered a hand being placed on his shoulder. "You all right there, mate?"

Andy turned, frowning. He gestured at the wicker man. "I was doing the thing. The scene."

"What scene, mate?"

"From *The Wicker Man*. You know, the film."

Gavin peered at him through the too-small lenses of his glasses, appearing none the wiser.

A middle-aged woman emerged from the house with the scarecrow wicker man in its garden. She was dressed in a plain white flowing dress, a garland of colourful flowers around her neck and a wreath on her head. Her feet were bare. She skipped past the scarecrow Christopher Lee in its tweed jacket and yellow polo neck sweater, past the scarecrow Edward Woodward in its police uniform.

"What do you think?" she asked Andy, tilting her head and revealing that her long, blonde hair was a wig. For some reason, she adopted an American accent to add, "Can I depend on your vote?"

Andy rose to his feet and looked beyond her to the wicker man itself, which was not even twice as tall as Edward Woodward. But the proportions were about right and somebody had worked hard on the spindly twig fingers and the blocky, suggestively blank head.

"I suppose," he said with a shrug.

The woman clapped her hands in delight. "Ed would be so proud."

Andy glanced at the police scarecrow.

"I mean my husband," the woman explained. "This was his favourite film. Had a real thing about Britt Ekland, his whole life. Hence my getup."

"Actually," Andy said, appraising her outfit again, "I don't think you're Britt Ekland. I think you're the young girl, um... Rowan? The one who's supposed to be the sacrifice but then isn't. Britt Ekland was mostly naked, at least in my mind's eye."

The woman squinted up at him, her pursed lips trembling.

"I never saw the film myself," she said. "I don't like shocks. And this was supposed to be a tribute to my Ed. I'm supposed to be Britt Ekland."

In response to a glare from Gavin, Andy said hurriedly, "Actually, I'm wrong. I'm wrong, okay? Now that I think of it, you look exactly like her. Like Britt Ekland. It's uncanny. And... and the wicker man is really outstanding." He forced a chuckle. "I hope you'll actually burn it?"

The woman's expression had been lightening, but now her eyebrows lowered again. "What? What the fuck did you just say?"

"Like in the..." Andy gulped. "Never mind. I say daft things sometimes." He turned to Gavin. "Shall we head on?"

They moved along the road, passing a scarecrow Boris Johnson and a scarecrow Duggee. When Andy looked back, the woman was spinning in circles before the wicker man with her arms stretched wide, making a low hissing sound.

"Don't mind her," Gavin said. "She's sensitive these days. It was pancreatic cancer that took Ed. Quite sudden."

Andy nodded. He looked around at the immaculate cottages, the immaculate gardens each containing a scarecrow.

"I suppose this is a tight community, though. Supportive," he said.

"Course. You probably think it's a bit twee, a bit claustrophobic, living somewhere like this. But the villagers live simple and pure lives, and I've come to respect that."

"Pure? Meaning pious?"

"Not in the religious sense. Just uncluttered, mentally. The people here believe in straightforward emotions, the purer the better."

It sounded like nonsense to Andy. City life suited him just fine. There, he could be anonymous and unjudged. He had no desire to meditate, or to take up Zen gardening, or whatever people did here.

A few other people were examining the scarecrows. They pottered along on the narrow road – there were no cars other than those parked on the keystone driveways.

"Does it get super busy?" Andy asked.

"You're asking does Roseberry Atherton get busy?"

"I mean today. On scarecrow festival day."

"Why would it?"

"Tourists. Offcomers."

Gavin shook his head. "It's not about that. We don't even promote it. It's not for other people, it's for us here in the village."

"You invited me, though."

"Yeah. Was your journey okay?"

"Sure. Long. Bumpy. It was an old bus."

Gavin turned to face him. "So... how long's it been, mate?"

Andy puffed out his cheeks. "Maybe twenty-five years?"

"Exactly twenty-five. Since we were last in school together, anyway." Before Andy could respond to this odd qualification, Gavin continued, "I was surprised you could come, thought you'd have other commitments. Family, et cetera."

Andy didn't think he'd ever heard anybody say 'et cetera' out loud. Gavin hadn't changed, not really. He'd always seemed from another era, always older than his years, reading the *Economist* instead of *NME* at secondary school, certain he was on course to become an accountant and a wealthy man. They'd bonded over nerdy SF shows, way back, and had continued to hang out sometimes during lunch breaks even after Andy's heart was no longer in it.

"I don't have kids," Andy said.

"Wife? Girlfriend?"

"Not right now. I've never been married. Hey, I know I should know this, but your wife's name is..."

"Flick." When Andy swallowed hard and almost choked, he added, "It's short for Felicity."

"Of course," Andy said, recovering himself, making a show of studying the scarecrow farmer in a nearby garden, whose straw hat was simply an extrusion of the straw of his head.

"She's looking forward to meeting you, putting a face to the name."

"Yeah?" Andy hesitated. "Look, I'm still surprised you invited me here. We haven't spoken in a long time. And now you're telling me that your wife knows me, that you've talked about me... To be honest, Gav, I haven't thought about you much. Is that a shitty thing to say?"

Gavin exhaled thoughtfully. "Still, you came."

"I didn't have much on this weekend."

"You're footloose and fancy free."

"That's right. I can do what I want. That's how I like it. Last September I just upped and went to Iceland for a fortnight. Didn't tell anyone. And I'm freelance, so I just kept on trucking with work, keeping the wheels spinning."

"No ties at all. I can barely imagine it."

"Are you envious?"

"Just curious." They moved along the road in silence before Gavin added, "It's been twenty-seven years since the other thing, you know."

Andy stopped walking. He'd wondered whether this would crop up.

"Look," he said, "there's no need to bring it up. It was a long time ago."

"It was important. It *is* important."

"I can't even remember what the argument was about – can you?"

Gavin shrugged. "That's not the important part."

Andy had started it, he recalled, or at least he'd raised the stakes. Whatever it was they'd argued about as they ate their jacket potatoes in the school canteen, he'd been determined to have the last word. He'd finished his meal, then stood and, very calmly, tipped a glass of water over Gavin's head before walking out of the room. But it was what had happened afterwards that was memorable. At lunch breaks they and their small group of friends played – or, more often, slumped against tree trunks and discussed canonical details of their favourite shows – in the small copse of trees between the tennis courts. That day, Andy had assumed Gavin wouldn't show up, but he did. Red-faced and shaking. He'd snatched a thick fallen branch from the ground and, with a long shout drawn from the belly, he'd chased Andy down and struck him on the head with the limb of the tree. Five stitches and a weeklong suspension from school, respectively.

"You really don't need to apologise," Andy said, only now realising the fingers of his right hand were touching the slight bump of stitched flesh on the crown of his head. He pulled his hand away. "We were just kids, full of hormones and rage."

Gavin watched him levelly for several seconds. Then he nodded and kept walking. Despite Andy's insistence about no apology being needed, Gavin's immediate acceptance struck him as callous.

A high-pitched sound attracted Andy's attention. The garden of the cottage they were alongside contained a large scarecrow cat. It wasn't well constructed – its body was wrapped in bin bags, presumably to hold the straw in place – but some effort had been put into its posture, bent forward with one of its paws resting upon a spherical bundle of straw meant to evoke a ball of wool. A young girl with short, dark hair, aged around seven, lay on the grass, stroking the front foot of the giant cat.

That same high-pitched mewl came again.

"Is that cat miaowing?" Andy asked.

"Yes," the girl said, raising her dark eyes. Andy balked, his question having been rhetorical.

"It's a clever idea," he said. When the cat miaowed again, he added, "It sounds really real."

"There's a CD player stuck underneath its tummy," the girl said. "And it *is* real. It's really Captain Crumbs."

"Captain Crumbs is your cat? Your real cat."

"Captain Crumbs is gone now." She stroked the scarecrow cat's foot again. "We recorded his miaow before he went."

There was something strange about that foot. Andy shifted to one side along the low garden fence, trying to make it out. The girl's fingers were stroking something soft that seemed to have been pushed within the coarse straw.

"You made a scarecrow cat as a freaky tribute to your real, dead cat?" he asked.

"Mate," Gavin said quietly. "She's a kid."

"Sorry."

"Dad says not to feel sorry," the girl said. "He says Captain Crumbs had to die."

"You mean because everything dies."

The girl gazed up at him impassively. She continued stroking the cat's foot idly.

As she did so, something came free from within the straw. Andy leant over the fence to peer at the small, furred shape. It looked like nothing so much as the paw of a real, normal-sized cat, severed from its body.

Before he could say anything, Gavin ushered him along.

★ ★ ★

Within a few minutes, they stood before a cottage that was noticeably larger than the others in the village. In fact, it was only the thatched roof that defined it as a cottage in Andy's mind. Alongside the house were outbuildings with doors all painted the same shade of eggshell blue. Offices, perhaps, or playrooms or guest quarters. In that instant, Andy told himself that he'd decline the invitation to stay over, that he would return home on the bus this evening, no matter the long journey. There was something eerie about the perfection of this village.

Alongside a driveway that contained a Range Rover and a Lexus was a perfect kidney-shaped lawn. A blonde woman stood on a stepladder held by a blond preteen boy. She was leaning over a bulbous scarecrow sculpture, weaving strands carefully. When she saw Gavin and Andy, she descended the ladder and hurried over to them, smoothing her smart green dress.

"Flick," she said, her hand extended. Pure, unthinking confidence.

"Hi," Andy said, taking her hand, which was far cooler than his own. "I'm Andy."

"Of course you are. I'm so glad you could come. We weren't sure you'd…" She laughed. "It hardly matters, does it? You're here now."

An awkward silence followed. Andy pointed behind her and said, "You're cutting it fine, still working on your scarecrow."

He tried to make out the shape of their creation. If he squinted, he could see a head, but it was oddly low on the body. Perhaps the part that Flick had been working on was a limb, raised above the head?

"It's quite an unusual one," he concluded weakly.

Flick smiled. "I wasn't certain we'd make one this year. Like I say, we didn't know for sure you were really coming."

Andy froze. "What do you mean?"

"I mean—"

Gavin laughed. "Pop your bag down – young Vincent will take it. I bet you could use a drink right now, mate."

Was that a deliberate jibe? No, Gavin couldn't know about his problems of the past decade.

"It's only early," Andy replied.

"Still. Let's head over to the fiesta." Gavin pointed across the road to the village green, upon which was a collection of striped tents that Andy had noticed as they approached the cottage. "It'll all be kicking off around now, and we'll have to move fast if we're to finish before the judgement."

"Finish what?" Andy asked.

Gavin laughed and clapped his hand on Andy's shoulder, in the same motion slipping his backpack from his shoulders. All of this camaraderie, the insistence of the use of the word 'mate', seemed entirely false. The two of them weren't friends. Perhaps they never had been, really, even before the incident in the copse that had ended their childhood relationship so decisively. Why had he agreed to come here?

He allowed himself to be led towards the village green. Flick spoke to her blond son, who climbed the stepladder and resumed work on the scarecrow, then she scurried to join them, linking her arm around Andy's so that he was flanked by the couple.

More scarecrows were positioned around the periphery of the green. An old woman carrying a large handbag, James Bond, a hamster, a pilot, a fish that might have been Nemo. They were all passable, but none seemed likely winners of the contest.

Deckchairs had been arranged before one of the tents. A few were already occupied by men wearing shorts and T-shirts, and women wearing summer dresses. Gavin gestured for Flick and Andy to sit amongst the group.

"Champagne?" he said in an affected tone like a nineteenth-century butler.

Flick giggled and nodded.

"Like I said—" Andy began.

"You don't drink," Gavin said. "Vimto?"

"Lemonade would be fine."

One of the villagers, a man in his sixties with a perfectly white beard, leant forward in his deckchair. "How're you liking the festival, Andrew?"

Andy blinked. "Do we know each other?"

"Gavin mentioned you were coming."

"Are you his dad?"

"Ha! His dad." Then, suddenly serious, "I'd be proud to be his dad. But no, just a nosy neighbour."

Andy forced a laugh. "A stranger coming to the village is newsworthy, is it?"

The old man simply nodded.

The woman sitting next to the man patted his arm. "What Niall means is that it's a pleasure to have somebody come and see us on our special day. It's rare to see a new face. And yours is interesting. Quite difficult to capture, I'd have thought."

"What do you—"

"I'm a photographer. Was, before I retired. I still dabble. Julia."

She held out her hand for Andy to shake. Then her husband did the same, so that both of Andy's hands were grasped and they performed an odd double-shake like the start of a complex country dance. He pulled his hands away and slipped them beneath himself on the sling of soft deckchair fabric.

He wanted nothing more than to leave this place. But there would be no bus for another two hours. *Pretend you're here to observe these nuts,* he told himself. *Pretend you're Louis Theroux.*

"It's a funny thing," he said, "but both of the people I've spoken to about their scarecrows said they'd created them as tributes." When neither Julia nor Niall nor Flick responded, he added, "Tributes to dead people, or dead pets."

"That's natural, isn't it?" Julia said calmly.

"Is it?"

"There's a great tradition of sculptures to remember those that have passed."

"Yes... but these are scarecrows. They're more in a tradition of scaring birds away."

"Two birds with one stone!" Niall roared, slapping his thighs.

Julia chuckled. "Yes, why can't they perform both functions?"

No answer came to mind. Andy was relieved when Gavin returned holding three glasses. He handed one of the flutes of champagne to Flick, and a plastic beaker to Andy.

"They didn't have lemonade," Gavin said, "but I thought I ought to bring you something."

Andy looked into the beaker to see that it was water. He raised it in an ironic cheers.

Gavin shuffled a deckchair to be positioned directly opposite Andy's, so that their feet were almost touching. Andy made to move away, but Flick shook her head. Behind her, Andy noticed activity within one of the striped tents. A group of teenagers were arranging what looked like set dressings, two-dimensional boards reinforced to stand on their ends. The pieces Andy could make out were cartoonish green trees with cloudlike masses of leaves.

"Is there going to be a play later?" he asked.

"We'll see," Flick replied.

More villagers were arriving at the village green all the time. They collected drinks from the counter within the nearest tent, then gravitated to the deckchair area. They all seemed to assess Andy as they took their seats or, when the deckchairs were all occupied, stood behind them in a ring.

Andy turned his attention to Gavin sitting before him.

"What is all this?" he asked.

Gavin smiled. "You look a bit lost."

"No, just weirded out, if I'm honest."

"I don't mean at this moment. I mean in general. You look like you've lost your way, mate."

Andy lowered his voice, uncomfortable due to the attention of the people encircling them. "What gives you the right to say that? I'm my own person. I've made my own choices. And I'm not your *mate*, mate, okay?"

Gavin smiled. "I'm not much of a social media user, but I indulged in order to check up on you. Failed career, failed relationships. And reading between the lines, failure to pay your rent, failure to stop yourself from indulging in vices... Am I wrong about any of this?"

It took some effort to rise from the low deckchair. When he'd managed to do so, Andy realised the throng of villagers had grown tighter around him.

"What the actual fuck?" he said.

"I pity you," Gavin said, gazing up at him implacably. "Not for those failures, but for the messiness in your head. If only you could find simplicity, purity."

"Like here in Roseberry Atherton? Meaning I should be like all these other grinning robots with their strimmed borders and scrubbed kids?"

"I mean only that these people appreciate untainted emotions. Perhaps you found it, for a time, in drink. But you couldn't allow yourself to feel it because even then the experience was tainted with fear."

"Oh Christ," Andy said wearily. "Then this is about religion after all? Are you trying to convert me?"

Faint laughter rippled around the crowd.

Gavin turned to look at the villagers. "It was twenty-seven years ago," he announced, "that I chased this man in a small forest with a stick."

Andy recalled the phone calls he was required to make as part of his own ten-step programme, the unreserved apologies he had been compelled to offer. That was what this was.

"I've already told you that you don't need to apologise for it," he said.

Gavin shook his head. "And I won't." Then, addressing the crowd again from his seated position, "Friends, it was the purest emotion I've ever experienced. Purer than the happiness of our wedding day. Purer than the joy of seeing Vincent for the first time when he was born. Purer, I suspect, than the grief that has informed your own scarecrow tributes. What I experienced was unadulterated rage. And it was beautiful."

Amid the polite applause of the crowd, Andy stared down at him in disbelief.

"These fine people have created tributes," Gavin said. "Grief is pure, and as I said, we all crave purity here. Sandra grieves for her husband Ed. Little Fi grieves for her cat, who was required to die in order to provide her with that necessary experience." He leant forward to take his wife's hand. "We have no knowledge of grief in our little family, more's the pity. For that reason, we had no intention of creating a scarecrow, initially."

I wasn't certain we'd make one this year, Flick had said. *We didn't know for sure you were really coming.*

Andy swallowed. His throat was dry. He glanced down at his right hand, which was still clutching the beaker of water.

Gavin was looking at it too. "It's not for drinking," he said. "Throw it over me."

"What?" Andy said stupidly. His thoughts were a slow trickle.

"Tip the water over my head."

"No. Why would I?"

"That's how it starts."

Flick rose from her deckchair. She put her hand on Andy's right hand. Andy was able to withstand the pressure she applied without any trouble, but then Niall stood and added his own strength. Andy watched in impotent horror as his hand was forced forwards until the beaker was above Gavin's head. Andy shook his own head and mumbled something that even he couldn't decipher.

The beaker trembled, then upturned.

Gavin stared up at him, water dripping down his forehead, into his eyes, along his cheeks. His lips parted in a toothy grin.

He stood. He opened his arms wide.

"It's returning to me," he announced. "That same feeling."

His eyes were gleaming. There was something very dangerous there.

"It's time," Gavin said.

The crowd behind Andy parted. Once again, Gavin and Flick stood on either side of him, guiding him, turning him around. Now Andy could see the centre of the village green, which had previously been empty, but no longer. The teenagers had left the tent containing the set dressings to arrange themselves in a circle in the centre of the green. Each of them supported a tall two-dimensional tree. Those trees on the far side were brightly and messily coloured, whereas Andy could see only the plain backs of those closer to him.

"Come, Andy," Flick said. "It's time to play your part."

Andy tried to struggle, but they were stronger than him, or he was weaker than he had realised. Gavin and Flick led him into the clearing within the ring of flat trees. The villagers fanned out to take positions around the exterior of the imitation forest – the *copse*, Andy told himself.

When they reached the centre of the clearing, Flick stood on tiptoes to kiss Andy's cheek. At this unexpected human touch, he burst into tears. Then she turned and skipped away to join her neighbours beyond the crayoned trees.

"I don't understand," Andy said.

"I think you do, deep down," Gavin replied.

He reached down to the neatly mown grass to pick up the thick branch that lay there. Unlike the trees, it was real.

Andy spun, looking for gaps in the ring of villagers, but there were none.

Gavin raised the branch high.

Andy crouched, cowering, putting his hands above his head to protect it, his elbows forward, his fingers pressing against the healed wound on his crown. The fact that his posture was a precise echo of the scarecrow on the lawn of Gavin's cottage only added to his certainty: his fate had been sealed the moment he arrived in the village.

He heard, rather than saw, the branch swing down.

THE WRONG ELEMENT

Aaron Dries

HUGO

First hates are the last hates.

I'm thinking this as I peer out my bedroom window, scanning the street for the green van again. The Tree Frog, Finn named it, two weeks earlier at school drop-off when the vehicle stalked us for the first time. Its paint job glowed in the apple-crisp morning, not a warm colour at all, a cold colour that would freeze-burn your fingertips were you to touch it, and trailing a question mark of exhaust that lingered in the air longer than it should. Prior to moving apartments, and moving so fast, almost *brutally* fast, I let Finn catch the bus home when I wasn't working in the office. He loved the adventure of the ride with the other students, how that half-hour of independence – which took him from the school gate to the end of our block – pushed against the image I have of him as 'the child'. He'd waltz inside, swaggering, unnerving me; he will be a man one day. But for now, Finn is angry. Because I am the one who has taken him away from his old room in Narrabundah. I am the reason he's mourning the fig tree across the road, the one that was so good for climbing and into which he'd carved his initials. And I haven't let him catch the bus since we saw it, The Tree Frog. The paint isn't matte as you might expect it to be, but shiny as tooth enamel. Only with an abscess within.

Guy has been released from the AMC.

The Alexander Maconochie Centre.

Prison.

"Hey, there's that van again," said my son, slender arm raised and pointing in the Bunnings parking lot where we'd been loading our car with paint cans and putty to mask all the wall gouges in our apartment – preparations for the about-to-be-broken lease. "Green tree frogs don't like it when you pick them up because the oil in our skin hurts them. Did you know that, Dad? Did you? Dad? *Dad*, you aren't listening. You never listen. Nobody *fucking* listens to me."

Finn is seven.

You don't have to be psychic to know where he learned the word. Right then, I didn't have it in me to scold him beyond a reproachful *hey*! We watched the van slink off, a chill on the back of my neck like someone gripping puppy scruff, forcing Spot's head to the carpet it shat on, rubbing its nose in the mess so it knew to never do it again.

I step back from the window in my bedroom in our new townhouse. It stinks of fresh paint. The street is empty. It's cold but staying inside is doing neither of us good. Finn exudes pent-up energy, and there will be screaming if he doesn't run it off soon. He's dressed and is on his iPad watching Bluey downstairs. I'm the one dragging the chain because I keep looking for the van. Because I'm thinking, again, how in the end, the first hates are the last hates.

It began like this:

Guy and I left the Vietnamese restaurant tipsy. The date, which took place four days after his initial tap on my Grindr account, had gone better than either of us expected. "Want to come back to mine?" I said. He answered with a smile, a touch of my wrist. Laughing, we stumbled up the street. A homeless, elderly woman was begging for money on Northbourne Avenue where we waited for the pedestrian lights to change. She kneeled on a flattened box, shaking a birdnesty hat. Guy elbowed my arm, and as if it were the funniest thing, whispered to me, "I wonder if her LinkedIn profile's up to date?"

We'd had a great time up to then.

I chose to ignore him, because earlier, our knees had brushed together under the table in a way that made me feel alive. And the taxi stand was *right there* on the other side of the road. And Guy was so charming, so handsome. And I wanted us to taste one another. Lips on lips. Lips on cock. Tongue to hole. Nipples pinched. Fingers sucked. Sweat mixed. Cum drying on our stomachs once we were done, as we slept. Because of this, all of it, because nobody had made me buzz this way in so long, I faked a chuckle. Yet I knew and ignored it. All these years later, I still remember the ride home that night, the two of us in the backseat, and how I thought: *Yeah, this man is pretty and smart and confident and I'm* obviously *punching above my weight.*

But there's something else there.

Geez, this man can be cold.

Dead cold. Inert flesh cold. Bruise me without apology cold. Throw everything away cold. Apprehended Violence Order cold.

Stalker cold.

That first date was long ago. Age isn't telegraphed in my body anymore. It's in Finn. I still dream about his surrogate, the woman we paid, one of Guy's old school friends. She ghosted us after the birth. Doing so must have been easier for her, as it was for us. Still, I often wonder where and *who* she is, and what of her is in our boy.

Do you think of him? Me?

Milk spurts across bub's cheek when he fought the bottle. Screaming. Hunger pains. Abandonment pains. Sleeping regressions. Songs on repeat. Routines. Nappy rash. Day care sickness. Vomit. Battery acid shit. The cupboard you forgot to lock. The scissors you thought were hidden. All the lessons Guy and I learned. Like how fatherhood turns you into your father. All the ways you want to say this is hard but aren't allowed to because you should be grateful you have a child when others don't – especially as two gay men.

I never thought I could love someone the way I love Finn. That's why it hurt so deeply when we parked the car after our trip to Bunnings, and I found him checking the wheels to see if the rim bolts had been tampered with again. Finn had been in the car when Guy did this the first time, and we crashed on the Barton Highway. People said we should be dead, that it was a miracle we survived.

(I wonder if her LinkedIn profile's up to date?)

Yes. *Cold.*

My knees pop as I crouch to scrounge through suitcases I haven't unpacked yet, looking for my thermals. I find a pair of trousers I haven't seen in eight years and wore only once on my wedding day. It's important I don't forget how much I've been hurt and humiliated, so I slip my hand into the pocket, into our past, and draw out whatever is rustling about inside. It's a fifty dollar note. I can't help laughing. It is the saddest laugh I've ever heard.

★   ★   ★

We're at Pialligo Redwood Forest, an artificial slice of another world near the airport. Finn calls it Endor.

He runs across browned grass, breathing out frosty ghosts. The air is brittle. Canberra winter is dry and gets between your joints.

He plays finger guns. Pew-pew. Watch me, Dad. Can I bring this stick home with me, Dad? Dad, look, it's a plane.

Here, he's not the kid I sometimes find loading his *Star Wars* sheets into the washing machine after wetting the bed. The kid who freezes, who doesn't speak, lips turning blue. The one who sucks his thumb and checks the wheels of cars.

I'm glad I spent those fifty bucks on him. "Whatever you want, buddy. It's all yours."

"Pho," he'd said, because his friend, Liam, told him about it. Not McDonald's. Not Hungry Jack's. Pho.

"So, how do you like it?" I asked, chopsticks in hand. "Nice, isn't it?"

"Yeah. But I don't like the white bits."

"They're called bean sprouts."

"I don't think I like bean sprouts, Dad. They're too crunchy."

"That's fine, mate. Are you going to tell Liam about us having pho together?"

"Maybe."

Finished, we drove in silence, listening to the radio. Quiet until:

"I don't like Mister Christie," Finn said without explanation. Mister Christie is one of his teachers at school. "He smells like smokes."

'Smokes': it's an adult's word in a child's mouth.

Five years ago, Guy stubbed his smokes out on Finn's eyelids when he was sleeping. Guy talked me out of taking our toddler to hospital, somehow convincing me that Finn did it to himself.

Shadow shame, together. Always.

Finn screams. I'm relieved when I find him in a clearing at the far end of the forest, fingers of gold light scrunching his duckish hair. I wonder if Guy is here, watching us with a spider's stillness from behind a tree. Finn stands above a dead rabbit on a bed of pine needles. It's too cold for flies and maggots.

"Maybe he's sleeping!" I tell my son.

"No. He's not." Finn turns away, an old man in a kid in a pea jacket. I'm the child here. Me. I do the breathing techniques Doctor Smalls taught me. If I close my eyes, I can see her nodding, legs crossed at the heels in the chair in the office in the house on a street where bad things never happen.

"Finn, not too far, I'm—"

White noise. A tinny taste drips onto the back of my tongue from my nasal cavity, similar to the decent cocaine you sniffed off your husband's chest on one of *those* nights, and more than once, back before you had a kid and realised how the first hates are the last hates. My brain says cough this taste up; my body swallows it down. Rollercoaster tummy, even though I'm standing still in this dank, fake forest. My eyes are drawn to twin chalky gum trees at the perimeter of the clearing. I take a step to the left, not because I have to. I do it because doing so just seems *right*, and their branches overlap in my line of sight, forming a perfect triangle with a smaller triangle at its core.

The drip turns sweet and rolls down my throat, like a kind of reward. I feel as though something I will never be intuitive enough to understand has clicked into place.

"Dad!" Finn's yell isn't a question. "Hurry up, I want to go-oooo."

My son may want to leave, but I don't want to move – ever. This is the centre of the universe. This is exactly where I'm meant to be. However, it's *his* day, and my fear of The Tree Frog snaps back. It takes effort to force my leaden legs to move, to shake off the invisible hands that have taken hold, not threatening, not as though disciplining me or offering caution, but fatherly. *Go to your son*, I tell myself. *Take one step after another.* Dead leaves crunch as I leave the clearing, my senses returning to normal, the white noise dissipating. Once the triangle within a triangle is out of sight, I feel gross and shamed, like the moment you finish jerking off but the porn still plays. *Gah!*

What the fuck just happened?

Is this vertigo? That is what happens to Mum, isn't it? Maybe it's hereditary. Shit. Wait. Did I just have a stroke, or something?

"Dad?" Finn says, leaning against the car, so casual. Again, I see a flash of the man he'll grow into – lanky and suspicious.

"Y-yeah?" I say, finding the words, shaking, touching the door handle to ground myself. This here is the feel of cold metal. This here in my nostrils is the smell of earth after a week of on-and-off-again rain. This is the taste of musky saliva and nothing more. This is the reality I share with my beautiful son.

This is me telling you everything here is normal.

I glance back at the woods, Endor. From where I'm standing by the car, everything looks so dark where we had been, like the inside of a great mouth. The inside of a closing mouth.

"Dad."

"What, mate? Sorry. You okay? What's wrong?"

"Do... you have a gun?"

Hearing this is a jab in the ribs. I wince. Shame twists harder, deeper. "What kind of question is *that*? The stuff you come up with, mate, I swear. Get in the car now, would you."

No. No, I don't have a gun, I don't tell my son. I also don't tell him that there was a time, and not that long ago, really, when I knew how to find one.

★ ★ ★

Later that night, Finn asks if he can have Sook, his teddy bear. Stitches and spit – that's all the old thing is now, and with one eye dangling on a thread.

"I seem to remember you telling me you were too old for Sook," I say, wanting to respect his choice but cautious of regressions. He corrects me with a glance. "Fine, fine."

I lift Sook from the toybox in the living room, trying not to trip over action figures and Tonka trucks I asked Finn to put away. I'm in no mood to school him now. Plus, I'd left unpacked boxes everywhere, so who was I to talk? I give my boy his toy, tell him I love him, and close the door.

Ice in the tumbler. The burn of good whiskey. I sprawl on my bed and am grateful our new rental has decent heating.

Monday feels far away. Mum is due at 8:00 a.m. tomorrow. She wants to get down from Jindabyne more often than she does, but her health makes travelling difficult. I miss who she used to be to me: my mother and not the person I see for thirty seconds on my way out the door when she comes to sit on school holidays, who I watch nod off on the couch once I'm home from Parliamentary Circuit after senate estimates. I don't resent her for the things she's said – like when she told me she'd always thought, when it came to Guy, that I was mixing with the wrong element.

Well, if that's the case, I'm the wrong element too, Mum.

Because I mixed back.

And gladly.

My wedding ring sits on the bedside table. I don't want to wear it, yet I don't want it far from my mind. It reminds me that Guy happened, and that he deserved his sentence. Even if the sentence was nowhere near long enough.

I found out about his release from my social worker who insisted I hustle to get an updated Apprehended Violence Order. But doing so required the disclosure of our new address to Guy so he would know what property to stay away from.

Being angry at the system doesn't change the system. I've learned that the hard way.

Whiskey works. I kill the lamp and roll onto my side, reaching under the bed to touch the shoebox. Just to know it's there.

★ ★ ★

A snake of cold air slithers over me in the dark. I know it is Guy by its wrongness. I inch out of bed and creep up the hall, telling myself that bursting into Finn's room will frighten him, and that will start the bed-wetting and thumb-sucking again. I push on anyway, tight as rope, clenching my jaw.

The door is open. My son's blankets are on the floor.

Sook is face-down on the empty bed.

Pulse-punch. Pulse-punch.

I rush to the window and look down at the courtyard between the front door and the open gate. Two silhouettes scuttle inside the green van at the curb. I rip the phone from the wall where it was charging in my room, the wedding ring bouncing out of sight.

Almost tripping over toys as I sprint downstairs. Leaves blow into the living room.

The door had been locked.

Wondering what Guy's done and how he did it will have to wait. I dial the police as I go, mashing the phone keypad and falling onto the footpath as The Tree Frog screeches away.

My car keys are on the granite counter inside. Force my feet into boots by a Welcome mat that must have belonged to the prior owner. I should have gotten rid of it when we moved in. These were the kind of details, the slights, which detectives note in their reports when something bad happens, the ironic comeuppance.

See, these people welcomed danger here.

They let it stroll in and take what it thought it had earned.

Danger thinks it owns everything. I know that now.

The van turns right at the end of the street. I follow, shoving the phone into the clip-holder as I steer, swerving to miss a dog that zooms across the road. Accelerator to the floor. Guy runs a red light, so I run a red light. The engine howls.

"Siri. Call the police."

"Calling the police now," says a female voice through the radio. The Bluetooth sync volleys my trauma through wires and off satellites in the sky as I wait for a dial tone.

Guy takes a left, away from the city, over – not through – a roundabout, going south. The airport exit.

"Police, ambulance, or fire?" says the operator. *"What is your emergency?"*

It's not real until I say it.

★ ★ ★

The police operator tells me not to pursue. I step out of the car at the entrance to Endor.

"Hugo, I repeat, do not—"

I lose Guy in the dark for thirty seconds when my phone slips from my hands. Fumble over gravel to find it.

"Hugo, are you there?" comes the small voice. *"Mister Helleyer?"*

Find it. Skid to the trunk and draw out a tyre iron, sensing its weight, flicking on the phone's torch feature, a silvery eye that reveals tree trunks, bushes, branches, all curdled with plumes of breath as I do everything the responder tells me not to.

"Finn! Yell if you can hear me. It's Daddy. I'm here, Finn. Jesus. SCREAM."

Footsteps. Rustling clothes. Crunching twigs like something chewing bones. I imagine Sook out there, grown large, its button eye hanging loose as it unstitches its mouth to reveal sharp teeth.

It scoops up my son and eats him alive.

Shadows swirl as I scuttle between trees. Why would Finn leave with Guy considering how frightened he was by him? And then it clicks. My boy has been forced. A hand on his mouth, maybe. A whispered threat. *Jesus, did Guy pull a knife on him? Please, not that.*

I funnel hatred into the tyre iron. Squeeze it. Punish it.

"Are you there, Hugo?" comes the voice from the phone. I'm on the same path from yesterday, the one to the clearing with its frozen rabbit. It's all familiar, yet different by night. But there is light up ahead.

The wind is stronger in the clearing. It churns the trees. They shush us.

Guy and Finn have their backs to me. My ex is dressed in a windbreaker with the hood up and holds our son with one arm. They stand between the two pale gum trees, which are stark against shadow, like something being dug up from the earth, dustings of white on all that black.

I take two steps, tyre iron raised, my phone in the other hand. Quivering.

"Guy. You leave him right there, you piece of shit. If you think I won't hurt you, you're dead fucking wrong."

Finn turns. Guy's torch dances across his face, time enough for me to see how confused my boy is – and it breaks my heart. Guy forces Finn to stare at the space between the trees, under the branches.

Triangles within triangles.

That sweet drip at the back of my throat starts again. There's an electric crackle in the cold air, that *come closer* sensation. It's stronger this time. White noise.

An invitation.

Endor floods with light. At first I think it's a plane, only the light is purple. It's not coming from overhead, either. The light blooms in front of Guy and Finn. They become thin silhouettes, scars on the brightness, between the trees. Immense wind. No, this is no passing flight. There is no word for what's happening here. This power, I can't help feeling, has its own authority, is its own element. My throat turns dry.

I rush forward.

Guy twists around. A gust pushes the hood off his head. Purple light flexes and in that flare I realise the man who took my son isn't Guy. This man has *my* face, and there are tears on his cheeks. *My cheeks*. Something inside me rips in two, and I want to reject both halves.

Purple rolls to white.

"I put it in the mailbox," shouts the man who looks and sounds like me.

Everything pops, then darkness. The white noise is gone.

I fall on my haunches, phone spinning across the ground, landing beside the dead rabbit. Gasping, my eyes adjusting to the dimness, I search the empty space where my son stood moments before – not held against his will, but where he'd held the man's hand. *My hand*. They have vanished. I'm screaming when red and blue light starts to paint the trees.

The squawk of radios. Their torches on my face.

Voices that instruct me to lie flat on earth that has never felt so empty.

FINN

Why is it daytime? Why is there a funny taste in my mouth?

Are you my dad?

I was so sleepy when he woke me, saying I had to keep quiet and leave, and no we can't go back for Sook. I couldn't tell the colour of the van he rushed me into, but I knew it was The Tree Frog. As he drove, I sniffed the man who looked like my dad and was relieved. No trace of smokes on him, like Mister Christie at school, like Pa. The whole van rattled as if it was about to shake apart, as if one of the wheels was about to fall off, sending us into a ditch. I got cut up in the last crash. Liam has asked me where I got my scars more than once, but I never tell. And then we were pulling up at Endor and running through a dirt cloud. Dad heaved me off the ground when I tripped, branches whipping my cheeks. Someone shouted my name behind us, pretending to be my father. Then came the purple light.

Now, I'm squinting because it's daytime.

Daytime.

It can't be. But it is.

Dad guides me back to the parking lot. There is no green van now. There is a black car and its wheels look okay. He tells me to hop in. Even though we're not in a hurry, I sense urgency beaming off him. I keep pointing at the forest, asking questions. Dad tells me to be quiet. "There isn't time."

We drive off. There aren't many cars on the road. Dad's hands rest on the wheel. I suck my thumb.

"Don't do that," he says.

I tap my bare feet on the floor. My skin is sticky with tree sap.

"Dad?"

"Yeah?"

And then I ask him. Because it can't be. And because it is. "Do you remember what we had for lunch yesterday?"

He pauses. Changes gears. Turns the strange car onto our street. It smells like an unwashed sink in here. A sick feeling wriggles in my tummy.

This isn't my dad.

We pull up out front of our old house in Narrabundah – it looks like a wooden toad. We haven't been in the new place for long, but I already miss having a common yard where I can bury my toys. I miss the fig tree across the road. My tree. I carved my initials into it, over and over again, with the metal point of my maths protractor. On this morning, which should still be night, the sky is blue like your tongue after you suck a gobstopper.

"Finn. I want you to stay here. We're going on a trip."

"Why are we here? I don't have any shoes."

"I've packed your stuff already. Our stuff," he says.

I peer into the back seat where gym bags sit on top of one another next to the suitcase with the wonky wheel we packed when we moved.

"I need to duck inside and grab a couple of things," says Dad, or whoever he is. "I'll be ten minutes. It's important you don't leave or talk to anyone. Are you listening? No climbing. No following me inside."

He smiles when I nod, a familiar-enough smile.

"Why are you crying?" I ask.

"...I'm happy, is all, mate."

He kisses my cheek and leaves, taking off his jacket and carrying it under an arm as he runs towards the front door, crunching over leaves. There's no gate at the old house. Dad is wearing a black shirt and is sweating even though it's cold.

Alone, I sit, wishing I had my iPad. I climb into the backseat and scrounge through the bags to see if Dad packed it. I sigh, empty-handed. Bite my lower lip. Suck my thumb, wondering how this man found our new townhouse if he isn't my dad.

Did you ask our social worker? Did you pretend to be Dad on the phone?

Why are you doing this?

Who are you?

★   ★   ★

The car door clicks shut. I look left, right, left again before crossing the street, just like Dad and Pa taught me when I was little. I hurry to the door, knowing I'm going to get in trouble. Sometimes doing the wrong thing feels right. There was a time at the Manuka pool when Dad yelled at me to stop swimming and come into the covered area because there was lightning about. I pretended not to hear him, and once I paddled to the ladder and climbed out I got in trouble, as expected. It was worth it, though. Pushing back is something I need to do. *This* is different. I'm doing the wrong thing because I need to know what he's hiding, and I'm doing it out of anger because he thinks I'm stupid – too young – to know that nothing about this is right.

Trying not to make noise. The front door is open. My feet swish over floorboards. It's even cooler inside our old house. All our things are here, as if we hadn't packed everything into boxes and moved. The couch is in the living room, as are the paintings, one of which I did with Nan when I went to visit her in Jindabyne one time.

My toy box isn't in the corner near the TV where we used to keep it. None of my shoes are on the rack by the door – just Dad's work boots with the heavy laces that click when he walks.

The smell of dead flowers and vase water rolls over me. There's a table I've never seen before set against the wall by the corridor to our bedrooms where I can hear Dad shuffling about. Old flowers rustle like cockatoo feathers you find on the ground – they are bound with faded purple ribbons. Above these bunches, almost tipping in the wind coming through the door I left open, is a booklet. I reach through the flowers to take it and flip it over.

Air seeps out of me slow. I'm a deflating birthday balloon. I'm a rabbit in the woods of Endor. I'm so cold.

Celebrate the life of Finn Patrick Downes-Helleyer, taken too soon, it reads.

Beneath these words is my school photo. Dad had made me do my hair that morning, but I'd tousled it as I waited for my turn to sit on the stool. This copy is black and white. The booklet slips from my fingers and slides across the floorboards, coming to rest between Dad's feet. I hadn't heard him come down the hall. There is a shoebox in his hand. I know what it is because I've snooped through it before. He keeps it under his bed here and at the new townhouse, too. It's full of trinkets and money. I expect him to yell like that day at the pool, only he just looks sad instead. He's breathing deep. We're empty now, the two of us. There's nothing left. Dad pulls me into a hug.

"You weren't supposed to see that," he says, running his fingers through my hair. I slip my thumb into my mouth. Salty. Dad is crying. Gripping me. "I'm sorry. I'm so sorry. Jesus, hold me, Finn. Hold me back. Please. This is real. You're real, right? I did this, didn't I? We're not dreaming. It worked. Christ."

A tap drips in the kitchen. The wisping of his jacket.

"Where's Pa?" I ask, pulling out of his grip. I'm not ready to give him what he needs. I'm not sure it's safe yet.

Dad wipes his tears away. He is pale. "You don't need to worry about him."

"Tell me or I'll scream." I spit the words at him, making him flinch.

He studies me, as if searching for who I used to be. I can still feel him shaking. "He will never hurt you again," Dad tells me, and I believe him. I believe him deeply. "I've made sure of it."

I hold my ground for as long as I can. His shakes don't trickle into me like they usually do. They bounce off. I won't let them in. I can't have his fear inside me anymore. It's poison.

HUGO

It's not quite dawn when the detectives leave the townhouse. Mum will arrive in a few hours. Everything hurts. Is dying better? The police said they'll want to speak to me again and advised me against going back to the forest, where I told them things turned bright and someone took my boy. If the details sound blurry, it's because the story I told them lacked focus. For all I know, there are conversations being had right now where I'm being described as 'a person of interest', just like in the movies.

They told me they believed me, these men and women, some in blue, others in black. But I didn't believe them when they said it.

The living room smells of instant coffee. Clots of warm air where police officers had huddled taking notes after escorting me home. Cologne clouds. Footprints on carpet, slowly starting to lift. A gum wrapper here. A long strand of brown hair on the kitchen counter there.

My bed screams for attention. I'm not ready. I need to go outside again, into the dark, and look in the mailbox. Because the *other* me – the one who took Finn into the white noise light in that place where there are triangles inside of triangles – told me. Right before they disappeared. All this, in the parts of the story I couldn't tell the cops.

I unlock the front door. Finn's shoes sit on the rack to my left. His toys are scattered across the living room floor where he left them the day before.

The dark stretch of pathway to the mailbox by the gate. My hand comes to rest on the latch and I lift the lid. Rattling metal. Reaching inside, I think about spiders, even though it's not the season. Parenting has trained my senses to be on alert for danger. For so long, Guy tried to convince me that my diligence was silly. I sought out the ugliness of the world to predict any threat to our son from that world.

"Everything will be fine," Guy would say, cupping my cheek, kissing me. "Please, don't be a drama queen. This town's got enough of them."

And all the while, the danger, the spider, was inside the house already.

"Weren't there signs?" Mum asked more than once. I told her no, even though I was lying.

The first cold.

My fingers settle on steel inside the dark mailbox. I withdraw a handgun.

The last cold.

A note is wrapped around the handgun's handle, bound in place with a rubber band. In twisting it free, the paper rips in two. The note is in my handwriting and reads:

I'm sorry but you should've been ready for him. Use the gun when he comes. He has knives and wants you dead. Finn will be safe with me here.

★   ★   ★

Inside, weary, waiting for dawn. It comes so late on these cold mornings. Itchy, red eyes. The loaded gun against my thigh.

I will never see my son again, a fact I approach with wonder, through a labyrinth of dead maybes, as immense as a miracle, or a devil's miracle. I have no religion yet pray at my bedside after searching for the wedding ring. God doesn't find me on this morning, but I do find the ring. It landed by the shoebox full of Guy's letters, our wedding invite, two rolls of cash in case we ever had to run. I place the ring on the living room coffee table. Every lightbulb in the townhouse – which never had the chance to become a home for us – is off.

Moments ache with tension.

A shadow moves across the blinds. Swallowing, I stand, gun in hand, as I hurry to the window and listen. Footsteps. Guy's raggedy breaths. His shadow is at my eyeline. He will try the door any second now, and I know he will have his knives, the ones he planned to use on me and Finn.

I have left the door unlocked for him.

Finn lives behind every blink now. I want to scream. Hold it in. It's so important I keep my pain intact for a little longer, like a wound with delicate stitching that might rip open at the slightest movement, like Finn's stitches after the car crash. Guy is shuffling across the Welcome mat. He's snatching at the door handle.

Again, I imagine that Guy is Sook grown large, hunched over and monstrous with its one dangling eye swinging back and forth on a sinew of string, spit-soaked fur all matted and kissed away in patches so the leather peeks through. Sook has blades for teeth.

And the blades are glimmering.

Hold the wound, I think. Keep the stitches in.

My boy. Finn, I will kill Pa with my love for you.

The door swings open and Guy's (Sook's) shadow spills into the room, thrown by dawn as it breaks at his back. I lift the gun and shoot him with rage in the shape of a bullet. The ringing in my ears from the bang is so intense I can't hear myself screaming. I've let it all go. The stitches are undone and the wound is free to bleed. A constellation of blood and brains on the wall, not cottony teddy bear stuffing. Purple smoke hazes the air, and I double over, the nose of the gun touching the tiles. Sunlight plays on my mother's face, and on the wet hole in the side of her head. Her eyes might be open, but they do not see. I grab her wrist and say her name and then say it again. And again. She's so cold.

MISTER REAPER

Annie Knox

Stephanie woke up at 11:59 p.m.

This was a bit of a shock. Largely, the shock came from the fact that she hadn't planned to wake up at all. As she blinked herself into the world, eyes crusted with make-up, she became aware of a dull, throbbing pain in her wrists. It was caused by the gashes in both, which she had torn open hours earlier with a box cutter from the warehouse.

She shifted upright. The box cutter sat on the floor in a puddle of cool blood. Her head was pounding. Her butt was numb. As she wiggled into a central position over the toilet bowl, both butt cheeks started to tingle as they came back to life.

Somewhere in the distance, bells chimed for midnight.

Her tights were clamped to her skin with dried blood. Her skirt was stiff. The space between the arch of her foot and the insole of her shoe was damp with it. As she pushed herself painfully up and off the toilet, her thighs unpeeled from the plastic seat.

Stephanie crept out of the stall, a criminal leaving a crime scene. Her reflection greeted her in the mirror above the sink; a white, expensive block that ran along one wall the entire way down the room to the entrance. No amount of gold tapwork, fancy air freshener or chime music could quite remove the sense of being a pig washing your hands in a trough.

She stared at herself in horror; she knew that a failed suicide would take a toll on anyone's looks, but even by that standard she was looking pretty hideous. Pale, gaunt, dark circles under her eyes, panda make-up smeared down her face, smudges of blood across her cheeks from where she had clutched them and cried. She tried to tuck her hair neatly behind her ears, testing out a smile. It wasn't great but it wasn't worse. She gingerly pulled her phone out of her bra; it was long dead.

Pushing open the entrance to the loos, she peered out into the shopping centre. Beyond the sanctuary of the toilets was a gleaming world: sparkling black and white flooring, walls towering up three storeys high to where diamond chandeliers dangled from the ceiling. Even though it was closed and empty, eerie meditation music floated through the mall.

The shops were shut. Brands lined the walls, stores sat in darkness behind barred doors. Mannequins peered through the windows, barely visible, ghosts in the gloom.

Shoes squeaking, Stephanie stepped out. The door slid shut behind her with an expensive sounding puff of air. The scent of white rose and eucalyptus cleaner tickled her nostrils. To her left, the mall veered off towards the perfume halls. To her right the mall opened up into a larger chunk of space dominated by women's lingerie. Beyond that it curved into a tunnel filled with overpriced coffee shops. Stephanie had the misfortune to have worked in most of the outlets as a temporary team member, hopping from place to place depending on where the agency sent her. Each tiny, dug-out designer hole was its own unique corner of Hell.

Stephanie headed to the right, marvelling at the emptiness now that the mall was deprived of customers. She hoped that one of the night security staff would have snuck out for a cigarette through the fire escape by the entrance to car park three and left the door unlocked. Being discovered wandering through the place after closing covered in her own blood was a sure way to a quick firing; and now that she had survived her impulsive wrist slashing, the problem of rent due still loomed large and real. Her next shift was at ten tomorrow morning. She needed to find her way home on the night bus, wash, try to eat something, then crawl into bed and sleep away the nightmare of her life for a few hours before getting ready to come back.

The exit for car park three was next to the store she had abandoned earlier that evening, *Sous-Vêtements Fantaisie*. As she passed by, her heart filled with rage; she despised the mall. But the truth was that she was aware that the real reason for her misery was herself. She was the one incapable of pulling together a proper life, she was the one who had chosen this lifestyle in order to pursue some money-less creative art bullshit. Although this place existed to suck cash from the depressed rich wandering it like zombies, and although it would always require desperate minimum-wage workers to keep it running, it was her own fault that she had become one of those workers.

Stephanie headed to the door tucked neatly into the space between *Sous-Vêtements* and *Joli Soutien-Gorge*. Her heart sank when she saw it was closed; the security box was lit red, which meant that it wouldn't open without a level four security pass. Hers was level two. Irrationally she tapped her card and rattled at the handle anyway. Her wrist twinged with the action and she gritted her teeth against a fiery wave of pain that washed out from the cut. Sweat broke out on her back and underneath her bra. She rested her hot forehead against the cool door.

Somewhere off to the right, from the direction of the *Gâteau et Café de Luxe* corridor, a door slammed. Stephanie panicked as footsteps echoed around her – the full-footed tread of a security officer on patrol. Did they know she was there?

Abandoning car park three, Stephanie scurried back through lingerie towards jewellery. Scurrying past perfume, thousands of contrasting smells invaded her nose. Oud and sandalwood from one, floral fragrances from another. Ingredients so expensive that they filled the air from behind shutters. She glanced back and saw a shadow appearing around the curve of the hall behind her. Making a quick choice she sped into a run, dashed up the escalator by *Beaucoup d'Odeur d'Argent*, and ducked behind the pot plant at the top.

Catching her breath, her pulse beating in the cuts in her wrists, she watched with tight lungs. A solid figure appeared at the bend of the mall.

She frowned, sniffed in confusion, and squinted, trying to clear her vision. The figure stood tall, solid, muscles stacked on muscles beneath his uniform. Clearly he was in no hurry to catch up with anyone spotted on CCTV, but she was a little too distracted to be relieved, because the head on his muscly shoulders was that of a moose. Huge antlers erupted from his head. Shiny brown eyes watched the empty mall with disinterest. Glossy brown hair coated his skull. The hands poking out from the sleeves of his neat uniform were those of a sloth, long claws reaching down to his thighs. From the back of his uniform a hulking shape zigzagged through the air behind him as he walked, swaying from side to side with weight. As his measured steps brought him closer, she saw it was a huge, reptilian tail.

He came to a stop. She watched with bated breath, unable to believe her eyes – what kind of monster was this? Why was it in a security uniform? Why was it operating the night patrol shift?

"I'm a little early," he called out, not looking in her direction. "Sorry about that." His voice was remarkably young. She stayed where she was, crouched on shaky legs. He couldn't possibly be talking to her. Maybe there was another monster security guard coming around the corner, and they were swapping from one monster night shift to another.

"I'm talking to you."

No way.

"Stephanie."

Maybe the other night shifter was called Stephanie?

"Yo. You. Up on the balcony. Behind the pot plant."

Well. Okay.

Stephanie crawled out awkwardly, grabbing hold of the metal rail and pulling herself upright, blinking away the headrush.

"Me?"

"Do you see another Stephanie hiding behind the plant?"

"...No?"

"Then I'm talking to you, aren't I? Jesus."

Stephanie shuffled. Her shoes squeaked embarrassingly. They were the classic minimum-wage worker shoes, a two pound pair of rubber shit that held up for a month at the most. She burned through pair after pair. It was a point of ridicule no matter which store she worked in.

"Am I dead?"

"Not quite. You used a shit blade. Didn't cut that deep."

"It hurt a lot."

"I'm not judging you." He held up his sloth claws. "No judgement here. You panicked and did your best. I'm not criticising your technique. I'm just saying... it wasn't a quick slash and dash for your soul. You've still got a little bleeding out and exhausting yourself to do. You're only about eighty-five per cent there."

"Right... eighty-five per cent?"

"Yeah." The moose head nodded up and down, solemn. "Not a bad effort. I'm just saying. You got a few more minutes on the clock.

Have a run around. Maybe trash a few things, you know. You hate this place."

"Yeah, but..."

"But what?"

Stephanie looked away from his piercing gaze. She was itching uncomfortably where her crusty tights were rubbing at the skin on her inner thighs.

"I kind of... I was going to go home."

"Go home? Now?"

"Yeah. I was just... looking for an open door. I was going to go have a bath. And maybe some food."

"Have a bath? Maybe some food?" His voice was flat, but she got the impression that she was being mocked.

"...I'm hungry. I didn't have lunch."

"Fucking hell. Are you telling me you've changed your mind?"

"I don't know. I didn't mean to wake up but now I have... so I was just going to go and eat and stuff before work tomorrow. And maybe try again another day."

"You're an idiot."

"Hey!"

"You are! Look at yourself! You tried to kill yourself in the *toilet* at work — which, can I just say, I *am* judging — and now you're trudging around here covered in your own blood, complaining about being hungry, and talking about going to have a bath? What was your plan? Bit of Radox? Cup of tea? Bit of *Brooklyn Nine Nine* on your phone? Come back tomorrow and act all surprised when people are gossiping about the mysterious bloody bathroom?"

"Something like that, yeah." The bath was pretty spot on, actually.

"Well!" He threw his sloth claws in the air, ready to argue, then sighed and dropped them back to his sides, shoulders slumped. "Stephanie, you cut your wrists. And you did it deep. I'm only an hour or so early. I was just going to wait outside the toilet for you, to be honest. I didn't think you'd be wandering around. I wanted to nab you before I head over to Westminster to catch the 2:00 a.m. drunk rush."

"Drunk rush? Like you want to go to the pub?"

"No, you... I'm your reaper, woman. I'm here to guide you to the afterlife, et cetera, et cetera."

"Right." Stephanie blinked stupidly down at the moose/sloth/ alligator. "But... you don't look like the grim reaper."

"There's loads of us." He started to sound annoyed. "I'm sorry I'm not some handsome skull in a fancy robe with a scythe. Do you want to die or not?"

"I'm not sure."

"Oh my god." He crossed his arms with a surprising lack of difficulty, claws folding neatly away. "I can't hang around while you choose. People are dying left, right and centre. If you don't want to die then I'll fuck off. But you've only got..." He looked at his wrist- watch. "You've only got another hour, I reckon. If you don't find a way out and get fixed up, I think you'll collapse and be done for. I can nip out and come back for you later."

Stephanie started to panic.

"Only an hour?"

"You're dying." He gestured at her wrists. "Don't you feel all weak and dizzy? Blood loss will stop you from moving soon. If you don't want to die you need to get to an ambulance. Either way. I'll come back if I'm needed. There's some kind of traffic accident happening down in Waterloo. Nasty. Lots of lost souls loose."

He turned.

"Wait!" Stephanie started down the still escalator, lost her sense of balance, and half-fell, half-walked, slumping into a sitting position. "Wait!"

"What now?"

She desperately tried to blink away the fuzziness, toes and fingertips tingling. "I don't know how to get out, my phone is dead."

"How is that my problem?"

"You're a guide!" She felt tears threatening. "Guide me!"

"That's not how it works."

Stephanie put both hands over her eyes. Her wrists burnt. She thought of her boyfriend, who always texted her goodnight, even if they were in the middle of a fight, as they currently were. Was his goodnight text sitting on her dead phone, never to be replied to? When would he even hear about her dying? He wasn't her emergency contact, no one from the mall knew him... would he just think she was a petty bitch for days before he got worried and went looking? She never said goodbye.

"You're so useless."

She peered through her fingers. The moose/sloth/alligator was watching her cry with disdain. "You literally work here. Think, moron."

"You're not being very nice and guide-y." She sniffed disgustingly. "You're not very comforting."

"That's because you're annoying." He rolled his big eyes. "I can't tell you directly. But you work here. Think. Think, dummy."

She stared at him dumbly.

"Think! What's next to the vending machine on the third floor? By the water station?"

Stephanie gasped. "The phone chargers!"

"Duh." He waved his claws at her. "Go on, then."

"Shouldn't I just go to the security office? And get help?"

"Where is the security office?"

"On the other side of the mall."

"Do you think you can make it?"

She started to stand up. Her ankle rolled and she nearly tumbled down the rest of the escalator. "Nope."

"There you go then."

Stephanie struggled up the steps, ignoring how weak her knees felt. When she reached the top, she turned round and saw the moose/sloth/alligator still watching her.

"Are you going to come?"

He stared, silent.

"I might die on the way." She tried to tempt him. "It would save you a journey to just come with me."

"You've got almost an hour, Stephanie. You can make it to the phone chargers."

"All right." She tried not to sound sad. "Bye, I guess."

"Stephanie!"

She turned back.

He had taken a step closer. "The chargers are next to the water station."

She waited.

"Water, Stephanie. The liquid of life. Do you see what I'm saying?"

"That I should hydrate?"

His big moose head nodded even as he rolled his eyes. Stephanie tried for a wobbly smile, and then turned and continued on her way, forcing her heavy feet to keep moving. Her eyes were wet as the magnitude of her situation set in. She wished she hadn't woken up, because now she had to deal with the reality of what she had done.

Hospital would mean stitches and bandages. There was no way she could hide it from her boyfriend, if he ever wanted to see her again. Maybe the hospital would lock her up for being crazy. What if they called her mum?

Her head span and she dropped to one knee suddenly, bracing both hands against the floor, forcing air into her nostrils and out of her mouth, whimpering. Her hands left red smears on the tiles beneath her.

"Stephanie." Moose/sloth/alligator grunted from somewhere behind her. "Get up."

"You left."

"Clearly not, woman. Get up. You have to get to the chargers."

"I can't." Tears splashed onto the ground, accompanying the bloody fingerprints. "I wish I'd died on the toilet."

"Fucking hell." There was a loud sigh. "Even I feel sorry for you. Even for a reaper, this seems quite pathetic."

A snotty laugh bubbled out of her. "I think I've gone crazy, Mister… Reaper?"

A long moment passed. Stephanie struggled to breathe through her stuffy nose.

"You're supposed to tell me your name now."

"I don't have one. Not for humans."

She sighed heavily. "Mister Reaper then."

"Stephanie."

She sighed heavily again. "It seems so far." She squinted towards the end of the corridor. "Is someone coming? Maybe they can call the ambulance for me."

Her vision was blurred by tears. Mister Reaper watched the approaching shadow with something akin to fear and anger on his moose face.

"What is it?"

"You really need to get up."

The figure at the other end of the hall dropped gracefully from their back legs onto all fours. A feathered crow's head with an unreasonably long beak and bright, beady yellow eyes poked out from a security uniform that weirdly didn't seem to be stretched. The rest of the body appeared to be that of a hugely overgrown cat. The feet belonged to a bird, talons braced against the floor, whilst muscular furry limbs vanished into the sleeves of the blazer.

"Leave her alone." Mister Reaper sounded pissed. CrowHead continued to approach gleefully.

"You're meant to be in Waterloo," it called back. Stephanie was stunned to hear a sweet, feminine voice coming from the crow's beak. "You're taking too long."

"I can take as long as I want." Mister Reaper sounded even more pissed. "You go to Waterloo, bitch. There's plenty of miserable dead sods there for you to fuck with."

"I want this one." The crow turned her eyes back to Stephanie, who felt a chill in her gut. "This one looks tasty."

"You're not supposed to eat them." Mister Reaper's voice was between exasperated and angry. "You're supposed to guide them."

"*Ma ma ma mah maaa mah,*" the crow mimicked. "Whatever. This is why your numbers are so low. You got called out in the KPI meetings four months in a row, loser. You couldn't afford to eat one even if you wanted to, you need all the souls you can get. You spend forever with them."

"They're dying! They're scared. We're meant to help. Some of them aren't exactly going to a very nice place, are they?"

"Am I going to a nice place?" Stephanie piped up, trying to ignore how weak she was feeling.

"You're not dying, Stephanie. You're going to charge your phone, and call an ambulance."

"Stop telling her what to do." CrowHead began to stalk closer. "We aren't meant to interfere. If I can't eat them, then you can't save them."

"I'm not saving her, she made her own mind up." Mister Reaper stepped slightly in front of Stephanie. "She isn't dead, so you don't need to be here. Go suck a dick down at the Westminster rush hour."

"So rude." CrowHead poked her beak around him and grinned at Stephanie. "Steph. Steffie. You cut your wrists, sweetheart. You want to die. You just made a mistake by cutting a little too shallow. It's fixable. You can finish the job, or you can wait here for a bit and shake your arms around to bleed out the last bit of life in you. Don't listen to this guy. He's always getting all upset and boo-hoo-y over the suicides."

"She isn't suicidal. Get out of the way."

"My hour is running out." Stephanie tried to get up. "I need to charge my phone."

CrowHead whooshed around Mister Reaper. Stephanie jerked back, falling and covering her head with a shriek as a beak came darting towards her head. A bunch of furious yelling and swearing erupted above her.

"Fuck off!"

"I didn't touch her!"

"You're messing with the process!"

"And you're not? Mr. Get Up Stephanie! Save Yourself, Don't Die! You were meant to wait for her to bleed out and then point her to heaven or hell, not sit around crying over the poor little wrist-slitter."

"If she dies, then I'll show her the way. She's not dead yet. So nobody needs to be saying anything to her, do they?"

"Fine!"

Stephanie peeked from behind her hands and saw CrowHead was back on her hind legs, towered high and skinny over Mister Reaper. Both had their animal arms folded like children throwing tantrums. CrowHead saw her looking and put on a very fake grin.

"Fine. I'll just wait for her to die. She won't make it. I don't think she even wants to."

Mister Reaper turned to look down at Stephanie.

"Just to be clear..." Stephanie hated how pitiful her own voice was. "...neither of you can touch me? Right? Or... eat me?"

"No, Stephanie." His voice was kind. His eyes were upset. "Just do your stuff. If you need me, I'll be here for that."

"Okay." She struggled to all fours, to one knee, to her feet. The world didn't feel solid, so she staggered to the closest wall and used it for strength, leaning her weight on it as she walked. Mister Reaper unfolded his arms and walked quietly alongside her. Behind, the clack-clack-clack of talons followed them.

Stephanie's headache was making her nauseous. Her hands and feet were numb. Her wounds were wet and sticky. She could feel the life oozing out of her and she wasn't sure if she was scared or relieved. Glancing at Mister Reaper, she saw frustration in his face and tried to distract him.

"How long have you been a… guide for?"

"Don't talk. Focus on getting to the chargers."

"They're just around the corner."

"Woman."

"I just… I feel… not good."

"That's because you cut your fucking wrists."

Stephanie went quiet. The talons went clack-clack-clack behind them.

Mister Reaper made a noise of unhappiness next to her.

"I've always been a guide. I was built to be one. Now stop looking so sad and focus."

"Okay."

She stopped to breathe deep for a second.

"Are you tired, Steffie?" CrowHead crowded closer. "Feel like giving up yet? It's a long way to the chargers, you must be exhausted. It would be easier to sit here and wait for us to take you, you know."

"It's twenty metres to the chargers," Mister Reaper said, voice flat. "Ignore her, Stephanie. Only stop if it's what you really want, not because she made it sound good."

Stephanie tried to ignore the wobble in her knees, leaning heavily on the wall. "Do you guys do other stuff? Like messages?"

The guides looked at each other. It wasn't the first time they'd been asked.

"Who do you want to send a message to?" CrowHead tilted her head to the side, asking out of curiosity rather than a desire to help.

"My boyfriend." Stephanie felt heat gather in her eyes. "Maybe my mum. Maybe not. Maybe she's better without some sad last message to cry over."

"What message?" Mister Reaper asked. "What would you want us to tell them?"

"My mum… just that I love her." Tears started to slide down her face. Her words felt stuck in her throat. "My boyfriend… I love him too. But also for him… that I'm sorry. And he's right. I should push myself more. Should have. But I'm also right. That he should eat healthier. But that doesn't matter now. Now all that matters is he knows I don't care about the fight, and I love him. And I died loving him, not mad at him." She sobbed a tiny bit, tried to hide it, then decided dignity didn't matter anymore and let the sounds of distress out.

CrowHead snorted. "Those are lame messages. What happened to revenge? What happened to See You On The Other Side, Fuckers?"

"Leave her alone." Mister Reaper shook his head in disgust. "Have some fucking class. Stephanie. We don't do messages."

Stephanie sobbed harder. "Why did you let me say all that stuff then?"

"If it's important to you that those people hear those words, there's only one way to make sure that they do."

Stephanie almost bent at the waist with her grief, but forced herself to look into Mister Reaper's eyes. He stared at her with meaning. "Do you understand, Stephanie?"

She nodded. Looked in the direction of the phone charging booth. She could see the corner of it, poking out from behind the water refill station. She had to get to it. Even if just to ring her boyfriend and tell him. Even if just to text her mum one more time.

Gritting her teeth, she forced herself back upright, closed her eyes and started to drag her feet blindly across the floor again, closer, closer, closer…

Her hands patted unfeelingly at the side of the unit. Slumping down to the ground in an ungraceful heap, she fumbled at the bottom locker, pulled out the iPhone cable, and plugged her phone in after several failed attempts. Then she sat back and closed her sore eyes.

There was a moment of quiet.

"She just isn't dying, is she?" CrowHead sounded bored. "That soul is stuck in there."

"iPhones take forever to charge," Stephanie murmured. "Don't give up. Although I'd prefer Mister Reaper as my guide. No offence."

"Did you decide what you want to do?" Mister Reaper crouched in front of her. Stephanie shook her head, brain loose.

"It's turned on."

Stephanie opened her phone, tapping at the screen with bloody fingers. She pulled up the phone app. Leave a death message or call for help?

She looked up at Mister Reaper.

"Life doesn't seem worth it sometimes."

He shook his head, eyes sad. "I can't tell you what to do."

She looked at CrowHead.

"I spend so much time thinking that I want to die."

"So die, sweetheart."

Stephanie looked down at her phone.

"I don't think I'll ever make anything of myself. I don't think I'll ever get anywhere. I can't stop crying. I cry all the time. At work, in bed, going to sleep, waking up. Hiding in the shower. I'm a loser. I'm a failure."

Her phone buzzed as it connected to the mall Wi-Fi and a slew of messages pinged through. Her boyfriend, telling her he was unhappy but wanting to know if she had finished work. Another from him, asking when she finished and if they could talk. One from her brother, asking if she was going to their nan's birthday. Spam emails. A couple of art gallery updates. A few bot comments on the last painting she had posted on Instagram. One nice comment, saying it was beautifully haunting. Another from her boyfriend, saying that the least she could do was text back that she was safe.

Even as she looked at her phone, one more came through from him, asking her to please just say if she was okay or not.

"He seems to care."

"What happened to don't interfere?" CrowHead hissed. Mister Reaper waved his sloth claw uncaringly.

"Report me at the monthly meeting." He winked at Stephanie. "It was just a statement of fact."

Stephanie looked down at her phone. Her fingers found the dial screen, and she found herself typing in 999 and pressing call. As she held the phone up to her ear with shaky fingers, she watched CrowHead roll her eyes, stick a middle talon up furiously at Mister Reaper, and prowl off out of sight, breaking into a run around the corner.

Stephanie finished explaining where she was and hung up on the emergency receiver, ignoring their requests for her to stay on the line. She smiled weakly at Mister Reaper.

"Thanks, Mister Reaper."

"Call your boyfriend. Tell him all that romantic crap."

She nodded gratefully, finding her boyfriend's number and starting to dial. "Will you still be able to catch the drunk rush?"

"Yes, Stephanie." He fidgeted awkwardly. "I'll be in trouble for this, you know. I hope you don't make me regret it by making me come back anytime soon."

"I'll try my best." She looked him in his moose eyes. "I think you're a really good guide."

"I'll remember that when they publicly mock my KPIs." He nodded, seemingly uncomfortable with the amount of friendliness between them. "See you."

Stephanie watched him turn his back and break into a jog, alligator tail swinging wildly behind him, vanishing around the corner. Then she held her phone to her ear and listened to a furious but very lovable voice come onto the line.

"You! You're in big trouble! You know you're supposed to let me know when you get home. I've sat here like an idiot all evening, worrying, while you've been doing whatever—"

"I'm not home."

"What?"

"I'm at the mall." She shifted, listened to sirens in the distance, hoped that they were for her.

"What? Why do you sound so weird? Are you okay?"

"Listen." She smiled helplessly. "I love you. Even when you eat junk all the time. I'm right about that, but I still love you. And you're right that I don't push myself enough, and I'm sorry. I got mad because I don't like talking about it, because I don't believe in myself. But none of that matters right now. What matters is I love you."

"You're scaring me." He sounded stern, but the fear was there. "I'm coming to the mall to get you. Why the hell are you still there?"

"I'll explain later." Tears of tiredness lined her eyes, she was dreading the oncoming conversations. "But everything will be okay. And I love you. That's the most important thing. Do you know that? That I love you?"

"Yes." Now he sounded uncertain. "You're really worrying me. I love you too, Stephanie, you know that. It was just a dumb fight... are there sirens near you?"

"Yes. Come to the mall and get me quickly, please."

"Okay. I'm coming. I love you."

"I love you."

The sirens stopped outside, and red and blue lit up one of the walls, light filtering in from the outside world.

Maybe everything really would be okay.

She was definitely calling in sick tomorrow, though.

THE CALL OF THE DEEP

Laurel Hightower

Keeper Ellis was already gone when Mel got to the Stack.

She searched the place thoroughly, but there was no sign of the man she'd been sent to relieve. She stood in silence and felt the weight of the empty facility. She was always alone out here, that was nothing new, but there was supposed to be a day's overlap when the Keepers switched out. It gave them an opportunity to exchange information, catch up on how the previous six weeks had gone. There was never anything new, but it was a reassuring little nicety. A final human interaction to tide her over during the long, quiet nights.

His bag was gone, though the bunk was unmade, musty sheets tangled at the foot of the sagging twin mattress. She left her gear and went back to the observation deck, checked the camera feed. All was still, the four screens filled with different angled views of the unbroken surface of the water. She breathed out, letting her shoulders relax. Sunk into the desk chair and stretched her legs out. Frowned when her shoes skidded. She ducked her head, peered into the dim space, and froze.

Water. A puddle on the concrete, hidden beneath the console's desk. Mel's chest tightened, her mouth going dry. Had it rained before Ellis left? Had he left a door open, or dripped dry while watching the screens?

That was the reassuring explanation. She wanted desperately to believe it. Even a pipe leak from the shower above would be preferable, considering the only other source of water in the Stack came from the Wet Room. Nine feet of salt water siphoned from the rocky beach far below, layered over the humming reactor core. Keeping it cool enough to prevent a meltdown, radioactive isotopes crammed in every drop. The level had to stay high enough to avoid a temperature spike, low enough not to slop over the edges of the in-ground pool. There were multiple layers of concrete slab beneath the pool itself, but if droplets escaped onto the surrounding deck, it was too easy to imagine them clinging to a shoe covering or sliding along divots and cracks until they reached groundwater. An excessive precaution – the Wet Room was sealed, requiring entry through two sets of doors with an airlock between.

And yet. Water, here, beneath the desk.

Her heart surged, a sickly feeling in her gut. If the water came from the pool, she was already exposed to radiation. She wiped her wet shoe ineffectually on the floor, holding her foot away from her body. She had no idea how to clean it, how to avoid further contamination. She leaned close to the screens, searching the feed for anything out of place. A puddle on the ground, a crack in the concrete edges. There was nothing, but she couldn't confirm the depth just by eyeballing it.

She looked over her shoulder at the plain, black phone hanging on the back wall. There were no number buttons, not even an old fashioned rotary dial. The phone only rang one number, and it was the sole method of communication with the outside world.

Mel took three steps toward it before she stopped. Ellis's absence was reason enough to check in, but she knew what they'd say.

What about the water? And they'd be right to ask – if there was some kind of leak, the risk to the core was of paramount importance.

Mel sucked in a breath and headed for the Wet Room. Pushed the button to open the first set of doors, changed into her slicker suit and mask in the airlock. She wasted no time opening the second set of doors, but as they whooshed closed behind her, she froze in place, held her breath.

A ripple crossed the onyx surface of the water.

The plastic face shield of Mel's mask fogged with her quickened breath. What moved beneath the surface of the pool? The only thing in there was the reactor core, nine feet below the surface. The room was hermetically sealed – there was no way air movement could cause the disturbance. Was the reactor melting down? Were those light ripples the first sign of a temperature increase? She wasn't trained in nuclear containment – the Keepers were glorified night watchmen, only there to keep tabs and sound the alarm. It was an oddity that bothered her when she was first hired – why have a nuclear facility with no trained personnel? But she'd let herself be lulled by Ellis's insistence that there was no real risk. And the job worked for her, allowed her to hide from her usual fears for six weeks at a time. Gave her anxiety plenty of opportunity to conjure new terrors, but at least they weren't of the human variety.

Sweat pooled in Mel's armpits and on the back of her neck. Her face shield was coated in condensation, and for a panicked moment she wondered if that was a result of increased humidity as the protective layer boiled away. She forced herself to move, to cross the room to where the depth finder hung on the wall.

'Depth finder' conjured images of something high tech, with precise methods of measurement. But tech and radioactive isotopes don't mix. They had to go old school in here, so the finder was a twelve foot titanium rod, its surface carved in pleasant patterns that made gripping it easier. Lightweight but unwieldy, Mel managed to unhook it and get to the water's edge without getting caught on the sweating stone walls. She stopped a foot away, unable to make herself go any closer.

There should be safety rails. Something to prevent her tripping over her own feet, or the rod, and plunging into water that might melt her flesh from her bones. But there was nothing, only empty space surrounding the perfect circle of black water. Ellis laughed at her when she voiced her fears, told her she'd seen too many movies. It was only water. Sure, it might increase her risk of cancer if she fell in, but that was just added incentive to watch her step during her daily trip into the Wet Room.

Ellis didn't get it. He must not feel that pull of self-destruction deep in his core. The grip of desire to speed catastrophe, to go ahead and get it over with. This close to the edge, she pictured it on an endless loop. Overbalancing as she placed the depth finder, its weight unable to keep her from going over the side. Splashing face first into the opaque water, powerless to stop a reflex to suck it deep into her lungs. And buried in her heart, a fear unacknowledged even to herself: that the water was not empty. That things lurked beneath the surface, always out of sight, keeping still only to lure her in. Once she was in their habitat, on their turf, they would rise, brushing against her flailing body, take her in their jaws...

Mel lurched in place, her stomach flipping with the sudden movement. She locked her legs, held one hand out to the side to regain her balance. Breathing hard, she made herself count to ten before moving again. Slowly, carefully, she placed the depth finder along the edge like she'd been taught.

"Never stick it in too far from the edge," Ellis told her. "You don't want to put it straight through the core."

Mel shuddered, pulling the rod as close to the edge as she could get it. Sunk it until she felt it make contact with the concrete bottom of the pool.

She squatted, squinting at the measurement. Nine feet, two inches. Relief flooded her body, bringing a wave of coolness in its wake. The level was fine, even a bit high, but she could correct that easily. This close she could tell, even through her suit, that the ambient air was no warmer than usual. The core was fine.

Her body still shaking once she'd left the Wet Room, she pulled the desk chair to the wall by the phone and lifted the receiver. She listened to thirty or so seconds of hushed white noise, then a series of clicks.

"Yes?" came the voice finally.

"Keeper two-four-oh, Melissa Ruth Proust."

"Keeper Proust. Your shift just started – what's the trouble?"

Mel kept it simple. "Keeper Ellis was not in the facility when I arrived."

Silence on the other end of the line, then: "Odd. Very well, is that all?"

"I'm... not sure," said Mel, looking over her shoulder at the black and white camera feed.

"Tell me everything."

Mel did so, leaving nothing out. The voice on the other end was quiet, letting her finish before speaking.

"So the level was fine."

"Nine feet two inches, yes. I'll bleed off the excess."

"No. Leave it," said the voice.

Mel frowned. "Leave it? But the level—"

"Two inches is no reason for concern. Better not to... disturb anything."

The lack of precision bothered Mel, but after a brief struggle she agreed. "And... the puddle? The water under the desk?"

"Do you have your Geiger counter?"

Mel swallowed. "I'll get it." She went to the wall where the unit was holstered, flipped it on with a wince. What if it started clicking like crazy?

"Keeper Proust?" The voice issuing from the phone's handset was small, tinny.

Mel took a breath and approached the puddle, holding the counter out as far as she could reach.

It stayed silent, and her knees went weak. Thank fuck.

"It's fine," she said as soon as she picked the phone back up.

"There you go. Feel better?"

"Yes, thank you. Keeper two-four-oh—"

"Keeper Proust."

The voice cut into Mel's sign off and she fell silent. "Yes?" she asked finally, when nothing else was said.

"It's best if you stay inside for the next few days. Can you do that?"

The relief Mel felt from the silent Geiger counter drained away. "Why?"

A long silence. "Storms in the area. You'll be fine in the Stack – that building's been there forever. But batten down the hatches, please. Run through your drills every day."

Mel wanted to ask why. But she wasn't sure she wanted an answer.

"Stay vigilant, Keeper Proust. Our safety is in your hands."

As Mel reached to replace the handset, she told herself she didn't hear a mournful cry in the patterns of soft white noise.

★　★　★

Mel woke from a dream of whales calling in the distant dark. Her cheeks felt tight, tracks of dried tears pulling her flesh. She sat up, trying to banish the deep sense of sadness that accompanied her up from her dream.

The sound came again, this time to her waking ears. Mel held her breath, heart pounding. She'd never heard whale calls out here, not in the six years she'd been coming to the Stack. Could their sound even carry out of the water? It seemed unlikely, but she was no naturalist.

Keeping still, she waited to hear it again. When it came it was much closer, deep and mournful, the lowest registers thrumming through Mel's teeth. She hugged her knees, making herself small. It hadn't sounded like a whale that time. More like the cries of something dead, no longer of this world. So close to her… was something in the building with her? But what the hell could make a noise like that?

She should check. It was an anomaly, and therefore her job to investigate. But it was dark in the old stone room where she slept. What if something waited beneath the bunk to grab her ankle, take her under? Was it Ellis? Dead in some horrible accident and back to haunt her?

The longer she sat there, the more sure she was that something shared the darkness with her. Listening to her breathe, hovering just far enough away she couldn't feel its touch. She couldn't stay here until morning, not wound as tight as she was. She gritted her teeth, reached through the clutching darkness and yanked the chain on her bedside lamp.

Its yellow glow banished the shadows closest to her, but brought little relief. A trail of water led from the cracked door of the room to her bedside.

"Oh, fuck," she breathed, wide eyes fixated on the water. Was it raining? Had the roof developed a leak? She couldn't hear a storm outside, but the old stone walls were thick. Shaking, she grabbed a hoodie from the end of the bunk and pulled it on, careful to avoid the water spots when her feet hit the floor.

Teeth chattering, she slipped down the stairs and into the main control room. More water out here, but not, she noted with relief, coming from the doors to the Wet Room. She hurried to check the screens and saw nothing but the monochrome view of a still pool.

At the Stack's outer door that led to the beach, she punched in her code with shaking fingers but was greeted with an array of red lights and an admonitory beep. The door stayed closed.

Frowning, Mel tried again, slower this time. She got the same response, and dread turned her to stone.

"No, this is bullshit. The code worked to get in," she said under her breath and tried a third time. Still the door remained closed, and a second later the phone gave a shrill ring from the wall.

Mel stood still, staring across the room. She'd never heard it ring before – her employers waited for the Keepers to call, not the other way around. She approached slowly and pressed the phone to her ear without speaking.

"Keeper Proust? Are you there?"

"I'm here. Why is the door locked?"

Several seconds of silence answered her. "We agreed you would stay indoors."

Anger flashed, heating Mel's face. "I needed to check something. Did you change the code remotely?"

"We're not sure what's going on. If the outer lock has been triggered, that means the system has identified a possible containment breach. I don't need to tell you how serious that is."

Mel swallowed hard, her gaze darting to the glass box on the wall behind the desk, protecting a flat black pull-down handle. When Ellis explained it to her on her first night of training, it dug a hole in the pit of her stomach.

Break glass in case of breach.

Last line of defence. She'd imagined what such a moment would look like. The desperation a person would feel breaking that glass, reaching in and throwing the switch for their own destruction. Inevitable death as a Hail Mary, the only thing preventing catastrophe.

"Protocol has been initiated, Keeper Proust. Remember your training. Straighten up and tell me what's going on up there."

The tone pissed her off, but Mel found herself responding to the admonition, falling back on her training. "More water."

The voice was tense. "Where? The Wet Room?"

"No. Sleeping quarters. I was woken up by something, a noise, and when I turned the light on there was water everywhere."

"What kind of noise?"

Mel took a breath. "Just whale calls, but the water—"

"Check the Wet Room." The voice was tight, almost shrill. Nothing like the calm responses she'd heard up until tonight.

Mel went to the monitors, scanned them for anything out of place. Nothing, except...

She leaned close, squinting at the screen filled with a close-up of the water's surface. Had something moved? A shadow in the pool, slipping from one side to the other?

"Keeper Proust? Is something moving in the water?"

Her mouth was dry. "It's the reactor coolant pool. Why would—"

"*Answer me.*"

Mel scanned the screens again. "Maybe. I can't tell if—"

"Then make sure."

Mel crossed her free arm tightly across her belly. "How am I supposed to do that?"

"Get in there and find out. Now."

Her heart thudded in her ears and she hung up the phone without answering. She'd been in the Wet Room plenty, at least once every day of her shifts, and with the safety protocols in place, she had nothing to worry about. But now there was a different protocol. If there was a breach that might end in her breaking the glass and throwing the switch, she didn't want to know. She cast a glance at the closed outer door and wondered if there was an override.

But Mel was nothing if not a rule follower, and in spite of her dread she set her shoulders and approached the Wet Room doors, bringing the Geiger counter with her. Pulling on her protective gear in the airlock, she looked down and saw more water pooled in several spots. Her breath came faster and she tried to make her mind accept that she wasn't getting out of this unscathed. Flipping the switch on the Geiger counter, she frowned when it registered nothing. It should have reassured her, but the world had been turned on its axis.

By the time the second set of doors slid open, she was hyperventilating, her mask so fogged she could barely see. And what was she supposed to be looking for? She knew fuck all about nuclear physics.

The thought made her frown down at the silent Geiger counter. She was in the reactor room, close to the pool – there should be some isotopes registering. In fact, there was always a minimal amount of background radiation in any environment – so why wasn't it making any noise at all?

The same deep, mournful cry that woke her from sleep sounded from outside, closer this time. The Geiger counter slipped from her sweaty hands and hit the concrete. Bending to pick it up, she caught sight of something pale piled out of sight on the far side of the pool, tucked behind a concrete pillar. Frightened enough to be sick to her stomach, she left the device there and drew closer, knowing what she would see.

Keeper Ellis. Some of him, anyway. His body was waterlogged, missing huge chunks from his torso, shoulder and thigh. The skin of his face had loosened and slid, leaving his mouth gaping, eyes swollen shut. Mel's gorge rose and she backed away as the call sounded again. She turned to the water. Whatever was calling, it came from within the pool.

She made herself inch closer, eyes fixed on the onyx surface, afraid to blink. It reminded her of staring at a corpse in a coffin, the way they so often looked like they were about to draw breath the moment your head was turned. Like Ellis on the grate behind her. If she kept focused on the water, nothing would breathe.

Something rippled along the surface, a ridged back cresting an inch or two out of the water as it travelled the circumference of the pool, bubbles churning in its wake.

Mel moaned and dropped to her haunches, afraid to lose her balance, certain she'd tip into the pool with whatever swam in its depths. Her imagination stuttered and stopped, overwhelmed with thoughts of undersea creatures exposed to years of radioactive water. Mutating, growing, changing into something more horrifying than nature intended.

A loudspeaker crackled to life in the far corner and Mel screamed.

"What's in the pool, Keeper Proust?"

"Ellis – he's here, in the Wet Room. I don't know how I missed him before, but he's—"

"What's in the pool?"

She looked up, searching for the speaker. "How did you know something was in there?" she asked hoarsely.

Heaving breaths took up space and made Mel's chest tighten, as though whoever spoke to her had taken all the air. Then a resigned sigh, and the voice sounded tired when it came again.

"It's always been there. Since the beginning, since the Stack was built around its containment. It's been... sleeping."

Mel scooted away from the pool's edge as the ridged back broke the surface again, circling faster now. This time she saw it was a pair of raised lines, the flesh between them dark and scaled. A preternatural growl like a crocodile's approach sounded, and a pair of impossibly big, dark eyes rose from the depths.

"Sleeping?" Mel said, her body shaking as she pressed herself against the concrete wall. "What is it?"

"Certain death. That's what it is."

"What the fuck does that mean?"

"It means what it sounds like. Ellis is only the beginning."

"What about the core?"

Another pause. "There is no reactor core."

Mel felt a flush of shame, of fury at her own gullibility. Of course there was no core. Why hadn't she questioned Ellis closer? But she knew why. Because he'd laughed at her, and she'd leaned into the assumption that, like usual, she'd missed something obvious to everyone but her.

"Keeper Proust, the danger is *real*. If that creature breaks containment and reaches the mainland, there's no telling how many people will die. You have to engage last line defence. Break the glass."

The eyes in the water stayed fixed on Mel's, and she couldn't look away. It had been here all along. Sharing space in the dark depths, slumbering while the Keepers puttered around it, not knowing what lay beneath. She shuddered, and the whale call sounded again, this time from outside the building.

The eyes in the water opened wider before dipping out of sight, the pool churning as it swam in agitated circles. It returned the call from outside and Mel clapped her hands over her ears.

Calls from inside. Calls from out. Something out there, communicating with the creature in the pool. Mel lowered her hands slowly, mesmerised as more of the creature rose from the surface. Never enough for her to gauge the full size of the thing, or to see its head or shape. It was big, and very old – she felt its age, its ancient intelligence. This thing had swum the oceans when the Earth was new, a force beyond her understanding. That was all the knowledge she had, beyond what the voice from outside had told her. That it was dangerous, that it had to be stopped. She fought the urge to look back at what it had done to Ellis, the jagged tooth marks she knew she would find in his flesh if she looked close enough.

The low, clicking growl sounded again and Mel saw the eyes once more. Immense, bottomless, vertical pupils glistening. She didn't bother telling herself she was safe out of the water. It had gotten Ellis. It could get her, too.

"Keeper Proust? You see it, don't you? It has to be stopped. Break the glass now, before it's too late."

Mel wondered if she'd even make it past the thing in the pool. Could it understand what was being said? Would it know what she was planning to do? If it killed her and there was no one to initiate self-destruction, how long would it be before it lumbered onto a beach, starving from such a long hibernation?

Why did it have to wake now, after all this time, and on Mel's watch? It suddenly made sense, the strange application questions about family and dependants, connections beyond what an employer had an interest in. They wanted Keepers who were unmoored in the world, more likely to sacrifice themselves. Regardless of what she'd signed up for, she didn't want to die.

The thing outside called again. There were two of them. That was why the creature in the pool had wakened after all this time, pulled by the call of its own kind.

"Who is that out there?" she whispered to the unblinking eyes. "Mama? Boyfriend? Kiddo?"

The creature didn't move or blink, its focus all on Mel. Did it sense hope for its escape in her hesitation? Or just its next meal?

"What's happening, Proust? You have to go, now, fast as you can."

"Why?" she asked.

"I told you, if it breaks out—"

"How would it do that? If it could break from the pool, why wouldn't it already have done it? Why is it still here?"

The Wet Room shook with the vibration of an impact to the structure. The eyes slid out of sight and the surface grew still once more.

"Proust. *Melissa.* There's no time to waste. You can do this. You must do this, it's your job. Your purpose."

Mel pushed to her feet and shuffled closer to the water's edge. "My purpose is to die?"

"To *save.* There's no higher calling, no greater act than the preservation of life, and—"

"Just not my life. Or hers."

"There is no *her,* only it, and you *must*—"

Mel would never get peace from that voice. Telling her what to do, what she was worth. Who and what was deserving of life, love. Happiness. It would grate in her ears until the day she died, and she would never have any peace as long as she could hear it.

She went to the water's edge and stared into preternatural eyes. Felt the sickening lurch of her stomach as her body fought to keep its balance while her psyche demanded she give in to the void. She'd spent her whole life afraid. Spinning outcomes both likely and far-fetched, the imagined risks keeping her hemmed in, unable to let go. It was exhausting, watching that water for movement. Watching dead bodies and waiting for them to breathe. Watching her future while braced for disaster.

Don't give yourself time to think.

She closed her eyes and stepped over the edge.

She felt its scaled, muscled body pass by her hip the moment she entered the pool. Terror kicked off, her heart-rate surging, and she waited to feel teeth clamp around her, inexorable jaws drag her deep. At this point it would be a welcome relief, an end to the silent, eternal scream of her mind. Her movements in the water were jerky, uncoordinated as adrenaline flooded her veins with no clear course of action. Why the hell had she thought this was a good idea? Legs kicking erratically beneath her, she looked at the slick stone wall of the pool and knew she couldn't take it back.

Her breath coming fast and shallow, she turned, looking for the creature. Squinting, she thought she saw shadows moving below, beyond the pale shape of her feet. Whatever it was moved quick, shooting up at high speed. She couldn't look away. *This goes much deeper than nine feet.*

She saw the open mouth, the widening jaw full of blunted, broken teeth before they closed around her left leg. Blood bloomed in the water around her and she sucked in a breath, but the scream never came. She was underwater too fast, her hip burning as the leg was pulled nearly from its socket.

I'm going to feel this. It's going to eat me and I'll feel every second of it.

She shot past a circular ledge of stone jutting out from the walls of the pool, narrowing the space. She knocked one flailing arm on the edge of it and knew the ledge was what she felt each time she used the depth finder. Like an idiot, never questioning her instructions, her made-up duties. She'd only ever been here for one reason – to die in the service of the greater good. The risk was still here, but so much older and more unknowable than nuclear contamination.

Then she saw a glow coming from below and wondered if there was a core after all. Wouldn't that be perfect – so many horrible ways to die bundled together. Still, it was better than breaking that glass and waiting to see what form of death would come for her. She squeezed her eyes shut, her head roaring with pressure as the creature pulled her downward.

Then the pull on her leg stopped and her descent halted. The thing must have bitten her leg off finally – the pain in her hip was excruciating, but she thought she'd feel her limb's absence more than this. She kept her eyes closed and waited to die, not wanting to see the creature consume her flesh.

But the need for air burned her lungs, her chest heavy and aching. Was she going to have to drown, too? She opened her eyes and in the glow of whatever lay below, she saw the creature eye to eye.

Mel didn't dare move. She floated there, who knew how deep, communing with something older than time. She looked down, saw the ocean floor below, lit by the soft glow of bioluminescence. Both legs still there, though the left one was mangled. How could she see? Was the pool open to the ocean after all? Had it broken open after all this time?

Another impact shook the Stack, its effect muted in the cushion of water where Mel fought against an increasing urge to draw water into her lungs. Something moved in the darkness below, big enough to shake the old stone building. How big would that be? Her panicked mind groped for an answer but slid off the walls of her fear. Another eye peered up at her. Kin of what swam in the pool with her, and Mel gestured downward.

Go. I won't stop you.

The creature lunged and caught hold of Mel's leg again, whipping her downward with a half body roll that churned the water. Then she felt what she hadn't been able to see. The bottom was glass. Thick, reinforced by the feel of it, which explained why the creature outside hadn't been able to break in. Though, did she feel a hairline crack in the glass beneath her foot?

How long had they been separated? How long had the one outside been searching for its kin, calling into the darkness with no answer, as its other lay slumbering? That was love. Commitment. Ties that bound closer than anything Mel had experienced. Lungs ready to explode, she struck out fast, swimming upward with no care for the building pressure between her ears and behind her eyes. Drowning, the bends, being eaten – it was all the same to her now. Breaking the surface with a gasp, Mel's vision was blurry, red. She found what she wanted without trouble – the long metal rod of the depth finder. With fading vision she looked around the edges of the pool one last time. Could she scale them? Maybe. It didn't matter – she'd committed to her course of action. The highest calling – preservation of life. Of love. Who said it had to be human? Humans were a plague on this planet. Maybe it was time to step aside.

With the metal rod in her hand, Mel dove deep. Her left leg hung unresponsive, the ligaments stretched past their capacity, but still she moved fast, feeling the ledge of stone brush her shoulders. The cold, alien scrape of scaled flesh against her own. Holding the blunted end of the rod before her, she bashed it against the glass below, where she thought she'd felt the crack. The water slowed her momentum, deadened her impact, but two or three more jabs gained her a spiderweb of splintered glass.

The air she'd brought with her from the surface was running out fast. Mel's chest hitched as involuntary action took over and she breathed in cold, dark water. The rod drifted from her hand, her bulging eyes watching the jerking movements of her body as it slowly, painfully died.

A vast change in pressure and the feeling of being sucked further downward. Muted pain as her back scraped against jagged glass, then she floated free in the dark depths of the ocean. Big, ancient things moved past her on their way to a long overdue reunion.

Mel's vision went dark, her struggle over. The corpse breathed no more and never would, no matter what eyes watched the Keeper's body floating in the silent ocean. The oldest form of life had wakened and been loosed upon the world. There was peace in answering the call of the void at last.

THE PLAGUE

Luigi Musolino

The trill of the alarm clock opened up a world of fever, nausea and pain.

Tullio Sandri crawled out of bed, his head pounding, his joints knotted by ropes of agony.

"For fuck's sake..." he gasped, and his voice seemed to come from an indefinite spot in the ceiling, sounding like the gasp of an old man.

In the bathroom mirror was a face he barely recognised: pale green, damp, with black circles around the eyes that crept down to the cheekbones. A quick examination of his tongue, rimmed with a white patina, accentuated the feeling that he was about to vomit his guts out.

"Not today, come on..." A thousand things to do, people to meet, posts to be published. And in the evening he was attending the dinner of the Party of Change, the Anti-Vax/No-Big-Pharma movement, of which he had become president just over a month ago. He had been working on his speech for a week. He could not miss it.

He opened the cabinet of homeopathic products. Aconitum, Belladonna, Nux Vomica, Eupatorium Perfoliatum, Gelsemium, Apis. He opted for fifteen drops of Eupatorium, hoping they would dull the ache in his bones, the exhaustion that pinned him to the sink.

"And fuck Big Pharma," he growled, shuffling back towards his bedroom. He hadn't taken any conventional medicine in five years or more, and he couldn't remember the last time he'd been sick.

By the time he reached the bed, with the room swirling around him as if he were on a rollercoaster ride, he was exhausted. He lay there for half an hour contemplating the Tibetan chandelier, the batik paintings, the framed poster of the Party of Change, as he waited for the Eupatorium to take effect. Then, without warning, he vomited a yellowish lump on the floor, an acidic flush rising in his throat like an eruption. He whimpered, thrashing around in the blankets, shivering. He felt like shit. Christ, he'd never felt so bad in his entire life. A giant, burning stove in place of a forehead.

He grabbed the phone from the bedside table and called Enrico Rizzi, friend, confidant, secretary of the anti-vaccine association.

"Hey, Tullio, ready for tonight?" Rizzi asked.

Tullio cleared his throat, and it was as if a nail had been driven into his Adam's apple. A pang went through his chest.

"Enrico... look, I don't know how to tell you this, but I'm really shattered. I woke up a mess, I must have a fever of forty. Flu, I guess."

"But can you make it tonight? You can't miss the dinner, everyone is expecting your speech..."

"You know how much I care, but right now I feel terrible. I hope to recover, but I wanted to warn you..."

"Did you take anything?"

"Eupatorium."

"Okay, but you also need to take something for the fever. Throw down ten drops of Belladonna, then pour a drop of cypress oil into a teaspoon of maple syrup and mix it all in a thyme herbal tea, boiling hot. And by tonight you'll be as good as new!"

"Let's hope so. I'll keep you posted, Enri. Thanks."

"You're welcome. Oh, I'll send you a crazy article later. A theory about the collapse of the Morandi bridge in Genoa. There's a hypothesis that it was blown up with micro-charges. An attack organised by the government to distract people from more important matters."

"I told you that something didn't add up!" exclaimed Tullio, forgetting for a second the headache, the vomiting, the fever. "Yeah, send me the article, I'm curious. I'll call you later, okay?"

"Get well. And remember, cypress oil!"

Tullio ended the call and stretched out his arm to place the phone on the bedside table. Under his right armpit he felt a presence, an abnormality; probing with two fingers he encountered a swelling, a pulsating bulge moving with every heartbeat. Lymph nodes. He discovered to his horror that they were all enlarged, the ones under his neck, in his groin. He didn't have the strength to drag himself back to the bathroom to retrieve the cypress oil. He realised he was scared stiff. He picked up his mobile phone again, then scrolled through the address book until he found the number of his doctor.

Although the idea of consulting a servant of the pharmaceutical companies did not appeal to him at all, he called the number, for the first time in over three years.

"Yes. This is Tullio Sandri, doctor, I don't know if you remember me? Yes. The one from the Party of Change. Um, listen… can you come by for a visit? I don't think I can make it to your office. Flu, I'm afraid. Bad. I don't feel well at all."

★   ★   ★

Doctor Riboni arrived half an hour later, the buzz of the intercom announcing his presence. Tullio got out of bed on shaky legs, cleaned up the vomit as best he could, and went to open the door of the apartment building. The doctor entered the flat in a black suit, holding a huge leather bag. He greeted Tullio with a nod of his head, looking at him sternly. Tullio did not remember the doctor being so tall, cadaverous.

"You don't look good, Mr. Sandri."

"I feel awful."

They moved into the room, and Tullio had the impression that the doctor was following him on stilts. Legs too skinny, too long.

"Strip to your underwear and lie down so I can examine you properly," Riboni ordered. Tullio obeyed, the effort of taking off his clothes drawing groans from him, and then he collapsed onto the bed while the doctor fumbled in his bag.

He pulled out a stethoscope, and donned a pair of latex gloves. Tullio shivered at the contact of the icy metal on his hot chest. The doctor's gloved fingers were just as cold. They probed under his armpits, in the crease between thigh and groin, behind his ears, on his neck.

"Open your mouth and say *aaahhh*. Now give me two coughs. There you go. Have you vomited? How long have you been feeling like this? Have you noticed these swellings in your armpit and groin area?"

Tullio obeyed the commands and answered the questions like a frightened child. When Riboni had finished his examination, he sat down on the edge of the bed, stripped off his gloves and placed his instruments in his bag. Then he stood, silently staring at his tapering hands, letting out a long, deep sigh. He pulled a handkerchief from his pocket and brought it in front of his face.

"Well, doctor?" urged Tullio. "What's the verdict?"

Riboni shook his head, stood up. He really was too tall. "The news is not the best, Mr. Sandri." He spoke through the handkerchief pressed to his lips.

"In what way?"

"I'm pretty sure it's the plague."

It was as if a shadow had suddenly slipped into the room, a creature of darkness that occupied the corners and engulfed the light. Tullio squinted, and with a tremendous effort he pulled himself into a sitting position, propping himself on his elbows.

"I beg your pardon?"

"Plague. Bubonic," the doctor confirmed. "You have probably been bitten by an infected flea. It's going to get worse and worse. Petechiae, boils, necrosis of the extremities, delirium. Of course, there are antibiotics, but I don't think you're okay with taking that stuff, are you? I'm sorry, Mr. Sandri, I really am. I am mortified."

Tullio opened his mouth wide, stunned, unable to utter a sound. He stared at the doctor, who was studying him with eyes like whirlpools from over his handkerchief, and suddenly burst into sobbing laughter.

"Very funny, doctor, very funny!" he coughed. "For a moment I almost believed you! Nice joke, but the plague was eradicated centuries ago. This is not the Middle Ages!"

Riboni, however, did not laugh. He walked away from the bed on his stilted legs, dragging his mammoth bag with him, an expression of pity in his deep, black eyes. On the threshold of the room he paused, lowering his handkerchief.

"The plague has unfortunately never been eradicated. But don't worry. We take care of everything. You just have to trust us. We are the only ones who know how to deal with the likes of you."

The doctor stepped into the corridor. Tullio heard him talking on the phone to someone in a whisper. He tried to get up and found he could not. It felt as if his legs had been sawn off and his torso stuck in a furnace.

"Hey, doc, the joke's only good when it's short-lived! Hey! Get back here!" he shouted with his last remnants of strength.

Then he collapsed back onto his bed, energy spent.

★   ★   ★

It was the sound of bells that woke him up. They tinkled in a disjointed, eerie song. Down in the street.

It took him a few moments to focus on the room, his head wrapped in a bandage of burning migraine. He managed to rise a little, pushing with his aching feet on the mattress, and saw the trio lined up at his bedside.

He screamed, huddling against the headboard.

In the centre was Dr. Riboni. Tullio recognised him by his suit and lanky figure. His face was concealed by a bizarre papier-mâché mask, from which emanated a sickly, sweet smell of spices. On his head was a shapeless cylinder, grey with dust. Behind two round holes covered by small glass lenses, he glimpsed the doctor's eyes.

"What do you want?" he breathed in a hoarse voice. "Who are they?"

The figures accompanying the doctor were the embodiment of decay. Hunched over, swathed in stinking rags, they peered at him from beneath hoods with porcine eyes embedded in faces chewed by disease, riven with scars and badly healed wounds, lips purple around rotten teeth. One of them was missing his left hand, his arm ending in a bony stump; the other had no nose, just a triangular gash of bright, wet red.

"Go away! Go away!" implored Tullio, and in response the doctor spread his arms wide in a gesture that set the two thugs in motion. They limped to the side of the bed and grabbed him under his armpits, wrenching sharp cries of pain from him. Unceremoniously they dragged him into the corridor, and then down the stairs as though he were nothing but a sack of potatoes.

"Help me! Someone help me!" Tullio called, but the apartment building was as silent as a mausoleum.

He wanted to rebel, to resist, but he was too weak. As the men dragged him into the street, he thought it must all be a nightmare, one of those horrible nightmares triggered by high fever.

★   ★   ★

Dishevelled clouds swung over the town of Pinerolo like a funeral shroud chewed by woodworms. A few metres from the door of the apartment block stood a cart drawn by a dissolute horse, its ribs so exposed as to resemble a birdcage. On the pavement Tullio tried to get his feet under him, to escape the grasp of his tormentors, but they pulled him to the cart, blowing breaths that stank of garlic and corruption into his face.

The doctor climbed onto the mangy steed, hoisting himself on his stick-insect legs.

Tullio turned and tried to bite the hooded man's stump on his right, but was lifted with ease and thrown onto the cart. Just below his skin he could feel things moving and swelling. He looked desperately around in search of a familiar face, perhaps a neighbour, but there was no one. All he heard were the bells that seemed to jingle mockingly around him, a soundtrack to the madness he was experiencing.

He pissed himself, and the hunched, twisted figures sitting either side of him snickered as if it were the funniest thing in the world.

He tried in vain to stammer a prayer, but the words were swallowed up by the hoarse cry of a crow that darted high over the rooftops.

"To the Lazaretto!" shrieked a voice, exultant. "To the Lazaretto!"

The lopsided cart splashed forward on the cobblestones, and Tullio wondered if he would ever return home.

*   *   *

Alternating between wakefulness and oblivion, Tullio saw Pinerolo's shops and squares, fountains and avenues, banks and ice cream parlours, lurch past as the cart jolted on. But he didn't see another human being. The only life evident in the streets were pigeons, stray dogs and the vague, scampering shapes of vermin, slipping around corners, or congregating near manhole covers.

The cart left the city and moved on into the countryside. It rattled along a long mule track lined with tall poplars, zigzagged through cornfields, crossed desolate plains rotten with fog, where the only human forms were the scarecrows built by farmers in the spring, and finally reached a huge brick farmhouse that looked abandoned.

"Where are we?" Tullio mumbled. The only response his captors gave him was to unload him from the cart and throw him onto a stretcher made of rudimentary sticks and red-stained sheets. As they carried him inside the farmhouse, he noticed gigantic bonfires burning in the distance, releasing monstrous bulbs of black smoke, which stank of burning flesh.

Tullio coughed and vomited blood.

Then he fainted.

When he rose from the waters of the void into the waking world, he was in the Lazaretto.

★ ★ ★

He had been laid in a corner of the vast hall that formed the necrotic heart of the structure, on a cot filthy with bodily fluids and overrun with ticks. The corpse carriers and the doctor were gone.

All around, Hell.

Hundreds of sick people were suffering and suppurating in the Lazaretto, some on improvised beds, others lying on the beaten earth floor, their putrid sores in contact with the feculent ground.

Tullio looked down at his own body: galaxies of boils dotted his legs, torso and arms, and some of the tumescences had burst, releasing black blood and pus.

The smell was intolerable. The stench of excrement and stale sweat mingled with the mephitic miasma of decomposition. The cries and groans, which echoed around him, were joined by the sound of distant bells.

Why was he there? What was going on?

He told himself that a new epidemic had broken out, a modern plague, swift and devastating, and he was nothing more than one of the many victims of a catastrophe that would see an end to the human race.

He remained in his corner, struck by the similarity between the scene around him and the depiction of Hell by Hieronymus Bosch.

He saw old nuns in shabby dresses, priests and doctors shuffling to and fro, attending with apparently little interest or care to the lame and the crippled, the disfigured and the hideously afflicted. From time to time, in the mass of bodies piled up, and in the continuous procession that swirled through the structure, he saw figures that had little or nothing human about them, with too many limbs, or disproportionate heads, some of which were concealed within nightmarish masks of wood and bone. He attributed those visions to the disease that was gnawing at his brain.

When he could summon up the energy, he screamed.

Clutching at the robe of a passing monk, he begged the holy man to put him out of his misery, but the monk merely spat on him and walked away laughing.

After some hours, a one-eyed child, a fellow sufferer, approached him and granted him the benefit of a wet cloth on his forehead.

Night came, and with it the melancholy hooting of owls.

Morning came, and with it new sick people, new bodies to pile up in the belly of the Lazaretto.

And then night again.

And so the days passed, endless and intolerable, with no let-up in the constant flow of pain and suffering.

Tullio's body suppurated, rotted and collapsed, but his consciousness remained alert, his mind clear.

One day he heard a doctor mutter: "We're no longer keeping up with them. There are too many! Christ, help us…"

No one was paying attention to him anymore. They were trampling him, dumping other sick people on him. He wished he could die. But when he looked down at his arms and saw that his hands were little more than metacarpals covered in parchment-like strips of sinew, he knew that he never would.

Gradually he felt himself seeping into the ground, infecting it, changing from a solid to a liquid state. Knowing he was destined never to die, he only hoped that one day he would mutate from a liquid into a foul-smelling gas, whereupon he would rise into the air and finally be free.

Oh, he knew it would take a long time. A very long time. But Tullio Sandri clung to hope as he rotted and leaked and changed.

One day, he was sure, he would escape from the damp, decaying embrace of the Lazaretto, and somehow return home.

Finally home.

JACK-A-LENT

Paul Finch

"Bless me, Father, for I have sinned." It was a male voice, but it sounded old and tired. "It's been so long since my last confession... I can't even remember it."

Father O'Shea gave it little thought. "Well, the fact you're here now is a good sign. It means you're serious about this. Remember, make a heartfelt confession and Jesus will forgive even your worst sins."

There was a pause on the other side of the curtain. "I wish I could believe that. Look, Father... there's a lot I want to tell you about."

"Go ahead, please."

"I don't think I can do it in here."

The priest was puzzled. "If you seek to unburden your soul, there's no better place than this."

"Yeah, but there are people waiting to come in after me, and this could take a long time. Could you meet me afterwards? I mean when confessions have finished?"

"Meet you?"

"I really need to talk, Father. But we don't have to go anywhere else. I'll wait out there in the church."

The priest chewed the inside of his cheek. He had other things he needed to do today.

"Please, Father. I'm desperate."

"Yes, of course." This was a soul in torment. And most likely a good one. Otherwise, whoever it was, they wouldn't have come here. "If you want to wait for me, that's fine. But I'll probably be another hour."

"That's okay, Father. What I'm going through has been half my life. Another sixty minutes won't hurt."

It ended up being more than sixty minutes. Nearly ninety. Even so, when Father O'Shea had removed his stole and cassock, and come round into the nave, a sole figure was still seated in the second pew from the front, his eyes locked on the towering window behind the altar, with its vivid stained-glass depiction of Jesus ascending in glory.

As O'Shea entered the pew, the man turned to face him. He was somewhere in his mid-sixties, but heavyset and wearing an old khaki combat jacket and jeans.

"Thanks for this." He offered a large, tattoo-covered paw. "The name's Michael Hagler."

The priest shook hands with him but was discomforted. There were tattoos on Hagler's forearms as well as his hands. His white hair was razored into a crewcut, he had a thick neck and broad shoulders. His face could once have been handsome but was now leathery and pockmarked. O'Shea sat down anyway. He was only in his late twenties, but thin and bespectacled. He'd never been a fighter and it was undeniable that priests had been robbed and beaten in their own churches. But these were the risks you had to take if you wanted to tend to your flock. And to be fair, the sense of threat wasn't huge. The man still seemed tired. His eyes were red rimmed as if he hadn't slept in a long time.

"That name doesn't mean anything to you?" Hagler said.

"I'm afraid not," the priest replied.

"I've been out of circulation a while, I suppose."

"How can I help you, Michael?"

"Father, I've got a story to tell that you might struggle to believe. But as God's my witness, every word of it is true."

O'Shea glanced at his tattoos again, seeing swords, pistols, clenched fists. All crudely done. "Before you say anything, Michael, I should warn you… if you're about to confess some crime to me, you're no longer protected by the confessional seal. Do you understand what that means?"

Hagler smirked without humour. "It means you can grass me up."

"In a nutshell, yes."

In truth, O'Shea wasn't sure whether this was strictly correct. The Apostolic Penitentiary might deem Hagler still to be in the process of confessing even though he had left the confessional and others had stepped into his place, but it was better to be safe and warn him. Either way, Hagler seemed unconcerned.

"Would you?" he asked.

"First of all, I'd try to persuade you to hand yourself over. But if this is something bad... well, I'm a priest and a spiritual counsellor, but I have a duty as a citizen too."

"You don't need to worry, Father. All my crimes have been accounted for."

Which meant that he'd been in prison, O'Shea thought, again with discomfort.

"How long have you got spare?" Hagler wondered.

"Well, tomorrow's Ash Wednesday. We have a full programme of services here at St. Lucy's. Today, though... well, it's all about pancakes. Not quite as much for the Church to do... is everything all right?"

The visitor had paled. "Ash Wednesday. Always thought it a miserable occasion, myself."

"Well, it's the start of Lent. Not exactly a celebration."

"Used to be, you know. Before your time." Hagler became distant. "Long before."

"Perhaps we should talk about what's bothering you?"

"Yeah... yeah, we should. You're not local to this area, are you?"

O'Shea feigned affront. "Michael, I'm a scouser born and bred."

"But you're not from Crocky?"

"Well, no. Childwall, but..."

"Used to be very different round here. Back in the early 80s, when smack was the thing."

O'Shea pondered that. His parish wasn't located in the most salubrious district even now; there was lots of unemployment and crime was high, but back in the day it had been truly woe begotten. "Were you involved in that, Michael?"

"Yeah. I'm sorry to say I was."

*　　*　　*

"What's Ash Wednesday anyway?" Bluto asked.

"I don't know," Doddy replied as he drove. "Some religious thing."

"Fucking heathens!" Marv said. "Start of Lent, isn't it."

Bluto, who was sitting between them, still looked nonplussed. "What's Lent?'

"Build-up to Easter, you dickhead."

Bluto didn't look as if he was even sure what Easter signified.

"Lent's the bit where you don't get any sweets," Doddy explained.

"Or more accurately," Marv added, "it's when you're supposed to mourn Jesus because he's gonna get put on the cross."

Doddy frowned. "Always wondered about that. I mean, Good Friday's the end of next month."

"So?"

"Why do we mourn about something when it hasn't happened yet?"

Marv shook his head. "It happened two thousand years ago. We already *know* it happened. So, each year... well, we mourn in advance."

Doddy hooted. "I can see why you were never a teacher, Marvellous."

Marv scowled. "What's difficult about what I've just said?"

Doddy stuck his thumb in Bluto's face. "Look at this dipstick. Doesn't have a fucking clue what you're on about."

"What's the ash bit?" Bluto asked.

"You not seen 'em all walking round with lumps of ash on their foreheads?" Marv said.

"Yeah, but what's it for?"

"Fuck's sake. I don't know. Marks them as sinners, maybe."

Bluto chuckled. "*We'd* be covered in the shit..."

"Here," Doddy interrupted, pulling up. A phone-box sat on the opposite corner. He turned to Marv. "You calling in?"

Marv, whose name wasn't actually Marvellous, or even Marvin, but whose surname was Hagler, went across the road. Doddy and Bluto watched him, the former so-named because, with his buck teeth and mop of black curls, he – sort of, vaguely – resembled one of the city's favourite sons. Bluto, on the other hand, looked a lot more like his Popeye cartoon namesake.

Marv came back and jumped in. "Black Dog," he said. "He's there now. So, get a spurt on."

They called them the Taxation Team. Their ordinary routine of a weekday night would involve prowling the district in their van, identifying the dealers operating without approval, carting them off, and... well, taxing them. Not every dealer was willing to give up even a portion of his money or stash, but the Taxation Team were old hands on young, fit bodies. On top of that, most of the characters they nabbed were pathetic specimens, users themselves looking to feed their own habits, working without protection.

Sometimes without protection. Which was why tonight was going to be different.

The Black Dog wasn't a pretty pub. Bang in the middle of a sprawling council estate, it had originally been built to provide a heart and soul for the community. They'd once had functions there, dances, live music. But these days the place was mainly known for trouble. Some of its windows were boarded; shattered glass sparkled on its car park. There were no cars there at present, though that was because the back alley, which was the only way in and out, was blocked by overturned bins and heaped with festering rubbish, preventing any kind of vehicle gaining access. However, tonight was going to be an exception.

Marv and Bluto got out. They were wearing their uniform trackies but now donned extra protective clothing: big thick coats (which worked quite well on a damp, cold night in February anyway), and heavy-duty gloves. It was easy enough heaving the bins out of the way, but the bulging plastic sacks would be full of needles, so they needed to be careful with those.

Doddy didn't reverse the van all the way onto the car park, but halted before the entrance.

"He knows *you* too well," he told Bluto through the open window. "*You* have to stay outside."

"He knows me too," Marv said.

"Yeah, but you don't stand out in a crowd."

Marv nodded. The logic was inescapable.

Bluto accompanied Marv along the car park to the pub's rear door, which stood open, a racket of shouting and laughter echoing from inside, even though it was only six-thirty. Bluto waited on the right-hand side, drawing his half-a-pool-cue. Marv went in, but almost immediately came out again.

"Nearly walked into him!" He darted left of the door, fitting his brass knuckles over his glove. "Gone to the pisser. But he's got his jacket on."

"Alone?" Bluto asked.

Marv nodded. They waited.

It was a bit of a joke really. Even if Clawson had come out with two or three heavies in tow, Bluto could likely have handled them. He wasn't much in the brainbox, but he was built like a shire horse, and he had a monster of a right hook, with or without his tool. Of course, the gun would be a factor. The gun was the reason they were here.

Clawson sauntered out, and Bluto's cue came down from overhead in a wild swinging arc, cracking on his cranium. The target's legs buckled and he collapsed. Marv didn't even need to throw one, but he did anyway, meaty impacts sounding as he slugged the target twice, once in the right temple, once in the right side of the jaw. Clawson was a lifeless heap after that.

Marv searched under his coat, finding the pistol, an old Webley, which, in truth, looked just as likely to blow its shooter's fingers off as kill someone, but he pocketed it anyway. They took Clawson's feet and dragged him down the length of the car park, watching the pub as they went. The few windows at the back that weren't frosted or boarded were too fogged. No one would see. Doddy now reversed into view, the van's back doors, which had already been unlocked, swinging open.

"Get him fucking in," Marv said.

Clawson's greying hair was a sticky, crimson nest, but he was coming round. He groaned, started struggling. Bluto raised his cue.

"Enough of that," Marv hissed. "He's gotta be alive."

They slung the half-conscious body into the back of the van and climbed in after it, slamming the doors. Marv yanked on a cord, and a flickery bulb came to life. Doddy hit the gas, and the van lurched forward, swerving out of the alley.

Clawson burbled something but it made no sense. His lips brimmed with blood.

"Too late, Johnny," Marv said. They turned him over, rummaged in a sports bag, and producing a pair of cuffs, fastened his hands behind his back. "You pay your fucking dues, lad. You don't pull shooters on people."

"Fucking dickhead." Bluto slammed a granite fist into the captive's ribcage.

"Should've known better, Johnny," Marv said, turning him back over. "Branching out on your own was never going to work. But pulling a shooter? That's against the rules. Bring a shooter, and what happens next? Every fucker does. Next thing, we're living in the Wild West."

Again, Clawson grunted something. His right eye was buried under a plum-sized blue swelling, but his left one had opened. It was weak and watery, but baleful. It fixed on Marv with unnerving intensity. But Marv merely shrugged.

"That's why we've got to make an example. We don't want to, you understand. But orders is orders." Bluto handed him a metal box. Marv yanked a glove off with his teeth, then flipped the box open and took out a capped syringe. Again, he caught Clawson watching him. "Don't worry. This isn't the same shit you've been selling. We wouldn't do *that* to you. It's not going to be great though, lad, I'll be honest." He glanced at Bluto. "Hold him still."

The captive only resisted feebly, but the giant leaned down, totally immobilising him. Marv produced a lock-knife, flicked it open and worked its blade along Clawson's left arm, slicing the anorak and shirt. He picked up the syringe again, flicking off its cap and applying the injection. "Just a little prick, Johnny. As the actress said to the bishop. In case you were wondering, this is called suxamethonium barbital. Used in general anaesthesia. Similar to succinylcholine, but not as likely to kill you. Got to get the dosage right, though. Which is why it's lucky we've got our own sawbones on the payroll, eh? Lucky for us, of course. Not so much for you." He shouted through the wooden partition: "How we doing?"

"Five minutes to the Scout Hut," came Doddy's muffled reply.

"That should do us." Marv dipped into the sports bag again, yanking out a bundle of pale green cloth, which, when he shook it out, was two-layered, and had been cut in roughly the shape of a human being. He glanced down at Clawson. Blood still ran freely from the busted mouth, but the single eye had glazed over. Marv shoved him a couple of times. He was so limp he might have been boneless. "Okay, strip him."

The Scout Hut was about the size and shape of a double garage and built entirely from wood, the rear of it accessible from the other side of a small grotto at the back of St. Lucy's Church. It faced down a narrow drive, and was separated from the rest of the world by a pair of wrought-iron gates, which, like the Hut itself, were never kept locked, because, apart from some cricket stuff and a few old footballs, what in there was worth nicking?

On the face of it, this should have been the easy part, but in actual fact it was going to be risky. The only place to park near the church was on a paved concourse at the front. Mid-evening on a weekday, there wouldn't be much traffic going past, while across the road stood a row of rubbishy shops – cycle repairs, second-hand goods and such – with flats above them, which all would be nestling behind drawn curtains. But there might be people coming and going to the church itself. So, instead of parking on its concourse, they'd opted for an unlit backstreet at the rear of the shops, which meant they now had to carry Clawson a significant distance. That was no problem for Bluto, but it increased the chance they'd be spotted. Not that anyone would recognise the captive. He'd now been press-studded into his head-to-foot suit of pale green cloth, while Doddy, Marv and Bluto had pulled balaclavas on.

Doddy went first, cutting along a side-passage to the front. He halted at the road, which was called Maitland Drive. Only the odd car went past, but on the other side, candlelight glowed through the stained-glass windows of the church. He signalled to the others. Marv came up next, Bluto behind him, Clawson's inert form draped over his shoulder.

"Anything?" Doddy asked.

"Dead to the world," Bluto grunted.

"Naw. He isn't that." Doddy leaned against Clawson's head. "I know you can't respond, Johnny, but I know you can hear me. You can feel me too, yeah?" He flicked at the cloth covering Clawson's ear. "Sorry, I know you can't wince. Shit when that happens, eh?"

"Road's clear," Marv said.

Doddy led the way over, the others following. They accessed St. Lucy's forecourt without incident, carrying the body down a narrow passage alongside the main building. In the grotto at the back, it was so dark they almost tripped over the low fence encircling the central flowerbed, in the middle of which a marble image of St. Lucy, holding the plate on which rested the pair of eyes the Romans had gouged from her head, stood on a plinth. On the other side of that, they opened a side gate and emerged at the rear of the Scout Hut.

"Piece of piss," Doddy chuckled.

"Yeah, but what's that fucking noise?" Bluto murmured.

When they listened, there was a rising hubbub of not-too-distant voices.

"That's what tonight's all about," Marv said. "You know, Jack-a-Lent?"

Bluto shook his head. He still didn't really understand why they were doing this, though it never usually stopped him. He turned up, did a job, got paid, went home. That was Bluto.

"Let's crack on." Doddy sidled around the Hut, found a door and opened it. It was dark inside, and not wanting to activate the main light, he pulled a torch and switched it on.

"What the fuck?" Bluto breathed.

In all honesty, it was the last thing any of them would normally have expected. Especially on Church property. It occupied the centre of the Hut, where space had been cleared, boxes thrown into the corners, sports gear kicked aside. In appearance, it was an ungainly wheeled structure, like an old-fashioned vaulting horse, but with no padding along the top, just rough wood, and an upright steel pole, a section of scaffolding or a piece of pipe, projecting upward about three feet. Most eye-catching was the figure seated astride the top of it. It sat with its back to the pole, its arms twisted behind it and knotted together at the wrists with twine. Faint hints of the same pale green cloth they'd put Clawson into were visible through gaps in its clothing, which mostly comprised a raggedy clown outfit: like a Pierrot costume, very old and dirty, one side red, one side blue, off-white ballet shoes on its feet, off-white gloves on its hands. A conical hat, like something a schoolkid would make, sat on its head, while a featureless white mask, held in place with an elastic band but daubed with exaggerated human features in blotchy, garish paint, covered its face.

"Meet the star of the show." Doddy pulled his balaclava off. "Jack-a-Lent."

"What's that fucking stink?" Bluto replied.

"*Him.*" Doddy grinned, his Bugs Bunny teeth protruding from his sweaty face like ivory pegs. "They stuff him with rubbish. Real nasty stuff. Rotten food, dirty nappies, all that."

"Fucking vile," Bluto said.

"I know. That's the whole point…"

★   ★   ★

"Excuse me …" Father O'Shea interrupted. He'd turned steadily paler during the course of the tale, but now looked physically sick. "This thing you describe was on Church premises?"

Hagler eyed him. "Course it was. At the start."

"Start of what, some kind of parade?"

"What else?"

"And what... what *was* Jack-a-Lent?"

Hagler frowned. "Aren't you supposed to be a priest? Don't tell me you're one of these trendy new ones?"

"Please, Michael! What are we talking about here?"

Hagler glanced down the length of the church. Briefly, the emptiness of it held his gaze, as if he'd just heard something odd. "I've looked it up," he finally said. "Had lots of time for stuff like that. There are different views."

O'Shea shook his head. "Whose views?"

"People who write about history, tradition, all that stuff..."

Before he could elaborate, a *boom* resounded through the building. The archetypal thunder of a church door. Hagler shot another glance along the nave, his mouth in a tight line. O'Shea looked too, but there was nothing to see. What they'd heard was almost certainly one of the cleaners going upstairs to the organ gallery.

"Michael?" he said.

With an effort, Hagler refocused. "Some say Jack-a-Lent was like an embodiment of the winter. You know, he was on his way out, so everyone was having a laugh at his expense. Were going to punish him. Good riddance to bad rubbish and all that. But that's probably bollocks, pardon my fucking French..." He reddened and shrugged. "Everything gets credited to pagans these days, doesn't it. Christmas, Easter... but mostly that's wishful thinking by sad little atheist bastards. Can't see why it would ever have been popular in old Catholic parishes like St. Lucy's if it was that. More likely, he was the personification of Lent itself. Parishioners who were due to have a hard time needed someone to take it out on."

O'Shea shook his head. "I can't say I'm familiar with this tradition."

"Medieval, isn't it. I guess someone here at St. Lucy's, some priest or teacher, liked the idea of bringing it back."

"Well, I myself would have been very uneasy with it."

"You do surprise me. Not even if it was supposed to be an actual person?"

"A person?"

"Because that's another theory."

"In God's name, who?"

Hagler gave him a pitying look. "Who do you think? Judas."

"Judas Iscariot?"

"How many Judases do you know, Father?"

★   ★   ★

Hillside View was a deceptively pretty name. It evoked imagery from the Yorkshire Dales; whitewashed country hotels; a vista of sweeping moorland. But the truth was different. A spartan 1950s tower block, located on raised ground overlooking St. Lucy's parish, it had been poorly designed and built with materials so cheap that, less than thirty years after welcoming its first residents, it had already deteriorated beyond human use. It now stood empty and condemned, but it was easy enough to access. A barricade of old doors had been erected around the site, but this could be levered open by simple use of a crowbar. Having left the van in an arched passage between two burned, boarded shops, the Taxation Team slipped through the gap they'd made and headed up to the fourth floor.

It would normally have been an unnerving prospect: bare concrete stairwells covered in graffiti, stinking of urine, scattered with beer cans and spent needles; on each level, shadow-filled corridors leading off, broken only by patches of spectral moonlight. But in truth, if Doddy, Marv and Bluto encountered any druggies there, or anyone at all in fact, *they* were the ones who'd be the problem.

On the fourth floor, on the north side, Doddy kicked his way through a door chosen at random. The shell of an abandoned apartment lay beyond it, though some items of older, heavier furniture had been left. They opened the slide window and stepped onto the balcony. Far below, a main street was visible. Further along it, terraced houses stood on either side, though down at this end it was slum clearance land, a cindery waste stretching into the darkness to both left and right. Despite that, excitable crowds were gathering on both sides of the road. There was cheering and raucous laughter, and a curious chanting.

The chanting grew in volume as the procession, which had just come into sight at the far end of the street, reached the first onlookers.

Marv waited with trepidation. He'd seen this numerous times, but it never ceased to unsettle him. Six blokes walked at the front in a horizontal line, each one carrying a burning torch. They waved at the crowd and shouted to people they knew. Twenty yards behind them, a team of men and boys lugged on ropes, which pulled taut over thirty or so yards before connecting with the cumbersome, wheeled vaulting horse, that distinctive garish figure still astride it, its arms locked behind the post at its back. The chanting grew louder, more voices picking it up.

Bluto looked puzzled. "What they saying?"

"What they say every time," Marv replied. "Innocent blood."

With that explanation in mind, the chant was now clear.

"Inno-cent blood... Inno-cent blood... Inno-cent blood..."

"What you fucking playing at, Marv?" Doddy asked. "Get the camera."

Marv dipped into the sports bag and took out the last item they'd need that evening. It was a Nikon F3, with a telescopic lens attachment. How much it would catch in this poor light was uncertain, but there'd shortly be plenty more to work with. The grotesque effigy now rode amid the people, whose cheers turned to roars as they launched projectiles at it. Initially, these were eggs and bits of fruit, but soon stones as well, cans and bottles, several of the latter missing and smashing on the road, though just as many scored direct hits.

Marv commenced shooting, managing to catch a sequence of three or four as a small kid broke from the crowd, raced forward and took a savage swipe with what looked like a clothes prop, smacking the object of their derision full in the face, knocking the mask askew.

"Ouch," Doddy tittered. "Nasty."

"What if some bizzy comes snooping?" Bluto said, his thoughts characteristically wandering. "Finds the van? And that thing in the back of it? And a pile of Clawson's clothes?"

"The bizzies are at the party." Doddy nodded down and grinned again. A Merseyside panda car was parked up about fifty yards along the street. A couple of uniforms leaned against it, arms folded, enjoying the show. Alongside them stood some kind of local dignitary, an older guy in a red gown and a chain of office. "Right under their noses, eh?" Doddy chuckled. "Right under their fucking noses."

Marv took more pics.

"Don't overdo it," Doddy warned him. "Don't run out of film before the big finale."

"Twat," Marv retorted. "Can't fucking please you."

Doddy cackled. "Just the good stuff, yeah?"

Below, the procession veered onto some wasteland, the crowd flooding in pursuit, forming itself into a huge circle, while the trundling vehicle and its single ragged passenger came to a halt in the middle. More folk scurried forward, unwrapping polythene sheets from great bundles of sticks and armfuls of loose planking, propping them up around it, building the whole thing into a massive combustible pyramid, from out of the top of which only Jack-a-Lent's sideways-lolling head was visible.

Doddy chuckled again. He'd always been one to enjoy his work.

The men with the torches now thrust fire into the kindling. Most of it caught easily, but just in case, a couple produced pails of what was presumably petrol. The crowd surged back as the accelerant was thrown and with a titanic *WHUMP*, the flames billowed, the entire ghastly structure now ablaze, crackling so loudly they could even hear it on the fourth floor. Marv peered through his lens, struggling with the glare, but closing tightly on the effigy's head as it was swiftly engulfed in flame. Within a couple of seconds, it was a blackened turnip; a couple of seconds more and it wasn't even that.

"How long before they notice the stink?" Bluto wondered.

Marv wrinkled his nostrils. "Speaking of which, there's a funny smell here." Glancing round, he was startled to glimpse someone walking past the apartment's broken-open front entrance. "Shit!" He hurried across to it but, looking out, saw only a deserted passageway filled with light and shadow. There was no sign of movement.

When he told the others, Doddy shrugged. "Some social reject. No shortage round here."

"What if he overheard us?" Marv tapped Bluto's arm. "Genius here mentioned Clawson's name."

Bluto looked sheepish, but Doddy shrugged again. "No biggie. Some fucking druggie who doesn't know what day it is."

"Or some druggie who's desperate to get his fix and knows he can get paid from the bizzies' grass fund."

Doddy worked his lips together as he thought on this. Silence was usually golden round here, but at present the big H had equal pulling power. He grunted and pushed them both out into the passage. "Go and see."

The figure had been headed left-to-right, so that was the way they went, rounding a corner into a small lobby area latticed with silvery moonlight, a number of black doorways standing on different sides. Even with weapons out, they hesitated.

"Come on!" Doddy shoved them from behind. He'd drawn his own weapon, a machete with its chopping edge honed like a razor.

They advanced, scanning the doorways. One, which stood just left of an upward staircase, was the jammed-open entrance to a lift shaft. When Doddy shone his torch through, the lift was present, a narrow metal cubicle, its interior scribbled all over as though some madman had been in there with a felt pen. A single frosted glass panel sat in the middle of its ceiling, but it was intact. No one could have climbed up through that diminutive gap anyway.

Doddy slashed his beam back across the lobby, highlighting more graffiti: skulls embedded with daggers, a devil head chewing an arm, a naked woman upside-down on an X-shaped cross.

"Christ," Marv breathed. "Fucking Romans…"

"What?" Doddy exclaimed.

Outside, the crowd was still chanting. *"Inno-cent blood… Inno-cent blood…"*

"This thing's fucked up, Dod," Marv said. "We shouldn't be doing this. We shouldn't even be here."

"Hear that?" Bluto interrupted.

They fell silent: a scraping or dragging sound filtered down the nearby stairwell.

"The fuck!" Doddy steered his underlings towards it. "Get up there."

They ascended warily, Bluto with the cue at his shoulder, the way the bizzies carried their truncheons when they were wading in, Marv flexing his gloved hand inside his brass knuckles. He now felt he could have tooled up with something better. He still had the Webley in his pocket, but suspected it was way past its best.

There was a sudden explosive *bang* from close overhead. Then another, and another, and they realised that something enormous was travelling fast down the stairway. They halted, tingling. The next switchback was about ten treads above them. Their eyes riveted on it as a massive angular object came end-over-end into view. It caromed from the facing wall, and descended again, driven with such force that it was all they could do to scamper back down into the lobby and dart one to either side. The colossal item of furniture, for it was an old bureau or sideboard, landed with a noise like a motorway collision.

The trio stared at each other agog as the dust settled.

"Bastards," Bluto breathed, that old psychotic rage slowly taking hold. He yelled it full-bloodedly, "*BASTARDS!*", before charging up the stairway, flailing with his cue. "*BASTARDS!*"

They heard him shrieking it again and again, increasingly muffled as he rounded switchback after switchback. And then his tone abruptly changed.

From roars of rage to screams of horror.

Marv stared at Doddy, whose eyes were bugging, whose curly mop looked almost to be standing on end. Upstairs, Bluto roared manfully again, bellowed in fact, as if he was still game for the fight, but it was shriller than it should be, tinged with terror. At which point it transformed back into a protracted, piercing screech, and then descended.

At shocking speed.

There was an immense crash from the lift shaft.

With a clatter, the frosted panel fell out and shattered.

Doddy swung his torch through its entrance. The lift was still empty aside from the reflective splinters on the floor, but Bluto's face was visible where the ceiling panel had dislodged. Torn and bloodied. Where the left eye once was, the butt-end of his cue jutted out.

They ran. It was more instinct than anything else. Just took to their heels, down and down towards the ground floor, only halting in the porch area, panting, sweating.

"How... how did that thing get through his head?" Marv stammered.

"When he fell down the lift shaft," Doddy stuttered. "What else?"

"Fell? Or was thrown?"

"What's fucking wrong with you, Marv?"

"What clothes was Clawson wearing?"

"How the fuck do I know?"

Marv tried to recall. Army Surplus kecks, he thought. A leather jacket over a denim shirt. He'd only caught a fleeting glimpse of that person passing the flat doorway up on the fourth, but damn it to Hell, if he wasn't sure that bastard had been wearing similar togs.

"We put the right one on that hobby horse, didn't we?" he said.

"Course we did. I carried the original back to the van, myself. It was light as a feather."

"Whatever's up there isn't."

"What do you mean, *what*ever?"

"You ever tried picking Bluto up?"

"Marv... Bluto fell. No one chucked him."

"How about the bureau? Did that fall too?"

Doddy glanced back to the foot of the stairwell. More silvery moonlight filtered down it. There was no sound from overhead now, but they weren't fooled. They knew what they'd seen. And that bureau had been one massive lump of furniture.

"Fuck it," Doddy said. "We've done the job. We're getting out."

They went to the front doors. The firelight that had previously flickered through the grimy glass panels was dimmer now. It was quieter out there too, the festivities dying down. Marv glanced back once as they went outside, not sure whether a shadowy outline at the foot of the stairway, which he was sure hadn't been there a second ago, was a silhouetted person standing just out of sight.

It didn't matter. He hurried after Doddy. They sidled through the fence of scabby doors and half-ran along the back alley to the arch where they'd left the van. But the first thing they saw were its rear doors hanging open.

They slid to a halt. Doddy shone his light inside. The effigy was absent, along with the scrunched-up ball of Johnny Clawson's clothing.

"This means nothing!" he said. "Some bastard's broken in, that's all. What do you expect, they're all fucking tea leaves round here!"

Marv ran his gloved fingers along the left door's edge, particularly over its mangled lock. "Smashed open from the inside."

"Bollocks." Doddy dug for his keys. "Get in."

The road took them around the rear of Hillside View, descending only gradually so that, when Marv looked up through his passenger window, the great monolithic structure, now atop a high concrete embankment, towered into the night. At first, he thought the figure standing on the embankment parapet was an old fence-post clad with tatters of windblown material, but then it leapt out.

The van shuddered under the impact.

"What the fuck?" Doddy shouted.

"Get us out of here," Marv replied. "It's on the roof."

They swerved onto a street where the houses were still occupied, careering recklessly between lines of parked cars. Once on a wider road, Doddy flung the vehicle from side to side. "Not fucking having this!" he shrieked.

But then a gloved hand snaked down onto the windscreen.

"*You bastard!*" He threw the wheel left to right again, the vehicle fishtailing, but the passenger clung on. "Gimme that fucking shooter!"

Before Marv could object, Doddy's left hand had burrowed into his pocket. It snagged the Webley, pulled it out and pointed it at the ceiling. And only then did the driver realise that they'd mounted the kerb, a concrete wastebin directly in their path. He yanked the wheel left, but still caught it a glancing blow, the impact terrific, the van veering crazily across the road on its nearside wheels, before tilting over completely and landing on its side.

Marv clenched his eyes shut as, first, the passenger window imploded on him, and then dirt and gravel flew into his face. However, by habit if not design, he'd fastened his seatbelt, so when the vehicle came to a halt, he was shaken but not injured. He couldn't say the same for Doddy, who hadn't put his belt on, and now lay half on top of him, his hair limp and wet with the blood leaking from a deep gash in his scalp.

However, the Taxation Team leader was still conscious and still raging with anger.

"*Fuck!*" He clambered off Marv, struggled upright, punched his door open and levered himself through it. In his left hand he wielded the Webley.

"D... Dod..." Marv stammered, so exhausted by shock that he struggled to unclip his belt and then had to fight with every inch of strength just to clamber out in pursuit.

When he dropped outside and stumbled around the vehicle, Doddy was limping along the road, the Webley in one hand, the machete in the other. There was no streetlighting at this point; demolition land lay left and right, a fire-blasted wilderness. This meant that the figure Doddy was encroaching on was indistinct.

Marv mopped sweat from his eyes, sagging against the van as his knees threatened to give.

Doddy shouted something incoherent, before throwing the machete. It spun, glimmering, hitting its target full on, but bouncing off. Doddy shouted again, levelled the firearm and pumped the trigger, and the blot of light as it exploded in his hand was searing.

The maimed man's scream split the night as Marv stumbled away. He was determined not to look back, though he did so anyway, perhaps a hundred yards from the crash site, and was just able to distinguish Doddy on his knees, right hand clasping his left wrist. But it was less like an accident scene and more like an execution tableau, because now that second figure was encroaching on him, its raised hand clutching that gleaming slice of well-honed steel.

★   ★   ★

"I didn't go straight to the coppers," Hagler said, his face ashen. "I was still in denial. But that night, as I slept at my girlfriend's place…"

"You just went to your girlfriend's?" Father O'Shea asked, incredulous.

"Why not? It was the code of silence. No one ever talked. That was our shield, our failsafe."

"You were worried that a drug addict in Hillside View might…"

Hagler made a dismissive gesture. "He could maybe have pointed the law in the right direction, but he wouldn't have given them a smoking gun. Anyway, there were worse things to worry about. That night, I heard the sound of Sue's back gate. It was locked but it was rattling, like someone was climbing over it. Then I heard someone in the yard. Steel-shod boots clashing on flagstones… and you know, I'd barely noticed it at the time, but Clawson had been wearing segs." He shook his head. "When someone tried the back door, I went out through the front. You look at me like I'm dogshit, Father. That because I left Sue behind? What did it matter? Wasn't her it was after. Far as I recall, she slept the whole night through."

A noise distracted him. He glanced up at the organ gallery. The priest looked too. A figure was visible there, standing with its back turned. Hagler's cheek twitched. But then the figure straightened up and moved along, and they saw that it was an elderly lady with silver-rinsed hair, wielding a feather duster.

★   ★   ★

It was anyone's guess what was happening in Liverpool. Marv made no effort to find out. He didn't even call Sue, because she'd demand to know what was going on, and the less she knew, the better. There was no way the bizzies wouldn't want to speak to him once they'd found Doddy and Bluto, especially as both were in the vicinity of Johnny Clawson's funeral pyre. The heat would be on, and at some point, he'd have to go and face it, but they'd lack the crucial evidence. Wouldn't even have enough to stitch him. If they tried, he knew people who knew people... no jury would convict him.

He shifted position. One of his buttocks was going numb. He was perched at the end of a jetty, looking out across the glass-smooth surface of Derwentwater, a pristine lake cradled amid craggy, pine-clad hills. Down its far end, the rolling treeless summit of Skiddaw brushed the salmon-pink clouds. On his left, the last of the setting sun's rays dissipated over the broken line of Catbells ridge.

He could almost have relaxed, if he hadn't been expecting an interruption.

Said interruption duly arriving.

The steady *clump-clump* of segged boots advancing along the jetty. And that smell, a ripe stink of putrid trash tainting the April air. By Marv's estimation, it was less than a yard behind him when he dived forward and hit the lake's surface...

★   ★   ★

"I swam to the western shore," Hagler said. "It's all woods on that side. No paths or roads. I made my way round the lake on foot, dripping wet, worried sick... because I could sense it coming, hundreds of yards behind me. But coming all the same, never resting. The die was well and truly cast, Father."

"So, that's when you went to the police?" O'Shea said.

"Turned myself in that night. Keswick nick. They didn't believe me at first, but then they rang Merseyside. The only way they could be sure I wasn't some nutjob, I suppose. And the only way I could be safe."

The priest blew out a long breath. "How many murders were you charged with?"

"Only Clawson's. Bluto and Doddy they put down to members of his crew. I got thirty years. Managed to extend it by constant misbehaviour, but the older you get in jail, the harder it is to keep the tough guy act going. Plus, these soft fuckers these days, they really want to let you out. It's not your fault, it's down to society. You deserve another chance."

"And so now you've got one."

"Or alternatively, I've picked up exactly where I left off. Because why wouldn't I? I've got a price to pay, and there's no way round that."

"Michael, would it help…" The priest wasn't quite sure how to put this delicately. "Would it help if I told you that you're simply wrong here? That God doesn't punish sin by sending demons to kill us? That's never been part of Christian doctrine. We don't even believe that demonic entities exist in this world."

Hagler looked puzzled. "What about possession and all that? The Catholic Church does exorcisms, doesn't it?"

"Even possession is a contentious issue. Not every priest accepts it. But even if possession is real, these entities don't manifest… don't take actual physical form as you've described."

"Maybe it's Judas himself, then, eh? He'd have a beef with me, wouldn't he? He used to come here every year… to get his just deserts. He needed to be punished for committing one of the worst betrayals in human history. And he took it on the chin. And then what happens? We suddenly get in the way, and not only that… we serve up one of our own mates instead. Just like he did. Talk about making a bad situation worse."

"Michael…" O'Shea smiled gently in an effort to demonstrate how deluded this was. "Think about it logically. This… *thing*, Jack-a-Lent, it was made of rubbish, rotting waste. It could hardly be walking around intact after nearly forty years."

"It shouldn't have been walking around at all, but it was. Anyway…" Hagler shrugged wearily. "Whatever will be will be. The main reason I'm here is to get some absolution. I've paid my debt to society, but not to the Big Fella."

"That I can certainly help with," the priest said. "You've made a very full confession."

Not that he thought it would make any difference, because this man was clearly in a state of complete mental breakdown rather than sin. However, reconciliation was always good for the soul. Taking him to the altar, O'Shea completed the sacrament and issued God's pardon, requiring only a simple Act of Contrition, rather than any kind of penance. After that, he undertook to walk him down the church towards the porch. When they reached the front door, Hagler hesitated, glancing warily outside. The paved concourse had never changed, though the row of shops across Maitland Drive offered different services these days, fried chicken, payday loans, e-liquids. It wasn't impossible, though, that the familiarity of it was a problem.

"If you'd rather, we can go the back way," the priest said.

"For old times' sake, Father, I'd rather not go past the Scout Hut."

"The Scout Hut's not there anymore. Nor is that deplorable statue of St. Lucy. It's an overspill car park these days, thank Heaven."

Hagler smiled to himself. "The front door will do fine." But still, he delayed going out. "I know you think I'm just a whacko…"

"I wouldn't say that."

"Careful, Father. Lying's only a venial sin, but it can lead to worse." The ex-con sighed. "The truth is… we did a lot of bad things in this city. I'm not just talking about Clawson. People like us turned huge tracts of it into a junkie sewer. I can't quantify the number of lives that were damaged."

"I told you. All your sins have been forgiven."

"We'll soon put to the test how forgiven I am. But you're wrong, Father, if you think everything should be nicey-nicey. You know… you feel bad about what you did so that means it's okay?" He smiled sadly. "I don't think so."

"Michael, you're not making sense."

"What doesn't make sense is trying to hide the reality of evil because it discomforts you. Or discouraging an appropriate response to it because these days we're too sophisticated for that. You've got things arse over tit, Father."

"I'm sorry you feel that way."

"I hope a time never comes when you're sorrier you feel *your* way.

Anyway, I've done what I came for. I'm off, I'm sure you'll be glad to hear."

He made a visible effort to steel himself and walked out of the church. O'Shea watched him trudge across the concourse. "Good luck," he called.

Hagler didn't look round but made a semi-coherent response, which sounded like "I'll need it." Then he turned onto Maitland Drive and vanished from view.

The priest went through to the presbytery and up to his bedroom, to change. If the fellow wasn't mad, he was plain wrong. Evil wasn't a totally outdated concept, but things weren't nearly so simple. Good Lord, Hagler himself was the proof of that. A terrible upbringing, most likely. Mental disintegration, which was now clearly in full force.

He glanced from the window as he buttoned himself into a clean shirt and collar, and spotted the penitent again. He was visible by his green khaki, down the far end of Maitland Drive, chatting with someone else. Whoever this new person was, Hagler seemed quite pally with him. An old mate? A partner in crime? Two idiots together? Had this other guy just been up the road, spinning a similar tale of gibberish to Father Magee at Queen of Martyrs?

O'Shea watched as the twosome walked off together, unsure whether to be relieved or irritated. Though then, rather than stay on the main road, they cut right down a narrow alley, which, as far as he knew, connected to a derelict underpass that now led nowhere.

It was disconcerting to see that the second man was leading Hagler by the arm.

THE ONLY FACE YOU EVER KNEW

Gwendolyn Kiste

We're standing in the cereal aisle at the grocery store, the fluorescent lights blinking nervously above us, a Muzak version of Barry Manilow crackling through the speakers, when Veronica vanishes.

One moment, I'm reaching for a box of Honey Nut Cheerios on the top shelf, making a crack about how I always have to stand on my tiptoes, an inside joke between me and Veronica. The next moment, I turn around, and she's gone, dissolved like sea foam. Like she was never there at all.

"Veronica?" My voice barely a wisp. It's a long aisle, and I'm standing in the middle of it. She couldn't have just walked away. She couldn't have gone anywhere, not without me noticing.

I abandon the cart, the gallon of milk sweating in its plastic jug, my heart a jackhammer in my chest.

I wander through the store, my head dizzy. "Veronica, where are you?" I try to keep my tone even, to keep myself calm. I don't want to be that person panicking in public. Especially since she's probably around the corner in the produce section, picking over the dragon fruit or gooseberries, some secret ingredient she must have forgotten for a new recipe she's planning to make tonight.

That's what I tell myself – that she's still right here. Her black hair the colour of spilled ink, her dark lipstick, her brown Docs. Everything about her more familiar to me than my own face.

Except there's no sign of Veronica. Not in the store and not outside either. Our maroon Subaru Forester is still parked in the second row of the lot, but she's not there.

My hands trembling, I sit inside the car, searching through my phone. I try her number first. No answer. I leave a message.

"Please," I say. "Text me or find me or something."

Then I start calling everyone we know. "Have you heard from Veronica?" I ask them, but it's always the same response.

"No, not today. Are you all right, Catherine?"

I don't say anything. I just lean back in the driver's seat and close my eyes.

★   ★   ★

It was Valentine's Day three years ago when Veronica and I met at a dive bar. There were paper hearts taped to the walls, all the overpriced drink specials dyed neon pink and rimmed with glitter. She and I were both alone until we weren't. Until we saw each other.

With a grin, she bought me a drink before I could stop her, before I could buy her one first.

"To the Lonely Hearts Club," she said, raising her gin and tonic to me, and I flashed her a smile, my cheeks turning red, because I only hoped I wouldn't be lonely for much longer. At least not lonely for the night.

She kept me waiting, I'll give her that. It wasn't until two in the morning, the bartender covering up the taps, before Veronica invited me back to her loft apartment. I drove us there, and she didn't say a word the whole time, her bright green eyes on the road ahead.

"It's on the top floor," she said when we pulled into the parking lot. Inside, her apartment was sterile and streamlined, all metal railings and hard edges. No houseplants, no pets, no sign of life at all.

"I move around a lot," she told me, and didn't say anything more about it. I could have asked then. I *should* have asked then.

But Veronica didn't seem to worry about questions. She had more than enough answers of her own. In her bedroom, she kissed me until I couldn't breathe, undressing me one careful piece of clothing at a time. My tight black jeans. My white tank top. Even the crow skull necklace I never took off, not even to shower, not even to sleep. She shattered me into pieces, and I loved every minute of it.

"This won't last forever," she said afterward, the sun sneaking up over the skyline, but with the sweet scent of her skin all over me, I pretended not to hear her.

★　　★　　★

It's dusk now, the lights in the grocery store parking lot flickering on, one by one, and Veronica's still missing.

I've called her cellphone a hundred times, leaving dozens of messages, my voice so thin and panicked I can't possibly sound like myself anymore.

I don't want to go to the cops. I don't want to file a police report. That was the one constant in Veronica's life: she didn't like people in charge.

"You can't trust them," she always said, but I tell myself this is different. This is something I can't do alone. Veronica needs me. And I need help.

I breathe deep and dial 911.

The men in uniform arrive over an hour later and barely search the store for Veronica before they haul me into the station, their shoulders broad, their eyes narrowed. They wouldn't normally do this, not if I'd called to report a boyfriend or husband missing. They'd tell me to wait it out, that he'll probably come home soon. I'm sitting in this station because I'm a woman and so is my partner. I'm already a deviant to them, just for loving who I love. And it doesn't help that I told the truth: I explained on the phone how she disappeared in plain sight. They've already decided that I'm lying or crazy or responsible for this somehow. This is why Veronica wouldn't have wanted me to call the police. She knows how they look at us.

They inch closer to me. "The woman who's missing – you said she's your girlfriend?"

"Fiancée, actually." I fold and unfold my hands in front of me, my diamond ring catching the light. "We just got engaged last week."

I'm still not used to saying it, not used to thinking it either. Fiancée. It's such a simple word. Such a complicated one too, so many hopes and dreams wrapped up in one person.

Veronica, the woman I'm going to marry.

Veronica, the woman who vanished into thin air.

I ask about the surveillance cameras in the grocery store, but of course, it turns out they haven't recorded anything in years.

"The owners just want to scare off shoplifters," an officer confides in me, as if we're bosom buddies now.

Everything goes silent in the station, and I hunch in my chair, waiting for it. For the question I know is coming next.

"Have you called her parents?"

I shake my head. "I don't know them."

The lead detective raises a sharp eyebrow at me. "You're engaged to this woman, and you've never met her parents?"

"She doesn't talk to them," I insist. "Not for years. Not for anything."

"Maybe you're wrong," he says. "Maybe she's gone home. She could be reconciling with them."

Instantly, my blood's boiling. The way they think they know us. The way they know nothing at all.

"Fine," I say and grit my teeth. "Call them."

★ ★ ★

"No one's ever looked at me the way you do," Veronica said, her voice the sweetest serenade, her heart-shaped face resting on my chest. We were at my apartment this time, three months into a relationship she'd wanted to write off after three weeks. But we kept finding each other, at little dive bars and art galleries and warehouse parties around the city.

I held her closer, our bodies in a tangle in my bed. "And how exactly do I look at you?"

"Like I've got a future," she whispered, "and not just a past."

★ ★ ★

The detective searches an online database, finding a home phone number for Veronica's parents in less than two minutes.

As he dials the number, I can't help but roll my eyes. This is a waste of time. It's been almost twenty years since Veronica spoke to her parents, walking out the door when she was twenty-one and never looking back. In the meantime, she's been doing her best to keep out of their sight. No social media, at least not under her real name.

"I don't want them to know anything about me," she told me a dozen times before, and my chest aches, because it feels like I'm betraying her now, drawing them closer, giving away her location. I'll explain everything when we find her. How I let the cops contact her family as a formality, so we could continue the search. So we could get her back.

She'll understand. She has to understand.

The phone rings once before someone picks up. "Hello?"

"Is there a Veronica Brody available?" the detective asks.

A long pause. "That's me," says a crystalline voice on the other end. "I'm Veronica."

Everything in me goes numb. This can't be happening. This can't be real.

I stumble forward, my feet knotted beneath me. "Let me talk to her."

With a snort, the detective passes me the phone.

"Veronica?" I blurt out. "Is that you?"

"Yes, it's me," she says. "Who is this? Do I know you?"

The voice sounds so familiar, so real, but it's still not quite right, something vaguely rancid in the timbre. Like it's almost her. Almost Veronica.

I want to ask her something else, to ask her anything, but there's a commotion in the background, and her parents are suddenly on the line.

The police put the call on speakerphone. "Can you confirm we were just speaking to Veronica Brody?"

"Of course," says her mother. "Our daughter's here with us right now."

The detective leans in closer. "Did Veronica just return home today?"

An agonising moment, the silence stretching thin between us.

"Yes," her father says at last. "She did."

The cops exchange smug glances, as though collecting on a silent bet.

"That's what we thought," the detective says. "Her fiancée claims Veronica was estranged from both of you."

A pair of harsh laughs, one from her mother and one from her father. "Our daughter doesn't have a fiancée."

My fists clench, my heart squeezed tight in my chest. "That's not true," I say, but it's already too late.

"Thank you for your time," the detective says and disconnects the call. Then he glances at me, pity in his eyes. "It sounds like maybe you were strangers to each other after all."

I try to argue, try to explain, but they aren't listening to me anymore.

They never listened, so they certainly won't hear me out when I tell them the one fact that can't possibly add up.

It's been three hours since Veronica went missing. Her parents' house is ten hours away. There's no airport nearby, not here or there, only a bus station and an interstate. She couldn't have gotten there already. That couldn't have been her that I talked to.

Could it?

★   ★   ★

It's Sunday afternoon when I take the long drive up the East Coast, the sun glinting off the Atlantic, my heart gone cold in my chest.

The whole way, I don't eat, don't sleep, don't make small-talk with strangers at gas stations. In fact, I tell myself I shouldn't do this at all. Everyone else told me the same thing.

"If she wants to take off," all my friends said, "you've got to let her go."

Then they'd add, with sneers on their faces, "What kind of person disappears in the middle of the grocery store anyhow?"

"Someone I don't know," I said. Because that woman on the phone didn't sound like Veronica.

Or at least she didn't sound *enough* like Veronica.

After the call in the police station, Veronica didn't text, didn't email, didn't send for her stuff. She quit her job over Zoom, and the Instagram account she had under a fake name was deleted by morning. Her whole life snuffed out in an instant. Now our apartment looks like an echo, everything in its place. Everything except her.

After three days, I found her parents' address online. This is the only thing I can think to do. To go to her myself. I arrive in her hometown at dusk, parking on the street in front of the little Cape Cod on the corner, not knowing what to say or do next.

But then I don't have to decide, because all at once, the front door cracks open, and there she is. Her hair's different now, back to blonde, back to her natural colour, and she's plain-faced in tennis shoes, but I'd recognise her anywhere.

I climb out of the car, my legs quivering. "Veronica," I call out, and she turns to me. Instantly, I want to run to her. I want to hold her.

I want to rescue her from this place that's sucked her back in. But as I start forward, one careful step at a time, a heavy wave of nausea washes over me.

Up close, everything about Veronica shifts. A cleft in her chin that wasn't there before. A longer face, more gaunt, more pallid. The green in her eyes faded to grey.

"Do I know you?" she asks as we stand two feet apart in the front yard, and I just stare back at her, because I'm suddenly not sure.

"What are you doing here?" Two strident voices in unison, their figures looming on the nearby porch.

Veronica's parents. They're exactly the way she described them. Her father with his eyes darker than sin, her mother with a smile like a snake's. But that's not what everyone else sees. They have a perfectly respectable life in a perfectly respectable neighbourhood. At a quick glance, they look so sweet, so apple pie American, and that's precisely why they're so dangerous.

"Please leave," her mother says, and I open my mouth to argue, but Veronica is already walking away, disappearing back into the home she spent her whole life trying to escape.

★　　★　　★

"I try not to think about that house," she said to me. It was our first Christmas together, my apartment decked out with stockings and garlands and mistletoe in every doorway, just for us, just for an excuse to kiss her. I was sitting at the table, writing out holiday cards to aunts and uncles and second cousins scattered across the country, family I rarely saw but still loved well enough. But Veronica had no one. Or at least no one she was eager to claim.

"Do you want to talk about it?" I asked, but I already knew the answer. There was only so much she could say about a past she wanted to forget. The late-night screaming matches, the broken dishes, the slurs about who she was and who she loved. The promises her parents made about how they'd never let her go, that she'd always be their baby.

"I can still feel them," she said. "The way they're trying to pull me back." A harsh laugh. "I'm sometimes afraid to even think about them. Afraid if I let my guard down, they'll be waiting for me."

"Don't worry," I said, as *How the Grinch Stole Christmas* buzzed merrily on the television behind us. "You're safe with me now."

She forced a smile. "That'll have to be enough," she whispered.

★   ★   ★

I get the cheapest motel room in town, the kind you can rent by the hour, and once I'm inside, the rusted bolt on the door, I call the accounting firm where Veronica was temping.

"Did you see her when she quit?" I ask.

"Sure," her boss says. "It was on a Zoom call."

"But did you see her *clearly*?"

"I mean, it was Zoom," she says, the white noise of the office crackling behind her. "It can be a little jumpy and pixelated, and her hair was different, but I'm sure it was her."

I hesitate. "What if it was only someone who looked like her?"

A long, awkward moment. "Catherine, listen," her boss says. "I know how hard breakups can be. Especially the way Veronica did it. Just leaving you standing there in a grocery store? I would be freaked out too."

"She didn't break up with me," I say, but I already know how this sounds. A jilted girl who can't take a hint.

I want her boss to come out here. I want her to see Veronica in the flesh, to see what's happening to her. But I already know nobody will make this trip. That's because nobody really cares enough about Veronica to bother.

"Thanks for your help," I say and hang up the phone. I shouldn't have expected anything different. Veronica always lived on the edge of the world. A punk rock band when she was in college. A punk rock life even once she finished her degree, jobs coming and going, friends flitting in and out of her orbit, never staying long enough to get to know her. Just how she liked it.

"It's safer that way," she used to tell me. Even on the day she disappeared, most of the people I called were my acquaintances, not hers. They only knew her because I did. There's nobody left to corroborate who she was.

Nobody but me.

*   *   *

The next morning, I wait until both her parents have left for work. Then I return to Veronica's house and knock on her front door.

A stranger in my lover's body answers. "You again," she murmurs, the quiet look on her face as inscrutable as the sea. "You think you know me, don't you?"

I gaze back at her. "I'm not sure anymore."

She leans against the doorway, her arms crossed. "My parents are talking about calling the cops on you. They say you're delusional."

"Do you think I am?"

She watches me for a moment before shaking her head. "No," she says. "I think you're lonely."

I wheeze out a laugh. "I think you're right."

"I know how that feels," she says. "We're all in the Lonely Hearts Club, right?"

My breath corkscrews in my chest, because this feels like Veronica. This feels like the woman I love. The words are suddenly slipping from my lips before I can stop myself.

"Would you like to get coffee with me?"

At first, I'm sure she'll tell me no. I'm sure she'll slam the door in my face, sealing me out of her life, out of the truth. But then something shifts in her, and she smiles.

And she says yes.

*   *   *

Veronica chooses a little place downtown, and we sit together at a corner table, sipping black coffee out of oversized mugs. I stare at her, the way her face is too long, too pale. It's not her. It can't be her.

"So you quit your last job over Zoom?"

"I guess so." She takes another sip of coffee. "I don't really remember the place very well. I wasn't there for long."

That's at least true. Veronica never held onto jobs for more than a few months at a time. Her whole life, she was ready to run.

But that's the problem: she was always ready to run away from her past, not straight toward it. Coming back here was the last thing she wanted.

"You were living in the city, right?" I ask. "What about your apartment?"

"I must have moved out." She gives me a coy shrug. "Like I said, it's all a bit of a blur."

I turn away, pain welling up in my eyes. She doesn't remember anything. She's no one to me now. And I'm no one to her.

But when I glance back at her, my chest tightens, because there she is. Veronica, my Veronica, the woman I woke up next to every morning for three years. Her hair's still blonde, but everything else about her has returned. Her heart-shaped face. Her bright green eyes.

Then a cappuccino maker hisses in the background, and she jolts toward the sound, and suddenly, that visage is gone, and she's only a stranger again.

This isn't Veronica. This is Veronica. I can't decide for sure.

We finish our coffee in silence. She looks ready to make an excuse, a reason to get away from me, but instead, she asks a question I'm not expecting. "Can I see a picture?"

"Of what?"

"Your fiancée," she says. "The one you lost."

My hands shaking, I pull my phone out of my pocket and scroll through the images of us together, showing her dozens of them. Hundreds even.

"But that isn't me." She takes my phone, holding a photo of us together next to her own face. "Does this look like me?"

"Sometimes," I whisper. "Sometimes it looks like you."

On the table next to her, her own phone buzzes. A new phone, one without the black glitter case, no crack through the middle of the screen. Another piece of her refurbished life. A gift no doubt from her parents.

She scrolls through the message. "It's my mom," she says. "She's trying to set me up with a guy from their church."

This sucks the air right out of my chest. "I bet she is," I murmur.

Veronica was going to marry me. Now her parents are doing their best to make sure she'll marry someone else. A nice boy for their nice girl.

I drive her home, my hands tight on the wheel. Her parents still aren't back from work, so she invites me inside and gives me a tour of the house. The place stinks of cinnamon potpourri and beef stroganoff, the curtains all drawn, as if protecting a secret. The dated orange couch is covered in plastic, and the turntable against the wall has a stack of records next to it, Barry Manilow's *Greatest Hits* on top.

"The house that time forgot," I say, and Veronica chirps up a laugh.

"My family likes to reminisce about the past, that's for sure."

In the living room, there's an old family portrait on the wall. Veronica was no more than five years old then. I stare at her face, that innocent face, doing her best to force a smile through the tears she won't let fall.

She fidgets in the doorway. "You don't like my parents, do you?"

I heave out a ragged breath. "You never liked them either."

A flash of pain on her face, as if she's remembering something. Her jaw sets, and she glances at the picture on the wall. "They don't look like monsters," she whispers.

I only shake my head. "They never do."

★   ★   ★

"I don't have any scars on the outside," Veronica said. "That's why nobody believes me."

The two of us were curled up in the bedroom of our new apartment, the ceiling fan whirring above us, the eggshell white walls bare with possibility.

I entwined my fingers with hers. "I believe you."

She exhaled a defeated laugh. "You're the only one."

But I told myself one person could be enough. This was our new apartment, our new future. Anything was possible now.

"This will be all right," I told her, and she smiled like she almost believed me. Together, we settled into a routine, bingeing reruns of *Mad Men* and *CSI*, ordering takeout from the Italian restaurant down the street, gnocchi for her, linguini for me. The two of us opting to stay in for the weekend and put together 1,000-piece puzzles on the dining room table, the pictures of faraway places. Of oceans and lighthouses and palm trees on desert islands. The two of us dreaming together, planning together.

"We're like an old married couple," Veronica said, and all I could do was grin back at her.

But then there were nights when it all came crashing back on her. She'd awaken in the dark, soaked with sweat and grief, crying out from a nightmare that wouldn't end.

"Sometimes, it's like they're all around me," she whispered, holding me tighter, as though I could anchor her against the world. "Like they're thinking of me. Like they're pulling me back to them."

"They don't get that choice," I promised her.

"What if you're wrong?" she asked, fear pinwheeling in her eyes. "What if I'm the one who doesn't get the choice?"

★   ★   ★

Veronica meets me every day for a week, always sneaking out when her parents aren't looking. A forty-year-old woman who still needs a permission slip.

"They're not like other moms and dads," she confides to me over club sandwiches at the downtown deli.

"I know," I say and do my best not to grit my teeth.

I ask her about her plans. When she wants to move out or get a job or start a life.

"I don't know," she whispers. She still doesn't remember me. She doesn't remember anything, the last two decades of her life a vague mist in her mind. But sometimes, when she turns her head just right, her eyes brighten, and she's still in there, flickering in and out like a firefly glow.

"Please," I say. "Try to remember."

"I am," she insists, but it's doing no good.

It's late in the afternoon when she invites me inside again and leads me up to her room. We sit on her bed, our thighs touching, a ceiling fan spinning above us. I glance around at the bubblegum pink walls, a CD player on the nightstand, a Blink-182 poster sagging in the corner. This place is still decorated for a teenager. For the person she was when she left this house.

"Don't you think any of this is strange?" I ask. "The way your whole life seems to have stopped. The way your parents are okay with that."

"All of this seems strange," she says. "But I don't know what to do about it, Catherine. I don't even know what's happening."

I start to say something, to tell her to leave with me, to leave right now, but a shadow passes over our faces, and the whole world seizes up around us.

Her mother, standing in the doorway, her gaze already black with rage. "Go downstairs, Veronica," she says. "Now."

With her head down, Veronica does as she's told, disappearing out into the hallway.

But I'm not like her. I won't back down so easily. "This is wrong," I say, "and you know it."

"Maybe," her mother says. "But you won't take her from us again."

"Again," I murmur, my guts tightening. That's as close to a confession as I'll ever get. And it's one that nobody but me will believe.

Across the room on the bright pink wall, there's a photograph of Veronica. She must be around twenty-one in the image.

"That's right before she left home, isn't it?" I ask, and judging from the way her mother grimaces, I know I'm right.

I edge across the room, inspecting the picture closer. It was taken at an odd angle, her face looking a little longer than usual, her hair a little blonder.

"That's how you remember her," I say slowly, understanding it all at once. That's why Veronica looks the way she does, a face that's not quite her own. Her parents don't know what she really looks like. They don't know who she is. All they remember is the girl who left home twenty years ago. She's their own makeshift creation, a Frankenstein's monster of a daughter, cobbled together with half-forgotten memories and faded Polaroids tucked in the back of yellowed photo albums.

"Why now?" I ask, sorrow churning through me.

Her mother gives me that snake's smile. "Why not?"

It's just like Veronica always feared. Maybe for one fleeting moment in the grocery store, she accidentally let her guard down. Maybe she thought of home. And maybe that was all they needed. After years of wanting to drag her back, to make her their own, to turn her into the obedient girl they expected her to be, they finally got their wish.

A parent's love. We say it like it's a good thing, like it's so beautiful and binding. We never think of the consequences, of what happens when someone takes it too far. When they won't let go.

"Get out of here," her mother seethes, pointing to the door. "Before I call the police."

I start out into the hallway, but Veronica's waiting there, her eyes wide and verdant. She overheard everything. It's not much, but it's enough.

"Pick me up at midnight," she whispers and squeezes my hand.

★   ★   ★

"You can't fight blood," Veronica once told me. "Everywhere you go, it's inside you. You can run your whole life – you can run a thousand miles – but you can't escape yourself. You can't escape family."

"That's not true," I said and held her close. "You're here with me now. We're here together."

★   ★   ★

Veronica is waiting on the sidewalk at midnight, the streetlight limning her in a halo. She climbs into the passenger's seat empty-handed, and we start down the street.

"This is probably pointless." She won't look at me. "They got me back once. They'll just do it again."

"Maybe," I say. "We'll drive for a little while. We'll see how far we can get."

The dark highway unfurls before us, neither of us speaking a word for a long time.

"I still don't remember you," she says at last.

"I know," I whisper, my heart twisting in my chest. All those years together, erased in an instant. Erased for good.

Together, we head out of town, past the signs for the city limits and the county line and the *Last Stop for Gas in the State*. Next to me, Veronica's face is shifting in the moonlight, between who she is and who they want her to be.

"And if they do pull me back?" Her faded eyes are on me now. "What then?"

I smile at her, at that face that's everything and nothing at the same time.

"I'll remember you," I say. "I'll remember for the both of us."

"And you'll come back for me?"

"Always."

"That'll have to be enough," she whispers.

Somewhere behind us, they've noticed she's gone. There are probably breaking dishes and a late-night screaming match and slurs about who she is and who she loves.

But right now, Veronica's not thinking of them. Her hand finds mine in the dark, the two of us tethered together. I hold her tight, and she holds me too, and with her bright green eyes on the road ahead, neither one of us is letting go.

THEY EAT THE REST

Jim Horlock

The antique gravy boat of the Du Pont family was widely renowned and certain to be the centrepiece of any of their parties. The Byrd family had their crystal chandelier, the Pratts had their ornate goose sculpture, and the Oglethorpes insisted on a walk through their portrait gallery after every meal, but for the Du Ponts, the gravy boat was the crown jewel.

It had taken many years of hard work and harder socialising to secure myself an invite to a Du Pont dinner party. Imagine my excitement when, finally, I took my seat and found myself within reach of that majestic vessel, resplendent in silver and mother of pearl. It was a sign of respect, I told myself, a sign of acceptance.

Imagine my horror when I saw something move beneath the surface of the gravy.

Of course, first I questioned my sanity. Such a thing could not be possible. But when I caught the movement again, I knew it was real. The question became how was such a thing possible? Had some servant slipped a worm or other foul creature into the gravy boat as part of some rebellious scheme? Had Magenta Oglethorpe orchestrated this? An avaricious old dowager, she had long held a not-so-secret scorn for the Du Ponts over a marriage proposal that went unfulfilled.

I scrutinised her while nodding along with the conversation, but she seemed none the wiser, her attention focused on Reginald Byrd, three years a widower and quite eligible.

The gravy boat stirred again, and this time the action was enough to rattle it slightly on the tabletop. I looked down at it in horror, then up into the eyes of Helena Du Pont, youngest daughter of the family, who was opposite me. She looked just as horrified. The glance reaffirmed two hard truths between us: firstly, we had both seen it, and, secondly, that we would each rather die than be the one to point it out. On all of Earth and across the heavens there was no wrath known like that of Lord Montgomery Du Pont.

I shot a glance at the head of the table, to where the grizzled old patriarch sat, monocle gleaming around his eagle-eyed glare. Montgomery Du Pont had singlehandedly wrought the ruin of the Montfort family after Ermine Montfort made the fatal error of clinking a teacup with his spoon while stirring. The last I'd heard, the Montforts were begging for money on the streets of Paris.

I averted my eyes quickly, before that piercing gaze fell on me. I could not risk bringing my own family, and the meagre wealth we'd scraped together, under the hammer of Montgomery Du Pont.

"You've outdone yourself, Monty!" Cornelius Pratt slapped his great round belly. He was the only person who could get away with applying a nickname to Lord Du Pont. They'd served in the war together, in some dark uncivilised part of the world, though which war and where exactly were unclear. The sword from the alleged conflict still hung over the fireplace. Pratt still wore his medals at every opportunity.

Lord Du Pont merely nodded. The suggestion that one of his dinners would be anything less than spectacular was unthinkable.

"The finest foie gras I've ever tasted," I added, then immediately realised my mistake as Magenta Oglethorpe shot a glare my way. She'd served foie gras at her party the previous month.

The gravy boat rattled again. Working overtime, my mind began to convince me that, as the newest invitee to this prestigious circle, I would be blamed if whatever was lurking within the rich brown liquid was discovered.

My brow began to sweat. Visions of destitution played across my mind. I caught my face in the reflection of the gravy boat, and wiped the sweat away.

"I see you've spotted the gravy boat, young Abernathy," Cornelius chuckled. "What do you make of it, eh?"

My throat went dry. The question was a knife and the answer balanced on the edge. Too much of a compliment would seem fawning, but too little would seem dismissive. I felt the eye of Lord Du Pont on me.

"Resplendent." I tried not to sound terrified. "So beautiful it's almost a shame to use it."

My answer hung in the air. The attention of the others turned from me to Montgomery, awaiting judgement.

"All things should have uses," grunted Montgomery. "I cannot abide a useless thing. Taskless beauty is a parasite, that feeds and feeds and contributes nothing of value."

Just for a moment, his gaze swept over Magenta Oglethorpe, who paled beneath her rouge. This was how it was amongst these people. Grievous wounds were inflicted just as often via unsaid words and subtle glances, than by outright slights.

"Here, here!" Reginald Byrd saw the opportunity to cleave to the sentiment, and earn himself some favour with Du Pont, unknowingly distancing himself from the dowager in the same breath. It was impossible to be ally to both.

"Bring out the next course!" Pratt boomed. "Before young Abernathy wastes away!"

He laughed at his own joke, and I forced myself to join in. A crack at my weight was a crack at my wealth, a reminder that I might sit at the table, but I was still a small fish in this pond. I had no choice but to endure it. In any case, I was far more worried about the contents of the gravy boat than the jibes of my betters. Was the creature growing agitated? The turbulence certainly seemed to have increased. I hoped one of the servers would notice it and remove it discreetly, but they simply laid the next course out on the table and vanished again without a word.

Rain lashed the windows as the other guests raised gleaming silverware and began to eat.

I'd cut only partway into my pie when the knife struck upon something hard. I paused. There was no way to explore my way through pastry and meat without looking like a savage. While the other guests were busying themselves with their own plates, I was sure all peripheral vision was directed my way. I glanced at Helena. Did she give me an almost imperceptible shake of the head? Was it a warning? Or did I imagine it?

I jabbed at the unyielding mass once more, but it had the consistency of a pebble and would not budge. Once again, paranoia nudged at me. Had it been placed in my pie intentionally? Was this a game by Du Pont or Oglethorpe or one of the others?

I had no choice. To dissect the pie was unthinkable and to leave a morsel behind might cause grave insult. I was going to have to eat it.

I raised the fork to my mouth and was thankful the object was small at least. I thought of Emily, and her doctor who needed to be paid. I thought of Michael, who was innocent but would need a good lawyer to prove it. I thought of Father, who didn't try hard enough and died a pauper, nearly dooming the rest of us. I wouldn't fail them like he had.

I forbade my curious tongue from probing the mouthful and swallowed.

It was then I realised Du Pont was watching me. I'd never seen him smile before. It was an ill look.

A bang and clatter from the hallway made me jump. Someone out there screamed. My first instinct was to rise from the table and investigate, but the other guests carried on like they hadn't heard anything. I forced myself not to fluster. One did not leave one's seat until dinner was concluded. Whatever was happening out there was a problem for the serving staff.

"A fine pie," Byrd mumbled, dapping at his lips with a napkin. He twitched a little and gripped his stomach, as a roiling sound came from within. I pretended not to notice, but he had taken on a grey look. Was there something in his pie too? What was the game here and who was in on it?

Another thud and more screaming from the corridors beyond the dining room, muffled by the heavy shut door. Du Pont looked around the table, as though waiting for any of us to make a comment so that he might have the pleasure of verbally skewering us. Rain battered the windows, and we sat in silence, not meeting his eyes.

I jumped again as the door opened, and serving staff came to clear our plates. They looked pale and sweaty, rigid in their movements, as though trying not to give anything away. I couldn't resist the urge to glance into the hall. Was there a strange mark on the carpet that hadn't been there before? It looked dark and wet.

The next course was more substantial than the last. Plates piled high with creamy potatoes, roasted vegetables and a great stuffed bird. Before the meal, I'd been worried about finding room for the infamous many-course meals of Lord Du Pont, but I found myself suddenly ravenous.

Byrd certainly wasn't holding back. He barely held on long enough for propriety before he started cramming food into his mouth.

With horror, I watched him pour from the gravy boat, any minute expecting to see some squirming creature fall onto his plate, but there was nothing.

"Good appetite, that man!" Cornelius Pratt boomed with a laugh, before tucking in himself.

I exercised all the restraint I could, determined not to make a spectacle of myself through gluttony, despite the demands of my stomach.

Byrd was only halfway done with his plate when a sudden convulsion wracked him, sending silverware clattering to the floor.

"Good lord!" Pratt exclaimed, as Byrd shoved himself up from the table, tipping his wine glass over.

"Well, I never." Oglethorpe turned away from the scene, as Byrd's body rocked wildly, sending him staggering left and right about the room. His belly was swollen like a balloon, buttons popping as it continued to grow. It hung from his body like a fat raindrop on the lip of a sill, fed by more water until it could hold itself no longer.

Byrd's stomach burst with a faint pop, showering the carpet with entrails. He slumped down the wall, one leg still kicking. He hadn't even had time to scream.

I stared numbly, feeling like all the blood had fled my brain. I turned to the rest of the table, expecting to see horror, to see serving staff rushing for a doctor. Instead, I met the cool gaze of Montgomery Du Pont.

Cornelius Pratt tutted and helped himself to more potatoes. Magenta Oglethorpe shook her head in disapproval and muttered, "For shame." Helena Du Pont merely looked sad.

I opened my mouth to insist that, surely, someone must do something.

"Please do accept my apologies," Lord Du Pont said, catching me off guard. "Mr. Byrd's behaviour is quite unacceptable for such fine company. Rest assured, he will not be invited again. There's no room at my table for those without manners."

I thought of Emily. I thought of Michael. I thought of Father.

I closed my mouth.

"Madness," I told myself, internally. "This is madness."

I ignored the voice, and the smell of Byrd's ruptured intestines, and continued to eat. That ravenous feeling lingered, despite all odds, but still I held my restraint.

"I hope it hasn't ruined your appetite." Lord Du Pont's smile was like a gangrenous wound. "Here, fill Mr. Abernathy's plate for him."

"Oh, that's so kind of you," I said. "But not necessary. I don't want to appear the glutton."

"Nonsense." Du Pont's words were cold iron. "If you don't accept my hospitality, I'm afraid I'll be quite insulted. Eat."

There was no choice. Whatever macabre game this was, I was stuck in it. I had to keep playing to the end, for my family's sake. One set of rules, at least, was clear: breach Du Pont's protocols, and die.

"Most gracious." I bowed my head to the maniac at the head of the table and prayed he wouldn't kill me.

I lifted a fork to my mouth, but a noise cut terror through my tendons and stopped me dead. In slow horror, I turned to where Byrd lay.

He was still eating, blood-soaked hands picking through his own viscera for pre-digested morsels. He smacked his lips and moaned as he chewed and swallowed.

I should have been revolted to the point of vomiting or terrified beyond reason. Instead, I felt only hunger. It gripped my guts like an iron hand and turned me back to my plate. Resisting the urge to eat was a Herculean feat. What was happening to me?

"Gravy for Mr. Abernathy." Du Pont's eyes were intense. I could feel them in my periphery but didn't dare turn to look. A servant reached out to pour gravy onto my plate. There was blood spattered on his sleeve. I realised the other servants had taken positions, one behind each of us. Their faces were set and grim.

Helena caught my eye, moving her lips just enough for me to glean the words she couldn't say out loud.

"It's not gravy."

There was a thump as Du Pont's fist slammed down onto the tabletop, rattling cutlery.

"Since you seem so determined to spoil the evening, daughter," he seethed at Helena, "we shall have to skip to the next phase."

While we stared in shock at this outburst, he began to unbutton his shirt. Only Pratt continued to eat, as though nothing were amiss. I glanced at Byrd but it seemed he'd finally expired. His hunger beyond death had only lasted so long. He lay there, mouth hanging open and full of his own guts.

"A shame," Du Pont continued. "I was looking forward to seeing what became of Abernathy as the hunger gripped him. Cornelius lasted several days but you appear of weaker constitution to me."

Pratt chuckled and patted his belly. "Never underestimate a man of appetite, I say."

"What is this?" I broke, finally. "Why is this happening?"

"We found it overseas during the war," Du Pont explained. "No idea the provenance of the thing but I became transfixed by it. The locals seemed to worship it. I couldn't bear to leave it behind."

"Had to kill the lot of them to get it," Pratt put in. "Nasty little blighters wouldn't give it up, you see? Can hardly blame them, I suppose. There's a fascination that grows in you when you're around it."

"It bonded to me quite quickly but, I suppose, I've always been an attractor of parasites." Du Pont looked about the table with hateful eyes. His shirt fell open and I couldn't help but gasp. The flesh of his chest and ribs was blackened, as though he'd been trampled by a horse.

And it was moving.

"Don't worry." Du Pont smiled. "You'll be useful too. As food, or as new hosts."

Pratt leant back and patted his swollen belly. "The latter for me. Of course, unlike Byrd there, my belly is made of sterner stuff. How do you suppose yours will hold, Abernathy?"

"Mine is just fine," Magenta Oglethorpe offered.

"Evidently not," Du Pont snarled. "You've eaten plenty this evening, but the worms haven't taken to you at all. They never have. Time and again, you prove less useful than I imagined. You're out of chances. This will be your last dinner on my dime, Magenta."

Her eyes went wide as she realised the danger she was in. She rose from her seat, preparing to make a dash for the exit. I expected the servants to stop her but it was Du Pont himself that moved. His body jerked upright, spine going rigid, and several long worm-like tendrils erupted bloodlessly from his chest. In my horror, I caught a glimpse of the wounds they made and the flesh beyond it. The inside of Lord Du Pont was a husk, a dried-out cave of squirming dark things.

Those that extended themselves from him whipped across the room and buried themselves in the body of Magenta Oglethorpe with such force that she was lifted from the ground and pinned against the wall. Before she could scream, one of them tore its way up her throat and out through her mouth.

"Guests shouldn't rise from the table until the meal is done," chided Du Pont.

"Bad manners," grunted Pratt.

"First Mr. Byrd and now Magenta Oglethorpe." Du Pont shook his head. "I cannot abide bad manners nor a useless thing." He turned his attention to his butler. "How many of the new staff did we lose, Wilson?"

"All of them, sir," the sallow-faced man responded. "It seems none could resist the gravy. We'll have the mess cleaned up immediately, and the bodies taken below."

"Excellent. I think that concludes this meal. Abernathy still hasn't had any gravy but I've run out of patience. Take him below as well."

Before I could ask what that meant, or make any plan of escape, something heavy hit the back of my head and sent me toppling into unconsciousness.

★   ★   ★

The hunger was what woke me. A terrible gripping, twisting sensation, deep in the gut. A fierce need, a desperate emptiness. I lunged into waking, flailing about as my senses bombarded me. Hungry. Cold. Wet. Hungry. Dark. Hungry. Hungry.

I was in a cave, some waterlogged coal-black cavern. I had to guess it was beneath Du Pont's manor. The space was huge, bigger than the house itself. At its centre, gleaming in the light of hundreds of candles, was an enormous jagged obelisk of black stone. Surrounding that structure were piles of bodies, placed in the shallow water. Their bellies, like Byrd's, were ruptured open from within. By their clothes I guessed they were Du Pont's staff. As my eyes grew more used to the gloom, I realised there were older bodies there too, decaying in the water. Ermine Montfort and his wife. The Arnauts. Others were too destroyed to recognise but I imagined every family that had ever displeased Montgomery Du Pont had been brought here.

Worse than the cave or the dread obelisk or the corpses, however, was the hunger. It was so intense that I caught myself moving towards those poor lost souls without thinking. Disgust filled me at the idea of what I might do if I got close enough.

I flinched at a sound behind me, and wheeled around, expecting danger. A line of Du Pont's still-living staff approached, but they ignored me in favour of the obelisk. Their movements were slow, reverent almost, as they neared it. Behind them, I saw a set of stone steps leading to a door. An escape. I could still get out.

Helena stood there, looking sad and broken. I caught her eye and thought to call for help, but she turned away immediately. She knew all along what my fate was to be. She'd tried to warn me. It was too late.

I took one step before the hunger turned me right back towards the bodies.

"No," I whimpered, tears of effort streaming down my face as I knelt down in the water.

"It's no good, lad." Pratt was hunched nearby. I hadn't noticed him behind the piled-up bodies. His mouth was smeared with blood. "You didn't have the gravy, but the eggs are still inside you. The hunger has you now. It'll never let you go."

"What is this? What's happening to me?"

"You've always been a parasite," Du Pont called out. He emerged from behind the obelisk. "I've always been a host. Might as well embrace the truth of it. Let the milking begin."

The servants surrounded the obelisk, pressing their bodies against it, feeling it with their hands. In no time at all, dark brown beads of liquid formed on the surface, and I knew at once it was what had been served in the gravy boat.

"Better to drink it, lad," Pratt said. "You might be lucky and end up like Monty, or me. They live in some of us, so long as we keep them fed. They eat the rest."

The cold water lapping at my thighs warmed as the dark liquid began to run in rivulets down the pillar. In those last moments, I should have been thinking of Emily or Michael, or even my father. I should have forgiven him in my heart for trying to keep me away from all this. Instead, all I could think about was the crippling pain in my gut, the terrible endless hunger. It was Hell, and there was only one salvation.

I cupped my hands into the liquid, then raised them to my lips.

THE NOTE

Paul Tremblay

After dinner, there was enough sunlight left to pretend we had more time to our Sunday. I suggested to my wife Linda that we walk the mile or so to the local dairy farm for ice cream. We had yet to go that spring, or, we had yet to walk to the farm to get our own ice cream. It's possible – scratch that – *probable* that some foggy number of weeks prior we had sent one of our two kids to fill our sugar fix. I suppose in the eyes of state and federal law Cal and Elly were technically adults, but they were young enough to remain financially umbilicalled to us. Cal would graduate from his college on the opposite coast in less than a month and Elly, a high school senior, was out with friends.

I almost pitched the walk to Linda as a preview of our fast-encroaching empty nesters' destiny, but she was already in the throes of the tomorrow-is-Monday blues, so I didn't pile on. Linda agreed to the walk, but without much, or any, enthusiasm. Was it the company or was she considering what the sugary dose of dairy might digestively wreak later in the evening's soft gloam? She rolled her eyes at the 'soft gloam' quip. Deservedly so.

We left our small dog, Molly, at home. Molly wasn't a fan of crowds, other dogs, or walks. She had never liked walks, but now, with her golden years descending as quickly as an autumn sun at dusk, she downright loathed them. No one in the family, myself included, was willing to verbalise the mundane yet depthless horror at how old and creaky Molly was getting.

So, it was just me and Linda. We walked, heading uphill and north – north if our house was the centre of a compass – through a suburban neighbourhood we knew well. That is to say, we knew it *physically* well. I could draw a map of the streets, but we didn't know any of the actual human neighbours. We weren't aloof or snooty – definitely not snooty, anyway. Our lack of conviviality with our neighbours to the north was more a quirk of happenstance and direction. Our kids made friends by coasting their bikes downhill instead of pedalling up. I don't intend that as a metaphor for their work ethic or future prospects. Not everything means something else, right? But, writing this now, I'm afraid the opposite is true. Maybe we need a new, better word to describe the slippery things we claim as true.

With no kids, no dog, no neighbours to chat up as we ambled past house after house, Linda detailed the latest shit pile the gaggle of old, out-of-touch white men, who comprised the board of directors for their chain of local seafood restaurants, had dumped on her all-women marketing department. It was a slight variation of a common theme at her workplace. Once her indignation and moral stance was clearly stated for the continuing record, she told me about another streaming true crime show, one of many that she referred to as her 'murder shows.' I didn't have much to add to the one-sided conversation. I was a listener, or *the* listener. That was my role in our relationship, and, frankly, it was my role in my handful of other close adult relationships. I used to think the people who were talkers, or tellers, could somehow sense I was a *listener* by just looking at me, as though reading the fine print on a nametag.

About a half-block away from the always-busy Bay Road, I saw the house first. We were across the street, the only side of the street that had a sidewalk, and I pointed out the house like I'd spotted a tiger and we had to be careful, make no sudden movements.

We stopped and stared at a modestly sized, boxy, white Colonial, not that different in terms of design than the other houses on the sleepy side street. Two storeys tall, the second floor had three windows; stacked below those were two more windows and the painted black front door. The only remarkable thing about the place was that its wild, overgrown grass and weeds were knee-high on me, and thigh-high on Linda. The abutting properties had well-manicured lawns kept as tight and neat as a fascist's haircut, which made the house with the rain-forest lawn stick out even more.

I asked, "Did the owner die? Foreclosure?" I just about wished death on whomever lived there, or once lived there, but not out of malice. At least death fit into the natural order of things, which was a weird way to put it. Everyone died eventually, right? But foreclosure? Talk about a fucking nightmare. In our insanely cruel economy, in which debtors were scythed like wheat stalks, all it took to lose your home was a little bad luck plus a wrong decision or two, the kind of wrong decision that had seemed perfectly reasonable at the time. What do you do and where do you go when your home was taken away? I didn't even want to consider those what ifs.

We crossed the street, slowly, not wanting to stir up the tiger in the tall grass. We swapped hushed I-don't-knows and does-anyone-still-live-theres. This house had been on our kids' trick-or-treat route in ye olde days, but I couldn't remember who had opened the door, or if the door had opened at all. Maybe it was one of those houses who left the lights off, not wanting to be bothered. Maybe it was one of those houses my kids told scary stories about.

Linda said, "Ooh, there's a note taped to the front door." She'd perked up. This new mystery was way more exciting than our walk through the 'burbs for pricey-but-worth-it ice cream.

"It's a no-mow manifesto," I said.

Linda twisted up her face in a what-are-you-an-asshole? expression. But I initially thought it meant what-the-heck-are-you-talking-about? They were similar and common looks, in my defence. I started rambling through a wholly unnecessary explanation of the *no mow* movement – gas mower and chemical fertiliser fuelled lawn maintenance being bad for the environment.

Linda interrupted. "I know what *no mow* means." She stepped ahead of me, almost onto an entrance for the driveway that carved a half-circle through the overgrown front yard. "Let's see what the note says."

"What if someone is home?" Yeah, I didn't want to trespass onto the homeowner's potential misery, but it was more I didn't want to trespass onto the property. I was a hopeless rule follower.

"No cars in the driveway." Linda was not a hopeless rule follower. At last year's college reunion, she had broken into her old dorm to see her freshman year room. I had waited and paced outside the dorm. She had later emerged victorious and disappointed with me.

The note was taped to the inside of a glass storm door that shielded the wooden one. The note was yellowed at its edges. I assumed it had been there for a while. I asked, "How long has the house been like this?" which I knew neither of us could answer. Even from that distance, I saw there was line after line of handwriting filling the note.

Linda said, "I know it makes me a bad person, but I want to read it." The way she said it, she was already reading the note in her head.

"How about on the way home? The ice cream line is getting longer by the second." I cowered back across the street and I was surprised that Linda followed me without running to the stoop and reading the note first.

On the final leg of our trek, we risked middle-aged life and limb traversing Bay Road. The posted speed limit was 40 mph, so add another five to ten mph for the vast majority of drivers. There were no sidewalks, only thin road shoulders and thinner patches of dirt and grass along the outside of fenced properties until we hit the farm. Linda marched forward, heedlessly on the shoulder, pressing her luck, and I couldn't help but imagine a driver futzing with their cellphone and then swerving – and it wouldn't take much of a swerve – onto the shoulder, scooping Linda up and away. I walked as far off-road as I could, even when it meant losing my head in low hanging tree branches. That we used to navigate this stretch of road with our kids when they were little, clutching their impossibly small hands that didn't always clutch back because they wanted to be on their own and were in a rush to walk balanced across the top of a stone fence right before the farm, seemed beyond reckless in retrospect.

★   ★   ★

Crescent Ridge Dairy Farm, where a kiddie cup was a small, a small was a large, and large was lactose intolerance. Cars jammed the parking lot and the lines behind the serving windows blobbed into a formless crowd. We played the losers' roulette of which window line to wait in. The reality of the wait-length dampened our ice cream enthusiasm, such as it was. I was glad we weren't any of the younger parents with impatient kids in tow, so clearly and loudly done with waiting. I couldn't blame the kids. I was done with waiting too, and since my own kids weren't with me, I didn't have to worry about modelling patient behaviour. I could say shit like, "We always pick the wrong line," and, "The kid working our window is taking his sweet ass time," and, "Selfish fuckers are getting frappés. Rome was built in less time than it takes to make a frappé." I counted the families ahead of us and I monitored the progress of the other lines as though I was an actuary, and I sighed, loudly.

Linda, as always, was more stoic in the face of the endurance test. She enjoyed my acting like a brat because she would appear more adult by any comparison. She asked if I wanted to switch lines when I grumbled that the one to our right was moving faster. I pouted, and I memorised the faces and clothing of people in the other lines, all to be forgotten later.

The sun completed its trip west and it got dark quickly. Finally, after forty minutes, we made it to the window counter. My order of chocolate chip with rainbow sprinkles didn't sound ridiculous at all. Since we'd be eating and walking, I asked for a cup with my cone. Which really wasn't necessary as I'd eat most of the ice cream before we left the parking lot. Linda always marvelled, and was slightly annoyed, at how quickly I ate my ice cream.

I'd forgotten about the house and the note as we flowed in the evening's current, until we drifted to a stop at the outer arc of the half-circle driveway. Our plastic cups were the only tangible evidence that we hadn't stayed rooted to that spot and stared at the house. The overgrown grass wavered in a breeze. The note was a rectangular shadow taped to the storm door. All but one of the house's windows were dark. On the second floor, there was one lamp on, the weak yellow light blurred by a lace curtain.

I said, "Light's on. Maybe someone is home."

"Sitting alone in the drawing room upstairs?" Linda asked.

"So Gothic. What's a drawing room?"

"No one's home," Linda said. "That light's on a timer to scare off would-be burglars."

"Or would-be note readers. Does anyone say 'burglar' anymore? Do they use that word in your murder shows?"

Linda handed me her half-eaten, soupy cup of ice cream, a wordless statement of intent to read the note.

I said, "You can't. What if they're home?"

She was already walking away from me, or, that is, toward the house's front stoop. Playing coy, she said, "What if who's home?"

"You know, *they*. The house people."

Linda didn't respond. I risked a glance at the lit-up window. And it was only a glance. I was convinced the longer I stared, the more likely someone would appear in the window and the expression on that person's face would most certainly be a horror.

I wanted to walk away, leave her there by herself, but I knew that would be unforgivable. I looked up and down the street to see if any other *house people* inside other houses were watching. In the full dark, the street was deserted, incongruously so, given the proximity of Bay Road and the crowded farm.

I wanted to suggest that we come back tomorrow, after work, because then we'd be too tired and defeated to do that on a Monday, so we'd put off the walk to the note house for another day, week, year, however long enough for whomever the note was meant to finally show up, read it, take it away, and then clean up the yard so it looked like everyone else's and I wouldn't have to think about this house and the note ever again.

Linda opened the storm door, gently, but there was a conspiratorial creak of rusty hinges. She looked once at the black wooden front door, maybe imagining it bursting open to reveal a Leatherface-adjacent nightmare. That's what I was imagining, anyway. With the storm door propped open against her hip, she peeled the corners of the note free from the glass. She couldn't read it in the dark so she took her phone from her back pocket and aimed the flashlight at the text. Judging by the time she spent spotlighted on the stoop with the note, she read it carefully.

I paced a rut into the pavement and had a conversation with myself about why I was a buzzkill, but also about why I was right to be upset and why Linda was wrong; nothing I'd ever dare say out loud. Those conversations with myself never ended in hurt feelings.

She finished reading and re-fastened the note to the storm door. Linda walked back down the drive and I watched the lamp-lit window for a face, knowing that people got caught doing inexplicable things in the new, irreparable moments after.

Linda walked past me and I had to jog to catch up. I thought she was angry or annoyed or disappointed, but now, I'm not sure what she was thinking or feeling.

I said, "Your ice cream is melting," and held her cup out to her. She took it. I turned and gave the note house one last look as it receded into the local horizon. I expected more lights to come on, and maybe the sound of an opening door. Neither of those things happened. Once we turned the corner, I presumed we were safe and I dared ask, "So what did the note say?"

"If you really want to know, you should go read it," she said.

I scanned for sarcasm or humour but I couldn't find either. She sounded distant, or detached. Detached is the best fit here. The words she'd said and who she was and what she was thinking, were separate, had been separated.

I said, "Wait. You're not going to tell me?"

"Nope."

Aiming for a levity that hid my exasperation I said, "That's the last time I take you for ice cream."

No response.

"You're really not going to tell me?"

She shook her head.

"I was your faithful lookout," I said. "I had your back and you're not going to tell me what was in the note? That's cold."

She shrugged and swirled the remnants of her ice cream with a plastic spoon.

"That's not fair," I said.

Linda laughed, but it wasn't a laugh, or it wasn't her laugh, exactly. Though my memory is tainted by what has since come to pass.

She said, "Life isn't fair."

We didn't full-on argue very often in our going on thirty-year relationship, and I don't say that in a braggy, we-were-so-perfect way. Sometimes arguments were avoided with one or both parties choosing to swallow our resentments or perceived slights instead of talking it out. When we did full-on argue, it was almost always over what we had said to our kids and how it had been said. When I say 'we,' I mean *me*. I'm trying to avoid the phrase *disciplining your kids* because it's such an awful phrase. Our last big row was years in our rearview mirror. The funny part is that I don't remember what our daughter Elly's request had been, one I had deemed unreasonable. I do remember saying, "No," and Elly then repeatedly asking, "Why?" and saying, "It's not fair." Instead of explaining the rationale behind my parental edict I pronounced, "Life isn't fair," with all the dismissive weight I could muster. Linda rushed into the room and admonished me for not explaining the why to Elly and for my tone, while Linda used the same tone on me. Everything rolled downhill from there.

Without relitigating the past, which I have no interest in doing as there's enough regret within these pages already, Linda's use of "Life isn't fair" during our walk home on that strange night, felt like a purposeful call back to that argument. I refused to take the bait, and instead pouted and simmered and seethed like the child I still imagined myself as sometimes, until those feckless emotions turned into something heavier and akin to sadness that could sink inside of me and stay at the bottom.

When we got home, Linda went to the living room, sat with our dog Molly on the couch, and watched murder shows. I retreated to my laptop, pretended to work on my novel and instead checked emails and social media feeds that didn't need to be checked, all the while thinking about the stupid note and how it had put us both in strange, pissy moods. Later, I wandered upstairs to our bedroom with a book, resolving to convince Linda to tell me what was written in the note the next morning. I read maybe about ten pages before the book flagged in my hands as I was nodding off. I rolled over to Linda's empty side of the bed, turned on her night lamp, then rolled back to my side and turned mine off and quickly fell asleep. I woke up a few hours later to pee. When I returned to bed, Linda was in her spot, lying on her side, facing away from me. I half-patted, half-rubbed Linda's shoulder twice, and I went back to sleep.

At some point in the early, night-stained morning hours, when I was still mostly dead to the world, the mattress creaked as Linda's weight lifted away. This and what follows might not be a real memory, but something I've imagined and willed into being. I can admit that, yet these sleep-hazed memories are real to me, as real as any other memory. I was lying on my back, eyes shut, and Linda leaned close to my head and whispered, "I have to go to the office."

I woke later with my phone's alarm. Molly was snoring and burrowed behind my bent knees. Molly didn't start off in bed with us, but Elly would drop her into our bed before she went to school. I got up, threw on joggers and a sweatshirt, plucked Molly from the bed and carried her downstairs. Because of lower back issues she wasn't supposed to walk down the stairs on her own anymore. I set about the morning routine, which included letting Molly outside and making both of us breakfast. It hit me as I sat at the kitchen counter, hunched over my bowl of cereal, that sometime during the morning routine I'd noticed something was off without knowing what it was. I looked around the kitchen and adjoining dining room and Linda's work laptop was open on the dining room table. The table was her workspace. Linda had been working remotely since the start of the pandemic, but she did occasionally get called into the office, like today. But why did she leave her laptop at home?

I abandoned my cereal and wandered over to her space. Folders and notebooks and her calendar were spread out on the table. She hadn't packed any of it up. Her shoulder bag full of more work stuff was still there, too. I thought I could maybe score some points by offering to bring her the laptop and bag. I took out my cellphone and texted her, "Did you forget something this morning?" In the abject quiet of the house, I heard the unmistakeable buzz of a phone upstairs. Was it Elly's phone? No, Elly would sooner forget a limb than her phone. I stood still, and listened, and the house's emptiness expanded inside of me. I typed another message to Linda: "Did you forget your phone too? Wrong answers only." I paused, then hit *send*. Somewhere upstairs, a phone buzzed. I ran up to our bedroom and found Linda's phone on her nightstand. I picked it up, touched the screen, and my two texts bubbled up before the locked screen went black again. I ran downstairs to the first floor, and didn't stop. I ran further down, into and then through the basement and out a side door and her car was gone. Yeah, sure, it was technically possible that she went into the office forgetting to take all her work stuff and her phone, but the instant I saw that empty spot in our driveway, that was when my memory of what she'd said to me earlier that morning, if she had said anything to me at all, changed from "I have to go to work," to "I have to go."

* * *

I'll spare you the details of my texts and panicked calls to Linda's office (there were no in-person meetings scheduled for her department that day) and friends and family and local hospitals and eventually the police. I'll spare myself a full accounting of the thirty-six hours over which it took me to convince the police that they needed to look for her, that something must've happened to Linda, that she wouldn't just up and leave us. I'll spare myself a full accounting of the thirty-six hours after the initial thirty-six hours, over which I was suspected of foul play, which, objectively speaking was fair enough given the appalling frequency with which men, husbands in particular, murder and disappear women. Those thirty-six hours were long enough to cause an online stir given my status as a minor writer. I ceased being a suspect when a gas station about a mile and a half down the road had surveillance footage of Linda pulling her car next to a fuel pump and minutes later driving away alone at 6:14 a.m. There was no question it was Linda in the video, with the clearest images of her being when she first got out of the car. There was a rectangular white patch with some sort of writing above the breast of her green jacket. I knew the coat but didn't remember that it had a patch. There wasn't a focused, clear shot of the patch despite Linda standing in unobstructed view of the camera as she pumped gas. The video quality degraded, went fuzzy the longer it played. No one explained to me why or how the footage became so grainy. By the end, the Linda climbing back into her car was blurred beyond recognition. It was as though she was disappearing on camera as we watched. After the gas station and one ATM stop at which she withdrew one-thousand dollars, Linda never used that bank card again.

Other than the gas station video and online conspiracy and rumour, there was no trace of her. Her car didn't turn up. Her cellphone records and email and socials showed zero evidence of Linda having carefully pre-planned leaving the house that Monday morning. Elly, Cal, and I wavered between imagining the worst had happened to her and hoping that she would return home. Given there was no reason that we could discern for her to go to the office that morning, and given the symbolism of leaving behind her work stuff and her phone, it became more plausible that she'd purposefully left us behind too. With each excruciating minute that passed without her contacting someone, anyone, was a condemnation of who we were, a judgement on something we had done or not done, which sent us circling the drain of the *where did she go?* and *who did she run to?* questions. Elly and Cal blamed themselves for her running away and they blamed me. I blamed me too, obviously. But mostly, I blamed the note she'd read. I had to.

★   ★   ★

Those first days and weeks after her disappearance, time was immeasurable and meaningless. It was as though Linda had fallen into the plot of one of her true crime shows, and I was a feckless character from one of the stories that I had written.

One night, I fell asleep on the couch with the television on. When I twitched awake, I reflexively checked my phone for a message from Linda that wasn't there. Instead of retreating upstairs to our bedroom, I walked out the front door. Everything outside the house was ambered in dark. The new spring leaves on the trees were as still as the stars dotting the night sky, forming their ineffable pattern. My footfalls and shallow breathing were intrusions upon the entropic reality of things. I was supposed to remain inside my house and sleeping, or trying to sleep. Instead, I was a glitch in the system, a blank spot in the universal mind. I was afraid that my transgression would be corrected somehow, but it was a thrilling kind of afraid that I clutched to, because at least I was feeling something other than grief, helplessness, and sorrow. I wondered if Linda felt what I was feeling and it was what had spurred her forward, or outward. Despite our thirty years together, I didn't really know what she was thinking or feeling.

I walked past the note house before realising I had. It no longer had a note taped to its front door and its yard had been mowed and landscaped. The note house looked like any other slumbering house on the street. There was one light on. That same lamp shining weakly through a second-floor window.

I stared at the window, an attempt at defiance, but an aimless one. I wasn't afraid of a face popping into view to look down at me, and if this was a story I'd written, my face would be peering down at me. I was afraid the window would remain empty forever. I stared, stuck in my own kind of amber, until tears turned everything blurry. Then I walked back home.

*   *   *

The following happened in the years before I saw Linda again.

Cal stayed in Los Angeles after graduation, moving into a small apartment with two friends. Linda and I had some money saved up, and I sent a large chunk of it to Cal to pay off his student loans. When I got back from my ten days in Los Angeles, I decided that I would not return to teaching in the fall, despite our household losing Linda's income. After the years of pandemic teaching and my imagining a cacophony of whispers about Linda from students and faculty, I couldn't face the classroom. Also, my stubbornly deciding to write full-time at an inopportune moment in my life was my way to fake that I had some control and to say fuck you to the universal mind. Moreover, I wanted to be home for Elly if she decided to stay home and take a gap year before going to college. I reasoned I could get another teaching job in the future, if needed.

That first summer passed without any clue to Linda's whereabouts or fate. Elly ended up going to her upstate New York liberal arts college in September. And I was glad she did. But the college didn't help us out as much as I'd hoped, given I was a single parent with a writer's twitchy, unreliable income. The college offered Elly more loans instead of cutting us a serious tuition break. I insisted that Elly turn down the loans. Like her brother, I didn't want her saddled with crushing debt. I told her not to worry, I'd figure out a way to pay it.

The rest of the break-glass-in-case-of-emergency money Linda and I had saved up went to Elly's first-year tuition. After that I took out a sizeable equity loan on the house, which doubled my mortgage payment. Elly's tuition became even more expensive because we were no longer on Linda's or my old school's shitty health insurance. The HMO I bought through the Writer's Guild featured a daily double of expensive premiums and high deductibles, plus it didn't fully cover Elly because she was attending school out of state. The college insisted I purchase a supplemental plan for $2,500 per year or she wouldn't be able to enrol.

My writing didn't go well despite my being home full time. Much to my publisher's displeasure, I stopped using social media to interact with readers and promote my writing. That was another fuck you to the universal mind, or another type of hive mind. Sales and marketing couldn't parse that I deleted accounts with a decent number of followers because the messages and tags and posts and DMs from trolls and randos wasn't good for my already-cratered mental health. Thirteen months after Linda disappeared, my next novel was published. According to my publisher, the novel had a soft opening as a direct result of my online hiatus. I was contractually obligated to write one more book for them.

For about a year post-disappearance, friends and family regularly called or stopped by our house or invited me out to dinner. I welcomed their emotional support and attention. But I could tell I was wearing on them. Being around me was a chore. I didn't have any news to share about Linda and my grief was a millstone they had to help me carry. I didn't have a sunny, positive outlook to make them feel better by proxy. One night, after having a few too many beers while at dinner with Larry and Jody, a couple Linda and I had met when Cal joined Little League, I told them about the note. I matter-of-factly told them I blamed whatever was written on the note for Linda's disappearance. I said it all in a rush and punctuated with a nervous laugh that turned into uncontrollable tears. The way Larry and Jody looked at me, or couldn't look at me, stopped me from telling other people about the note. But I thought about the note all the time, especially when I was supposed to be working on my next book. The note, the note, the note. Cutting my grief and confusion with obsession over the note was how I would continue surviving my one and only life.

After that night out with Larry and Jody, I made excuses to everyone and anyone as to why I couldn't talk on the phone or have them over or go to dinner. Everyone *did* take my *no* for an answer. I don't blame them. No one liked to be around someone who was receding, pulling away. I did it for them as much as I did it for myself. I didn't want to take any of them with me.

Our dog Molly died somewhere in the middle of Elly's college years, and I can't write another word about that. Those college years went quick, and so did the money from the equity loan and my old school's retirement IRA from which I'd also borrowed. Elly moved to Portland, Maine, with two friends after graduation. I stubbornly stayed home. I couldn't sell our house, even if I wanted to, as I owed more than what I could sell it for.

Eventually, I squeezed out enough pages for my last contractually obligated book, a book I turned in two years late. It was titled *Lost and Found*; plotless, metafictional, ambiguous, recursive, hopeless, with morose, irredeemable characters, according to my editor. Instead of dickering over edits and changes that would be required to make the thing remotely palatable to a general readership, my publisher dropped it into the world with zero marketing behind it. There wasn't any need to explain its soft sales opening this time.

★　★　★

About a month ago (or a month from the writing of this note), a well-meaning friend insisted that I take part in a library panel discussion in central Connecticut. I'd been saying no to event invites for years, but I said yes to this one. The long drive appealed to me, and I fantasised driving past the library's highway exit and into the next state and the state after that. Of course, reality struck back, and I got stuck on I-95 traffic, the kind that killed wanderlust and spirit-of-the-road vibes.

I exited the highway, and with the aid of GPS, wormed my way through cookie-cutter suburb after suburb toward the library. This was not how I'd imagined disappearing onto the wide, open road. I might as well have been driving loops around the neighbourhoods in my own shitty town. It was downright depressing.

I didn't make it to the library because I had to pee like a racehorse. I pulled into a random shopping plaza's parking lot. I walked/jogged into the chain supermarket, and me and my middle-aged, balky prostate made a beeline to the restroom. With a piss-my-pants crisis narrowly averted, I headed for the exit and was about to step through the automatic doors when I saw Linda pushing a grocery cart around the end of an aisle.

I'd seen wishful-thinking flashes of Linda elsewhere, ones that had proved false as soon as I'd paused for a double-take. But this wasn't one of those flashes, wasn't my mind manipulating an image into what I wanted to see. I saw Linda. It was her.

I sped-walked through the front registers and dodged sales displays and other shoppers. I found her more than halfway down a canned goods aisle. Her back was to me as she pushed her cart past a man stocking the shelves. She wore jeans and the same green coat she had worn when she left, but I couldn't see if it had a patch on the front. Her brown hair was streaked with grey. She swivelled her head, eyeing the shelves, showing each side of her profile, a profile I knew better than my own.

My heart stopped and filled at the same time. I jogged toward her on unsteady legs as though mired in the molasses of a dream. I was scared without being able to explain why I was scared. I had fantasised about this moment and had imagined crying tears of relief, regret, joy, and recrimination, but I had not imagined fear. My lizard brain clamoured at me to turn around, return to my car, drive to the library, and pretend I had seen a stranger who looked like Linda. But I kept moving toward her and I was about to call out her name when a white man, the one who was stocking the shelves, stepped between us. He was my height and build, and as I mumbled, "Sorry," and "Excuse me," his movements mirrored mine so I could not pass him.

His smile was neither friendly nor helpful, and his teeth were as grey as newspaper. His hairline was at low tide, and when I quit attempting to move around him, he rubbed the top of his male-pattern baldness head. The close-cropped black hairs encircling the islands of his ears looked as though he'd spraypainted them on. "Can I help you?" he asked.

I said, "No, thank you, just trying to catch up to—"

"I don't believe," he said, and paused to arch both eyebrows, which looked as painted on as his hair. I had the urge to press a finger into the ink as he continued, "that you are familiar with this place." He sounded like his throat was full of something other than words, like he was holding down his gorge. He swallowed heavily after speaking.

"Yeah, well, I don't need help," I said. He continued mirroring my movements so I couldn't navigate past him without ploughing through him. Dumb, animal anger bubbled up and I shouted, "Get out of my way, please!" *Please* said with all the inchoate fuck you I could muster; a poor camouflage for my growing unease.

His eyebrows collapsed over eyes that were so deeply brown as to be almost purple. "Are you sure?" he asked and swallowed again.

"Yes," I said.

He wore tan khaki pants, a white shirt with a blank white apron. There was no name or logo of the supermarket etched on the apron. A nametag over his breast read *Welcome, my name is* and below that an array of black bars, slashes and dots, the sum of which, when viewed as a whole, turned into static in my head. It was as though I'd read sheet music and could hear the dreadful song.

He spread his arms and said, "We've rearranged some items." He didn't quite roll the double r's in *rearranged*, but he lingered over and across the expanse of the word, as though speaking it was an unfathomable pleasure. Then he said, continuing to enunciate carefully, whatever it was he really meant hiding in the low grass of the syllables, "While we acknowledge previous items of preference will be difficult to find, we ask for your continued patience, and we ask that you be mindful of our work." The man tapped his skull by the temple with two fingers, turned, spinning on his heels, and returned to stocking the shelves.

My dizzy, slouching shuffle away became an awkward, staggering jog by the aisle's end. Succumbing to an impulse similar to the urge to smear what I assumed were his painted-on eyebrows, I flashed out a hand and knocked cans of beans off the shelves.

Linda was not in the next aisle, nor was she in the one after that, and I wanted to scream. She wasn't in the freezer section or perusing the baked goods or at the deli. She wasn't back in the fresh fruit and vegetables area and she wasn't waiting in check-out. I paused at the registers. The workers all wore red aprons, not white, emblazoned with the supermarket logo and advertisements from local businesses. They wore nametags with their handwritten first names.

I went outside and wandered the parking lot. Linda wasn't there either.

I went back into the store and walked the aisles in order. When I made it to the aisle in which I saw her, Linda wasn't there. The man with the blank white apron wasn't there. The cans I'd knocked to the linoleum had been returned to the shelves. One of the cans that had fallen was dented.

I continued searching the aisles until the supermarket manager and security guard asked me to leave. I asked to see their surveillance footage to look for my missing wife, and I have to assume that because my manic request was a harried and wild-eyed demand, they refused and asked me to leave. I wanted to sit in my car and survey the parking lot but the guard was now joined by a cop, and they were both watching me so I left. I didn't drive to the library event and instead drove to another small town's supermarket and wandered the aisles until I was asked to leave again.

Later, much later, I returned home, and pulling into the driveway, even in the dark, I noticed that my grass was getting tall, well over my ankles in height, and needed to be cut. I joked to the Linda in my head that maybe I would write a no-mow manifesto and post it on my door. The Linda in my head didn't think the call-back joke was funny. Then, the Linda in my head was replaced by the man in the white apron and indecipherable nametag, and he grinned at me. I wandered my empty house in the dark until one of the lamps in the living room went on. That timer had been set by Linda and I'd never changed it. With the automated flash of light came an idea. Maybe the slashes, bars and dots on the man's nametag was what was on the note that Linda had read, and maybe also written on the white patch that was on her green coat when she was at the gas station. Maybe those symbols created some type of code, the knowledge of which was as dangerous and irreparable as the fevered sets of equations that allowed for the weaponised splitting of the atom.

As fearful as I was about stumbling onto such a mind and reality warping code, I spent two days and nights attempting to replicate the slashes and dots from the man's nametag. I think I got close once because staring at what I'd written reproduced a static noise of a dead radio station in my head. Granted, the noise was at a much lower level than what I'd experienced in the supermarket, like groundwater low. I could only hear it if the house was totally silent. I tried changing and tweaking the symbols and scratches and the static went away. I was unable to make it louder.

I gave up trying to perfectly replicate the markings, and instead wrote the one that worked, or worked a little, onto an index card and safety-pinned the card over the front pocket of my jacket. I then spent the better part of two weeks wandering through supermarkets and malls and libraries and town and city parks and parking garages. The hope was my version of the note would be like, I don't know, me placing a phone call to Linda, or even the awful man in the white apron, and they'd answer. But no one answered. I never saw either of them again.

However, I discovered that with the card fastened to my jacket I could haunt public spaces for hours and hours and I'd be left alone. No one asked if I needed help and no one asked me to leave. No one even looked at me. It was as though I wasn't there.

★   ★   ★

I could make a pithy observation about these pages – and all writing in general, secret code or not – breaking the rules of time and space (i.e. you reading these pages in your present, which is my future and also, at the same time, my past), but I'm not feeling up to pithy.

I will leave these pages, this rather long note, in an envelope (the one you opened) taped to my former house's front door. So as not to infect the family and friends I have left, I will leave this house and fully recede and lean into being forgotten. I cannot tell you, now, what a balm the idea of being forgotten has become.

You, the one holding this note, I don't know what might or will happen to you. As ominous as that reads, maybe you can take comfort in the idea that none of us know what might or will happen to you, whether or not you've read this note. Life would be an unremitting horror, otherwise.

Yes, my house is in foreclosure. I assume you knew that already. You might've looked up the house online. Maybe you're the nosy neighbour from a few doors down, who complains that the neglected yard is a terrible look for the neighbourhood and you believe you're entitled to read what's in the envelope taped to the door. Or you were walking through the neighbourhood, on the way to get ice cream, and judging by the yard's neglect and the manilla envelope taped to the front door you put two and two together. I could come up with hundreds of scenarios attempting to explain why you are here. I'm a writer, after all. Maybe I'd hit on the correct one. Maybe I wouldn't.

I've already shared some theories about what any of this means, and I have more, but they are only theories. They are not answers. I haven't been able to figure out the exact connections, if any, between Linda and the note and the man with the weird, buzzy nametag and my own low-grade homemade version. I still don't know what comprised the note Linda had read. I don't know how the note works. At first, I suspected the note was some Monkey's-Paw-like form of sharing misery, of attempting to shed it to others as evidenced by my economic downfall and my house now appearing just like the neglected house Linda and I had walked by. But I didn't read that note so how did that misery get shared to me? I suppose the misery was shared to our family, but that's not narratively satisfying. But this isn't a narrative. Is it?

I am afraid that my insipid writer's brain – one too often given to flights of worst-case-scenarios spun within the prism of postmodernism and metafiction – took a concatenation of real-life events that didn't make any sense and puzzled the jagged pieces together into a narrative that I could better explicate, if not understand. I am afraid my own actions followed the rules of narrative. I am afraid I made the string of poor fiscal decisions so my economic crash could act as a narrative call back to the foreclosed note-house Linda and I had found. Assuming the note-house had been foreclosed, of course. I did not create nor fabricate the man stocking shelves at the grocery story, but I am afraid that, as he appears in these pages, he is an exaggeration, or an extrapolation. I've written other stories with characters experiencing static filling their heads due to exterior and possibly supernatural or extradimensional forces. I am afraid the reoccurring static-filled motif in my fiction has wormed its way into my real life because I wanted or needed it to.

Now, I do not believe or think the above paragraph is the truth, or even a partial truth. I mention it here to honestly acknowledge its slight possibility.

That the unending end of this note is nigh, and that, as a traditional narrative this ending being, perhaps, unsatisfyingly open, is a shred of hope you and I should cling and clutch to. Because what I am most afraid of – and I can't state this strongly enough – what I am deathly, pants-shittingly afraid of, is that the events of my life (and yours) and the people I love have been *rearranged*, have been moulded into narrative not by me but by the universal mind. Or worse, someone or a collection of someones – solipsistic, obdurate fools incapable of seeing the world beyond their fingertips – have hacked their way into the collective mind, have roughly and coarsely split our existential atoms.

I have to go.

UNMARKED

Tim Lebbon

I knock on the door before opening it and entering the house. I do this every time, even though old Ronnie is almost deaf and probably won't hear, and he leaves the front door unlocked so that his carers and visitors can gain access without him having to get up from his chair. Mostly housebound and very unsteady on his feet, Ronnie is still as sharp as they come where it matters. His mind is vastly populated with memories from his century on this planet, and though he sometimes gets confused, he's aware when it happens. That makes a big difference. He's a good kind man, and beneath the aged countenance and occasional muddled thoughts, I know that he cares.

It's morning, and his living room door is still open. Ronnie is a man of habit. If I'd come after lunch the door would have been closed, and more likely than not I'd have found him asleep in his chair with some inane afternoon TV blaring. But the morning is his time for reading the newspapers and drinking his one and only coffee of the day.

I pause just outside the door, always a little afraid of what I'll find when I enter. *I'm way past my sell-by date*, he often tells me, and even though I'm quite sure I was here fairly recently, I worry about the decline I might find.

My knuckles graze the living room door, and as I enter Ronnie looks up from his newspaper. His smile is open and honest and it knocks thirty years from his age.

"You again!" he says.

"Me again."

"It's been... not long. A month? Six?" He taps his head. "Losing it, a bit."

"I don't believe that for a moment, Ronnie."

He laughs, coughs, waves a hand, then struggles upright. "I'll get the damn kettle on, then. As you're here I'll have another coffee, just for today. And there's some Victoria sponge."

I smile and nod, and follow him out into the kitchen. He fusses at the kettle and the cake tin beside it, and asks if I want anything, but I'm never thirsty or hungry. It's the same charade we always play. He cuts himself a small slice and makes a cool cup, then we return to the living room.

Ronnie places the cup and plate on his small table and drops into the chair with a deep sigh. He sits up straighter, then brushes his hair and straightens his shirt. On the arm of his chair is a notebook and pencil. It's a thick book, the ribbon marker two-thirds of the way through. I think he uses it to remind himself of appointments, visits and thoughts he doesn't want to see flitter away. Sometimes I wonder whether it's actually a notebook just for me, and if each page is filled with a name and a location. That's impossible, of course, though I can't recall exactly how many times I've been to see Ronnie. In the hazy memories of my past I think perhaps he was a much younger, stronger man when I first whispered into his ear, but still considered old by most.

I take a seat on his sofa. He picks up the notebook.

"Maybe today's your last visit," he says. "That time's got to come soon, you know. I'm not as young as I used to be." He laughs, because it's what he always says. I laugh also, because it's one of the greatest truths. There's a saying that the only certainties in life are death and taxes, but there's also time. Most people spend their lives hardly noticing it passing by until it's too late. Some dwell on it too much. Ronnie knows the dance of time better than most, and he's as close to being friends with it as anyone I've ever known.

"I'll be here again," I say, and Ronnie's smile slips.

"Oh. So not this time then."

"Not this time. Not yet."

"Never mind." He actually shakes himself a little, like a dog shrugging off an itch. He sits higher in his chair, straightening his aged back. "You'll find what you want soon."

"Soon." Ronnie is my ticking clock. Each time I visit I fear he might be wound down and sinking into his true old age, with the years leaching his life and dulling his sharp mind. Yet here he remains, mind as sprightly as ever. "I don't know, Ronnie," I say. "Maybe I'll never find it."

"Come on, now. Don't talk like that. It's not as if… well, you've got plenty of time to look."

"That's true, my friend." I smile and nod.

"Ah," he says. "Of course. Plenty of time, but I'm the only one who can hear the truth from you. And I'm not here for much longer."

He has verbalised my fears. I'm glad I didn't have to say it; thinking it is bad enough.

Ronnie grunts a little, then takes a good swig of coffee and a big bite of cake. Crumbs patter onto his shirt and he wipes them away. He dabs jam from his top lip with a napkin. Old he might be, but the man still has his pride.

"So you have something for me," he says. It's not a question. It never is. He knows how this works.

"Melanie Groves," I say. He starts to write, slow and meticulous because of his twisted old hands, concentrating on the notebook in his lap. "She's out by the old railway arch at the end of Sordon Road."

"Uh. I know it. Used to play there with my brother."

I keep talking, Ronnie keeps writing. I give him the details of how I found her, and the way she sang to catch my attention. The same way they always sing.

One day perhaps I will recognise my own voice.

★ ★ ★

I walked along the same road that I'd walked countless times before. It was a mile outside of town, a narrow lane curving around the base of a low hill and leading eventually to the small wharf on the canal that took our town's name. I was neither too warm, nor too cold. The air around me felt still and stale. I'd come to recognise the lack of any real stimulation for my senses as just another side-effect of being dead.

As I neared the canal I heard the first whisper of a strange voice. I paused, a lonely wraith frozen in surroundings I could barely feel or experience, and tilted my head to one side. The voice was so distant that I wasn't sure if I was imagining it. I often heard such mutterings from beyond, sometimes in languages or dialects I did not know. But this was closer, and more immediate.

I left the road and headed across a field, wading through tall damp grass that I barely felt. A butterfly was startled aloft at my approach. It fluttered around and settled on my arm. As I neared the far corner of the field where a rough farm track passed beneath a railway line, a small herd of cows stopped munching on grass and raised their heads to look at me. They didn't seem unsettled. Still chewing, they watched as one as I passed them by.

The voice was louder now, and it ebbed and flowed like a gentle summer breeze. It was a woman, and she was singing. For a moment I paused, feeling guilty about intruding on a living person's private time. She wouldn't see me – Ronnie was the only person I'd ever found who I knew for sure could see me, perhaps because he was closer to death than most – but I'd still feel bad. Watching the living often felt like spying. That was partly why I wandered in quieter places and sought out the dead.

Her voice rose and fell in a song I did not recognise, and then I sensed something different about it, something that made me continue on into the short tunnel beneath the railway arch. Though she sang, there was a flatness to her tone that I recognised, and none of the words quite made sense.

"Who are you?" I asked, my voice echoing from the arched brickwork above.

The singing stopped. It was as if I had never heard it at all. I looked around, knowing what I was going to find because I'd discovered places like this before. I couldn't help but come across them as I searched for the resting place of my own earthly remains. I walked further beneath the bridge and through the gate on the other side, and the landscape opened out into a large field, given over to wild fallow growth and scattered with the remains of several old tumbled sheds and storage barns.

"Keep singing," I said.

No reply.

"Keep singing and I'll find you."

She started singing again, this time with something resembling hope in her voice. And I found her.

★ ★ ★

"Do you recognise the name?" I ask.

"Melanie Groves." Ronnie shakes his head. He puts down the notebook and nods at the phone he keeps on a small table beside his chair. "You want me to…?" he asks, and I know what he means. He could search for the name Melanie Groves on the internet, discover where and when she disappeared, but I don't want to know. There would be grief and misery attached, and I've come to learn – as has Ronnie – that what I do sometimes reignites both.

But it also gives closure, not only to those I find in shallow graves or buried in silt on remote river banks, but for loved ones who have struggled to continue with their lives even though something is missing. Love always invites grief eventually, and everyone I've ever found has been loved.

I was also loved, though my past is so distant and hazy that I only have vague memories of the man who used to smile at me, kiss me, hold my hand. And I have yet to be found.

"Maybe do it after I'm gone," I say. Ronnie's eyes betray his sadness that I won't be staying with him for long. He has plenty of company – his carers every day, his children and their children from time to time – but I'm different, and something quite special. A man his age has few secrets, and I am one that he treasures.

"Do you have to leave so soon?" he asks. "You've only just got here."

I want to leave. I don't like being with the living, and speaking with Ronnie… it doesn't quite hurt, but it's uncomfortable. I'm intruding into the world I left a long time ago, and breaking rules comes with consequences.

I relent. "I'll wait while you make the call, if you like," I say, and Ronnie smiles. He's grateful. That makes me feel good.

As Ronnie calls the police and gives them Melanie's name and the location where she's buried, I imagine him typing my own name into his phone as he searches for my story.

I've been missing for a long time, and none of this is fair.

★ ★ ★

I wait outside Ronnie's house until the police arrive. They're wearing plain clothes and come in an unmarked car. The history of police finding missing remains with the help of psychics or others is not a flattering one. I once asked him what he tells them about the information I relay, and he said that he tells them he sees these places in dreams. They suspected him at first, of course – old murders, given up by a man close to the end of his life – and he took that on the chin. But then more recent disappearances were solved through Ronnie's 'dreams', and they slowly drifted from suspecting him to… well, he says he thinks that they fear him, just a little.

It's hardly surprising.

But they're solving crimes, and bringing closure, and in three cases the discovery of buried remains has led to them capturing and convicting killers. Ronnie and I are providing a good service, and however the police are managing and processing the arcane nature of the knowledge Ronnie provides, they must accept that.

It's a man and a woman this time. I've seen them once before, and as they step from the car they stand at Ronnie's front gate for a while, facing each other, heads close as they talk. I can see their trepidation. They're about to confront something that neither of them can explain, and yet they're driven to go through with it because they know that there's a good result on the other side. They look confused but determined. Afraid, but set on the course they know is right.

Huh. Welcome to my death.

★ ★ ★

The passage of time is strange for me, like a river that sometimes flows upstream. I remember this from when I was alive – time exists to stop everything happening all at once, I read somewhere – but it ceased meaning so much to me when I had passed away. This strange post-death existence feels like it's happening all at once. I leave Ronnie's house and drift from here to there, and I have just found Melanie's sad resting place, and I am with Ronnie for the first time, and there is a fog of memory and emotion and anger at whatever happened to me so many years ago. Everything has already occurred and is still happening.

I've been like this for quite some time – I can judge that by how much Ronnie has aged since I first visited him – and I've come to understand that my own eventual fate must be bound up in the remains of those I sometimes find.

I have seen or met no one else like me. I am dead and yet I wander, and perhaps I am as unique as Ronnie. He is the only one who can see me and hear my voice. The idea that we are both special is pleasing to me.

I don't know where my own remains are buried, only that they are undiscovered. There must be loved ones who miss me and want to know what happened to me, but my living past is vague at best. Shadows and hints; that face, that smile. I wish it was not this way.

In finding others, I seek to find myself, and lay myself to rest.

★   ★   ★

The valley and the town it nurtured was often too busy for me, too bustling with life, so more and more I found myself heading into the hills. Every time I crossed the canal and started up the slope towards the low mountain bordering the valley to the east, a song echoed inside and drew me on. I thought it was the memory of something I might have once sung. It made me feel good and free. I thought perhaps I liked coming up here when I was alive.

I always followed the song but eventually lost it, and never found anything of note.

I had no reason to believe that today would be different.

Perhaps the change came from finding the sad remains of Melanie Groves. Each time I found one of these missing unfortunates, they seemed to mutter in my memory before I revealed their location to Ronnie and they were discovered, excavated and taken away. They were words I didn't know, little more than mere suggestions. Perhaps they had been building a picture in my discorporated mind. A map of whispers.

Today I followed that map, and it was up on the hillside, higher than I usually went, and so close to the trig point that marked the summit, that I heard three people starting to sing. Two of those voices were strange, and I already recognised them as remnants from long, long ago, from a time before the town huddled in the valley ever came into being. The words were in languages I did not recognise and they were so, so faint, a mere memory of sound and cadence. Wherever I trod there was deep history, and the remains of those gone into the ground many hundreds or even thousands of years before I walked these roads and hillsides. They never acknowledged my presence. I'm not even sure they were aware of themselves anymore. I could do nothing for them, and I hoped that over time they might have found some sort of peace.

The third voice I recognised.

Little fly upon the wall
Ain't you got no clothes at all?
Ain't you got no shimmy shirt?
Ain't you got no blouse or skirt?
Poor fly.
Ain't you cold?

I paused on the hillside, listening to that song again and again, until I remembered someone singing it to me a long time ago.

Mother, I thought. She used that song to nurse me to sleep. The memory brought a rush of images and emotions. But the voice I heard reciting this old beloved song now was my own.

I scampered across rocks and heather and through tall ferns, leaving the well-trodden paths and climbing a steep slope until I reached the old railway track. Open-cast mines hauled thousands of tonnes of coal from these mountains a century before, and the tracks used to transport it down to the canal far below were long gone. But the stone sleepers remained, and I followed them as the voice grew louder.

The old track passed around the top of the mountain, and I had flashes of a strange déjà vu that is only experienced by the dead – I remembered my life, and walking here with the sun on my face and a cool, wintery breath on my skin.

The track eventually disappeared into a stone structure that marked the beginnings of a tunnel through a shoulder of land, and I felt the curious sensation of a heart beating in my chest as the singing ceased and an old memory came.

★ ★ ★

I was here on my own, hiking these hills I loved so much. I'd come this way a score of times before, always passing by the old stone tunnel. I'd looked inside once or twice, but I had never ventured in. I was too careful for that. This place was close to the town, but it still had its dangers, and I was aware enough of mountain craft to know I should avoid such dangers at all costs. I had my phone, and my partner knew where I was. But it would have been irresponsible to risk hurting myself, and causing all the worry and trouble that rescue from the mountainside would cause.

Despite that, this time… this time something lured me closer. The darkness inside, warm and rich. The thought of old times buried there in that tunnel, unknown secrets hiding away from me and smiling from the shadows. I tested the stone, and it seemed solid. I hesitated for several minutes, taking a drink, nibbling on one of the sandwiches I'd brought with me, telling myself again and again that of course I'm not going to crawl in there, of course I'm not that foolish.

I crawled in there. A shimmer, a shake, a rumble, pressure from above, a moment of shock and pain.

And I never crawled back out.

★ ★ ★

Here I am, I thought, *I've found myself at last.*

The memories swished around me on the tides of time. I approached the tunnel and pushed my way inside, startling a small lizard which skittered away, froze, and then looked back at me. It seemed to realise that there was nothing to fear, because I was barely there. It watched as I squeezed through the fallen entrance, drawn by the echo of my own voice. I clawed at the moist ground buried beneath a fall of rocks, and though I had very little sense of touch, it moved beneath my fleeting fingers, rucking up and rolling aside until the first faint yellow smear of a bone was revealed.

Found me. I've found me.

I sat back against the curving stone wall. I didn't know how long it had been since I'd visited Ronnie, but time pressed in and surrounded me, and I knew that discovering where my remains were buried had also started a ticking clock.

I rushed back down the hillside.

★   ★   ★

There is an ambulance outside Ronnie's house. Its back doors are open, but there's no movement. His front door is ajar, and I move closer. As I approach, it opens fully.

They don't see me as they slowly, carefully, wheel the stretcher out, lifting it over the door's sill. The shape on the stretcher is covered with a sheet, its edges tucked in beneath the body. There are two paramedics, a man and a woman. I'm touched by their reverence as they pass me by and push Ronnie's mortal remains towards the waiting vehicle.

"Oh no," I say, but they don't hear me. "I'm too late." I feel a rush of grief and loss, partly for Ronnie but also for myself. I've been looking for so long, but even though I've only ever known Ronnie here at home, sitting in the chair or pottering in his garden as he follows his old man's rituals, he has been with me from the beginning of my search.

Right up to now, when he has gone and left me behind.

Who can I tell? Who will listen? Who *can*?

I walk into his house. There are two people in Ronnie's living room, sitting on his sofa and filling out forms. They talk softly, and one of them laughs. It's respectful. The items of a man's life surrounds them. Medical paraphenalia is scattered on the floor, but I don't think any of it has been used, and I hope Ronnie passed away in his armchair, quiet and asleep.

"I'm here," I say, but they don't hear me.

I move through to the kitchen, and there are several half-drunk cups of tea and coffee by the sink. I remember Ronnie fussing around out here, offering to make me a drink even though he knew I could not touch it. He'd always been quite accepting of the fact that he could see me, hear me, and speak with me, but sometimes he'd conducted his own familiar routines, perhaps to make himself comfortable with the idea that he was talking with someone who had died long ago. Neither of us tried to understand, and I think that was why it worked between us.

I miss him. Though I always found it hard being so close to the living, Ronnie was different. He was my friend.

I see something moving in the back garden and there's a flicker within me. Maybe it's a spark of hope. I step through the open back door and there's a man sitting on the garden bench. *Ronnie!* I think, and I wonder what he will be like as a ghost. I hope he'll retain that same sense of worldly-wise humour. In truth, I have no idea.

But this is not Ronnie. The man is younger, and as he turns and leans back against the bench, looking across the garden with a heavy sigh, I recognise some of his features – the heavy hooded eyes; the slightly hooked nose; the wide mouth and strong jaw. I'd always told Ronnie that he was handsome, and he'd laughed almost until he couldn't breathe.

As I watch, a tear escapes the man's eye and runs down beside his nose. He does not wipe it away. *Ben's a good boy*, Ronnie once said to me when he was telling me about his son. I liked that he called him a boy, even though Ben was retired and edging into his seventies.

As if he can hear me thinking his name, Ronnie's son turns and looks at me. He frowns for a long few seconds, and his eyes seem to flicker a little to the left and right as if he's trying to bring me into focus.

I hesitate, thinking of stepping back into the house. I don't want to frighten him.

Then Ben offers me a sad smile.

"Are you here for my dad?" he asks.

He really can see me! I think. I nod. "I saw what... I'm sorry."

Though he frowns at my voice, Ben is still smiling. I think perhaps it's a common expression for him. Just like his dad. "He was asleep when I arrived. I could hear him snoring. So I made myself a cuppa, made one for him too, and when I took them into the living room he wasn't snoring anymore. He wasn't..."

"It was peaceful," I say, to myself as well as him.

"Yeah, peaceful," he says. "So who are you?"

"I'm an old friend of your dad's. And I've got something to tell you."

RED MEAT FLAG

David J. Schow

Here's a sentence I never thought I'd express in a zillion years: Mister Tweezers really makes my sinuses hurt.

I'm punching the speed limits – pantsing them, actually – en route to the latest crime scene. The gumball tells onlookers I'm privileged. Modern LED flashers are tarted up with adjectives like 'tactical' this-or-that, but the light you stick on the dashboard of an unmarked, standard-issue patroller is still called a gumball, a reference that's at least fifty years old, which places it comfortably within my realm of sociological irrelevance.

Go figure.

I know a shorter route to the target because I am wiser than the know-it-all GPS, which speaks to me in an Australian woman's voice as though I've just groped her or something, a very schoolmarm-wielding, steel-ruler tone of disapproval, especially when I don't follow her directions or perform as exactly ordered. This is another facet of my personality known well and understood by my several remaining friends and exes. No disrespect, but a machine can rarely tell me what to do, even when it's right.

It would be more entertaining, though, if it bossed me around in the voice of the Wicked Witch of the West, or Morgan Freeman from *Se7en*, or the *Goodfellas* incarnation of Joe Pesci: *"What the fuck did I just tell you? Turn LEFT, fucking asshole, LEFT! Are you fucking stupid, you fucking remedial cheeseball dickhead, turn fucking LEFT... fucker! Fuck you!"*

Central knew to hail me once it was clear our star psycho had struck again. Our infamous nutbag-du-jour. This summons always comes between midnight and dawn, without fail, thus far on the hit parade. How I wound up with Mr. Tweezers on my plate is also the usual frustrating tale of personal involvement, emotional engagement, and outrage at the calibre of horror that so-called humans can inflict on other humans, other lifeforms.

Under normal circumstances, the only aspect we share in common is that we are all Earthlings. Specifics of gender or colour or creed or bias or nationality must be taken into account in any investigation, because not everyone is so generous when it comes to sizing up humanity.

Be practical, but never divorce yourself from compassion. That's good, solid baseline thinking with which only an imbecile or a crazy person could disagree or find fault, right?

Or a killer that just plain *wasn't* an Earthling. It would be like expecting compassion or empathy from a praying mantis… which only appears to be praying. For prey.

I thought we would catch a breather during August, the only month to feature no official national American holiday. Wrong; no respite. Mr. Tweezers simply *invented* his own goddamned new holiday – Cleavage Day, which turned out just about as wrong as you are imagining it to be, right now. For you fans of language, 'cleave' is one of the few words in English that has two exactly opposite meanings; things can cleave together just as they can cleave apart… and by now you've pretty much got the whole, lurid picture, in a Giant Golden Book sense.

Not that anybody remembers what Giant Golden Books were.

Mr. Tweezers quickly developed a knack for turning you against your favourite things. Do you like chocolate? Not so much, after the Easter Sunday killing – a re-enactment of the Crucifixion using a morbidly obese black woman whose blood had been evacuated and replaced with chocolate syrup. Then he opened her up with a shotgun. I've heard that in the days of black and white film and TV, chocolate syrup was often used to simulate blood. That blood spiralling down the shower drain in *Psycho*? Hersheys or Bosco, choose your favourite… and then try not to think about that every time you see the product, thereafter, no matter how tasty it might have been. Vomited blood is not Technicolor red, usually, because your body has tried to digest it. It is more often a ruddy brown thanks to the dead blood cells, the bilirubin – the same stuff that makes faeces a brown colour instead of russet. Kind of chocolatey.

You get the idea.

Are you one of those people who consults that oh-so-precious, sensitive website to determine whether animals 'die' in the movies?

Animals in general, pets in particular, and *especially...* dogs. *Does the Dog Die?* Then Mr. Tweezers concocted a holiday special just for you, right after the Fourth of July. You would probably not wish to see your favourite household pet's head mounted on a plaque like a hunting trophy, with bright, alert-looking glass eyes that are more horrible because they are *human* simulacra, not animal. The whole torture show was designed to mess up your brain. Candy sprinkles, in red, white and blue. Another image I would never be able to un-see, every time a cute pet video flashed across my feed. Every time I looked at a cupcake, I would think: *That poor, goddamned dog; I know it suffered.*

The worst was the baby. Right after Thanksgiving. Eviscerated, laid out on a pizza crust like so much mixed meat, and cooked, head intact.

Pizza. Mr. Tweezers has made me and many others hate the sight of *pizza.*

I mean, how much longer would it take you to become enraged?

One afternoon I realised the index card box on my desk had been sitting there for over six months, since I had first opened it and stocked it with a supply of vari-coloured blank cards, and then begun to fill the cards with notes and information. I dislike computer organisers. A PowerPoint presentation flattens the data to a bland sameness which, to me, seems to dishonour the lives lost, to under-serve the gravity of what is being investigated. People and animals with lives, taken. Their suffering needed to be recorded by hand, methodically, to honour the gravity. The time it took to write information down longhand, to thumb through the cards until the top edges became smudged and furry – all that time is needed to assist the process of concentration. I don't need short-cuts. I need fewer distractions.

Neither the holiday playbook nor the pitch-black humour of the food references were dependable, either. Mr. Tweezers had no fixed victim profile. Like Peter Kürten, the Düsseldorf Vampire of late-1920s Germany, he struck at men, women, children, animals... and this suggested two things. First, perhaps like Kürten, Mr. Tweezers was one of those ordinary-looking individuals who could inspire rapid trust in total strangers; second, also perhaps like Kürten, maybe Mr. Tweezers missed as many as he hit. Many of Kürten's victims – the ones who survived – never reported the attacks *because* they survived. Humiliation, embarrassment, social status all contributed. Once

Kürten was in the docket, the adjudicators seemed surprised at the sheer number of victims who then came forth. Kürten merely smiled and advised the court that his last wish, upon being beheaded, was to retain consciousness long enough to hear the sound of his own blood dripping into the basket.

Maybe Mr. Tweezers had a few survivors walking around, keeping mum.

Maybe he had terrorised them so badly that they would never step up – that is, those collateral people not required for his extravagant murder displays.

And over time, he became my quest. I wanted to fist up his throat and get close enough so my spit went into his eyes. *I'm on to you, you fucking subhuman. I figured you out.*

The day after Christmas, he did a whole group working at a pop-up discount store. These days, people frequently dismiss 'Exmas' as a consumer nightmare. Well, Mr. Tweezers made the nightmare flesh, so to speak: heads and limbs, eyes and hands, torsos on tripods revolving under multicoloured gels, tinselled viscera, big bulb ornament earrings. Mouths stuffed with cookies; blood mixed with milk; those little scored, six-way disintegrating price tags stuck to still-oily human flesh to alert the browser to discounts and mark-downs. From now on, every time I saw the tchotchke rack change seasons in a local drugstore or big-box circus, I'd remember. People had died so I would remember.

Which was a strange thought; almost *too* logical, for this guy. Or gal. Or group. It was a motive that normal folk could understand and sympathise with – a protest, of sorts. *Don't commercialise the holidays. It upset little Bunky and he became a serial killer.* That made sense, *common* sense, and caused us to recognise a diversion when we saw one. The public, and especially the authorities, needed Mr. Tweezers to remain a super-villain with motives comprehensible only to the insane.

Not 'common', not ever, not by a long shot.

I had not invented the 'Mister Tweezers' moniker; that had been Forensic Donny Frakes. Our perp, apparently, never left hair or fibres. It was as though he had gone over his own crime scene not with the proverbial fine-toothed comb, but with tweezers, picking away every last micro-bit of incriminata. We could forget about fingerprints altogether. DNA, too, for that matter.

I blew a stoplight on the way in; not the first time. That's my sad privilege, as I hurry to readjust my own limits for fright and disgust.

Skinner's rats. Pavlov's dog. And me – performing as expected, racing too late to the next atrocity, all for the apparent amusement of a killer who watched all the *CSI* shows, who read all the crime books, and who decided to be the latest contestant to one-up everybody else in the sweepstakes for what was socially unacceptable and morally outrageous. This being – the he/she/it-or-them – was trying their hardest *not* to be a fellow Earthling. Doing their damnedest to be superior and untouchable and unfathomable to the likes of me.

I especially wanted him when he made me dance, like this. But *wait...*

Had I split? Was my psyche cleaved right down the middle into the most dreaded, Norman Bates territory of multiples? Believe me, I began to fear that possibility six killings ago, catching my own gaze in the rearview, wondering whether I had concocted Mr. Tweezers out of my own frustration as a do-gooder cop, lumbering myself with the ultimate challenge: I had to get into the skin of a psychopath in order to recognise and apprehend him. It fucks with your head. But it's also a convenience of thrilling fiction, that salon of what-if where people must make wrong choices and embrace the worst possibilities in order to drive a plot-twist that hopes to snare some reader or viewer unawares. Surprise! The fiend is actually the cop obsessed with catching the fiend!

Except that, too, was a cliché on the order of how amnesia functions, in stories. Or the blow on the head that knocks a character conveniently unconscious on TV. (After being cold-cocked fifty or more times, don't you think Our Hero would suffer permanent brain damage and be retired to stud?)

Plus... too easy.

Plus... my sinuses were throbbing now. Like having expanding, toxic bread dough trying to push your eyes out. Sixty milligrams of one red pill, thirty of another yellow pill, and still the voice taunted: *If your brain had nerves, this is what an aneurysm would feel like, sucker.* How much longer before I came to a full stop? How many headaches and odd little inexplicable pains? When did they total up to a surprise sum? Was this the stew of botched memory, ghost pain and weird smells that signalled the starting flag for dementia?

Yeah, Mr. Tweezers made my sinuses hurt, all right.

The Marine he murdered for Veteran's Day had drowned in urine. His lungs were distended with piss, like water balloons. At first we thought it was simple contempt for humanity, again – a humiliating desecration. Or a kind of dog-in-the-manger statement: *piss on it so no one else will want it, either.* Urine doesn't reveal DNA unless it contains blood, or epithelial cells. The urine that soaked and bloated the late Master Gunnery Sergeant Steven Ian Church had revealed *ninety-three* DNA trails.

Mr. Tweezers had harvested urine from over a hundred sources.

No wonder my head was throbbing.

Yeah, I wanted him. I wanted him to know that, yeah, I really *had* gone that far just to put my hands around his throat. I really *had* gone the distance of checking out his piss trail, when everyone else just shrugged and thought: *Oh great, another psycho loon, who knows why they do what they do?*

Who knew why people pretended to be completely different people on social media? The pretend celebrity, the fake artist, the influencing name-dropper. Make-believe versions of an inadequate self, with Photoshopped eyes and filtered complexions. Curated exposure… just so long as they didn't expose their real personalities, or lack thereof, which could hit a dozen times worse because most people are predictable, ignorant, frightened, hostile, broke and dull.

Whining in public was never attractive. Yet here I was, toasting my own pity party.

You already know the run-up. Two cruisers, flashbars painting the exterior of a dry goods warehouse – yet another cliché, a dusty storage facility about the size of a city block, full of pallets and forklifts, and probably teeming with rats. A uniform admits me through the yellow cordon tape. Another officer with a special coffee lid to keep latte foam off his moustache directs me to the detective who was first-on-scene, the guy who had known I needed a heads-up. His name was Fleck; I'd never met him before. Sandy hair, mid-to-late thirties, married, glasses that looked to be bifocals in stylishly squared-off aluminium frames, blue eyes, straight white teeth, about 160 pounds. Still took pride in his wardrobe; still eager. He was packing a beefy .357 revolver in a nylon belt holster – a fast, quiet draw and dependable loads (probably wadcutters). Most modern cops had gone to nine-mil semi-autos; this guy didn't want to risk a jam in case there was a misfire. I appreciated his choice of sidearm.

Me? For all my love of old things and forgotten rituals, I was a fast-forward futurist when it came to firepower. Forty-five auto, extended mag, hollow points. It was overcompensation, sad and predictable, but I had never yet killed anyone I had been compelled to shoot.

I note that because I saw Fleck glancing inside my jacket. He was assessing me, too.

"Chesley? I'm proud to meet you but not happy about the circumstance."

We shook. He explained that he was Robbery Homicide out of Hollenbeck Division; he had arrived first because his turf was right on the border to mine. The LAPD's restructured Homicide Special Section didn't have to fret about jurisdiction.

"Let's see it."

Fleck gave the nod to another officer, who made way. The warehouse was in Boyle Heights, birthplace of Mickey Cohen, Anthony Quinn, and Jack Chick, the guy who used to do all those annoying (but inadvertently hilarious) religious comic tracts; nearly everybody still has one stashed somewhere.

The front office was abandoned but had been opened after-hours. The fluorescents made everything seem a dim green. Another uniform stepped back and muttered "sir" as we passed.

"Look at this," Fleck said, directing his light toward the floor.

It was a pastel-blue 3x5 index card.

It was one of *my* pastel-blue 3x5 index cards. I knew it even before I flipped it over.

Vets. Veterinarians I consulted back in July. Several entries, different pens. *Dr. Julie Montrose. The Hollywood Cat & Dog Hospital. Dr. Steven Martineaux. Dr. Jessie Bernstein*, circled. All recorded in my hand.

Fleck nudged my arm. About seven feet along the office corridor to the main warehouse space was another card, this one pinkish. Also mine. I had bought the cards in a packet that offered red, blue, green, yellow in softer shades, plus the inevitable white. He held the card up so I could read it, but just from the header I knew what it listed.

Mr. T.

Compare to Kürten, Holmes, Bundy – charming – trustworthy – ordinary-looking – victims don't suspect him (her?) – not attractive or noteworthy but not hostile either...

"Chesley? What is this? Fill me in?"

"These are my case notes. Right off my desk, downtown."

"You're shittin' me."

I sniffed hard, my heart already pounding. Nope.

"Total red meat flag."

I felt my sinuses spike again. "Translation, please." I didn't have the time for cute jargon, not now, nothing special or woke, thanks.

My request actually screwed up his stride; I'd caught him in half-step and he had to look back at me. "Oh, red meat flag. It was a health thing, I mean, that's how it started. Flagging the dangers of red meat. Trans fat, cholesterol, E. coli in processed beef, high blood pressure, low sperm count..."

"Frying is bad, chicken is better, that sort of thing?"

"That sort of thing."

"You said that's how it started. Then what?"

He actually stopped and turned back to make his point. "C'mon, Inspector. Follow the red flags. Beef has always been a short form metaphor for American manliness – red meat, blood-rare, shredding T-bones with your teeth."

"Macho carnivores."

"You have it exactly. You know a manly crime from a wimpy crime when you smell it. And Mr. Tweezers is a total red meat flag."

Fleck was filling the air up with jabber because he knew he did not want to see what came next. I'd already been on that carousel – eleven times.

High-profile, sensational murders seem impossible because they are magic tricks. Sleight of hand to direct our attention away from what we should be looking at in the moment. Just the way Fleck deflected me with razzle-dazzle about... meat.

It was *all* meat, so far, and would continue to be meat.

"You know what they say about people who eat rare meat," said Fleck. "They're better tippers."

Was he pushing some kind of paleo diet agenda?

I should have paid more attention to *my* senses. I said it right upfront: *Mister Tweezers really makes my sinuses hurt.*

There before us on the floor was a third card, sure enough. Part of a breadcrumb trail we were supposed to follow. Fleck already had his gun up.

"Don't worry," I said (uselessly, but it felt good saying it). "It's already happened."

"Fuck. I'm sweating like a pig." He mopped his eyes.

When I bent to pick up the third card, that's when he hit me.

When he snapped an ampoule under my nose, that's when I woke up.

"How analog," he noted of the index cards, which were sitting on a table, in the box from my desk. "You know, you can find out a lot more about people by just hacking their phones, nowadays. But there's something to be said for the old-school approach. You've got my respect."

Apparently, contrary to convention, I had been knocked out cold. Air touched fresh blood somewhere on the back of my head. I couldn't focus my eyes; everything in the room was doubled. I had a migraine of Rammstein concert intensity dragging out an encore in my skull. I was bound to a chair with my own cuffs. No latitude for wiggle; the chair had been secured to the floor by somebody who knew how to do it right.

Plus, my sinuses were trying to kill me now.

Yellow card: *Very likely male Caucasian… eclectic education… possibly a degree in a field like psychology or social science disciplines… average-looking (circled twice)… very likely knows firearms, mantrapping procedures, takedowns or restraint… maybe ex-military? Knows internet structures and burner phones – knows how to stay invisible amidst increasingly digital transparency. Probably has zero online footprint or a variety of pseudos (encryption?).*

I tried to speak. The sentence came out mushy. Blurred.

"I know, Chez. You're trying to remind me of the police presence here. Let me chop that one off at the knees. Those guys you saw outside? The uniforms? They're actors. They've checked out and gone home. They thought they were bit-parting for a reality show; I set it up with fake contracts and day rates – yeah, they all got paid. You see them nod at me? That was the signal that they were released for the day. I signed them out while you were napping. There's nobody outside now, and they wouldn't hang around because there's no craft service table to pillage. The cop cars are movie rentals. You didn't bother to look closely enough. Four hundred bucks per day from Reel Wheels."

Another yellow: *No DNA (scribbled out). No hair. No prints. No fibres. Very cautious about spoor – obsessive? Maybe ADHD? Clean freak? Feet that don't leave footprints – how hard is that to do?*

"I even know your buddies in Hollywood Division call you 'Chez.' Yours is the older desk, the one that used to belong to a junior high school vice-principal. You fought the longest before you'd let them put a computer screen on your desk. It was just you and your file box, and all that hard-copy, ancient paper data to sift. How analog."

I could no longer feel my legs. Fleck had jammed me with something. *Mister* Fleck. Today's pseudonym.

"You're not the crimestopper on the brink of retirement, running one last case to ground, DeeTee. You're done, and you know it. You wonder whether you have presenile dementia, like your mother did. Or diabetes, like your father. Your cock hasn't worked correctly in three years; it's one of the reasons Amy dumped you. Have you heard the one where half a hard-on is called a 'Hollywood Loaf'? No? This isn't Holmes versus Moriarty. This is me, running rings around your bureaucracy and common sense for ordinary people and Us versus Them.

"Slick, am I right?"

I wanted a psychotic. I got the opposite.

At least I could acknowledge that no more of my life would be wasted in coping with child-proof packaging on the sinus pills.

You want the reason, the rationale, the explanation, the punchline… and there isn't one. Without Google you don't even know the difference between a Dirty Sanchez and a Hot Carl.

"I only have one thing to say to you," he said in conclusion. "Happy New Year."

A REVIEW OF *SLIME TUTORIAL: THE MUSICAL*

P.C. Verrone

How can we revive the American musical? This question had been posed to our industry long before theatres were forced to shut their doors due to COVID-19, and it has only become more urgent in the wake of unprecedented closures, dire financial straits, and the shuttering of numerous workshops, salons, writers' groups, and legacy organisations. How is the American Theatre to proceed? Many have parroted tired clichés of the 'power of the theatre to bring people together.' Yet, again and again, we have seen the empty seats, the runs cut short due to low ticket sales. The fact is, now that theatres have reopened, audiences are still not flocking back.

And why should they? What unique communal experience will greet these eager theatregoers upon their return? Some Frankenstein's Monster of existing IPs, hip hop-inflected composition, a reorchestrated 80s popstar's catalogue, a stunt-cast lead, and a book more preoccupied with convincingly using 'mid' and 'rizz' than telling a decent story? Frequent readers of this column will be well aware of this reviewer's feelings of alienation from the contemporary musical. Rest assured; this is not out of malice. I spent lockdown replaying *The Sound of Music* and *Hair* to death to escape the paranoia and isolation. If the Nazis and Vietnam War could inspire masterpieces like these, I was eager to learn what great works would emerge from our own hellish episode of history.

Theoretically, I agree with the theatre-makers who assert this institution's ability to unite us in a time when we feel so estranged from one another. I am hungry for such an experience. But each time the final curtain drops on a new play, I am left with a bland taste in my mouth.

Slime Tutorial: The Musical has been on my radar for some time. Those of us who braved the digital theatre and Zoom performances that themselves became endemic when venues closed will likely recognise the name Ricky Herron-Mayers, *Slime Tutorial*'s writer, composer, lyricist, and director. Herron-Mayers rose to prominence in experimental circles during the height of the pandemic. Their (Herron-Mayers uses they/them pronouns) interdisciplinary combination of performance, organic chemistry, and quasi-synthetic bioengineering could perhaps only catch the theatre community's eye in a moment when the line between 'Drama' and 'Technology' became blurred beyond distinction.

Herron-Mayers' digital performances took place in their studio, though it is perhaps reductive to refer to this space as merely that. It was more of a warehouse combining aspects of a laboratory, terrarium, aquarium, and film set. From the limited vantage point offered via Herron-Mayers' webcam, you might glimpse a fume hood, lab stands with flasks and beakers, heating mantles and stir plates, thorny green vines creeping in from the corners, exotic potted orchids, fresh and saltwater fish tanks, black-lit tanks containing various reptiles, amphibians and invertebrates, tables littered with script pages, or hangers with enough masks, hats, wigs and costume pieces to outfit a drag queen for a lifetime. According to one of the rare interviews that the infamously reclusive Herron-Mayers has given, the warehouse also contains a bed and a kitchenette where they eat and sleep. I'll let you decide whether that is simply hyperbole.

It is difficult to imagine Herron-Mayers' work existing outside of this highly specific space. Their piece *The Quiet Sublime of Things Lost* involved a blend of behavioural training and harmless environmental manipulation to direct a sextet of cephalopods to change colour while Herron-Mayers recited six monologues. Lucas Cohen of *American Theatre Magazine* was the first to put the artist's name on the map when he wrote an article likening this performance to Ntozake Shange's seven multi-coloured Ladies in *for colored girls...* Another piece devised by Herron-Mayers entitled *Unimpeded Undulation* featured the climax of an operatic aria coinciding with an explosion of thick, pink foam that doused Herron-Mayers' entire body.

Perhaps Herron-Mayers' most famous work is their adaptation of *Antigone*, Sophocles' tragedy in which the titular character seeks to

202 • ELEMENTAL FORCES

unlawfully bury her brother's body. The first Herron-Mayers-led production to incorporate other actors, this gripping staging depicted the artist's studio being slowly filled with soil. Watching the livestream from my laptop on my kitchen counter, I feared this might veer into maudlin. (Let's bury the stage in a play about a burial! Groundbreaking!) But then, in the second of the five acts, I noticed the waist-height soil begin to ripple. Before my eyes, seedlings wiggled their way out of the dirt at the speed of a multi-week timelapse.

The live chat lit up. Were they real? Was it some practical effect or accelerated growth hormone? Was it safe for the actors to be immersed in this dirt wearing only togas? I kept my thoughts to myself and observed. By the third act, the stems were at the actors' elbows. By the fourth, they had bloomed into a rainbow of flowers. By the time Eurydice's body was discovered in the final scene, the blooms had withered and shrunk back into the soil. In a play that pits the Laws of Nature against the Laws of Man, Herron-Mayers had fashioned a spectacle that seemed to have joined – or maybe disobeyed – both. I was intrigued.

Once traditional venues began to tentatively reopen, Herron-Mayers seemed to follow their flowers underground. But it wasn't long before the theatre world was rocked by an announcement in *Playbill*: Herron-Mayers' next project would be – of all things – a musical premiering Off-Broadway. The fact that Herron-Mayers would be taking on all major creative roles, entirely writing and directing the piece themself, seemed laughably absurd. But the producers of the show expressed no qualms, saying, "If we can pull this off, the theatre you know will be a thing of the past."

The only aspect of *Playbill*'s report that was not utterly baffling was the title: *Slime Tutorial*. Given Herron-Mayers' online beginnings, it seemed fitting that this musical would reference the bootleg recordings of stage shows hidden in plain sight across YouTube and Vimeo. 'Slime tutorials' (so called to evade censors that would otherwise take down the unauthorised films) proliferated during the pandemic as fans searched for some way to sate their cravings for *Legally Blonde* or *Heathers: The Musical*.

But the title alone gave little hint as to what the content of this musical might entail. Would it centre on the controversy of these bootlegs? Would it argue for their potential to democratise a prohibitive industry, giving those who cannot travel to New York or pay Broadway prices the chance to see their favourite shows? Would it lampoon the industry itself, the way that *The Producers* had twenty years ago? I must admit, I assumed the worst. I had nightmares of a reference-heavy parody of every hit musical from the past ten years. What could be worse than one soulless, unoriginal Broadway show? How about a mash-up of them all!

By the time the first advertisements for *Slime Tutorial: The Musical* appeared, little about the show's content had leaked from casting calls, rehearsals, or production meetings. Whatever Herron-Mayers was planning, they were making sure that no one would see it before the first night of previews.

Herron-Mayers appeared in a single promotional interview for Broadway.com. This was the first time I saw them outside of their studio, or even out of character. Dressed in layers of blue-grey fabric with a shaved head, they looked more like a monk than a playwright. Speaking in their breathy tenor, Herron-Mayers hardly touched on their personal background except for a brief mention of abandoning a PhD from 'a school in Boston' to live with a group of Radical Faeries.

When asked about their inspiration for *Slime Tutorial*, they said, "At its core, the show is about desire. We understand our own desire through these walls, these blinders – gender, race, the body. Sexual organs and erogenous zones. What does it mean to take those away, to give yourself to something without arbitration? When two anglerfish mate in the darkest depths of the ocean, they fuse their tissue together. That's what I'm interested in. What does the anglerfish desire?"

It was with this perplexing description in mind that I took my seat at the Slow Pony Theatre last night as part of the first audience to lay eyes on Herron-Mayers' Off-Broadway debut. The curtain rose on a quaint suburban cul-de-sac, beautifully designed by Martine Robinson. The façades of the houses were highly realistic, just short of uncanny with an unnervingly pastel palette. Part of me had expected the set to recreate Herron-Mayers' studio, and I couldn't help but feel disappointed that it didn't. Zola Monks and Blossom François took the stage as your run-of-the-mill gossipy neighbours, whispering about a new family moving into the house next door. Then, the slime appeared.

It was difficult to tell exactly what I was looking at as it oozed out from the crevices of the set. It pooled stage right for a moment before rising just a little taller than Monks. I must commend lighting designer Kat Xho for finding a way to suitably light both the human actors as well as this translucent, blue-green mass that stood before us. After a moment of silence (emphasised by a pause in the orchestration), its unctuous body shuddered. The vibration was not the same as speaking, not quite like the hum of vocal cords, and yet I could perfectly understand that the slime was saying, "Good morning, neighbours."

A low murmur throughout the audience told me that everyone else was just as bewildered by this thing – this being – that had just spoken. However, the play gave us no time to marvel or question. Monks and François broke into the first song, 'Not Like Us,' an upbeat pop/rock duet about change coming too fast. The song could have been plucked from any other recent musical from *Be More Chill* to *Six*, but it was difficult to concentrate on the music when a human-sized slime was swaying along to the beat. Then, during the final chorus, the slime began to sing along. Its body once more quivered, though the resulting sound was more melodic than its speaking voice.

And it did have a voice! It wasn't too bad, either, though I am hard-pressed to describe it. It was something between a mezzosoprano and smearing jelly on your ears.

I tried my best to follow the rest of the story, which largely centred around this slime having moved into a closed-minded neighbourhood. Quique Gonzalez, fresh off his Tony-winning performance in last season's revival of *Zoot Suit*, played the town's fire-and-brimstone patriarch, warning against the evils of soiling the purity of the community. It was unclear to me whether the show was aware of the irony of having a Mexican American actor sing a song entitled 'Why Don't We Build a Wall?' Seasoned Broadway baby Lauren Swanson played a spiritually lost recent widow and performed an emotional ballad that may perhaps be some of her best vocal work ever. But this was all overshadowed when midway through the first act, the slime split into two. These two slimes, equally sentient and independent, performed a comedic duet that left the theatre audience in stitches. At the end of the number, the two slimes merged back into one and exited to a standing ovation.

A common word of wisdom for actors is, "Don't work with children or animals." I am tempted to add slime to this list.

The slime (which I can only refer to as such, as it was criminally absent from the cast list) truly was the centre of attention. I know prima donnas with less individuality. It had singing chops, comedic timing, and dare I say it, *star quality*. All of these were evident during the final scene of the first act.

Monks' character, who despite her earlier distrust had clearly taken a shine to the slime, found herself alone with it in the intimate dark of the town's gazebo. Streetlights haloed the scene, and the two actors' chemistry became so palpable, I could almost run my fingers through it. Monks' character said, "I'm tired of being this person who feels so separate from everyone around me." The slime vibrated in agreement before leaning in and consuming Monks entirely. The music swelled as the curtain fell on the image of Monks' body dissolving inside the slime like a tablet of Alka-Seltzer. The applause was deafening.

I have never been part of an audience so impatient to get through intermission. My fellow members of the press leapt from their seats, immediately dialling their phones or hurriedly typing out emails to announce that this was the most extraordinary must-see experience in decades. Forget about that 2,000-pound King Kong puppet, this was *singing slime!* Most of the audience was trying to figure out the secret to it. What was the slime made of? Where was its voice coming out of? And what about that trick, where Monks' body seemed to disappear inside it?

I, however, tempered my reaction. I wasn't here on behalf of *Life* or *Science*, debating whether this slime was a miracle of modern biochemistry. I was here to report on the merits of the *musical*, its direction and staging and composition. If I am to be honest, all were lacking. The script was thin – in the past eight years alone, how many of us have sat through some version of the 'stranger comes to a bigoted town and we have to learn to get along' story? The music was nothing to write home about, except for the fact that it was coming out of a bluish-green blob. From a financial perspective, a star or a gimmick might be enough to carry a production. But is it enough to carry the American Theatre?

After thirty minutes passed without us being called back to our seats, the impatience bloomed into hostility. Audience members began shouting for the performance to resume. Ushers ran around frantically, promising to get to the bottom of the delay before disappearing backstage. Some patrons seated in the orchestra began to throw their programmes or drinks onstage. A physical altercation broke out in the mezzanine, and the culprits were promptly escorted out. Many have written about the sharp decline in theatre etiquette in recent years, though I tend to argue that this trend has more to do with the quality of the shows than the content of the audience. A truly great performance will stay a sneeze.

After another ten minutes, the intercom announced that Ms. Monks would be unable to continue the performance, so her understudy would be going on in her place. Murmurs spread throughout the house. Many wondered if that last effect had injured her in some way. But there was little time to speculate as the curtain rose again.

The second act began with the song 'How to Make a Slime,' which addressed one of my lingering questions: we'd seen the slime, so where was the 'tutorial'? However, if anyone hoped that this number would offer a window into the creation of Herron-Mayers' being, we were sorely disappointed. Rather, we were treated to an introspective 'I Want' song from the slime – which now seemed to have doubled in size. It expressed homesickness for a country from which it had fled, or perhaps been exiled? The lyrics of the song were vague and contradictory, and the slime's diction had become muddied, like someone trying to sing while chewing.

At the end of this song, Monks' understudy Cori James entered. It was immediately clear that James lacked the charisma and chemistry of Monks, timidly reciting her lines and often refusing to get within two feet of the slime. This undercut what might have been a dramatic scene in which her character confronted the slime for not having called her after their one-night stand. The slime's voice remained garbled, which made the entire scene almost undecipherable. It ended with the two in a tight embrace, so they must have worked it out. As the lights faded to black, James let loose an unnervingly graphic moan.

When the lights came up again, Herron-Mayers themself stood centre stage. Their name did not appear amongst the cast in the programme, so I hadn't expected to see them until curtain call. Portraying what I can only describe as a disgraced scientist, the slime's father, and a vengeful god from its homeland, Herron-Mayers addressed the audience: "In the primordial days of theatre, the roiling masses yanked acts off the stage, incited riots if they were dissatisfied. You are no different. At the slightest inconvenience, you revolt. You only desire what your tongues have already tasted. Everything you consume is palatable. You claim to challenge yourselves, but see how ugly you become when you are really challenged? You've always been this way, entitled and unwilling to love the abject. But *you* are the abject. *You* are the hungry mass demanding meat—"

Herron-Mayers' monologue was interrupted by Gonzalez bursting onstage and screaming, "It's coming! God, that *thing* is coming!" The musicians screeched to a halt as the slime burst through the set, encasing Gonzalez as it formed into a single mass once more. Through the slime, I watched Gonzalez's shocked expression morph into one of orgasmic ecstasy just before he dissolved.

The slime now towered over Robinson's pastel set. There was only a moment to appreciate its sheer magnitude before François came tearing through, knocking one of the flats askew.

"Run for your lives!" she shouted, showcasing her famous vibrato. "It ate Lauren and Cori!" François leapt into the pit before scrambling up into the aisle. Other members of the ensemble streamed out from backstage and into the audience.

"Someone call the police!" one of them shouted.

"Someone call Equity!" screamed another.

While I might appreciate this breakage of the fourth wall as a nod to Wilder, the 'immersive experience' has become entirely played out. Once you've gotten a lap dance from a spandex-clad cat, the 'actors in the aisle' gimmick becomes old-hat – though, I did admire this reversal of it. Rather than welcoming the audience *in*, this cast was begging us to get the hell *out*.

The immersion was so wholly felt, some patrons in the front orchestra also began to scream and race towards the exits. Those of us more seasoned theatregoers remained seated, watching the slime vibrate at a low frequency. It seemed disturbed by the noise in the aisles. Many of us have seen the viral videos of actors who have had to stop a performance to personally address a disorderly audience member. The slime's reaction to the interruption was to split into multiple globules, hopping into the pit and carrying musicians back onstage before rejoining together. Herron-Mayers watched stone-faced as this all played out before going into their torch song.

'Primordial' was the first number in *Slime Tutorial* that I can attest is totally unique. With the entire pit emptied – either absconded or dissolved within the slime – Herron-Mayers technically sang it acapella.

However, they were accompanied by the slime, whose mumbled voice now seemed to have incorporated the tones of an oboe, the thrum of a cello, the whistles of flutes, and the bass of a kettle drum. Whether electronic or live, I have never heard a sound like this. As the song progressed, the slime ballooned so large, it threatened to overflow off the stage. Herron-Mayers belted their final note, took a breath, and then dove head-first into the slime.

You could have heard a pin drop. The towering slime emitted a low hum, something between a tuba and a belch. It shuddered for a moment before releasing a torrent of globules down the aisles into the house.

This seemed to give everyone left in the audience permission to panic. Patrons tore out of their seats, rushing the exits. The doors quickly became blocked with bodies clawing at one another like crabs in a bucket. Those who were slow or trampled by the stampede were snatched up by the bouncy globs, which whisked their dissolving bodies back to the main slime onstage.

I watched as the central slime began to absorb the architecture of the theatre itself. The wooden beams and proscenium and faux-baroque murals of the Slow Pony Theatre disintegrated before my eyes within the growing mass of this bluish-green gel. But I just wasn't convinced.

The invitation of chaos, the uniting of the audience against a common enemy, the destruction of the traditional monument – these were powerful ideas, but was this really Herron-Mayers' answer to the future of the American musical? I had felt a glimmer of hope in that final number before they dissolved themself in their own creation, but was it enough? Would a slime solve the rampant issues of diversity and representation, oppressive 10-out-of-12 tech schedules, or the threat of New York City being underwater in forty years or less? Would any of that matter if the slime couldn't tour or be replicated in high schools with no arts funding?

Flashes of red and blue approached through the slime's body. Evidently someone had called the cops, and the slime had eaten so much of the building that we were basically outside. I heard gunshots and looked on as the NYPD lobbed smoke bombs into the gooey body. These were all promptly swallowed and dissolved. The slime continued to expand, absorbing its satellite globs back into its main mass. Nothing could stop this thing, not bullets or attack dogs or blockades. Herron-Mayers had created something immense and impractical, yet indestructible and – above all – demanding.

The slime was a work of pure art.

I realised that I hadn't left my seat. I was alone, watching the slime perform just for me. So, I stood and applauded. The slime trembled, which might have been a bow. Then a jelly-like tendril shot out from its body, grabbed me in its tacky grip, and pulled me inside of it.

I hesitate to refer to this as an 'exclusive,' as nothing feels especially exclusionary about the slime. The slime wants everything, takes everything. It is inclusion in its final form.

Unfortunately, I cannot divulge how Herron-Mayers developed the slime, or the reasoning behind its relentless consumption. But I do have some insight that my colleagues who left the performance early lack. To be in the slime is to be of the slime, to be everything that the slime has eaten. There are no barriers between me and the actors, the musicians, or the other patrons. There is no separation between the performers' emotions and my own, between Herron-Mayers' vision and my interpretation, between the designers' imagination and my mind. When my skin and bones and muscle dissolved into slime, I experienced an intimacy with my fellow man that was euphoric. This understanding would be impossible if I were fleshed, if I could conceptualise myself as a separate ego, but the slime has removed all walls.

In fact, this review is as much a part of the slime as everything else. The review, the critic, the art, and the artist are all one! The specifics of how to publish a review made of slime or compensate a writer whose corporeal form has been dissolved is a task my editor will have to work out. Hopefully the slime will spread fast enough that by the time I finish, we won't need publications to mediate interpersonal communication. That's the beauty of the slime! If you won't come to it, it will come to you.

For those who might criticise the slime as a work of biochemical terrorism or a re-skinned Audrey II from *Little Shop of Horrors*, I want to offer this final thought: When you become the slime, you do not die. Rather, you meld with everyone else sharing this unique, living experience. And in the end, isn't that what theatre is all about?

THE DOPPELGÄNGER BALLET

Will Maclean

There was once a man, a very bad man. A gangster in fact, the very worst kind of bad man – a man who dresses up what he is in some kind of spurious moral code that means absolutely nothing, but justifies any action. Such a man is capable of anything.

He lives by one rule and one rule only, the most ancient, reptilian rule, that whoever dares to do, will prevail. By this rule, if anyone opposes him, they must not merely be stopped but broken, destroyed, snapped in half. He understands this completely, without words. He has understood it since he was a child. So he makes his money, illegally, and he builds his criminal empire through extortion, protection, theft, prostitution, drug dealing, and, almost incidentally, murder.

Grinning round a cigar, he recounts the first time. *Me and the lads had some bother with this shopkeeper...* (the story is old by this point, worn smooth as a pebble). From, I dunno, some fucking place. We offer him the usual policy, he says no, he didn't come here from the old country to be intimidated (faded map of the old country on the wall, roughly square, with a jagged river through it, like black lightning). So after a week we smash the place up, we threaten his family 'cept he don't seem to have one. The bloke doesn't bend. Stubborn. Another week, then we go back to first principles as it were and I let the boys – my boys – go to work on him.

I watch, but only seeing as it's work. The man, the shopkeeper, suffers under a variety of tools and tortures. *We fuck him up something awful, like that, for four hours, do anything we can think of to the prick.* He still won't break. White shirt, red with blood, black with burns, still he don't see. Before he dies, he becomes something else, someone no one ever thought of before, not even in a nightmare.

Fucking mess. After that we wrap him in a curtain and dump him in the canal. Next week, someone else takes over the shop. Someone… (he pauses to find the word) …someone *pre-approved.* A gale of sycophantic laughter. He pauses to exhale foul cigar smoke, lost in fond reminiscence.

And so, built on the dead, his empire grows. After a few years this man – this monster – becomes so powerful he doesn't have to do any first-hand monster work anymore and his life starts to resemble that of any successful CEO. He goes to the gym, plays golf. He eats out, Michelin star restaurants, puts on weight, goes to charity dinners. A little shiatsu, trips abroad, some more golf. All the while, all the cruelty and murder and broken lives pile up in his wake; he, now far removed from it, disconnected, an executive, his hands grown soft.

Disarticulated bodies turn up in bin bags on the banks of the river, minor hoods and those who oppose him, turned to rot, stinking sludge falling from greening bones, blue flesh at low tide, food for seagulls. He takes up tennis. He's crap at it. Seven times a millionaire, nine, thirteen, twenty-four. Seven cars, a wife, a mistress. Four overweight Rottweilers, a vast, sprawling house that looks like a Tudor mansion might if it had been designed by a disturbed child and assembled over a weekend. *Things,* he remarks one day, fork in hand, *are going well.* What else is there? What lies ahead? Years of idleness. Years of comfort.

Then, one day, his mistress suggests they go to a fairground, because she wants to go, so they go. It's terrible. Fucking toerags running rusty machines with glazed amphetamine indifference, shit sweets and treats, the horrid stench of doughnut batter, the din. He hates it. He shoots three bullseyes, wins her a grotesque pink chipmunk with a leering, skull-like grin. *Can we go now.* Strolling away from the whirl and the noise, they see a lone caravan. Set apart from the rest of the fair. A fortune teller. She says he should see one, he's always wondering about his future, reading his horoscope and stuff.

So, laughing at his destiny, ha ha ha, he goes into the tiny caravan.

Inside, bad light. Bead curtain. Smells of cat. Not much furniture. Faded map of the old country on the wall, roughly square, with a jagged river through it, like black lightning, which stirs a memory, but it's gone as soon as he thinks of it. Behind a table (a piece of plywood covered with a satin cloth) sits a scowling woman of seventy, face as wrinkled and unwelcoming as a clenched fist. She smokes long, cheap, cleaning lady fags, and she sucks on one now. She regards him, unblinking, takes all of him in. His haircut, his Armani shirt, which fails to hide his paunch, his grey trousers and black loafers. She looks him up and down, and suddenly he realises that his defences, the million behaviours that tell the world to leave him alone, to *fuck off* or *get fucked*, that tell you he's *a someone* – they're all deactivated here, and he is naked. She looks him up and down, says something in a language he doesn't know. He goes *Wha?* Finger to his ear, pantomiming ignorance to raise a cheap laugh from a nonexistent sitcom audience, confrontational but feeling foolish, and she shakes her head as if clearing it of a bad thought. He ignores this, and sits down, but she's still looking at him, with the level, matter-of-fact hatred with which a venomous snake in the zoo glares at its captors. Her eyes are almost all black, no white at all, they seem huge to him.

In tart vowels and long consonants she gives him the prepared speech. *You can have Tarot, palm readings, crystal ball, or something a little more...* (she hesitates, her dark gaze darts to his face, then back to the table) *...direct*. He is confused (scared) and a little bit freaked out (scared), so he tries to recall the half-a-Business-Management course he went on years ago. If faced with someone proffering unbearable alternatives, you should, he recalls, choose the most unbearable and see how they like *that* (in his heart he dearly wishes he was outside, with his mistress and the pink lights and the skull-faced chipmunk and the candyfloss and the frying smells). So he says, *the last one*, and she smiles nastily and he smiles back, a false smile hurting his overfed face, and tries to look confident. She tilts her head left to right, looks this way and that, as if to say, *well, it's your funeral*, and proceeds to grind her Superking out on the heel of her shoe.

She instructs him to place both hands palm-up on the table in front of him. Smirking (scared) he does so. With a suddenness he associates, somewhere deep in his mind, with predatory, many-limbed, female things (squid, octopus, spider), she places her cold bony hands over his. He wants to whip his own hands away, to run outside, he's in way over his head, he knows that now, but he can't move. He feels something running through his body, something it has never felt before, something deeply and viscerally unpleasant, like worms squirming through him. He looks to her face, her bold, ancient face with its triangles of black skin under the eyes, looking for reassurance, possibly, but she is in a trance already, so quickly, and her eyes, so black and piercing, have rolled over to white, and her mouth gibbers and starts, forming words, not-words, bits of words, things that should never find expression. As she jabbers, saliva pours from her mouth, crumbs of thick pink lipstick, and he so desperately wants to run now but he's clamped down, held there.

She starts to speak. The voice that issues from her lips is awful, not hers or even like it, older by far, and deeper, like some heavy antique machine that has somehow ground into speech.

In short, clipped words, it speaks.

It tells him his name. It tells him his wife's name, his mistress's name. It tells him how old he is, the name of the first and only woman he has ever loved, the name of the first man he ever killed. The vitals. Omitting all that cannot be proved, deleting all falsehood. The voice tells him his secrets; the money in the safe under the sauna, the trio of dead men concreted under a house on the coast, the offshore accounts. Information that he has shared with no one. And he sits, panting, unable to move. Silence and the smell of silence, overpowering. *Things no-one could possibly know.* And he is beyond scared now, fear has made a child of him, but he can't stand, can't run, he knows that he will hear something he wishes he hadn't, but he cannot move, all he can do is sit and tremble. And the voice informs him that his movements and actions, his empire, and all the steps he has taken to build it, have met with the approval of a thing, or rather, a thing that is not a thing, a terrible, abyssal absence, two broken sets of teeth against blackened gums, open in perpetual mirth, but bravado is always his first reflex, even here, and he simply twitches in the furnace of that moment and says *Wha?* again.

On it goes, this voice, this strangulated snarling of giant gears, inexorably, toward a conclusion. Done with past and present, it starts to foretell the future, which is what it is here for.

In not so very much time from now, the summer of your life will end, and your life with it. You will be killed, murdered.

He stammers, blurts questions, but he can't even hear them himself. The experience is flowing through him now, in all its reality, like an electric current. *This is real. It is happening.* Dirty, sick thoughts. Electric stench of river rot, the kind of aroma that reaches into you and pulls out your last meal. Still it talks.

It will happen soon. It will happen with terrible precision, by magical means. It will be, as if it were already done.

He will be killed by one in eight billion, by a man with his face, his exact double. His Doppelgänger. *His Doppelgänger.*

This last detail – the alien sound of the word – is too much, and he rips his hands from the table.

And there it is – a worst nightmare he never knew he had. Stunned, her eyes fill with human being again, and she briefly sags like a puppet before becoming grotesquely animated, her face quivering and juddering like the wattles of agitated poultry. Her hands are claws on the tablecloth, tearing it, rending it. He crashes into the bare bulb on the way out, scrabbling at the door, and when he looks back she appears to tick like a metronome, back and forth, swathed in a membrane of pulsing shadow, tick tock.

He screams and slams the caravan door behind him. What's wrong, crows the mistress, what's wrong?

Jump-cut to a few weeks later. Dark hollows under his eyes now, he hasn't slept for days. He has lost a lot of weight. Whisky by his side, all the more potent for being a cliché. He has become obsessed with the experience, with the absolute reality of it; he cannot dull it or buy it off or rub it out with the usual distractions. Its power in his mind seems to grow rather than diminish as time passes. The thought preoccupies him, riddles his every waking thought like a disease. *His executioner will arrive one day, soon. Wearing his face.* In that moment, he will know total fear, and the anticipation of this is killing him.

One day, he is alone in his enormous house, apart from the men in suits, the human oak trees he hires to guard him. Both his wife and his mistress, have, by this point, left him, disturbed and upset, both separately picking up instinctively on things other people, hamstrung by delusions of their own rationality, would deny.

He wanders to a marble bathroom, rubs his stubble, looks at his face in the mirror.

The face of the betrayer, of the executioner yet to come.

Fucking face, he thinks.

He begins to shave, foaming his jaw up. All around him, bad things. Shadows where shadows should not be. Creaks and cracks in the air as if time itself were watching, dirty, filthy intentions climbing spiderlike around the doorframes, eyes pale yellow like tartar or old ivory.

He peers out of the open bathroom window. Two of the security goons, the human oaks, are involved in monosyllabic confab on the immaculate lawn. They remind him of characters in a fairy tale, but why he thinks this and what it means he doesn't know. It is broad daylight. No silent assassin, features all too familiar, skulks across the grass. A full security staff. Surrounded by oak trees. Still he doesn't feel safe. A pistol in his pocket, six bright brass-tipped bullets in it, still he doesn't feel safe. He stares into the mirror. His own face, tired, soaped up with shaving foam, so he looks like a cheap department store Santa Claus.

Fucking *thing!* Fucking *face!* That this should be the thing that marks him out for extinction! The razor glitters in the cold sun. The sunlight is pearly, lethal, madness dances in it, and it is at this point he has the idea.

Before he can think better of it, he slices the razor across his cheek.

A second of nothing, the world hangs suspended, things are almost as they were, and then time and space march on in unison, and a curtain of blood descends from the cut.

The blood, the sheer amount of it, breaks him out of his trance. *Fuck, there's loads. Fuck, what have I done? Fuck!* He presses wads of toilet paper to it, pats the bloody foam from his face. He swaps the wad of damp paper for a towel, makes his way uneasily down the stairs, heads out to the car.

If the oak trees are surprised, they don't show it. One of them drives him to hospital, in silence, asking no questions. When they get there, this same mysterious lack of curiosity also grips the doctors: they've seen enough cuts to know that this one is self-inflicted, and know enough about who their patient is to keep this assessment to themselves. They tell him it will scar, that he will need plastic surgery, but he tells them he doesn't want it. The weirder and more distinctive the scar will be, the more distance it puts between him and the rest of the human race, the better.

Twelve stitches. A hideous thing, like a centipede, crawls across his cheek.

Two weeks later and he's almost accustomed to it, he feels better already, sleeping better and drinking less. The fear, whilst not entirely gone, has subsided to manageable levels.

And yet.

Doppelgänger. It's one of those words, imported from the German, like *poltergeist*, that is *unheimlich* by its very nature, it sounds as if it did not originate on Earth, or any Earthly place. And then, some days later, he looks into the mirror, and again sees dread. He sees that, far from being distinctive, his new scar is, after all, a fairly ordinary scar, of the type anybody might have. Worse still, it is healing nicely. All his past misdemeanours, and the executioner in the shadows, wearing his face, ready to step out of the wings and snuff him, send him to the void. Bearing that same scar. He runs a finger along his cheek and thinks *it's not enough*. It's too humdrum, too much like anything else. And that word, *doppelgänger*, haunting him, barely there, turn around and glimpse it, made of steam, of smoke, of air, it'd be gone.

He rummages in the bathroom cabinet till he finds the cut-throat razor, a heavy thing, ornate, the blade like a miniature cleaver. It was his dad's.

Now he stands before the mirror, like last time, razor in hand.

Like Van Gogh, he thinks, and he smiles, the last complete smile he will ever make.

One decisive, untrembling wrench of the blade rightwards, like the carriage return on an old typewriter. Something plops into the sink. He fishes it out and quickly, quickly, into the toilet bowl, flushes it, so there is no going back.

Two minutes later he's out on the lawn. The oak trees are disturbed, they have nothing in their experience to help them process this. They cluster, leaning toward each other in conference, like a dolmen that's lost its capstone. He, another crimson wet curtain consuming his lower face, red smeared teeth, smiles and grimaces, smiles and grimaces.

One of the oak trees expresses concern, places a hand on his shoulder, but he tells the oak tree to go *huck himself, don't hucking touch me.* They are rattled but, as before, they take him to hospital, a different one this time. Again, however, the doctors and nurses there aren't stupid, they know who he is. And if he wants to cut his face up, who are they to stop him? They tut and fuss and do what they can, but the lip has gone, and when they send him home he has a face that perpetually drools and sucks, a face that will forever, now, show the machine-like grille of his bottom set of teeth. Every second breath, he sucks the scab inwards, agitates it. A black ragged line, like a dog's lip, like a slug that's been doused in salt.

His reward for this? Four days of almost-peace, and he feels the madness dissipate, though not enough for him to quite accept what he has done. Nonetheless, his brain begins to unclench, to organise itself. He stares out of the window onto the empty green lawn, dribbling whisky onto his collar, gun in hand, alert to any movement at the edge of things.

But then, on the fifth day, alone again, in the bathroom, staring at his lipless face, bathed in the lethal, pearly sunlight, the awful alien word runs through his mind again, and he knows it isn't enough. Something more is required. Something final.

He heads down to the enormous garage, where he keeps two of his lesser cars, and a speedboat on a trailer.

There is also a workbench, with an extensive rack of tools.

At the workbench now, moving fast so he won't think about what he's doing. From his jacket, he takes three items: a brand-new razor blade, wrapped in card, a pocket mirror, and two grams of cocaine, the closest thing to anaesthetic he could find, folded in squares of British *GQ*. He rubs a lot of the cocaine on his upper gums until they start to go numb. When he is satisfied with the numbing, he takes the razor blade from its packet.

He carefully chops out three colossal lines of coke, pausing momentarily before snorting them through a rolled-up fifty pound note, one after the other, methodically, right nostril, *bang*, left nostril, *bang*, right nostril, *bang, bang*. He waits five or six seconds until the first terrible, fantastic belt of apocalyptic euphoria thrills through him and his palate is numb. Then, he reaches for the pliers.

He places the metal jaws of the pliers around an upper left-hand canine. Both tooth and pliers feel reassuringly solid, as if all of this were really happening to someone, somewhere. His heart is galloping in his chest now, tripping over its own rhythm to keep up with itself. He grips the pliers as hard as he dares: the tooth, caught in the metal jaws, becomes, for a second, the focus of his whole being. It feels alternately large and small, huge and tiny.

He gasps and wrenches it with all his strength, to the left.

A tiny sound, like a stem of celery being snapped, as the socket cracks around it. To the right (the pain enormous, more than even muted nerves can describe), and before he can fully take note of the situation, he yanks it sharply to the left again. Lots more rich red blood. The gum tears in a ragged strip as it surrenders on the fifth wrench, the tooth an inch long including the root, the bloodied enamel gleaming in a stray rod of pearly sunlight. He is crying, his shirt is covered in blood, he feels fucking amazing. He smears coke into the ruined gum, chops out another enormous line (difficult, as he's shaking and bleeding so much, but he does it) snorts it at once.

And why stop here? A tooth is only a tooth. It won't be enough. Is it enough? The very fact of thinking this, a weird kind of creeping guilt. Again the feeling that jaundiced eyes are watching, whilst his back's turned, sticking their fingers in the pool of his blood, licking and tasting.

Of course it's not enough.

What else is there on the tool rack? Numerous knives and saws. A roll of chisels. Every variety of hammer. A blowtorch. He is particularly drawn to the blowtorch. Grimly, he chops out another enormous line. He's laughing now. The cocaine has been cut with something, as usual, and he feels as if the barrier between this world, the quiet afternoon garage divided by queasy sunshine, and the world where the chattering jabbering things live, is being dissolved. There is a nailgun, a bolt cutter, a power drill. He doesn't really have a nose to speak of to sniff the final, enormous line into, but, heroically, he manages.

Halfway through cauterising his new face with the blowtorch, he dies, of course, falling backwards onto the concrete, heart stammering, consumed by the moment, a lethal fit of shock. He lies on the floor, his face ruined once and for all, a skull wrapped in loose bloody muscle, three teeth gone, one eye put out, the other staring manically, lidlessly outwards from the red mess in comical surprise.

But just before he dies, a strange thing happens. The garage falls totally silent, free from any noise at all, free from the distant chatter of birds or the furnace roar of the blowtorch, running out of fuel as it rocks back and forth, on its side.

As he lies on the concrete floor, the sunlight thickens inexplicably, takes on the sickly quality of that other world, from where he felt he had an audience; the air becomes thick and brown, like rank water. And a figure coalesces in one corner of the garage, filthy rags unfolding out of space. Roughly a person, bound in a stinking, rotten robe.

On broken limbs, in angles that aren't human, it shuffles its painful way towards him. The figure is cowled, stench of riverbed, of dead leaves, flesh turning to mud, and he can't move or scream now. He's already dead, but that fact seems suddenly irrelevant. The thing, unmistakeably a man at some point, now become something else, inches toward him. Rags and waterlogged lilac flesh, one bloated hand opens, a gesture of salutation, of recognition. The light thick as soup, heavy with significance. And it is here, now, in front of him. *Something else. Something no one ever thought of.*

And in that flash he knows everything. The thing beneath the cowl. White shirt, red with blood, black with burns. Not even in a nightmare. *Fucking mess. After that we wrap him in a curtain and dump him in the canal.* The shopkeeper, the one he tried to extort, the one he had tortured to death, all those years ago. The first man he ever killed. Two riverbed-rotten hands reach up and bring the cowl of the curtain they wrapped him in down, around the shoulders, but he knows already what is under there, what he will see, and see he does.

The remnants of a face. Burnt. Sliced. Drilled. Destroyed. A lip is missing. Three teeth. An eye is out.

He was doomed all along. Every step he took away from this moment, his destiny, has been a step closer to it. *A man with the same face.*

He laughs, until the enormity of the joke crushes him off this plane once and for all.

When the oak trees break down the door and find him, they see the face that is no longer a face, they see the tools and the blood and the cocaine, and the blowtorch, still roaring, but the thing they will take away forever is that laugh. Silent, two broken sets of teeth against blackened gums, open in perpetual mirth.

EIGHT DAYS WEST OF PLETHORA

Verity Holloway

"He won't lay a hand on us."

Mancino could choose to be offended. The old priest had considered him for all of four seconds before telling the girl he's as good as neutered, but Mancino could – he could lay a hand! He could lay two. Even so, the strangers have food and a tent, and Mancino has no horse, no water, no gun. The black desert night will kill him. Hear that? The coyotes are howling to chill a man's blood. He has a story of bandits, of desperate, ruthless men, and he, poor young Mancino, in the wrong place at the wrong time, as always. Not strictly a lie, any of it.

Ned always did say he had a wretched look.

"Just a moment at your fireside, Padre. Then I'll be on my way."

The girl's brow creases. She's savvier than her companion. "There's nothing for thirty miles. In any direction."

Mancino ignores her. "Where are you headed, Padre?"

The priest casts his weary eyes across the distant sandy hills, fading into the twilight sky. "The sea."

The answer surprises Mancino. He has only seen the sea once, when he crossed it. People here don't mention it, the way people don't mention Mars, or whatever stinking hole they came from. It's a saltwater chasm between the old and the new, and Mancino cast off the past a long time ago.

The girl is a nice piece of meat. She's well-muscled, glowering, and wears a gun belt over her skirts. Mancino is svelte and dark, with long legs nimble from his boyhood in the foothills. He knows his green eyes garner looks. This priest's girl might notice his eyes if she drops the attitude.

Seated around the fire, they say grace before their canned meal. Mancino declines with a curl of his lip.

"He's done nothing for me, the Almighty."

The girl meets his eyes coldly. "What have you done for Him?"

They say their prayers without him, but he eats, and more than he ought. Detritus always did call him the trash can. Detritus was built like a steer and dressed like a child's drawing of a man. Her waxed coaching coat brushed the dirt and her hair was a black halo framing her smiling face, though what anyone had to smile about out here in the dustbowl was a mystery to Mancino. Detritus had led gangs across all the country, that much he did know. She collected people, curious categories of them. It satisfied some urge in her to pack them together into a tight crew and teach them how to hold up mail trains and drain banks. Gangs of mean Spanish women with pox-pitted cheeks; of buck-toothed redheads; of men with green eyes full of guile. That was how she met Mancino, sidling up to him across the sticky floorboards of a nameless bar.

"How's a man like you feel about the redistribution of property?"

He had opinions, as it turned out. They lived in the mountains, he and Detritus and the other four Green-Eyed Monsters, all rootless men like himself, learning to shoot straight and keep their heads. With Ned as their leader, post offices all over the frontier knew to fear them.

What are friends but guys who haven't got around to screwing you over yet?

The priest and the girl are guarding something. They don't tell Mancino so, of course, but he recognises the rabbity look of a bank teller with a stuffed safe and no backup. Mancino scrapes the last of the bean sauce from his can and watches as the girl goes to the little tent, pretending to fetch a shawl. She's checking on it, the valuable thing. She sketches a cross from shoulder to shoulder and closes the tent flaps behind her.

"No bed roll?" the priest asks Mancino.

He rubs at his bruises, which are real enough. "The *banditti* took everything. I was lucky to escape with my life."

The priest offers him a blanket, at least. When the pair retire, Mancino sees a box between their bedrolls, plain and black, asking – pleading – not to be noticed.

He grants them an hour of peace before quietly preparing the horses. Inside the tent, the priest sleeps open-mouthed. He'll have money sewn into his clothes, but he's all too sober. The girl scowls through her dreams, one hand curled around the bone handle of a knife tucked into her belt. The box rests on the sand, small and tempting between the warm bodies of his hosts. Coin, he hopes, or even jewels. Priests always have jewels.

He creeps on the toes of his boots, edging closer in the tent's near-perfect darkness. He bends his long back, his hand a pale star against the box's black lid.

Wait.

He flinches back before he fully registers what he sees. A snake, bright and deadly in a sliver of moonlight. His sudden motion startles it, and it reacts the only way it knows how. Mancino's flesh is safely out of reach, but the priest's hand lies limp on his chest. The snake gets him in the wrist, little more than a pinprick. That's all it takes.

Mancino grabs the box and gets moving.

The girl can survive without a horse. She's capable; call it a compliment. Besides, she's the type to come after him, and he can't have that. He lashes the spare behind the other horse, moving fast. With the box – heavy, he registers happily – safely in the saddlebag, he goes to mount as the girl comes falling out of the tent, wrestling with her pistol.

"Stop!" she shouts. "You don't understand."

The horses respond to his spurs, kicking up sand and rock. A bullet zips past his shoulder and the last he hears of the girl is a despairing cry:

"Throw it into the sea!"

★　★　★

Mancino is thirteen and the sun is a brand on the back of his neck. Sheep will not watch themselves, but Mancino has been awake since before dawn and their fat white shapes bob in and out of his sleepy vision like bubbles in beer. He settles his rangy body under a tree and leans his head against the warm bark. When two of the sheep wander off and a third is found dead in a wolf trap half a mile from the pasture, Mancino receives a belting for his carelessness and his younger brother is sent in his stead next time: little Damiano, always delighted to point out his mistakes. When a wolf takes him, Mancino wonders at his own luck.

*   *   *

He knows a hollow where he can stop before dawn. No one will see him, nor the horses pawing at the red dirt.

The box sloshes with coin. Mancino's tongue flickers over his lips. The priest really didn't want anyone getting inside – he can't see a keyhole or even a hinge. It's one of those trick boxes the Chinese silver-miners give their children, he supposes, and he gets to work with a rock, smashing it down with all his strength.

When the lid finally cracks, Mancino frowns.

He turns the box upside down and shakes it, feeling a fool for doubting his own eyes. The weight! The sounds of shifting cash.

The box is empty.

"*Vaffanculo.*"

The saddlebags, at least, contain a couple of handguns, a few coins, and a flask of warm water. And ammunition. Armfuls of it. Mancino holds out a bandolier jingling with shells. What was a priest doing with a private arsenal? Still, it's something to show for his efforts. He can defend himself if the girl follows him – or worse, if his old friends show up.

He rests as the coral sun creeps over the crags, examining the box, running his fingers over the oiled wood for a hidden compartment or a false bottom. When he's done, there's little left but splinters, and he curses the priest and the girl for their duplicity.

Throw it into the sea.

Puttana probably got bitten. Snake venom can take some that way, trigger a sudden delirium. If she's dead, she won't come after him, at least. Mancino finishes the water in the priest's canteen, letting it drip down his sun-blistered chin.

He can't chance stopping at the nearest town. Someone will recognise the horses, or worse, Mancino. He thinks of Ned and the rest of the Green-Eyed Monsters, plotting behind his back. They probably think he's vulture jerky by now. He brings his heel down on a rock, imagining it's Ned's treacherous head. The rock splits, revealing a fossil. Some butt-ugly sea creature, coiled up like a turd.

"This was all ocean," Ned told him once, sweeping his arm across the desert vista. "A million, billion years ago."

Mancino kicks the fossil away and takes a piss before his journey.

* * *

He is nineteen and his mother is close to death. She's a husk of a woman, not a drop of juice left in her, and she barely fills the straw bed, sharp with sweat and wizened herbs. She presses the Saint Christopher into his palm, her cracked fingers rasping unpleasantly against his skin. "A mother will do anything to protect her children." 'Even you', he hears, though only her eyes say the words. The medallion fetches a little cash from the pawnbroker. He looks fine in the new jacket it pays for. "One day," says his father as they trudge home from the church on the hill, "the farm will be yours." There is no time for mourning, they both understand that. The crops know no waiting.

* * *

Plethora is a grand name for a dull town, but it's a good distance from the Green-Eyed Monsters' stomping ground. Mancino hitches the horses and pays for a room in an inn that leans like an eavesdropping crone.

The innkeeper's squinty eyes give him an apprehensive look, but he accepts Mancino's false name without incident and leads him down a bare corridor to his room. "You on your way to the Lizard?" he asks, wafting away a brace of flies.

"The what?"

The innkeeper raises his voice, assuming Mancino has sand in his ears. "The shrine."

Mancino grunts. He doesn't know any shrine.

"You'll have to scrounge up breakfast elsewhere," the man goes on. "Our cook's dead."

"Dead?"

The innkeeper shrugs. "Life became a burden."

The room hasn't been cleaned since the last residents left, or perhaps the sorry souls before them. The bedsheets are coarse and grey, and the smell of stale sweat clings to them, but there is a chair for him to throw his clothes over, and the innkeeper eventually comes lumbering back with a basin of yellowish water and a sliver of soap.

Mancino frowns. He's paid good money. "That it?"

"Hasn't rained in a while."

Mancino is all too eager to strip and wash and sleep for as long as his bruised body desires. As he peels off his shirt, he is reminded of the marks left by Ned's boot as the other Monsters tied him like a hog and left him to fry.

"A good-for-nothing tick is what you are," Ned had said. "Dead weight."

Porco Giuda. If Mancino lays eyes on Ned again, the little bastard better have a swift horse.

There's an old playbill down by the washbasin. Something about a harvest dance; there's an illustration of couples arm-in-arm amongst jolly mounds of pumpkins and squash. Mancino vaguely remembers Plethora being known for its good soil, a microclimate of regular rain and kind sun. His mind darts to Italy, to his father, his cracked hands the colour of barren earth.

Enough of that.

Yes, looking at the playbill, he recalls the stories. People used to visit Plethora to taste the produce and take it to trade across the state. Pumpkin beer poured by sweet, fat women looking for husbands. Glancing out of the dusty window now, down at the listless men with the street's dry red earth on their boots, he wonders when the town's luck turned. A wagon draws up outside the undertaker's shop, laden with plain coffins.

Mancino will leave first thing in the morning.

★   ★   ★

He is twenty-one and his new wife is nagging him about the top field. They could plant oranges there, Maria insists. Or figs. If Mancino would only get off his backside, she gripes, work with the other men to get an irrigation system in place, think what they could make of the place. Dig an underground aqueduct like they did in the Bible, bringing water down from the hills. She'll do it herself if she has to.

Mancino waves away the flies. She'll quieten down when she's pregnant.

★   ★   ★

The night is hot and the Plethora streets are alive with breaking glass and the shrieks of squabbling harlots. Mancino's aching body is buffeted through formless dreams. In the singing of the mosquitoes, he hears the *whizz* of the priest's girl's bullet, her desperate cry.

Throw it into the sea.

Mancino rolls onto his back, seeking the part of the sheets he hasn't already soaked with sweat. To have paid for a bed and be unable to enjoy it—

There is something in his mouth.

His hands fly to his face, but the sizeable object is already slipping over his teeth. He wrenches his head from side to side, kicking out at his assailant with both legs. He figures it's the innkeeper come to kill him – his own fault for being too tired to wedge a chair under the doorhandle – but the darkness of the room is so complete, he can't make out the shape in front of him, and his flailing feet connect with nothing more substantial than his own blankets.

Panic meets pain. The thing in his mouth pins his jaw so wide he can hear the cracking of the hinges. His fingers scrabble where it protrudes from his lips, solid and thick as a man's wrist, yet slick, briny against his tongue. He feels his face turning red, and he flips onto his stomach to try and dislodge the thing as it nudges experimentally at the fleshy opening of his throat.

He is reminded of the twisting knots of lampreys sold in buckets, waiting to be diced and fried in a broth of blood and wine. Vampire fish, born to mindlessly latch on and suck.

A fresh surge of fear. He bites down with all the savagery he can muster, but the skin – and that's what it is, he realises then, a rubbery glove covering coils of heaving muscle – refuses to yield.

And then there are more. Oily tendrils weigh his bucking body down and make easy work of his most private defences. He is open, a passage warm and slippery. With a strangled cry, Mancino finds himself tossed onto his back once more, facing the ceiling where something dark and colossal masses above his spread legs. Through a blur of tears, there is a flash of light like a photographer's bulb. A lightning storm blown in from the desert, perhaps, though the only thunder he can hear is the clamour of his own heart. It's no more than half a second's illumination, enough time for Mancino's terrified brain to shout, nonsensically, *"Woman!"*

On the outside he is tough and scarred, but under the skin he's an overripe fig. She loves him for it – *She* – for every sumptuous curve and pulsing cranny. All his uselessness rendered luscious, a fecund network of warm passages from his ears to his cockstand. His skin is sticky with every fluid he possesses, and there's more for her the moment she asks, bubbling below the surface, anything she wants of him: sweat, seed, blood, every drop is for her. She's making a map of his bowels, squeezing the sponge of his lungs with such affection that he spends, arched and whining around the roiling mass filling his throat.

At last, sing his cells as he drops into unconsciousness. *At long last.*

★   ★   ★

The sun is low. He has slept all night and most of the day, and he stinks worse than he's ever stunk, which is saying something. After lying inert, listening to the rumble of the carriages outside, he gets up and pads to the grimy mirror. Each step sends a clatter of pain through a different set of muscles. Sunstroke, he tells himself, but he doesn't look as bad as he feels. Nowhere near, in fact. His skin is clear and smooth, and the prints of Ned's boots have faded almost to nothing. His hair – though sticky – curls around his ears in a comely fashion, with pedigree shine.

The dancehall, the butcher's shop, and the general store all greet him with closed shutters and fading signage: Plethora is half shut up. There's a fever burning through the population, the innkeeper tells Mancino, and it's cutting down the youngest and the old. If it would only rain, he sighs, at least they'd die clean and cool. Mancino strikes out and asks the gravediggers if they're in the market for a new horse, but they curse him for tramping over babies' graves and he leaves after stating a few opinions of his own.

Last night's fever dreams have left him randy. Down a side street he finds an agreeable woman with almost a full set of teeth, and he visits her room for a few minutes of rummaging. He is not an imaginative man, but he hopes he's still sunstruck enough for one more hit of those fabulous, surgical sensations. All he gets is a moment's relief and a throb behind his eyes from dehydration. Later, he tries a man. The rough-hewn farm boy treats him nicer than he treated the whore, and it's something akin to the strange dream, if only in a mechanical sense.

What are you doing with your life? his brain asks of him at the crucial moment. Hangover philosophy. The worst.

After he extracts himself from the stable – plus a few coins from the dozing man's wallet – he is accosted by a beggar sitting on the porch of a boarded-up house. The poor specimen is a noseless victim of Venus, and he shakes a can with a penny in it, though Mancino suspects the tremor is involuntary. Mancino likes beggars. If a town has vagrants, it means he's not at the bottom of the pile.

"Stranger, hey," the man calls. "You on your way to the Lizard?"

"Some shrine, right?"

The beggar nods, earnest as a drunk. "I don't want your money. No, when you get there, will you tell them I've always been a devotee? In my way? I mean, I've never been out there, but my old man did, and he was a churchgoing man, don't get me wrong, but he always maintained, *always*, 'til the day he died—"

Mancino interrupts. "They'd buy horses at this shrine, you think?"

The man wipes at the flared rim of his single nostril. "What's it eat, your horse?"

"Oats, apples, whatever I give it." Mancino scowls. "It's a horse."

At this, the beggar breaks into a dry cackle. Mancino leaves him to his delirium. He has to get rid of the spare horse. If by some miracle the priest's girl has followed him to Plethora, she's sure to ask around about a man with one steed too many, and he's drawn enough attention to himself already.

Only it's hot and dry, and the empty saloon is making eyes at him.

The beer is bad, and after the second glass he scoots into an alley to throw up. He leans against the wall, wiping the sweat from his eyes, and pauses, squinting. In the puddle of ejected ale, something stirs. At first he takes it for one of the bright little snakes that did for the priest, and he steps back. But the skin of the thing is like black glass, untouched by the red dust of Plethora. It slips through the saloon's shadow, a pristine string of jet beads tugged by an unseen hand. Alarmed by its speed, Mancino retreats. The alcohol has barely touched his blood, but he swears the creature loses its shape as it glides away, becoming insubstantial, as if shedding its shining carapace in favour of a dirty grey vapour. Mancino remembers cold mornings in the mountains when his breath puffed from his nostrils.

He resolves to quit drinking, in this town at least.

★   ★   ★

He is twenty-five and his children number three. It is puzzling to Mancino how impatient Maria is with the little ones, how she seems to find so little joy in her life on the farm. Mater dolorosa. When she sweeps the floors, the children cling to her legs, heavy and tumescent. She never expresses pride in her handsome husband, nor their little home. She prepares the spezzatino for supper with all the delight of a prisoner picking hemp.

He spies her standing in the arid riverbed one morning, at the deepest part where the water once flowed at the level of her eyes. Standing there in the dress she's mended a hundred times, doing nothing. Saying nothing.

There is an itching in his boots.

★   ★   ★

Garlands of dried gourds cross the main street from the rooftops, casting grimacing shadows in the deepening twilight. He's glaring back at them, wondering what he's still doing here, when a voice startles him.

"I figured your bones'd be picked clean by now."

His hackles rise. Detritus is smoking her long pipe on the front porch of the drugstore, watching him with a wry smile he does not feel inclined to return.

"Were you in on it?" he demands.

She sucks on the pipe, allowing a tendril of smoke to slither from the corner of her lips. "No. But I heard. I can't control how my babies turn out once I set 'em free." She sniffs, jerks her chin. "Ned got his, if you want to know."

A nudge of disappointment. Mancino wanted the pleasure of strangling Ned himself. "Who shot him?"

She snorts; it's not a bad guess. "I dropped him off at the infirmary earlier today. It's the fever. I found him forty miles east in a miners' encampment. The others abandoned him. Here's the first town with beds available." She nods at a passing wagon, wobbling its way to the cemetery. "The wells are good as dry. Anyone with a lick of sense left long ago."

"You should've left Ned to rot."

"I care about my babies, little monsters though they may be." Under the porch light, she considers him. "You look good."

"I slept."

The infirmary windows are shuttered for the night. Ned never could sleep in anything but pitch darkness. In happier times, he would wrap his neckerchief around his head and Mancino would delight in making obscene gestures at him until the other man grinned. *I can hear your evil thoughts, you little dago.*

"Which room is he in?"

Detritus rolls her dark eyes. "Come on now, Mancino…"

"I want to say goodbye."

"I have a job for you. Figure I'll need an escort, being the delicate female that I am. I'm heading out to see the Lizard."

She tosses him a folded map. He sees Plethora, a cluster of farmsteads against the yellow vastness of the desert, fringed by distant hills. Far out into the sands, he sees it marked with a black spiral coiled up like a sleeping gecko – the Lizard. An eight-day journey if his beer-sore brain has the calculations right. How interesting could a lizard honestly be?

Detritus sucks at her pipe. "I'll buy your spare horse, too."

He has nothing better to do. Only one piece of business to attend to.

★   ★   ★

Mancino slinks into the infirmary, a handkerchief over his nose and mouth. Hanging bunches of herbs give the place an apothecary odour, but not enough to overpower the animal stink of decay. A dried pufferfish dangles from a ceiling beam, glass eyes agog, while a taxidermy crocodile, small enough to cradle, grins at the scene.

He finds Ned upstairs in a back room. It's him, all right, laid out like a dead man. Mancino's first instinct is to snatch the pillow and crush it into the man's face, but Ned hears his boots on the floorboards and cracks open one green eye.

"There you are, you little dago."

Ned's clammy face breaks into that smile they shared so often, stealing moments in caves and bars and stables. "That's a nice tan you got," he adds. Mancino detects the rattle of water on his lungs.

"You left me to die."

"Boo hoo. I was sick of you. Always was a do-nothing, take-what-you-can... barnacle." Ned pauses, frowns. "You didn't tell me you remarried."

"What?"

"Her."

Ned's fever-bright eyes travel over Mancino's shoulder. There is no one there.

Mancino won't let Ned weasel out of it. "I never even got my final share."

Ned laughs weakly. "That last post office? You hung back where you figured you'd be safe. Benny took a bullet in the thigh 'cause of you. It went green. Green!" He jabs at his eyes, the same cold jade as Mancino's, the reason Detritus brought them together. "You spread nothing but shit wherever you go."

He sounds like Mancino's mother.

In a surge of rage, Mancino lunges. Only then does he notice the shape of the gun Ned is pointing at him under the sheet. As the blast deafens him, he swears he sees the bullet sail through the air like a stately bumblebee. Shock, he supposes; his brain slowing in dumb surprise at the unfairness of being murdered by his old friend twice in one week.

Mancino knows there's something up when the bullet turns a corner mid-air. He gapes, ears ringing, as it picks up speed, ricochets off the wall and is flung back in the direction it came from, catching Ned's jaw in a spray of blood and bone.

As Ned falls back, he's trying to speak, his arm flailing, pointing at nothing.

★   ★   ★

Mancino is twenty-six, watching the tiny figure of his father ride the mule out over the badlands. It hasn't rained for nine weeks. The fields are barren, but

Maria is expecting for the fourth time. Mancino's father speaks infrequently and cries when he thinks no one can hear him. It's always been his way, but now he's taken to riding out into the wastes to scream.

The old man's howls echo in the impassive caves. It is Christmas Day, and on Christmas Day in Italy, everyone knows any baby born will become a werewolf. Mancino smokes on the hill, listening to his father cursing Christ for withholding the rain he needs, telling Him He is a werewolf, consuming tithes and praise, giving nothing in return.

Mancino's youngest son stumbles over on stubby legs, intrigued by the distant noise. "Babbo cry?"

Crying won't fix anything. In the woodshed, Mancino has stashed his saddlebags with some clothes, a couple of fennel sausages, and whatever money was under the loose floorboard in the bedroom. It'll take Maria a week before she notices the mule is missing, let alone her husband.

★   ★   ★

He flees the infirmary like a man pursued by the devil, but no one tries to stop him. It is as though the rest of the patients are under ether. Even the physician grinding his mortar and pestle keeps his rheumy eyes on his work. When Mancino tumbles out into the street, Detritus is there in her long coat, preparing the horses for the journey.

"Satisfied?" she asks neutrally. He realises she never heard the shot. He feels eyes on him, and whips around, but it's only the woman he tumbled earlier, leaning against the general store with her shawl loose around her shoulders. That missing front tooth is repugnant, he thinks, staring. A black hole in her sallow face. There is something behind it, billowing and fibroid.

"We'd better get going," he mutters.

★   ★   ★

The gourd fields of Plethora are a sorry sight. Even the rats don't bother with the crisp, colourless husks. As Mancino rides through the furrows, followed by Detritus, a shabby rabbit thumps a warning, *pum-pum-pum*, against the parched earth.

The journey is long, and Mancino was never one for idle chitchat. Above him only sky; below him, the sweating hide of the stolen horse. Half-dreaming, Mancino's brain slides away to thoughts of the trick box he took from the priest's tent. How unfair that it turned out to be empty. In his reverie he tosses it into the sea and watches it dissolve like a paper boat. Under the sun's glare the seawater rises into clouds blowing back over the land, over the mountains where he was born. The clouds burst into the rainfall his father prayed for, rolling like sweat down the foothills and into the arteries of the rivers passing once more into the sea. He sees the whole cycle forming a great ring over the earth like a snake devouring its own tail.

He could have been a hundred miles away by now, drinking wine in a good suit. Doesn't he deserve a little luck?

They camp for the night. A ravine has risen up around them, the same guilty red as dried blood. Detritus hitches the horses to a dead tree and starts clearing the ground for a fire.

Mancino sniffs the air. "If I were *banditto*, this is where I'd wait for travellers."

Detritus snorts. "You are *banditto*."

"We should move on."

"No one's going to bother us."

She seems sure of it, but he keeps his gun close all the same. The sky is a vast canopy draining blue to indigo. He lies on his back to look at the stars, imagining them as diamonds he can pluck one by one and stuff into his pack. Robbing God, wouldn't that be something?

Later, as their stew bubbles on the fire, he asks: "Why'd you care about this Lizard anyway?"

"People in these parts used to make the journey and pay their respects." She keeps her eyes on the stew pot. "Lately I've been having these… thoughts."

"Bad dreams?"

"Why, what dreams you been having?"

He stiffens, like she's caught him with his hand in her purse. "I don't dream."

In the firelight, her skin shines like oil. He makes to kiss her. It would pass the time, drown the clamour in his head and guts. But her hand is on his chest, gently pushing him away.

"You're my baby, remember?"

They eat in silence. Somewhere above, a bobcat revs and grunts, but the fire keeps it away. Detritus spits a chunk of gristle. "Back at Plethora, in the good old days, they used to make this pumpkin curry. Roasted seeds sprinkled all over like stars. I'd shoot a man for some of that curry right now."

"No one in this country knows how to eat."

"You've never been to Plethora. Not when it was worth it. People came, and never left. That good."

Mancino picks his teeth. "Everybody leaves."

The map is spread open by her boots. He sees the sea, the edge of it, a slice of goading green.

*　　*　　*

He wakes just in time to roll over before he throws up.

Detritus, feeding the horses in the dawn light, chuckles silently. "We ate the same shit last night. Don't you blame my cooking."

He wipes his mouth with his sleeve. "That sickness back in Plethora – is this how it starts?"

Her smile disappears. She pats the horse's flank. "Nah."

He's cold despite the sun peeking over the mountains. Their camp is in a valley where once a river carved a course through the land. He finds himself thinking of Ned and his ancient ocean again. It's hard to reconcile that old friend with the man inhaling his own blood in that infirmary bed. Harder still to consider how it happened.

Best not to dwell. That sort of thing leads to screaming alone in the badlands.

Detritus interrupts his thoughts: "Can you ride?"

He growls at her, and they are on their way.

*　　*　　*

They're a few days into the journey when they cross a railroad dividing the plain. The ground would usually be dotted with brittlebush and sand verbena at this time of year, flowering yellow and pink. All that's left are last season's tumbling brushes tossing empty seed shells to the cracked earth. Detritus suggests they follow the train tracks for a while; kinder for the horses on the cleared ground.

They ride in silence. The dancing haze of the horizon promises towering temples and fountains, but Mancino knows better than to hope for such things. Late in the day, they come to the site of a train wreck. The engine and its carriages have come off the rails. They sprawl there, rusting in the heat. A herd of wild horses gather at the metal carcass, all ribs and rolling eyes, and as Mancino slowly rides past, he swears he can hear their great yellow teeth grinding on the steel like it's a sweet mountain of hay.

A shiver passes through him. *"Che cazzo?"*

"Weird, huh?"

He looks at Detritus. She's staring ahead, as if she's seen the strange spectacle already and would rather not repeat the experience.

"You've not felt it? Empty sensation," she goes on. "Like a hole in the gut. Things haven't been right for a long time." She casts her dark eyes over the wild horses, working together to tear a sheet of steel from the train's carcass. "A while back, someone stole something from the shrine."

"Anyone we know?"

"Not our type of thief. There was... a relic, I guess you could call it. Meddling folks confiscating something they didn't approve of, or didn't understand. About a year ago, I caught wind of rumours the loot was buried someplace in the desert, like the thieves were planning to come back for it when the heat was off."

"How valuable?"

"Money?" Detritus snorts. "You ever see a shark pay for something? Or a whale, for that matter? Forty feet long and seventy tonnes, old as God, worried about what something's worth?"

Mancino thinks she's touched by the sun. "And these thieves – they come back for their relic?"

"They sent people who'd know what to do with it. By then, the harvest had failed. The rains never came. Out-of-towners stopped coming to the fairs and the dances, so the businesses went under. People left. The ones who stayed got sick, or just sick of trying."

He recalled the innkeeper, what he said about the cook and his burden. "That's just life."

"And that over there…" She nods grimly at the wild horses, fighting now over a flaking fragment of wheel and piston. "Is that just life to you?"

He always did hate it when she talked like she knew something he didn't.

"Thou breakest the heads of leviathan in pieces, and gavest him to be meat to the people inhabiting the wilderness." She catches his quizzical look with seriousness. "I'm a preacher's daughter."

"You're full of shit is what you are," he says, and turns his face away from the wreckage. For another long mile, he swears he can still hear that wretched metallic crunching.

★   ★   ★

They make camp at an oasis. Boot prints decorate the sand around the mounds of tall cacti. People have been here before them, and recently.

"You should bathe," Detritus tells him. "If you'll pardon my honesty."

"They particular at this shrine?"

"You'd wear a clean shirt to the Vatican."

Mancino grins. "It's like you don't know me at all."

She busies herself picking rocks of the same size and colour to line their fire pit. Rocks, old socks, people: she always did feel the need to match things up. Mancino wonders what could be troubling her enough to send her eight days deep into the desert to consult some hokey oracle. He knows she was born down in the South with no idea of her own grandparents' names or faces. She talked about it once when Ned passed a bottle around the campfire. Must be nice, having no past hanging around your neck. Mancino's ancestors had lived and died on that pitiful farm in the foothills since the time of Caesar. Some nights he could feel them crowding into the yard to peer at him and mutter their grievances; how the fields had gone fallow and the house was a sty. Between that and Maria wordlessly haunting their dusty rooms, it's a wonder he didn't shoot himself.

He's sweating an absurd amount. He replenishes his canteen and downs it, wincing as the cold spring water coats the heat of his insides, pulsing like an oncoming headache.

"They say there's no rain in these parts?" he asks Detritus.

"Not for a long time."

He squints up at the clear sky. "I feel it, though. I feel rain."

★   ★   ★

A coyote is singing in the dawn. Its hitching cries wrap themselves around Mancino like a thread and tug him from his fitful sleep. His clothes cling with sweat, and his guts clench in time with his heartbeat. He thinks of the slaughtered pigs hanging in his father's barn, their exposed bowels alive with tapeworms. He tries to push the repulsive image aside, but it's replaced by a memory of Maria in childbed; the amniotic tang in the hot air; the amphibian kick of the baby's slick purple legs.

His retching wakes Detritus. She stands over him with a look he can't quite read.

"I told you I'm sick," Mancino snarls.

"You're not sick." She rubs the dust from her hair and helps him stand. She points to the yellow horizon where the heat makes dancing shapes. "See that ridge? A day's ride. Then we're there."

"I'm not weak." He spits into the dirt as he wrenches free of her, tasting salt so strong he can feel his lips pucker. "*Vaffanculo*, woman!"

The impudent heifer has the nerve to look affronted. But with a couple of blinks of her great dark eyes, she's in control again. She regards him, from the peeling soles of his stolen boots to the sweat rolling down his brow. She huffs. "Better hope you're not."

★   ★   ★

They are eight days west of Plethora when they finally see it.

There's an encampment up ahead, two dozen weather-beaten tents pitched in a semi-circle around what looks to Mancino like a wide, deep crater. He stands in his stirrups, shielding his eyes from the spiteful midday sun. It's not like any shrine Mancino has seen before; no statues, no priests. He thinks he spots someone emerge from one of the tents, but the figure either ducks back inside or was a trick of the heat.

"Is that—"

"The Lizard," Detritus answers. "Almost."

"I can't go in."

"Nah, you're not flaking on me."

"I'm going to shit myself." He's not exaggerating. Everything feels tender, his flesh too large for his skin. Sweat prickles down his spine, hot and cold at once. When he dismounts, his gut lurches like there's a ball of lead inside, and he groans so loud it startles his horse. "I'll wait here. Find a bush to squat behind."

"The hell you will. What was it you said yesterday, about not being weak?"

He grumbles, but they hitch the horses together at the camp's entrance. He can hear people inside, talking softly. The horses dip their long noses into the sorry drinking trough prepared for them in the shade. Some shrine. After eight days of travelling, Mancino was expecting more than two dozen tents and some whispering. He's about to make a joke to Detritus when a wave of nausea hits him, and he jostles the horses aside to get to the brackish water, splashing his burning face.

When he's steady enough to look up, water running down his neck, he freezes. Between the gaps in the tents, the view into the crater is clear. Mancino wipes his eyes to be sure it's not a fever playing havoc with his brain. Lizard, they call it? It's a skeleton. Longer than a whale, coiled up like a snake, it's a bleached cathedral. A man could stand inside the ribs and reach up without touching them. Great spindle-fingered hands and feet spread out in the sand as if the creature is swimming through the dunes. The skull is propped open with flaming torches, the long pincer snout bristling with crocodilian teeth.

The leaden thing in his gut churns with recognition.

Mancino flinches. He forces his gaze back to the trough with its rusted edges and reflections of the horses either side of him. And of Maria. Maria at the table in their farmhouse kitchen, feeding their youngest, her cheeks wan and her eyes dull as if the baby is contentedly draining her life's blood. No, he was right to leave. She was faulty, not put together like other women. His parched lips part to tell her so, and in the water's surface he sees the flapping of his tongue, black and billowing. Startled, he cries out, and a flash of light from the entrance of his throat sends him scuttling back from the trough. He's blinded, scrabbling for his gun with both hands—

Hands on his shoulders. "Hey. Steady now."

Detritus is gently taking the gun from his shaking hands.

"When I was thirteen—" he gasps. "I was sent— to watch the sheep—"

"The wolf and your brother, yeah. Very sad."

Something shunts inside him. He retches, bringing up nothing but a grey dribble of sputum. Detritus is unfazed.

"We do this every time you have a drink, sweetheart," she says, rubbing his back as she steers him away from the horses. "The Saint Christopher you pawned before your mama had her last rites, and how your daddy had a fall in the badlands and froze to death in the night, and how you up and left your wife and kids without two pennies to rub together and none of it was your fault. Honestly, when I heard Ned and the Monsters strung you up and left you, I assumed they'd had enough of your whining."

She leads him through the shrine's canvas entrance. Mancino totters, rubbing at his smarting eyes. He'd forgotten about his father. Tossed that memory somewhere deep and lightless along with the rest.

In the crater below, the Lizard's bones are dazzling in the sunlight. The sweat is pouring down his face now, dribbling hot into his eyes and mouth. People are emerging from the tents: men and women and a few wide-eyed children. He stumbles on the shale, kicking up a shard of white shell.

"This was the ocean once," he mumbles, his tongue dry and thick against his salty teeth.

Detritus is half carrying him, and he tries to pull away, but when he opens his mouth to curse her, there's a flash from inside and the assembled people cry out and surge for him, pulling him deeper into the pit.

There are too many of them. He can't see. Someone shouts to be gentle with him, and he feels his feet leave the ground with the help of a dozen hands.

Detritus' voice against his ear: "Those dreams I talked about. She told me to look for a girl burying a preacher in the desert."

"Who did?" There's another blast of light from inside his mouth, and the people carrying him moan with excitement.

"I bring people together, sweetheart, you know that. Look how happy you've made all these folks."

Panic surges. *"Che cazzo dici?"*

"You let her out," she tells him, shouting above the rising din of voices. "They stole the spirit from her bones. They bound her in that box and they were going to take her to the sea and throw her in, but you stopped them, didn't you?"

"Who are these people?" His heartbeat is a roaring tide inside his ears. "They worship a... a fish?"

"I don't pretend to know all the ins and outs," she says, "but the men of science are saying there was a race of dragons a million years ago, or somesuch. Land ones, sea ones, things that could fly. This desert was her ocean. She doesn't want any other – she belongs here. And all the while the people here take care of her, she'll take care of them. You get it?"

He doesn't. But as they stumble down the beaten track to the crater's base, someone is peeling off his jacket and sodden shirt, and the relief is almost too much. The Lizard's incisors are stalactites bearing down on him, and his heart lurches with the same stupefying fear he felt back in the infirmary, watching that bullet take a corner mid-air like it had its own mind. Spirits in boxes, stuffed crocodiles watching over dying men's beds, no – Mancino needs a doctor. Strange fingers struggle with the fastenings of his trousers, but when the cotton tears, he barely notices. He falls on his knees. The Lizard's clean, dead jaws accept him as he crawls inside, curling with his knees to his chest as his guts continue to fight like a rat in a sack.

He is dimly aware of Detritus crouching outside the row of teeth. She's packing her pipe, chatting in his general direction as if they're enjoying a cordial evening by the fireside. "The moment I first saw you in that bar, I said to myself, 'What a waste of skin that one is'. If it weren't for those eyes, I'd have passed you over for useless. Which would've been a mistake, as it turns out."

Mancino's bladder gives way. He puts a hand between his legs. It comes away bright with blood, and when he finds his voice, it's shrill with fear. "It's killing me."

Detritus smiles around her pipe, as if he's simple. "Why would she kill her own bride?"

Someone shrieks and claps. Mancino tries to lever himself onto his back, but his limbs won't take his weight. Something is forcing its way out of him, solid and smooth against the slick contours of bowel and throat. The applause gathers weight: a hard carapace clicks against his back teeth as one of the things ventures up and out. He gags, but the shape quickly dissipates, becomes insubstantial as it spreads against his tongue and past his lips like a wet, fibrous cloud of cheesecloth.

Four, five, six. As more of them wriggle free of him, the crowd keeps count. More maddening still, someone starts to play a penny whistle. The people seem to know the tune, and soon the air is hazy with sand where their dancing kicks it up. The refrain whirls and repeats until it is all Mancino can hear or even think of, replacing the thoughts inside his own head as the strange expulsions reach double digits. His world has shrunk to the size of the Lizard's bone mouth, sheltering him, keeping him close.

They are emitting from him steadily now, unfurling from his every tender opening. They bob into the sky where they cluster together: fat black clouds, heavy with rain, flashing joyous white lightning against the hard blue sky.

With time, the blood on his thighs and chin dries and cracks like desert mud. The people gathered around the Lizard's bones dab their tears and give thanks for the receptacle of his body. After many hours, when the sun is swaddled in cloud and the gentle rain opens his aching eyes, he can no longer see Detritus anywhere.

THE DAUGHTERS OF CANAAN

Kurt Newton

Everywhere Mary-Alice looked she saw dog-headed men. There were dog-headed men on the city bus that she rode to work each night. Tonight, there were at least three that she could count. She sat near the front of the bus and watched them in the driver's mirror. They disguised themselves well, because no one else on the bus seemed to notice them. In fact, when Mary-Alice gathered the courage to turn and look one of them in the eyes, their head would reshape and look human again.

When her stop arrived, she hurried out onto the sidewalk. Fortunately for her, the building in which she worked was less than a block away and well lit. The doorman let her in.

"Good evening, Ma'am." The doorman tipped his hat.

"Thank you, Gerard. Good evening to you, too." Mary-Alice hurried in, risking a glance over her shoulder to see if the dog-headed men had followed her.

But no. The sidewalks were free of them. Mary-Alice breathed a sigh of relief.

Gerard closed the door behind her and locked it. Gerard was an older gentleman. He had been the doorman for this particular office building since before Mary-Alice was hired. His head was far from dog-headed. In fact, he had a nice round head with soft eyes and a kind smile.

"There's a fresh pot of coffee in the lunchroom," Gerard told her. "And some superb cinnamon buns from the bakery down the street." He nodded his permission.

"You spoil me, Gerard." Mary-Alice unbuttoned her coat and headed for the maintenance closet.

"Somebody has to," said Gerard with a chuckle under his breath.

Mary-Alice reappeared minutes later pushing her cleaning cart, her hair tied in an unglamorous knot on top of her head, her coat exchanged for a light blue smock. She aimed her cart toward the elevator.

"Don't forget the cinnamon buns," said Gerard with a wink and a smile. Mary-Alice tried not to blush.

For Mary-Alice, her job at the office building was her sanctuary. During her shift, dog-headed men rarely entered her thoughts. The only things on Mary-Alice's mind were empty waste bins, vacuumed carpets, shiny desks and clean, well-stocked washrooms.

Each floor had its own janitor's closet (all except the penthouse, where Mary-Alice wasn't allowed access). The closets supplied the toiletries for each bathroom. She could safely put the argument over which bathrooms were messiest to rest – ladies' or gentlemen's? The answer was both. Each had their challenges and each were equally disgusting, at times. People were people.

Except when they revealed their true identities. Such as the dog-headed men who revealed themselves to Mary-Alice.

There was a time when Mary-Alice believed there was a reason why the dog-headed men appeared to her and her alone. Although it frightened her, it made her feel kind of special in a way. But then she realised she had never told anyone about what she had seen. Perhaps there were others like her, only they, too, chose not to speak of their experiences. There might be a whole group of people out there living in fear of dog-headed men. A conspiracy of silence. So far, Mary-Alice had not been physically harmed by any of these creatures. Who were they? What did they want? Why her? These were all questions that worried her and reshaped her waking life into one of nightmare, and, in her darkest hours, forced her to question her own sanity. Which was the prevailing reason why she kept this horror to herself.

But tonight Mary-Alice was not thinking about any of that. Instead, she was lost in the pleasant monotony of spraying and dusting, tidying and bagging, and the rhythmic dance of vacuuming. The music she played that streamed from her MP3 player to the buds in her ears also helped. She preferred the music of the 70s. It was a happier, more innocent time for her, before the tragedy came and took her mother from the Earth and left her father in a near-vegetative state for more than a decade. As she vacuumed one of the many narrow conference rooms, the overhead lights began to flicker. She turned toward the doorway and saw Gerard pointing to his watch. Mary-Alice smiled and stood the vacuum upright.

"Break time!" said Gerard.

"I'll be right there," said Mary-Alice. She pulled the buds out of her ears and stuffed them into the pocket of her smock.

★   ★   ★

The lunchroom was typical of any small corporate break room. There were vending machines along one wall, a table outfitted with hot coffee and tea, and a microwave for reheating food. Gerard sat at their usual table, the cinnamon buns proudly displayed. "Twenty seconds in the microwave. Magnificent!" He kissed his fingertips like a French chef. "So? What's new?"

Mary-Alice thought about the increasing frequency of the dog-headed men and was tempted to tell Gerard everything. But she decided to broach the subject in the way a student might ask a professor, out of curiosity rather than concern.

"What do you know about dog-headed men?"

Gerard laughed. "Dog-headed men?"

"I know, it's silly. Never mind."

"Mary-Alice, no question is ever silly. A question is a thirst for knowledge. Now, let's see…" Gerard brought a hand to his chin and adopted a more serious tone. "Did you know that Saint Christopher was said to have had the head of a dog in his sinful youth? Only when he was baptised did his head change to what we see on all those Saint Christopher medals people wear."

Mary-Alice thought about the dog-headed men she'd seen and wondered if they were somehow caught between a sinful life and a righteous one. But then weren't we all? she thought. She sipped her coffee.

"No?" said Gerard, humoured by Mary-Alice's response or lack thereof.

Mary-Alice smiled. She stared at Gerard. His eyes were the kindest she'd ever seen. Surely, he could be trusted. "You're going to think I'm crazy."

Gerard took a bite of cinnamon bun. His eyes lit up, intrigued. "Go on."

Mary-Alice took a deep breath, then blurted it out before she could stop herself. "I've seen them."

"Who?" A morsel of sugary confection clung to Gerard's lip before his tongue darted out to retrieve it.

"The dog-headed men. I've seen them."

Gerard stared at her as he licked his fingers. He sighed. "You're not supposed to tell," he said, his voice hardening. "They will come after you now."

"So, they *are* real?" Mary-Alice grabbed her chest to keep her heart from pounding through.

Gerard burst into laughter. "Mary-Alice…" Tears rolled down his cheeks. When he realised she was serious, he quickly retracted his grin, unsuccessfully. "I've hurt your feelings. Forgive me. I thought you were joking."

"No, I've seen them," said Mary-Alice, "and they've seen me. What should I do?"

Gerard struggled to answer. He pushed the cinnamon buns away to achieve a better level of concentration. "Well, fortunately for you, I am a loyal friend and good listener. My advice is: tell no one, for they may not be as understanding as I. I will research the subject further and maybe together we can get to the bottom of it. Until then, mum's the word." He pursed his lips and pretended to lock them shut with an invisible key. Then he smiled. "Did you know the expression 'mum's the word' has nothing to do with the mummies of ancient Egypt but originated in the fourteenth century, and is closely related to the word 'mime' which means to keep silent?"

Mary-Alice was always amazed by Gerard's breadth of knowledge. It was as if he had lived several lifetimes.

★   ★   ★

When Mary-Alice's shift ended, it was time for her to go home and brave another bus ride. Something she dreaded. The morning sun was just creeping into the city as she waited at the curb.

Behind her was an alley. Along one wall of the alley sat a series of large cardboard boxes and over-stuffed shopping carts. There were noises coming from one of the boxes: growls and scratching. Mary-Alice tried not to look but fear compelled her to. She gripped her carry bag and dug her fingernails into the canvas. She glanced toward the alley one more time.

One of the cardboard boxes bulged near its entrance and a large dog-headed man crawled out from inside. It immediately locked eyes with Mary-Alice and began approaching on all fours. It arched its back and howled.

Mary-Alice was frozen in place, her chest heaving. The creature's howl sounded like the cries of the damned. Mary-Alice was about to run when the bus pulled up in front of her, its brakes shrieking, its doors offering escape. When at last she sat and the bus doors were closed, she chanced a look into the alley.

What she saw was only a homeless man standing, stretching in the morning light.

★   ★   ★

Mary-Alice Tuckworth lived on the fourth floor of an old apartment building. Her neighbours often cracked their doors to see who it was in the hallway when she passed. Mary-Alice would usually greet them with a wave or a whispered, "Good morning," to which they would respond with a *tsk* or an eyeroll. She didn't know any of her neighbours' names, except those shouted during arguments or when the Super came to issue an eviction notice. Which was fine with her.

This morning she made it down the hallway without a single door opening.

With her apartment door closed and locked behind her, Mary-Alice could at last relax. This was her domain. It wasn't much, but every morning it felt like she was returning from the wilds of the city to a den of peace and solitude.

The first thing she did after kicking off her shoes was put the water on for some tea.

The apartment was spare. A visitor might even say it was cold. There was very little colour. The furniture was two decades old, the upholstery patternless, as if the pigments had been drained from the weave. Lampshades, curtains, paintings on the wall – all purely functional. The only thing out of place was the bookcase. There were no books on the shelves, only photographs, framed portraits going back in time to the beginning of photography. Her family: mother, father, aunts and uncles, grandparents and great-grandparents – a lineage of Tuckworths dating back to the late 1800s. Some of the frames were just as old and likely more valuable than all the other items in her apartment. But, for Mary-Alice, her most valued possessions were the photos themselves – the faces that looked out at her from across time, that watched over her – reminding her of her lineage: her family, of which she was the last living member.

A change of clothes, a cup of herbal tea while sitting in the well-worn recliner… her eyes soon closed and sleep came like a soothing mist creeping up out of the darkness. Her dreams often took her to places she had never been. Other cities around the world, smaller towns and outposts on barren, forbidding landscapes. She attributed these 'flights of fancy,' as she liked to call them, to the presence of her ancestors' photographs and her own imagination conjuring what life might have been like for each of them. After all, she was the sum of the blood and the genes, and perhaps even the memories, of all who had come before her. She didn't know why she believed this, but it was a comforting thought in a life that was, for the most part, unadventurous and, at most times, uneventful.

Except when she encountered the dog-headed men.

Thankfully, the dog-headed men had yet to populate her dreams. But she could sense them, lurking in the shadows, waiting just beyond the periphery of her vision. She knew it was only a matter of time before they showed themselves and she would learn their true nature.

Today, her dreams took her to the hot, dry grasslands of the African savannah. She and her clan were stalking their prey: a wildebeest. It was large, muscular, meaty. The grass protected them like a shield. The breeze carried their scent downwind. Through an invisible communication, the moment came and they struck. Mary-Alice could feel the movement of her body through the grass, feel her heart pumping as she rushed with an explosive burst toward the unsuspecting animal. The next thing she felt were her jaws sinking into warm meat, crushing the bones beneath, and the taste of blood flooding her senses…

She awoke panting, beads of sweat on her brow and an uncomfortable, yet not unpleasant, ache in her loins.

She went into the bathroom and ran the shower. While she undressed, the hot water steamed, returning her to the fog of her dream. Naked, she stepped under the shower head and let the water blanket her with heat and sensation. She reached down and caressed her engorged clitoris. In her mind, she returned to the savannah and replayed the hunt. Moments later, her legs shuddered as she orgasmed.

Afterwards, Mary-Alice looked at herself in the mirror. Her clitoris had always been unusually large, embarrassingly so, appearing, for lack of a better word, like a small, semi-erect penis. In high school, she found reasons not to take showers with the other girls after gym class. As for boyfriends, some found her anomaly repulsive, while others were obsessed with it once it was discovered. After a while, she simply gave up men and focused on pleasing herself when needed.

But as she examined her body, moving her clitoris from side to side, there was one thing for certain. It appeared to be growing larger.

★ ★ ★

"Good evening, Ma'am," said Gerard.

Mary-Alice quickly closed her umbrella and slipped through the doorway. "Thank you, Gerard."

Rain had come to the city, wetting everything with a glistening, clear coat. The rain, however, did not stop the dog-headed men from coming out, showing themselves briefly to Mary-Alice on her evening commute. The rain reminded her of her shower earlier that day and she was reluctant to meet Gerard's eyes for fear of him looking into her soul and seeing her naked. She hurried off to the supply room and got to work.

When break time came, Gerard was waiting for her. Today he had avocado toast and chocolate-almond Danish. "I researched your dog-headed men a bit further," he said, broaching the uncomfortable silence that had developed between them.

"You didn't have to," said Mary-Alice, biting into a piece of avocado toast. "Like you didn't have to bring this. Although, it is scrumptious."

"And full of vitamins K, C, B5, B6, B9, E. Plus potassium. Good food, no matter what it is – as long as it is prepared in a way that preserves its natural nutritional value – is good for you. Good for the soul."

Mary-Alice eyed the Danish with scepticism.

"Even chocolate has its beneficial properties. Almonds. Raw sugar. Sweetness does not automatically demote a snack to junk food status."

Mary-Alice smiled. Gerard had a way of always presenting things in the best light. She lopped off half the Danish and slid it closer. "So, what did you find out?"

"The dog-headed men. Ah, yes. I found many excerpts and accounts from travelogues and encyclopedias. Fascinating subject."

"You make it sound like you have your own personal library."

"I do."

Mary-Alice laughed but this was one of those very few occasions where Gerard was serious.

"You should see it some time."

Mary-Alice blushed.

Gerard broke off a corner of the Danish and popped it into his mouth. "Are you ready for this? Did you know the Egyptian god Set possessed a man's body and the head of a dog? He was master of disorder and warfare. According to Egyptian mythology, Set and his brother, Horus, battled all the time. On one occasion Set was said to have sexually violated his own brother. On another occasion he tore out one of Horus's eyes. A whole cult of worship evolved around this jolly fellow. Imagine that."

Mary-Alice was still recovering from her blush. She tried to avert her eyes from Gerard's insightful stare, but to no avail. Gerard continued.

"Another fun fact. The Egyptian dog, the Basenji, is the only breed of dog that doesn't bark. It's relatively mute."

Mary-Alice nodded, mesmerised.

"Did you know there was a sacredness to being mute? Monks went years without speaking. It was a purification process – a way to eliminate the outer voice so one can focus on the inner voice, which, in ancient circles, was the voice of God."

"I would very much like to see your library," Mary-Alice said. She felt she was committing to some kind of date and felt a girlish swirl tickle her stomach.

Gerard sized her up. It was as if he was peering into her very soul. He nodded. "Soon," he said.

★   ★   ★

The cavern was as large as a multi-storey home. She could hear the drip of water. She could smell the sweet aroma of grass bedding.

The clan was resting after a night's hunt, the daylight a golden shimmer outside the cave entrance.

Restless, she ventured deeper into the cavern. A scent caught her nose and she followed it, until she came upon a pile of bones where the stripped skulls of the clan's enemies stared at her. Her nostrils flared and she instinctively bared her teeth, even though the bones posed no threat.

She sniffed at the pile and found a morsel to sink her teeth into. The taste of blood and fetid meat filled her senses...

Mary-Alice awoke. In the past several days she had experienced an increase in the dreams that visited her with visions of hunting and killing. It was as if some violent alter-ego had infiltrated her psyche. When she awoke, she was exhausted. Only hot tea and a long shower seemed to relax and cleanse her mind of the awful images and restore her energy. That and sex. Self-gratification untangled any remaining knots the dreams may have left in her.

However, with her hyperactive libido, came a marked increase in the size of her clitoris. So much so she began to question whether she should see a doctor about it. It could be the onset of a tumour. Or an imbalance of some hormone she wasn't aware of. Either way, it worried her as much as it excited her – this newfound plaything that now rivalled the size of an average man's penis when engorged – albeit, thinner and without foreskin. It was also extremely sensitive. Mary-Alice took to wearing two pairs of panties to keep it trussed in place to avoid any unplanned stimulation.

Meanwhile, the sightings of the dog-headed men had also increased to the point where she kept her head down at all times when she was outside, her eyes only lifting to navigate the bus steps or the sidewalk curb. The office building had become as much of an oasis as her apartment, Gerard's understanding eyes and kind smile a refuge she looked forward to every evening.

Like tonight.

Mary-Alice hurried in as Gerard held the door. She had found it harder and harder to meet his eyes as she responded to his pleasantries.

"A beautiful evening, isn't it?" he said with a smile in his voice.

She wanted to say, *I wouldn't know. I can no longer enjoy the evening knowing dog-headed men lurk at every corner!* Instead, she offered a quick glance and an even quicker response. "Yes. Yes, it is."

"Mary-Alice?"

The tone of Gerard's voice stopped her. It possessed a firmness she wasn't used to. "Yes, Gerard?"

"Meet me in the break room at our usual time?"

"Of course," she said. "See you then."

★   ★   ★

When Mary-Alice finally came down to the break room, she noticed a square box on the table where she usually sat. Gerard was waiting for her with a small platter of confections for her to indulge in.

"You have to try the baklava," he said. "The filo is like thin layers of heaven. When you bite into it the honey oozes between your teeth like the sweetest kiss."

"You make it sound so decadent."

"It is. Here – have a bite." Gerard leaned forward. He lifted a piece of the baklava and held it for her, cupping his hand beneath her chin to catch any crumbs.

Gerard's description was accurate and then some. Along with the honey came the woodsy flavour of pistachio and cinnamon spice. Along with another flavour she couldn't place. She took another bite before turning her attention to the box.

"What's this?" she asked.

"That's for you," said Gerard, watching her enjoy the pastry as if he'd made it himself.

"What is it? A gift?"

She examined the box. It was about six-by-six inches square and about ten inches tall. It appeared old, made from a fancy type of cardboard once used for hat boxes or for premium grades of liquor.

"No, not a gift. It belongs to you," he said. "Or, I should say, it belongs to your lineage… of which you are the last remaining member. I've been holding onto it all these years, waiting for the right moment to present it to you. From what I see, that moment is now."

Mary-Alice blushed. "I don't understand." She felt the first subtle wave of drowsiness hit her, but she attributed it to the strangeness of Gerard's words, and her recent lack of sleep.

"Did you know that there has been a battle ongoing for centuries between two clans?" he said, launching into another diatribe as if this one was no different than the many historical footnotes he was fond of relating. Only, this time, the glint in his eye was missing, replaced by a seriousness she hadn't witnessed before. "Forgive me, Mary-Alice, but the dog-headed men you have been seeing are, in fact, real. But they are here to protect you."

"Protect me? Protect me from what?"

"Members of the other clan, should they be so bold as to take matters into their own hands. But such breaches in the Code of Succession are rare."

"Clans? Code of Succession? Gerard – you're scaring me. If this is some kind of joke, please tell me now. I don't think I can take much more of what you're saying."

"Then let me prove it to you. Open it." Gerard's eyes flitted to the box. He smiled.

"Okay. But if this is some kind of elaborate prank, I don't think I can forgive you."

Mary-Alice pulled the box closer. She lifted the top flap and peered inside. She then reached in and lifted out a large jar. Inside the jar was a thick fluid, and floating in the fluid was a tubular-shaped thing, at least ten inches long, that looked to be made of flesh.

Another wave of drowsiness hit her. She knew what it was in the jar, but she was too afraid to vocalise it. She'd seen similar jars in the photographs of her ancestors, held in the laps of the women like a prize-winning jar of preserves from a local fair.

"Mary-Alice, for years I have tried to keep your identity a secret. But they are here – those who want to unify the two clans. You have been challenged."

It was all too much. Mary-Alice felt her head spinning. She was close to passing out. A part of her wanted nothing to do with this. Gerard was mistaken; she was not who he said she was. She just wanted to live a normal, boring life without complications. But another part of her, the part that came alive in her dreams, knew she was destined for greatness, knew her ancestors didn't just pass on their special gifts but expected her to use them to their fullest potential.

Mary-Alice tasted blood and realised she had bitten the inside of her mouth. It roused her to action. "When is this supposed to happen?"

Gerard's eyes never left hers. With a dire-sounding sigh, he said, "It is happening as we speak."

The lights grew bright and fuzzy, like the hot sun beating down upon the savannah. Mary-Alice felt the world closing in. Her head felt heavy. She was unconscious before her cheek hit the table.

★   ★   ★

When Mary-Alice awoke, she found herself in an underground arena. Ancient columns stretched from floor to ceiling. There were strange symbols carved into the columns, sculpted profiles emerging from the walls. The noise of many murmuring voices echoed in the large stone chamber. Gerard was by her side, supporting her, as were a cadre of dog-headed men, some of whom she recognised as those she'd seen about the city in recent weeks. Across the arena was another group of dog-headed men, and among them a fierce-looking woman wearing only a plain cloth strip across her breasts and a wider band around her waist.

Mary-Alice looked down and realised she was dressed in the same fashion. She still felt sluggish, as if moving underwater, but another sensation was building, a sensation that was too surreal to be embarrassed about. She turned toward Gerard. "Gerard – what have you done?"

"No, my Queen, this is about what you are about to do. It is time for us to be united."

Gerard stepped forward and raised his hand. A collective howl rose up from Mary-Alice's corner. Across the arena, their second-in-charge stepped forward and raised his hand and a similar howl erupted. Mary-Alice watched as the man's head transformed, brow sloping backward, ears pointing upward, his snout elongating. And then she witnessed the same transformation happen to Gerard – sweet, round-headed Gerard. He was one of them, too.

What happened next came in a flurry of ceremonial preparations. Her 'opponent' was stripped of her clothing. To Mary-Alice's amazement, the woman's clitoris was also large, engorged, pointing downward like a weighty sword. Her seconds surrounded her and began to paint her with mud. Meanwhile, her opponent's 'Gerard' dipped what looked like a pig's tail into a small bucket filled with what looked like blood and marked her forehead and chest with symbols similar to those that appeared on the stone columns.

Mary-Alice felt her own wraps being pulled away. The dog-headed men surrounded her and began painting her in likewise fashion. What Mary-Alice thought was mud was actually faeces; its pungent scent flared her nostrils. Faeces, no doubt, collected by her cornermen and applied as an offering to their Queen. Gerard held a similar bucket of blood and, while speaking in a low monasterial chant, he dipped the pig's tail in and painted a series of symbols on her forehead and across her chest.

"Gerard, I haven't trained for this!"

Gerard's smile still showed through his transformation. He gripped her face. "Oh, but you have, my Queen. Every dream… every scenario you saw yourself in – the wild hunts and the chasing and the killing – was preparation for this moment. Think of your ancestors and they will be with you – in your mind and in your spirit."

There was something in what Gerard had said that struck her deeply, in a place where truth had lain dormant all these years. A place she always knew was there but had never had the need to tap into… until now.

Mary-Alice's anxiety lessened, her breathing slowed, her heart-rate adopted a more regular rhythm. The clash of noises and the raw smells all contributed to elicit an electric feeling that felt as if she were about to burst through her skin.

Mary-Alice looked down. Her clitoris was as large as she had ever seen. Out of fear. Out of excitement. Out of purpose. Her display did not go unnoticed. Howls erupted from her 'pack,' and she felt her own howl, emanating from deep in her body, fill her chest and exit her throat. She let out a volley of shrill yips as the energy of her ancestors inhabited her. Without any external signal or call, the fight began.

Her opponent came at her in a blur. She felt the pressure of several blows, on her ribcage and face, that sent her staggering backwards. She tasted blood and the flavour of it recalled her dreams… that first bite into warm flesh... that rush of hunger flooding in and the wild abandon that followed. She turned that wildness upon her opponent and fought back.

She set her feet and charged forward, landing blow upon blow, arms and legs working in concert as if with a mind of their own. She heard herself growling, deep and feral. She not only wanted to beat this opponent, she wanted to destroy her. She clawed until her fingernails peeled skin. She bit until she tasted the oily bitterness of blood. She fought like the animal she needed to be.

It wasn't until she felt herself being restrained that she realised she had won. Her opponent lay on the floor unconscious, bloodied and battered. Her clitoris had been removed; the place where it had been was now a ragged stump. It was then Mary-Alice realised she had the amputated organ clenched between her teeth.

She was lifted up into the air and carried around the arena on the shoulders of her followers – her disciples – all howling, "Long live the Queen! Long live the Queen!" Gerard merely nodded to her with that look of knowing she had grown accustomed to.

*   *   *

Mary-Alice awoke from a restful sleep in a large king-sized bed. Sunlight streamed in through tall windows. She sat up. She was in what looked like a very old penthouse apartment, based on the height of the ceiling and its ornate ceiling tiles, and the large stone fireplace in the corner with its inlaid filigree and decorative mantle – a luxurious relic of the past.

She was wearing a silk top. She pulled back the covers and saw she was wearing matching silk panties. She felt naked. And a bit confused. *Was it all a dream?* she thought. The jar Gerard had given her? The fight in the underground arena?

She pulled the covers back further and saw the bruising on her legs and arms. Her ribs still ached. Her fingernails had been trimmed down to the cuticles. The violence of the fight – the noise and the brutality – came back to her and she winced.

She heard the rattle of a service tray in the outer room. There came a knock on the bedroom door, then the door opened slightly and Gerard poked his head in. "Good morning," he said. "Breakfast is ready." He disappeared just as quickly.

There was a matching silk robe lying neatly on the upholstered bench at the foot of the bed. She slipped it on and joined Gerard.

"There she is." Gerard bowed. He stood by a circular marble table that was nestled in a breakfast nook bathed in sunlight. On the table was a small bouquet of fresh-cut flowers in a crystal vase, and a breakfast for two: eggs, ham, blood sausage, sliced tomato, home fries, orange juice and a very aromatic tea.

"You don't expect me to eat all that, do you?" said Mary-Alice.

"A queen must maintain her strength."

She sat at the table. The bay window jutted out over the city. The breakfast setting, the surrounding apartment, the nightgown she wore – all of it made her feel majestic, on top of the world. "So, this is the penthouse I was never allowed to enter. Your penthouse, I assume?"

Gerard smiled. "Eat. Then we can talk about the future."

"What about my apartment?"

"Everything you need is here."

She noticed her belongings were now in Gerard's living room: her photographs sat atop a baby grand piano, assembled like an army of guardian angels. Her family. She also noticed, on Gerard's bookshelves, the jars of her ancestors, their contents floating like strange biological specimens.

"We're not staying in New York, are we?"

"No," said Gerard, "we're leaving tomorrow."

"To where?" she asked. But she could already guess by the artifacts hanging on the walls and decorating every niche in the penthouse: tribal masks, carvings of canine deities, handmade musical instruments. She could hear the drums beating across the Serengeti.

"Home," Gerard said, "to reclaim what is rightfully yours."

And Mary-Alice knew that this was just the beginning.

A HOUSE OF WOE AND MYSTERY

Andy Davidson

If she slept, she woke early. Shaken from fragile dreams. The sun broke, and she sat those mornings, like today, in her robe in the living room, alone. She drank a sludge that you could not call coffee, and through the picture window, she watched golden leaves drop one by one from a tree whose classification she had never bothered to know. It would have been so easy, thumbing a few buttons on a screen. But there were no screens now. No buttons.

The last of their cats – the one who stayed after her husband turned the others out – sat on the table by the window, zeroed in on some poor, wretched creature among the pine straw. A rat, maybe. They had rats aplenty. Drawn out of field and sewer to roam the footprints of houses, Pestilence playing pied piper to them all. The cat went out into the neighbour's deadfall across the street, and brought them back from burrows and holes, left them turned inside out on the porch. After all, the humans could not feed themselves. Little offerings on the altar of love, nostrils leaking red. Eyes black and dead as buckshot pellets.

She drank her not-coffee, which had been brewed in a pot over the little firepit they had dug in the dirt beneath the house, after busting through the kitchen floor a few months back. She sat on the couch facing the picture window, the squat ranch house across the way, and thought of random people who had passed in and out of her life like ghosts. A mechanic who had serviced her mother's Oldsmobile thirty years ago, the magnificent way he'd eaten a fast food hamburger on his lunch break, fisting up French fries, jaws working like an oil well. A poet she and her husband had driven to dinner a few years back, on behalf of the Department, long legs in fishnet stockings, a wedding ring yet on her finger, though she claimed it was all over for the poor sap, him unaware and scribbling bad fiction back home, somewhere on Michigan's Upper Peninsula. "There is no man who can satisfy me within a thousand miles," the poet said, over tacos. She'd won a prize of some sort. She forgot which one. Finally, she thought of sex at sixteen. That first, awkward plunging in her parents' boat house up on Lake Minot. How her boyfriend slapped a mosquito on his face when he looked up from between her legs, there on the deck of a pontoon barge.

At the window, on the table, the old cat's tail flicked. Its ears flattened.

Outside, there was a fog.

In it, things crept back and forth. Huge and baleful shapes.

The cat was losing its hair.

She sipped her not-coffee and thought of the early years of their marriage, when she and her husband had still believed this place, a Sixties ranch on Rose Street, to be haunted. Deep-in-the-night knockings, mutter and creak of wood. Skittering in the walls. They lay awake with the bedcovers tugged up and rubbed bare legs together like sticks to make a fire. A few times, he got up to look. The brave husband in sagging boxers and ankle socks. But there was only ever a cat or two or three, skulking around, eyes gleaming in the flashlight beam. Once, in the backyard, a possum, belly heavy with babies.

Suicide, the story went. Some old man shot himself in the guest bedroom, which had become his sick room, the wife no longer capable of sleeping near him for all the hacking. Fevered dreams made him kick her in his sleep. A room with weird stains whorled in the red oak floor, which had been covered up by the previous owners with hideous orange shag. After they bought the place, they'd pulled it up and there it was: a wine-coloured stain in the shape of Australia, confirmation of the rumours, or the closest thing to it, short of a ghost materialising in the hallway at 3:00 a.m., half its head blown away. Which did not happen.

It was an odd house. They learned this over time. Iron water pipes in the crawlspace patched with concrete mix. In the laundry room a second breaker box, only it affected no currents, all the switches thrown. Water stains appearing, from time to time, on the ceiling, no leaks found. Out in the backyard by a muscadine vine, there was a shed, roofed and walled, unfinished inside. The length of every rafter, every stud covered in ten-inch nails, spaced three inches apart. Nothing hung on them, save a single lantern and an old prosthetic leg.

It was all very interesting and made her want to write scary stories. She spun a few up, had the knack, while he – a dull grammarian by trade, a dissector and diagrammer of other men's sentences – loved her and was proud. She won a contest or two. Would have won more, had she only started before people stopped reading stories. Before people stopped reading. Before people stopped.

Do I regret? she wondered, suddenly.

She could not say that she did.

Example: they had turned the cats out not from cruelty; they loved all animals. It was unfair, he argued, to watch them waste and suffer. To allow them to devolve and prey upon one another. Better they risk it out there, where each could stalk and catch and eat its own fill of tiny horrors. She hated how much sense it made. Later, when things got truly bad, they could eat the last of the cat food straight from the tins, he said. Beef in gravy, she imagined, would be the most bearable. Turkey hearts, horrible. Forks or spoons?

In truth, she was not the kind of woman who would have tried harder, been better, loved or lived or laughed more, if some secret knowledge of the end had been shown her. When the world began its long winding down, she, like everyone else, was merely forced to live in the moment. Suddenly, there was nothing more but to dig trenches inside the chain link fence and line them with sharpened sticks and buried glass. Years back she'd been gifted a pistol from her father-in-law, along with three thousand rounds of ammunition. Now, there was only a surfeit of bullets. No past that mattered, no future to pine for. A single breath drawn, and the next, and the next. One foot in front of the other. One day at a time, sweet Jesus. Et cetera.

And so they had kept their lives, if not their dignities. Sheltered, still, from the beasts that roamed day and night. Great lumbering, shambolic things, red eyes burning high up in the creaking pine tops. They would not starve. Even if the cat food ran out. The man who came into their yard last month – hobbling in rags and hollering out for his dog, armed with an ancient pitchfork – was salted and stored in cling wrap beneath the guest bedroom, his bones buried beneath the shed, where the cat would not dig them up. Each having been first cracked and stewed in a pot of rainwater. The broth already drunk. She remembered a time when she had loved to cook.

Something creaked in the back of the house. A foot upon a board, an attic beam bending. She sat up on the edge of the couch, set her not-coffee down, and listened.

Nothing.

She sipped. Thought on. Of her parents, the last time she'd seen them. They'd come for Christmas, a week in the guest bedroom. Her father spent whole days stabbing his finger at games on an iPad. Her mother at the kitchen table, cross-stitching. They barely spoke to one another, and she to them. She did not know why. She had never decided: was it comfort or estrangement?

They left, and after New Year's, a great whirling hole opened in the Atlantic off the coast of Massachusetts. "Like God pulled a stopper," her husband said, glued to the news on television. She'd thought it was funny. Such a stupid way to say the world was ending. At the bottom of the hole was a blackness, impenetrable. Aerial photos splashed across CNN, a vortex like a bottomless black eye. Shortly after, the first people started going mad. A man in a truck stop in Rhode Island throttled another man to death over a jukebox song. A woman in Pennsylvania, driving home from a business trip out of Pittsburgh, crashed her Acura through a storefront and ploughed over three children. Delivery men with knives and neighbours with nail guns. Murders. Suicides. It took the experts a while to figure out it was airborne, the insanity. By then, of course, it was too late.

At least, she thought, *we did not have children.*

One dusk, not so long ago, they stood in their sun room that looked out upon the backyard and watched, over the chain link fence, as their neighbours slunk out of the house next door wearing army surplus gas masks. The woman wore exercise tights that hung like loose skin. She carried something small and swaddled. She'd just started her first trimester when it all began. The husband – he wore Oakley sunglasses and a pink polo shirt tucked into khakis, his Sunday best – got a shovel from the toolshed beside their deck, and they dug a hole in a garden of day lilies and perennials that had yet to bloom. When it was done, they carried one another inside and were never seen again.

In the days that followed, all up and down the street, where once she'd heard the cries of children bouncing on trampolines, or the rip and snarl of a dirt bike tearing through distant fields, there was only the peculiar silence of human absence. The stillness of poisoned air. Together, they sealed up every crack, every crevice, with Gorilla tape. They wore N95 masks from a box under a bathroom sink, leftovers from some lesser plague.

For a while, planes from the air force base to the west streaked the skies like arrows shot by gods. Their passing made the panes in the windows jump. Deep in the night, she and he woke to the sound of bombs exploding amid the trumpet cries of monstrous things. Creatures in the skies. Thunderous wings flapping in the night. But there were no news programs anymore to explain it all. No pundits, no anchors, no commentators. All they knew was that after the madness and the first wave of dying and the breakdown of everything, after the April rains, the monsters arrived like a midnight carnival blown into town. Hungry, slavering, they roamed the empty rooms of the world. This house of woe and mystery—

On the table beneath the window, the cat gave out a low growl and jumped down and slunk away, into the kitchen. Tail big, it dove into the hole in the floor, where the broken joists jutted like the ribs of a great and meaningless carcass.

She set her not-coffee on the coffee table and got up from the sofa, crossed to the window.

Down at the corner of the street, something loomed beyond the burned out shell of a church. It rose up out of the fog and cut a horned shape against a sliver of purple October sky. So big, she had to crane up, to see it. White birds passing behind it.

Between it and her was the tree she had never bothered to identify, to name. What was it? Some kind of maple? A tulip tree?

Down the street, the creature turned its massive, shadowy head, and the earth trembled as it took a step, then another. The glass in the picture window shook.

A creak, again, from down the hall.

In the bedroom.

A shadow fell across the yard, big as the end of the world.

It was never a haunted house, she thought, *until we made it one.* Who knew a ceiling fan was strong enough to hold a human's weight? To hold him, dangling. Creaking. From a length of electrical cord. His own cup of coffee – no, you just couldn't call it that anymore, could you? – set full on the bedside table. Getting cold forever.

Outside the picture window, the darkness bent low, filled the window. Red eyes like miniature suns blazing. Glass fogging with breath. She looked past it, to the tree, which was the last mystery of her heart. Bereft of all the leaves that were going to fall this season. The last had dropped just a while ago, and the ones yet clinging were brown and withered. They never fell.

Only waited for the new growth to push them out, come spring.

Like always.

I MISS YOU TOO MUCH

Sarah Langan

Through the rabbit hole.

"I miss you too much," the old woman said.

These words had always been presented to Stella as love words. A language that meant Stella was her mother's world. She was her sun and earth and moon; she was her inside and outside and reason. Stella was supposed to appreciate this declaration and reply in kind: *I miss you, too.*

But even as a child, the words had felt more like an accusation, as if by going to school or falling asleep or even by leaving a room, Stella had pained her mother: *I miss you too much.*

An imaginative person, Stella had sometimes wondered whether she was real, or simply an extension of Mom – a liver or marrow gone rogue, that had burst from its source body, leaving a mortal wound, an insult that could only be healed upon her return; her physical nearness to her mother.

…*Were they the same person?* she'd wondered in nursery school, as her teacher had taught *left*, *right*, and letters of the alphabet, and all the other children had seemed so very happy, so thrilled to define themselves, to trace their mirror images, and shout their own names, while she'd counted the seconds until she was back home, a heart without a house.

★   ★   ★

Years later, Stella forgot about growing up inside Baltimore House. She forgot about the half-person she'd been, the whispered words, the frog-footed bird (so terrible!), the yellow shadows that had moved at night, the house that seemed to shrink around her, so that she was too ungainly and big to fit inside it.

She made an adult life – kids and a husband and a house and a job and a dog and sometimes fish but usually the fish died. Though she suffered from phantom aches and mystery illnesses that doctors told her were not real, she considered herself happy. She passed for happy. She pretended to be happy.

Her first and only rebellion: in her teenage years, she'd sneaked the application. Packed her bags for college on the sly, waiting for but never finding the right time to tell Mom she was going. Still, Mom went through her things and found out. Stella'd stood in the hallway of Baltimore House, feeling strange and too heavy; unreal. Also, terrified.

"I'll miss you too much. Don't go," Mom said, her eyes set inscrutably deep and dark. Surely it had been a reference to their shared love language. Surely it had not been a threat that she was going to kill herself, or trap Stella here for the night, then set the house on fire and murder them both while they slept.

"Please," Stella said.

"No," Mom said. "Your place is here."

Maybe it was the repetitive thoughts (the frog-footed bird! the shrinking house!) that had only gotten worse since kindergarten. Maybe it was Stella's survival instinct, kicking in at last. To this day, she had no idea how she found the courage to tear the heart free from its host and walk out.

Escape!

College was awful. She was terrible at school, at making friends, at setting an alarm, at living in the world. She got through two and a half semesters before quitting to work full time at the CVS. Life didn't get easier after that. Bad roommates, hungry nights, loneliness. She didn't know how to negotiate. No one had taught her the grey space between one person's wants, and the other's. She slept with men who didn't call back, and pretended not to mind. Didn't bother her a bit! She lent money to friends and strangers because she was afraid to say no. She never asked for a raise, and consequently only ever got the standard cost of living increase every January.

She was ashamed of this – that she was weak, the type of person others victimised, who then smiled and said *thank you* because it was embarrassing to acknowledge her own hurt feelings – her lack of life skills that indicated a strange upbringing. But then, a miracle! She met

Bruce, a confident and oblivious pharmacologist who told her she had a jawbone sharp enough to cut glass.

They moved to New Jersey. She unpacked, got a part-time job proofing AI newsletters for the local real estate agency, signed the toddler up for half days at Loving Garden, and met the rest of the local moms, from whom she learned she wasn't alone. They all felt bad sometimes; felt wrong, like pieces of them were missing.

Stella suspected that unlike her, they'd once been whole people; captains of industry, math geniuses, track stars, night club party animals with killer moves. But by the time their lives delivered them to preschool drop off, they were not these things. They were nervous, tired moms who may as well have had worn signs around their chests that read: *WHATEVER HAPPENED I'M SURE IT'S MY FAULT AND I'M SORRY.*

If only people knew, Stella thought when she learned it herself, that the feminine blight of suburbia was not entitled Karens, but women who blamed everything on themselves! Husband a drunk, you divorced him, and now the kids are messed up? Your fault! Is your son a bed-wetter? You shouldn't have sleep trained him! Now he has an insecure attachment! Feel bad about not making enough money, which in turn gives you less say in your marriage? You should have leaned in! Why didn't you lean in?

Together, they formed a feminist book club where everybody read novels written only by women (mostly). In their bravado, they made jokes about their husbands, who got cranky when undersexed. Didn't the husbands know that cranky was the opposite of seductive? Could the husbands (and sometimes wives) please learn more than just that one move? They made jokes about their kids, who were pieces of work, every damn one of them. They made jokes about their jobs, which were going nowhere. Most jobs, ultimately, went nowhere. And even when they did go someplace, wealth didn't magically make you well-adjusted and awesome. You were still you; a person (or sometimes just a heart) wrapped in weird skin, looking out through marble eyes.

Over the years of their friendship, these women confessed their histories; their heartaches; their porny desires; and even sometimes, their hidden bottles and pills and affairs. Stella, grateful at last to have discovered friends, tried to do this, too. But she couldn't remember her history. Couldn't think about Baltimore House (the sounds and smells, the feeling of disproportionality, like she'd been a giant inside it), without everything fading to black.

She stayed in touch with Mom. They talked on the phone once a week. These calls were polite and uneventful. Normal, in other words. Twice a year, Stella and her family visited Baltimore House. They never slept over. Stella had the irrational fear that the house was a kind of fairyland, and if she let down her guard, she'd be trapped. She'd never leave. Upon returning to Jersey, Stella often had nightmares that something terrible, something too needy, was kneeling on her chest.

"What's wrong?" her friends would ask when a thought or word or bird in the sky made Stella remember Baltimore House (not Bruce. He'd given up on questions, though not on Stella). "Why are you sad today?"

Stella wanted to answer, but she didn't know how. The feeling inside her was an undefinable black murk she was afraid to touch. Better to isolate it so it didn't contaminate her friends, her family, her new house with its working garbage disposal and smooth ceilings.

This went on. Years and life. She engaged from a remove, like an alien anthropologist. When the kids cried, it took her an extra second to hear them, her thoughts skimming surfaces of notions, catching images through a sieve from long ago – of birds and beds and cut trees. Sometimes she forgot that this was her house in Jersey, her family. She'd startle, as if they were all strangers.

Bruce was soft spoken and decent. Genuinely gentle, and a good cook. He respected her privacy and her moods, seeming to believe that her gender was, by its very nature, mysterious and emotional. So long as she looked up and noticed him from time to time, he allowed Stella to remain an island.

She read all the child-rearing books, did her best in the best ways she'd known. Apparently, her children were normal. Their teachers and her friends told her they were normal, which meant they *had* to be. The lawn outside their house was mostly green. A happy marriage, food on the table, healthy kids, a roof. These things seemed like more than anyone like her ought to hope for. She ought to be content.

But she had the feeling that a clock was ticking. Something awful was about to happen.

It wore her down, this secret, ineffable terror. She went to doctors to check her colon and heart and brain and stomach and oesophagus. They drew blood. They took scans. They told her she was fine. They proscribed Prozac, then Klonopin. These things helped a little, but didn't change the fact that it felt to her that her organs were not truly hers. They were foreign, pulsing bodies over which someone else had laid claim.

She went to a therapist who suggested she talk about her childhood. This was what she remembered:

Mom was amazing! She'd raised Stella all alone and she'd done it with so much love! Even though she'd worked full time at the library, she'd sewn all Stella's Halloween costumes. She'd done the laundry and the errands and the extra-curriculars. She'd helped with the homework and listened and supported. She'd cooked nutritious meals!

"I had a perfect childhood!" Stella told the shrink. Then she went home. Those unwelcome repetitive thoughts she'd had as a kid, of birds, of Baltimore House shrinking around her, returned. Only now, these wild notions had uprooted, chasing her hundreds of miles to Jersey. She imagined that the sheets she shared with Bruce were just washcloth sized, the bed not long enough for her legs, her body too big for the kitchen table, too tall inside the low, clean ceiling. For days after therapy sessions, she doubled the Klonopin, walking carefully just like she'd done back at Baltimore House, terrified that the weight of her would break through the floors. She'd fall down, down, down until she was gone.

What's that word? Alienation? She felt alienated. Or maybe like an alien. Her lapses in attention grew. She imagined birds and broken trees and crawling things. She stopped pretending to feel her life, because in truth it had never felt like anything. She lived with people who didn't know her. She didn't know herself.

You ever wake up and it's the same as going to bed? You ever think: *Why not have a shot of vodka for breakfast? The other moms'll never smell it, and why the fuck does someone like me need to stay sharp?* These were thoughts she had; uncontrollable. This was what happened to a heart separated too long from its body.

When her therapist pointed out that for a person who'd had a perfect childhood, she seemed pretty unhappy, Stella fired her. And why not! She didn't take insurance and charged $250 an hour!

★   ★   ★

The mystery here was the absence of evidence.

During the regular calls back home, Mom acted like a normal, not remotely needy, person. She was nice to Bruce, interested in the kids. "How was that soccer game?" she asked, cheerful and enthused. "Now, I hear you like sushi, is that right?" She showed a kind of attentiveness that Stella lacked, remembering every detail about them, as if she kept meticulous notes in a journal and there would one day be a test.

When Stella and her family visited Baltimore House, it was nothing like Stella's memories. It didn't smell like chlorine and ashes and it wasn't claustrophobically small. No stick figures hung from the ceilings. No secret doors led to cubbies and crawl spaces and disturbing hidey holes. Nope. It was a rundown two-bedroom ranch with chipped paint that smelled like Lysol and squeeze-tube cookies. Mom was always thrilled to see them all. Ecstatic, even, like every grandmother ought to be. The kids were friendly, if bored. Bruce looked at his screen. He loved his screen. Stella felt comfortable. Her old room was the same. The couch with her butt indentation was the same. Still, she never slept over.

★   ★   ★

Interminable, this went on. She kept waiting for the bad thing. The inevitable thing. And then one week, Mom didn't call. It was the first missed call in fifteen years. Stella paced her kitchen, with its garbage disposal and its broken marble counters. She'd been researching how to replace them herself, pouring cement, which, from the YouTube tutorials, sounded tricky but doable. She drank two glasses of wine. She picked up the phone, thinking she ought to finally be the one to call. But she was afraid. So she dialled her friend Martha, who was training for a half-marathon. They talked about which kind of collagen to use for joint health and the fact that if their kids ever dated and got married, they'd be related.

Before first light the next morning, her cellphone rang from a strange number. It was a doctor at the hospital at Baltimore General with bad news. Mom was sick. Terminal, in fact. Then Mom got on the phone. Her voice was pleading. For the first time in fifteen years, she said: "I miss you too much. Please come home."

With those words, it was like the umbilicus rope connecting Stella to Mom snapped her right back to Baltimore House.

★   ★   ★

Eat some cake. Drink some potion.

Instead of phone calls, she visited every week. Upon arrival the first time, alone, the house wasn't menacing like she'd feared. Why had she thought that it would be? No vines attached themselves on and around her, trapping her within the walls of Baltimore House. Mom was visibly emaciated since Stella's last visit, her eyes sunken, but she was still upright. Standing and walking and breathing and delighted to see her daughter. She wrapped her arms around Stella and held her, and for a moment it felt to Stella like they were separated magnets, joined at last.

The house was the same as at every other visit – neat and sterile, if also old. The first few weekends, Stella didn't stay over. She took the early train, arrived before Mom was awake, cleaned, filled the fridge, scheduled the doctor appointments and rides, reviewed the accounts, ate dinner with Mom, who insisted on cooking, then took the midnight train home. But this got silly. The kids were older and could get themselves to their various weekend activities. If they needed help, Bruce was utterly competent.

Her first overnighter, she slept on the fold-out couch. But it was uncomfortable. No nightmares – since she'd been visiting, all the nightmares and repetitive thoughts had stopped. It was as if, by returning home, seeing for sure that nothing was amiss, she'd cured herself of wounds so undefined as to be invisible. But the mattress was too thin, the metal bar a mean, smooth mouth on her back.

The following weekend, she opened the door to her old bedroom. Remembered, vaguely, the sense of everything getting too small, of falling through and down. But then it was fine. Just a bedroom. There was still that Backstreet Boys poster. She'd gotten it at a garage sale when she was thirteen, thinking it would make her appear like a normal teenager. Then she'd listened to their music obsessively, even though boy bands were no longer cool. Stella laughed at the memory and the sound echoed within the small, pink-decorated room and the single bed that really did appear small, as if made for a doll.

Sleep was comfortable that night. Her belly full of her mom's good stew, her worries hundreds of miles away, it was the best sleep she'd had in years.

Why had she thought she'd find totems? Stick figures tied with string and hung all over the ceilings, dangling both separately, and also joined like mobiles? Why had she remembered a yellow, musky smear against the second storey plaster?

It wasn't like that!

Though she was sad that with every visit, her mother's eyes sank deeper, she loved coming home, loved being back in her hometown, watching people in Orioles caps, panhandlers drinking hot coffee at the Western Union, hipsters with weird facial hair slow-sipping foamy caffeinated beverages. Mom was so happy to have her around that it made her feel special. The two of them didn't have much in common – with Mom so sick and tired, they could barely keep a conversation going – but that was fine. "I needed this," Stella told Mom one morning, after a perfect night of sleep. "I needed a break from my life so I could see it clearly. Someplace I could feel safe."

"You'll always have Baltimore House," Mom answered, and Stella's eyes got wet from the bittersweetness of it: she had a home. She had a place. This strange, impossible past (the birds! the totems! the yellow smears!) she'd imagined was irrelevant.

In rare moments, when all the work was done, they talked past politeness. Stella told Mom about Bruce, about their marriage. He could be stubborn and he didn't admit when he was wrong. When it came to their relationship, he was happy to let her take the lead. Trouble was, she didn't quite know how to do that. The kids were good, but she'd been bad about boundaries. She needed to set them more often, needed to maintain them and deliver consequences when they transgressed.

"You're doing a wonderful job," Mom reassured her, and Stella felt good. Warm in her belly like she'd eaten a perfect meal, which was often the case – Mom was an excellent cook. She still had questions.

For instance, why did she remember so little? Why did she have this feeling of unease, this sureness that she must not trust Baltimore House, no matter how much she wanted to trust it? But she didn't ask these questions. Like she told her kids when they were working up the courage to confront teasing friends, it would happen eventually, when they were ready. They'd hit a point where they had no choice but to articulate their feelings. She would ask Mom these questions when she was ready. And if her mother died before that happened, well then, it didn't matter anymore, did it?

So, it was good. It was healing. And Mom's food, her curries and soups, were so damned delicious.

Still, the cleaning, the appointments, the living and managing of someone else's life, drained her energy. Even when she wasn't at Baltimore House, she was thinking about it, worried Mom might trip or eat something bad or just get scared, all alone like that.

She and Bruce discussed a nursing home or hospice. They agreed these were good ideas. They also agreed there wasn't a rush.

Though the cancer had spread all over, three months after the diagnosis, Mom still loved to roll her walker around the kitchen and make meals. Together, they'd eat in the quiet just like old times. Stella got used to the ritual, the breakfast and lunch and dinner that stretched and extended, so that the meals felt as if they rolled into one. Time passed strangely. Sometimes she'd look at her phone and it was morning. Then she'd look again and it was night. She stayed longer, missing work. She slept deeper. She missed soccer games, missed outings with friends, date nights with Bruce, a man from whom she'd always felt just slightly removed.

She liked Jersey, but she felt better in Baltimore House. She felt safe and real there.

There were other changes that happened so slowly as to be imperceptible. That strange scent returned – an old scent like tannis root and liver that Mom started adding to the stews and porridges. About six months into Mom's sickness, Stella found a stick figure in her dresser drawer just behind an old spelling bee participation ribbon. The wood was carved smooth and pale, as to almost appear like bones. The creature had four arms and four legs, but in an ineffable way, appeared human. Tortured, but human.

Stella untied it and took it down. "Mom? What is this?"

Mom was in bed, her breath rising and falling in the darkness of dusk. "I don't know. An octopus? I don't know, you win. You tell me!" she said.

Stella held the thing. Was she real? Was she crazy? Why did her chest hurt so much? She tucked it into the back of her closet under a pile of old clothes, like something radioactive.

Seven months in, the repetitive thoughts returned. She and Mom were watching the old *Alice in Wonderland* cartoon, where Alice eats cake and gets larger, drinks potion and gets smaller. "I used to think that," Stella said. "I thought I didn't fit."

"You didn't," her mom answered. "You never fit."

Stella turned. Mom's eyes were closed. She appeared to be sleeping.

That night, she imagined that Baltimore House was getting smaller. She wondered, when she found the second stick figure hanging from their shared bathroom ceiling, which was thick with angry black threads of mould (when had they grown? had they always been there?), whether she was really Stella, or someone else, someone ghostly and unknown.

Stage three didn't reverse, but it didn't progress. Mom's skin got even looser. The cooking continued, only it was weird, half raw meat. Stella slept more deeply, missed more time. This was grief, of course. This was normal. Wasn't it?

No matter how much Lysol she sprayed, the house stank. Was this what dying smelled like? Then why was it so familiar?

"I should get back to them," Stella told her mom. "I think we need to consider hospitalisation."

"They don't need you," Mom answered. "He doesn't love you. The kids don't want you. You can't even keep them in line." Stella had looked at her mom, stirring that awful turkey meat stew with tannis root and carrots, her expression so flat it was hard to believe she'd uttered such cruelness, and she'd thought: *this is the pain talking; the cancer. She isn't herself.*

Stella's hair began to fall out. Always her pride, the lush, black gloss thinned, running down the shower drain and sticking to her pillow. More totems made their way along the halls of the second floor, away from prying, rare visitors' eyes, but not from Stella, who was no longer a guest, but beginning to feel like a resident. Branched, deformed things like bony sea creatures. Like men turned monsters.

An inversion occurred: the house in Jersey began to feel too large. When she slept there, she'd wake up to make breakfast, skip the vodka, stare at the crummy table, thinking: *I'm too small to sit there. I can't reach it.*

Something awful is about to happen, I know it.

Travel days were the worst. She hated sitting on the train, heading to Baltimore. What would she find? What new ailment or calamity had befallen Mom? She hated the train back home to Jersey, too. Because by then she'd gotten used to Baltimore House, where there were no rules, and civilisation had fallen apart.

A problem happened. Stella noticed in a vague, distracted way. Her youngest, Denise, came home from soccer with tears running down her dirt-streaked face. She gave no explanation for her mood, no matter how hard Stella pried. Over the following days, Denise got quiet. Though Stella was back at Baltimore House by then, she heard from Bruce that Denise had refused to go to the game. Wouldn't get out of bed all day. Over the following month, her grades dipped. Then Ben, Stella's older child, got into a fight on the bus. He slugged a kid and was expelled.

"What the hell?" Bruce asked them both at dinner.

Sitting quiet, thinking about her mom (Was she okay? She'd winced so much when she'd rolled in her walker last visit. More than ever before!), Stella had only listened, wondering if she, too, had ovarian cancer. Was that why her groin hurt so much?

But vaguely, like a smoke signal wafting through her subconscious, she also thought: *I need to get out of this.* What *this* was, she couldn't say. But the following day, after the doctor in Jersey told her that her scan was clean ("Please, stop getting scans. You don't need them!" the doctor begged), she thought about her children.

Was it possible that the numbness she'd felt for so long, this worsening hollow inside her, wasn't because of the life she was living? What if Jersey, with the lawn and the kids and the job and the husband and the friends, was her real life? What if it was the other life – the life she was carrying – that didn't belong to her?

Just like it had done years ago, Baltimore House was making her sick. She needed to get out of this. She needed to put Mom in a home. "I'm done with this," she said out loud, a resolution and a promise.

★   ★   ★

This thought, perhaps a revelation, was undone by a phone call from that same doctor. At last, the cancer had progressed. The doctor was certain, this time, that Mom had weeks, if not days, to live. "She doesn't want a hospice," the doctor said. "She wants to die among family. She wants you."

"It's not for long," she told Bruce, who was tired of hearing it. But he was the kind of person who did the right thing, whether he wanted to or not. They both were.

To Stella's dismay, Denise and Ben were fine with her extended departure. At first, she imagined that they were being brave for her. But soon, she understood they were glad to be rid of her. You treat people like obligations for long enough, they reply in kind.

In a moment of clarity, she gathered all three of them together before she left. "I've been bad," she said. "I've been wrong. You're the most important people to me but I haven't been giving you my attention."

They'd looked at her with a kind of horror she recognised. When you've been living inside something for long enough, you can't see it, and when someone points it out, you're utterly shocked. More than that, you're angry.

"I love you," she said. "And I want us all to think about the ways I can prove that to you once I'm home."

Bruce had looked at her, and then his beer. Then he drank his beer. She felt sad for him. Realised that just because he never confronted, never complained, didn't mean nothing was wrong. He was lonely. They were both lonely. Because she'd been thinking that this Jersey life was pretend. But all along, it was her only real thing.

Ben smiled a strained smile, a fresh bruise over his eye from yet another fight. "I don't know what you're talking about," he said.

"Why are you saying this?" Denise asked.

Stella thought then about the day Denise had come home tear-streaked from soccer. What had happened? She hadn't been the same since. These secrets, she was so tired of them. Even when you tried to isolate them, they broke free and lashed out, invisible cuts inside arms. "Because it's true," Stella answered.

Denise glared, then blinked.

A kind of electricity ran all through the house and the room and between all four of them. The electricity was new and scary and for the first time, Stella felt connected. She felt a part of something other than Mom and it was glorious.

"I've been treating you all like a burden. But you're not the burden. You're the gift."

Uneasily and with confusion, they saw her off.

★   ★   ★

Off she went to Baltimore. To ease her mother into the undiscovered country.

On the ride, she thought about how this trip might resolve everything. She'd give her mother what she needed, and in death, they'd both be free. She smiled at this thought, consoled.

★   ★   ★

The Queen of Hearts Desires an Audience.

Carrying her bag, she keyed her way into Baltimore House. It would be two weeks at the most, the doctor had told her. No one ever rebounds from something so serious at such a late stage. She was quiet, didn't want to wake Mom. The hospice aid was sitting in the kitchen, scrolling her phone. "Is she sleeping?" Stella asked.

The aid shrugged. "She didn't want me. She only wants you."

"Who cares what she wants?" Stella shot back. "You're supposed to sit with her." Well, no. She didn't say this. She thought it. But she didn't want to make a scene. So she headed up the stairs, where more totems hung. They twisted in the air, sharp wood-bone points. How had bedridden Mom gotten them up there?

She went into Mom's room (which had once been Dad's room, too, though she didn't remember Dad). The bedsheets were crinkled. She turned on the light and became unexpectedly frightened. Her heart beat strange and arrhythmic. No one was in the bed. She set down her luggage. Where was her mother?

Creeping, creeping, she thought. Always creeping. A kind of terror overcame her, swallowed her, spit her back out, wet and reborn. She knew, then, where to look. She went to her childhood bedroom, with its reassuring and unfashionable Backstreet Boys poster. There was Mom, covers pulled to her nose, breathing softly, eyes closed. But awake. Stella could feel it. On her pillow, a scraggle of long, black hairs. Stella's hairs.

"Mom?"

Mom opened her eyes.

"Why are you in my bed?"

"I asked the girl to help me," she said. "I missed you too much. I wanted to be near you."

★　★　★

Late that night, after feeding Mom some broth by the spoon, and taking her blood pressure and pulse (both bad, both low – yes, she was definitely dying. This would not last!), she called home. Her home. Yes, she had a home. It was real. Bruce answered, groggy. She worried, suddenly, that he'd found a girlfriend. Someone present and happy.

"How is she?" Bruce asked.

"I don't know. I'm confused," she answered.

"Oh," he said. Then, for the first time in a long while, he asked a serious question. "Why?"

She pressed the phone tight. Whispered now. "Did I ever tell you that I didn't like it here?"

He didn't answer and it made her scared. But then again, he was Bruce. Bruce was not a guy who knew what to say. Never had been. In the delivery room when she'd pushed out Denise, whose head had been as big as a basketball, he'd cried, "That's awful! Doc! You gotta help them!"

"I can't explain it. But something's wrong."

"Yeah," he said. "It's strange there. Bad."

"You think so, too?" she asked.

"Yeah. I always thought it. No offence."

"What's strange?" she asked, and mostly she was afraid he'd answer: *You. You're strange.*

"I don't know. She seemed fine. Your mom. But I was always glad you never let the kids stay too long. I appreciated that."

"I don't want to stay," she said. "I lived here eighteen years and I don't want to live here again."

"So don't," he said. "Come home."

She thought this might have been the most honest and open conversation they'd had. It startled her that it came so naturally.

"It's not forever," she said. "They told me days. I'll stick it out. If I don't, I worry I'll regret it. Closure and all that."

"Sure," he said. "Love you." Then he put the kids on. Denise had quit the team but refused to give more details. Because of another fight, Ben was going to ride his bike to school from now on.

Because Mom was in her bed that night, she went to sleep in Mom's bed. She was too tired to change Mom's skin-shed-dirty sheets. So she wore her socks and a turtleneck, slept above the covers with a big towel as a blanket. In the night, everything went wrong. Mom gasped and shouted – a death throe? – and Stella comforted her, wetting her lips with ice. Later, the bed she returned to felt too small. Because of her socks, her feet were too warm. The mould-riddled ceiling was hung with stick figures on nooses.

And then, something slurking, slurking. She squeezed her eyes tight as it slid across the floor. The sound was familiar. From her childhood. The only thing that was different was the size. Last time, she'd been much smaller. She'd been a little kid. She opened her eyes and the slurking thing was upon her chest, its wide mouth encompassing her legs as slowly, it kept crawling.

*　　*　　*

In the morning, the memory was vague and awful. A clump of her hair had come out and stuck to the old pillow. She left it and made breakfast, which Mom was too sick to eat. She spoke with the visiting nurse, who told her that the end was within a day or two. She directed the aid, whom insurance had agreed to cover for four hours, to go sit with her mother, then went out to the grocery store. She cried as she walked the aisles, desultory and confused.

*　　*　　*

She'd forgotten about the slurker. For how long had that dream followed her? She wasn't sure. As far back as she could remember, probably. A wide-mouthed thing.

"Stella Munsey?" someone called. By the yoghurt and cheese appeared a woman with dyed-blonde hair in a belted pink trench coat. Stella's married name was Goyer. She hadn't heard Munsey in years.

"Yeah?"

"I thought that was you! It's me, Skyler!"

Stella still didn't know her.

"Kindergarten? No, before then! Preschool with Ms. Dolly. We went all through. All the way through high school. My last name's Moews. Alphabetic. We always sat next to each other! How have you been?"

Stella thought this was probably a redundant question, because she was sure her eyes were red and wet. "Fine?"

"I hear you moved away. Good for you!"

Stella shrugged. "I guess? What about you?"

"Me? Oh, you know me."

Stella didn't. She had no memory of this woman. What the hell? Why didn't she remember this woman?

"I still live with my parents. I took over their house. I know, I know. I ought to be ashamed I never left the nest. But I love it there! I got married for a little while. But it didn't work out."

"Happens," Stella said. This conversation was a welcome one. It took her mind off sick Mom. The slurker, too.

Skyler seemed genuinely interested and nice, like any of her friends back in Jersey, who didn't understand what she came from, so there was no point telling them, but they *wanted* to understand, and that was precious. Skyler lowered her voice. She seemed earnest and innocent, perhaps a little slow-witted. "I thought about you a lot."

Stella raised a brow.

"I mean, it was so weird. What she did. So wrong. Someone should have called the cops on her. Child services, at least."

Stella had no idea what this woman was talking about. But she did, a little. Because this was about the animal, wasn't it? The class pet. "Yeah," Stella said.

Then the woman smiled brightly. "But you're okay now. I can tell!"

"I'm great!" Stella said. She let the woman hug her, even hugged her back and promised to stop by for a beer sometime. Then she waited until the woman was gone, and burst into the most awful tears.

★ ★ ★

That night, she helped Mom onto the commode and wiped her. She set her back into her own bed, where she wheezily slept. She wasn't taking food anymore. Hardly sipping water. In the quiet, Stella returned to her pink bedroom and looked through old dresser drawers. Found a yearbook. Opened it and saw her own picture from a long time before. People she didn't remember had signed it. They seemed to like her, though they didn't seem to know her particularly well.

She went through her other things. Old books and drawings. She found a diary. Most of the pages were blank. Except on one, she'd written: *Madam Slurkins won't leave me alone.*

She called home again. Said the end was any moment. She was going to try to get some sleep while she could. She talked to Bruce who said he missed her and wanted to make a plan for a date night when she returned, which was new. He wasn't an initiator. She said, *Yes, I'd like that more than anything.*

She talked to Ben, who said that it was too cold for his bike. "So ride the bus," she said.

"I can't."

"Why not?"

"This senior. He said I'm weird. I don't like him."

"I don't like him, either," she said. "This guy should mind his own business. Also, *he's* weird. He's eighteen and he's riding the bus. You're fourteen. What kind of loser senior picks on a freshman?"

"Yeah," Ben said, seeming suddenly to realise that this was correct: the guy was a loser!

"But probably you shouldn't hit him," she said. "Unless he hits you first."

"Yeah. But I get mad."

"I know," she said. "It's good somebody in this house has a temper. I just don't want it to bite you in the ass."

"I love you, Mom," he said.

"I love you, too."

She talked to Denise, who still wouldn't explain what was happening at soccer. Then the call was over, and Stella ate the stew in the pot on the stove – not the gross kind Mom had been making lately, but canned from the store. Only, had someone dropped pieces of tree bark in it?

Had Mom instructed the aid to do this? This seemed unlikely. The aid preferred scrolling her phone to helping. Who had done this?

She put her dish in the sink, walking slow and exhausted. But wait! Was that a new totem? Had someone hung totems in the kitchen? Had someone smeared yellow cream on the walls?

She called the hospice centre. Asked for the aid. They said this wasn't possible. Aids don't receive direct calls. "Can you ask if she hung stuff in my mom's house?" Stella asked.

She climbed the stairs, noticed more waxy smears. Had the notion of something slurking, leaving slug trails. More totems dangled. Enough that their limbs weaved as they spun, even though there wasn't a breeze. Their collisions sounded like rain sticks.

She checked on Mom, who was sleeping. Felt bad about it, but opened Mom's private nightstand drawer. Inside, a giant, leather ledger. The contents: notes on every phone conversation between Stella and Mom they'd had over the last eighteen years.

For instance: January 14, 2016: *Stella says Denise switched best friends: Sharon's out, Asher's in. Asher often has runny noses.*

These notes were incredibly detailed.

Stella replaced them. Went to her bedroom. It felt too small. She swallowed three Klonopin, even though it meant she might not wake up if her mother called, and in tears, went to sleep.

Slurkins returned, laying on Stella's chest, her jaw underneath Stella. Her eyes were doll's eyes. Marbles.

★   ★   ★

The next morning, she'd lost more hair. So much that she cut the rest into a bob with dull shears. After, she sat by Mom's bed. "What's happening to me?" she asked.

The old woman wheezed. Her eyes were like marbles. Her skin was waxy, greasy yellow.

The phone rang. It was the aid. She said she hadn't smeared anything or hung anything and Stella better not lie about her, because she hadn't stolen, either. And by the way, that spiced food Mom cooked was ugly magic. The aid wasn't coming back. She didn't mess with witches!

Stella hung up. Returned to Mom's room. Only, the hall didn't go there. It wound and opened into a room she hadn't seen for years. A small, low room with mouldy ceilings that led to a smaller room and a smaller room, all adorned with swaying totems, all stinking of rotten spices.

She got to the centre of it, found jars and potions that lined an entire wall. Inside were dead, pickled creatures, some of which had been cut and sewn and experimented on. A bird with a rabbit's head; a mouse split in half; a squirrel with a tarantula in its belly.

Prominently displayed was a leather-bound book called a Necronomicon. She lifted it, decided right then. Ran with it, through rooms like hobbit burrows, winding and winding, until she was at the familiar stairs, and then down. She set fire to it, watched it burn.

She remembered, then, church as a kid. It had been at an old church, closed down with fallen beams. Everything had been painted black. A crucifix had hung upside down. Had she been there? Had Mom taken her there?

I miss you too much.

She remembered a group of people standing over a dead bird – a bird like any from those jars. Its wings had been sliced, its feet cut and replaced by frog feet. She remembered that the dead thing had shivered, then gotten up and flapped its wings.

She remembered why Skyler had stopped her yesterday. Her mom had killed the fifth-grade class pet. A rabbit. They were supposed to take care of it for the weekend. A class project on community. But her mom had snapped its neck, cut off its ears, and brought it to the church. Only, it had been too big to revive. So she'd blamed it on Stella: *Stella killed the rabbit. She's very sorry. She doesn't know her own strength.* She'd said this at drop off, holding the thing's mutilated corpse, loud for all to hear. And the teacher, God bless her, had said, "No she didn't, Mrs. Munsey. Stella's not like that. I'll bet money you did this."

There was a stir after that. Phone calls and even an interview with a soft-speaking man. But nothing came of it.

*   *   *

Stella didn't sleep that night, despite the two Klonopin. No aid came in the morning. Hospice apologised. The previous aid was angry about the false theft accusation. They hoped she'd understand. They also hoped she'd be more careful in her accusations in the future, despite these trying times.

"Is my mom a monster?" she asked.

The woman paused a long time. "She's dying, that's all."

"How would you know?" Stella asked. "You don't live in Baltimore House."

Stella went up the stairs. Saw her mother on the hall floor, a totem clutched in her hand, pulling herself by her arms back into Stella's old bedroom. Slurking. Slurking. Her skin left a trail of yellow grease.

Was her mother Madam Slurkins? Or was it worse than that? Did something called Slurkins live inside her mother?

She helped Mom up, lifted her to her bed even as she clutched the ugly totem she'd been trying to hang. She was light as a sack of empty corn husks. Stella tried to think of a time she'd spent, a good memory with her mother, but it was all a blank.

"Mom? Are you a witch?"

"Runs in the family," she said. "Long, long line."

"Was Dad?"

She laughed. "You know what's funny?" Mom asked.

Stella waited.

"The more you do something, the less you care about it."

She felt a terrible chill, then, that this lack of conscience was about her. She was, in some way, disposable. Her belly hurt right then, her chest, too. The pain ran all through, and for a moment, in her mind, she and Mom switched places. Stella was in the bed, Mom ministering to her.

Stella got the water, the pills. Gave her mom some extra morphine to keep her from wandering, sponged her clean. Saw, for the first time, the swirl inside a pentagram etched over Mom's belly. It was an old scar, healed long ago. She took the totem from her mother's hand. It was smooth and freshly whittled. Shaped like Stella, wearing a piece of Stella's nightgown.

★   ★   ★

That night, she didn't dream of Slurkins, but when she woke she couldn't move. She felt wrongly proportioned, as if her body didn't fit. What was most strange, most horrifying, it seemed that she had moved in the night. She had crawled into bed with her mother, who was holding her close, mouth open and drooling.

*   *   *

Exhausted, she extricated herself. "What's happening?" she asked Mom. "What have you done to me?"

The old woman didn't answer. But her hair had grown. No, it was stranger than that. She was wearing Stella's hair, the hair that had fallen out. She'd knit it together somehow, and was wearing it like a wig.

"Why are you doing this?"

"It's what you owe me," Mom said.

And Stella remembered that the rabbit hadn't stayed still. In class, it had twitched, its neck broken, and the kids had cried. She'd cried. She remembered Skyler, clasping her hand. "It's my fault," Stella had told the girl. "I'm sorry. I did it." But no one had believed that.

The outside world, she'd understood even then, had been better than Baltimore House.

*   *   *

That day, she searched the house, the too small house. But it didn't feel as small as it had. Or she was shrinking. She returned to the secret rooms of potions and jars with the intention of setting everything there on fire. The lights in the small, hidden room went out but that was fine. She'd brought matches, gasoline. She lit a match. Saw Mom, looking back at her, and then the match blew out. Everything went dark.

She lost time, somehow. Lost the day. When she looked around, it was night and the secret rooms were gone. She was standing in the hallway.

Frightened, she packed her bag. Mom could die alone. That was fine. She went to the door. Couldn't open it. Literally, it stayed locked. She tapped lightly on the window, then slammed a pot against it. The glass was unsmashable. She called for help – to home, to the hospice, to 911 – there was no reception.

She screamed. No one came. Exhausted after hours of trying, of raging against Baltimore House, she came back up the stairs in the stark daylight. The totems danced like skeletons. The walls were all yellow now, smeared from Madam Slurkins' nightly romps. This had happened before. Her mother had tried this before. But back then, it hadn't taken. Stella's body had been too small. Her mother had needed to wait. Needed Stella to grow up.

Stella looked in on her mother, whose eyes were marbles. "I love you too much," she said, and Stella understood at last that *love* meant *covet*.

Weeping and exhausted, she sat on her childhood bed. And then lay down. And prayed. She tried once more to call home, because a solution occurred to her. The day Denise came home from soccer was the same day the new coach had started. It could be coincidence, but then again, it could be a reason. Denise was the only girl on the team. Sometimes, certain coaches didn't like that. Or not even *like*, they didn't know how to handle it.

Like she'd done so many times before, she imagined she was far away from here. She was a grown up who'd left her past behind, where it belonged. She was free. She was crying as she thought these things, and Madam Slurkins appeared. She fought, but Slurkins was so slippery, her mouth so impossibly large.

★　　★　　★

In the morning, everything hurt. It hurt awful. It hurt like nothing had ever hurt before. She would have cried but the moving of her body would have hurt, too. She stayed frozen, watching shadows dance as the sun got high and then low. The bedroom was pink. All around, pink and girlish – such a contrast to everything else in this awful house. In eyesight: the Backstreet Boys.

"Help," she whispered, praying to Bruce and the kids and the nurse and the aid and Skyler and her Jersey friends. "Help me!"

That night, she felt a hand on her shoulder. She opened her eyes, believing help had come. But it was Mom who leaned over her. Mom, looking fit and well. Rosy cheeked. Her hair was black. No, wait. It was a wig. Mom was wearing a wig of Stella's hair.

Mom spooned bitter soup Stella didn't want into her mouth. But she was so thirsty.

★   ★   ★

Slurkins came again. Praying to the people she loved was too sad, so she prayed to the Backstreet Boys. Wished they would hear and save her. She made her mind a blank, a nothing, as Slurkins' jaw enveloped her.

★   ★   ★

In the morning, so much pain. Her body like fire. She opened her eyes and found she'd moved. She was in Mom's bedroom. But where was Mom?

Then, someone leaned over her. She didn't want to believe. It was too awful. The person looking back at her was Stella. Rosy cheeked, this Stella's hair was restored to its glossy, gorgeous glory.

"Take this," Stella's voice and body said, only its eyes were black marbles. The medicine it was holding was liquid morphine.

Stella tried to see but this was hard. Her hands were wrinkled. Everything wrinkled. Everything tired. The pain in her abdomen was fire.

"Give me back," Stella mouthed.

Stella's body turned. It did a dance of joy. A kind of mean-spirited, monstrous jig. Then it waved an exaggerated goodbye to bedridden Stella, the way you might wave at an infant or someone very old.

A new aid arrived. She ministered to Stella. "I'm the daughter," Stella said.

"Yes," the aid answered, scrolling her phone. "Of course you're someone's daughter."

"Help me," Stella said. "Call my family."

Stella recited the number. The aid made the call. Bruce answered. Stella burst into tears. "Hello?" Bruce asked. "Hello?"

"It's Stella. Come get me. Please come get me," Stella wept in muffled horror. "I'm sick. My voice is bad because I'm sick."

"Stella?" he asked with confusion. "This sounds like Stella's mom."

"It's me!" Stella cried. "Help me. Come get me."

"Okay," he said, bewildered and not quite believing. "I'm on my way." The trip was four hours if he drove straight without stopping. She cried with relief, and then fear. Would he recognise her?

"You're an odd one," the aid said once the line went dead.

★   ★   ★

After the aid left, new Stella returned. She'd gotten her gorgeous black hair styled the way Bruce liked it, in ringlets down her back. She'd painted her nails glossy black. She was holding the ledger Stella'd spied. The detailed inventory containing the facts of Stella's life. She held up Stella's phone, which was now her phone. "He's not coming," she said. "I told him I'd meet him. We'd have that date."

"He'll know," Stella said. "Even if he doesn't say, he'll know. They'll all know."

"Just like you," new Stella said, smiling mean.

Looking closely, there was a difference. New Stella's eyes were dull. She moved strangely, as if unaccustomed to her limbs, her space, her skin. Had Stella's own mother been just as unsuspecting? For how long and through how many generations had this creature blighted the Munsey line? Real Stella couldn't begin to guess.

New Stella slid her foot against the floor, walking backward, smiling too wide. Then the other foot. It was odd. Ceremonial. She stood in the doorway, facing Stella. Still that grin. Then the door shut, hard.

With the sound, Stella felt Mom's sick, withered body tighten around her, like a shirt dried too long, that shrinks. Through dying eyes, she glimpsed the Backstreet Boys, those young angels, and the pink walls of Baltimore House, slicked with yellow.

She hadn't asked Denise about the new coach. She hadn't replaced that marble counter with concrete. In her mind, she screamed a warning to her family, because she could see the future:

This creature wearing her skin would install itself at Jersey House, turning the Goyer family home into a haunted, needy place. She would act the part of Stella, all the while, taking notes. There would probably be a divorce. A break, and confusion; new less happy homes established.

Ben would get mad and leave. Bruce would find someone new. Denise, who took after Stella, would linger, trying to fix this mysterious thing inside her mother, that had broken.

"I miss you too much," the creature would tell Denise. And Denise, sweet Denise, would not know how to get away.

They say you can't go home again. But what they really meant was that you should never go home again. Not ever.

BIOGRAPHIES

Poppy Z. Brite is the long-time pen name of Billy Martin. Since beginning his career in the small-press magazine *The Horror Show* in 1985, he has published eight novels including *Lost Souls*, *Exquisite Corpse*, and the Liquor series, as well as several short story collections and assorted non-fiction work. Brite is also the editor of the erotic horror anthologies *Love in Vein* and *Love in Vein 2*. He has recently completed *Water if God Wills It*, a non-fiction book about religion and spirituality in the works of Stephen King. In addition to writing, he runs the online curio shop PZBaubles New Orleans, specialising in vintage Tarot cards, quirky jewellery, religious objects, and more. He lives in New Orleans with his husband, the artist Grey Cross, and their cats.

Andy Davidson is the Bram Stoker Award-nominated author of *In the Valley of the Sun*, *The Boatman's Daughter,* and *The Hollow Kind*. His novels have been listed among NPR's Best Books, the New York Public Library's Best Adult Books of the Year, and *Esquire*'s Best Horror of the Year. His short stories have appeared online and in print journals, as well as numerous anthologies, most recently the Shirley Jackson Award-winning *Hideous Book of Hidden Horrors* from Bad Hand Books and Ellen Datlow's *Best Horror of the Year Volume 15*. Born and raised in Arkansas, he makes his home in Georgia, where he teaches creative writing. He lives with his wife, Crystal, and a bunch of cats.

Aaron Dries is a Bram Stoker and Shirley Jackson Award-nominated, and Ditmar, Australian Shadows and Aurealis Award-winning author based in Canberra, Australia. His novels include *House of Sighs*, *The Fallen Boys*, *A Place for Sinners*, *Where the Dead Go To Die* (with Mark Allan Gunnells), plus the novellas *The Sound of His Bones Breaking*, the highly acclaimed *Dirty Heads*, and *Vandal: Stories* *of Damage* with Kaaron Warren and J.S. Breukelaar. *Cut to Care: A Collection of Little Hurts* was described by author Paul Tremblay as "heartbreaking, frightening, and all too real". Dries is one host of the popular podcast, *Let the Cat In*, and co-founded Elsewhere Here Productions. His fiction, art, and films have been celebrated domestically and abroad. Aaron Dries is represented by the Annie Bomke Literary Agency and can be contacted at X @AaronDries / Insta and Threads on aarondries / TikTok @aarondries_writer and on Bluesky on @aarondries.bsky.social

Paul Finch is an ex-cop and journalist turned bestselling author. He first cut his literary teeth penning episodes of the TV drama, *The Bill*, and has written extensively in the horror, fantasy and historical epic genres, including for *Doctor Who*. However, he is best known for his crime/thriller novels, of which there are twelve to date, including the Heckenburg and Clayburn series with HarperCollins (the first Lucy Clayburn novel, *Strangers*, making the *Sunday Times Top 10*) and two stand-alone novels with Orion. Paul lives in Lancashire with his wife and business partner, Cathy.
Website: paulfinch-writer.blogspot.com

Christina Henry is a horror and dark fantasy author whose works include *The House that Horror Built*, *Good Girls Don't Die*, *Horseman*, *Near the Bone*, *The Ghost Tree*, *The Girl in Red*, *The Mermaid*, *Lost Boy*, the *Chronicles of Alice* series (*Alice*, *Red Queen* and *Looking Glass*) and the seven-book urban fantasy *Black Wings* series. Her short stories have been featured in the anthologies *Cursed*, *Twice Cursed*, *Giving the Devil His Due* and *Kicking It*. She enjoys running long distances, reading anything she can get her hands on and watching movies with samurai, zombies and/or subtitles in her spare time. She lives in Chicago with her husband and son. You can visit her on the web at christinahenry.net
Facebook: authorChristinaHenry
Threads: authorChristinaHenry
Instagram: authorChristinaHenry
Goodreads: goodreads.com/CHenryAuthor

Laurel Hightower is a bourbon-loving native of Lexington, Kentucky. She is the Bram Stoker-nominated author of *Whispers in the Dark*, *Crossroads*, *Below*, *Every Woman Knows This*, *Silent Key*, and the upcoming *The Day of the Door*, and has more than a dozen short fiction stories in print.

Verity Holloway lives in East Anglia. She is the author of the novels *The Others of Edenwell*, *Pseudotooth*, and *Beauty Secrets of the Martyrs*, the graphic novel *Gore*, and *The Mighty Healer*, a biography of her quack doctor ancestor. She writes folklore features for *Hellebore Zine* and her short fiction has appeared in *British Fantasy Society Horizons*, *The Shadow Booth*, and *The Ghastling*, among others. Find her at verityholloway.com and on Twitter/X as @verity_holloway.

Jim Horlock considers himself less of an odd duck and more of a wobbly goose. He loves all things dark and weird, and you can find his dark weird stories at The NoSleep Podcast, Crystal Lake Publishing, Eerie River and elsewhere. There might be one in the room with you right now. He also has a short horror collection of his own coming soon from Quill & Crow Press, and his first horror novel, *Masks*, is on the way too. Jim is a ghost collector, a cryptid enthusiast, and a wiki-hole spelunker. He also appreciates a good hat.

Gwendolyn Kiste is the three-time Bram Stoker Award-winning author of *The Rust Maidens*, *Reluctant Immortals*, *Boneset & Feathers*, *Pretty Marys All in a Row*, and *The Haunting of Velkwood*. Her short fiction and non-fiction have appeared in outlets including *Lit Hub*, *Nightmare*, *Best American Science Fiction and Fantasy*, *Vastarien*, *Tor Nightfire*, *The Lineup*, and *The Dark*. She's a Lambda Literary Award winner, and her fiction has also received the This Is Horror award for Novel of the Year as well as nominations for the Premios Kelvin, Ignotus, and Dragon Awards. Originally from Ohio, she now resides on an abandoned horse farm outside of Pittsburgh with her husband, their excitable calico cat, and not nearly enough ghosts. Find her online at gwendolynkiste.com

Annie Knox is an author based in London. Working primarily in genre fiction, she focuses on horror and all of its subgenres. Her previously published works include *Incorporeal Tax*, featured in *The Perfectly Fine Neighbourhood*, and *A Sister's Love*, featured in *Terrors from the Toybox*. Her favourite books include the *Monstrumologist* series, *Salem's Lot*, and *Jurassic Park* (yes, it was a book). Recently Annie started her own company, Snake Bite Books, looking to create a home for horror with an emphasis on interesting stories, deep emotion, and fun spookiness. Aside from writing scary stories, she is an amateur boxer!

Sarah Langan is an award-winning novelist and screenwriter. Her most recent novels are *A Better World* (April 2024) and *Good Neighbors* (February 2021), which Gabino Iglesias at NPR called: "One of the creepiest, most unnerving deconstructions of American suburbia I've ever read." She's won three Bram Stoker Awards for her fiction. Her previous novels are *The Keeper*, *The Missing*, and *Audrey's Door*. She has an MFA from Columbia University, an MS in Environmental Health Science/Toxicology from NYU, and lives in Los Angeles with her husband, the writer/director J.T. Petty, their two daughters, and two maniac rabbits. Mailing List: sarahlangan.com/contact.
Twitter: SarahVLangan1
Facebook: sarah.langan.90
Instagram: sarahlangan

Tim Lebbon is a *New York Times* bestselling writer from South Wales. He's had over forty novels published to date, and hundreds of novellas and short stories. His latest novel is *Among the Living*. He has won a World Fantasy Award and four British Fantasy Awards, as well as Bram Stoker, Scribe and Dragon Awards. He's recently worked on the new computer game *Resurgence*, acted as lead writer on a major Audible audio drama, and he's co-writing his first comic for Dark Horse. The movie of his novel *The Silence* debuted on Netflix in April 2019, and *Pay the Ghost* was released Halloween 2015. Tim is currently developing more novels, short stories, audio dramas, and projects for TV and the big screen. Find out more at: timlebbon.net

Will Maclean has been writing professionally for over fifteen years. As a comedy writer, he has written sketches, one-liners and gags for many of the leading lights of British comedy, such as Al Murray, Peter Serafinowicz, Tracey Ullman, and many others. He's also written a great deal of children's TV, writing for well-loved characters such as Shaun the Sheep and, on one occasion, Cookie Monster. He is perhaps best known as the author of McKitterick Prize-nominated novel *The Apparition Phase*, a 1970s set ghost story which utilises many of the tropes of popular hauntology. It was Will's idea to place one single word inside each of the one thousand limited edition Goldsboro editions of the book which, when put together, will make a short story, a stunt which generated worldwide interest in the novel. He's almost finished a new book, and, if his agent's reading this, it'll be with you soon, Alex, jeez.

Tim Major is a writer and freelance editor from York. His books include *Jekyll & Hyde: Consulting Detectives*, *Snakeskins*, *Hope Island*, three Sherlock Holmes novels, short story collection *And the House Lights Dim* and a monograph about the 1915 silent crime film, *Les Vampires*. Tim's short fiction has appeared in numerous magazines and anthologies, and has been selected for *Best of British Science Fiction*, *Best of British Fantasy* and *The Best Horror of the Year*. Find out more at timjmajor.com

Mark Morris (Editor) has written and edited over fifty novels, novellas, short story collections and anthologies. His script work includes audio dramas for *Doctor Who*, *Jago & Litefoot* and the *Hammer Chillers* series. Mark's recent work includes the *Obsidian Heart* trilogy, the original *Predator* novel *Stalking Shadows* (co-written with James A. Moore), the official novelisation of the Doctor Who sixtieth anniversary special *Wild Blue Yonder*, and the anthologies *New Fears* (winner of the British Fantasy Award for Best Anthology) and *New Fears 2* as editor. He's also written award-winning audio adaptations of the classic 1971 horror movie *Blood on Satan's Claw* and the M.R. James ghost story 'A View from a Hill'. His novel *That Which Stands Outside* was published in 2024 by Flame Tree Press.

Luigi Musolino was born in 1982 in the province of Turin, where he lives and works. He is the author of several short story collections of weird fiction, horror and rural gothic. His first novel *Eredità di Carne* was published by Acheron Books in 2019 and the novella *Pupille* was published by Zona 42 in 2021. He has translated works by Brian Keene, Lisa Mannetti, Michael Laimo and the autobiographical writings of H.P. Lovecraft into Italian. His latest publication in Italy, *Un buio diverso – Voci dai Necromilieus*, is published by Edizioni Hypnos. His works have also been published in the United States, Canada, Russia, Ireland, Hungary, Spain and South Africa. In 2022 Valancourt Books published the collection *A Different Darkness and Other Abominations*, a finalist in the 2023 World Fantasy Awards.

Kurt Newton's short fiction has appeared in numerous magazines and anthologies, including *Weird Tales*, *The Dark*, *Vastarien*, and *Cosmic Horror Monthly*. His most recent collection of short stories, *Bruises*, was published in 2023 by Lycan Valley Press. *Dreadful Seasons*, a collection of young adult horror, is scheduled to be published in late 2024 by PsychoToxin Press. He makes his home in the northeast corner of Connecticut, where nothing really scary ever happens.

Nicholas Royle is the author of five short story collections – *Mortality*, *Ornithology*, *The Dummy and Other Uncanny Stories*, *London Gothic* and *Manchester Uncanny* – and seven novels, most recently *First Novel*. He has edited more than two dozen anthologies and is series editor of *Best British Short Stories* for Salt, who also published his *White Spines: Confessions of a Book Collector* and follow-up volume *Shadow Lines: Searching For the Book Beyond the Shelf*. In 2009 he founded Nightjar Press, which continues to publish original short stories in the form of limited edition chapbooks. Forthcoming is Royle's third short story collection for Confingo Publishing, *Paris Fantastique*.

David J. Schow is a multiple award-winning West Coast writer. The latest of his ten novels is a hardboiled extravaganza called *The Big Crush* (2019), and the newest of his ten short story collections is *Suite 13* (2024). He has been a contributor to Storm King Comics'

John Carpenter's Tales for a Halloween Night since its very first issue, as well as three multi-issue graphic novels for *John Carpenter's Tales of Science Fiction* – *The Standoff* (2020), *HELL* (2021-22) and *The Envoy* (2024). He has written extensively for film (*The Crow*, *Leatherface: Texas Chainsaw Massacre III*, *The Hills Run Red*) and television (*Masters of Horror*, *Mob City*, *Creepshow*), and his non-fiction works include *The Outer Limits Companion* (1998), *The Art of Drew Struzan* (2010) and *The Outer Limits at 60* (2023). Thanks to him, the word 'splatterpunk' has been in the Oxford English Dictionary since 2002.

Paul Tremblay has won the Bram Stoker, British Fantasy, and Massachusetts Book awards and is the nationally bestselling author of *Horror Movie*, *The Beast You Are*, *The Pallbearers Club*, *Survivor Song*, *Growing Things and Other Stories*, *Disappearance at Devil's Rock*, *A Head Full of Ghosts*, and the crime novels *The Little Sleep* and *No Sleep Till Wonderland*. His novel *The Cabin at the End of the World* was adapted into the Universal Pictures film *Knock at the Cabin*. He lives outside Boston with his family.

P.C. Verrone is a writer of page and stage. His fiction has appeared in *FIYAH Magazine* and has won accolades from the Bridport Prize and Black Creatives Fund (We Need Diverse Books/Penguin Random House). His theatrical work has been featured on Off-Broadway and regional stages. His play *Crocodile Day*, a Native American reimagining of *Peter Pan*, was published by Playscripts in 2023. He was a Many Voices Fellow at the Playwrights' Center. He holds a BA from Harvard University and an MFA in Creative Writing from Rutgers University. He currently lives in Newark, New Jersey with his husband. Find him at pcverrone.com.

FLAME TREE PRESS
FICTION WITHOUT FRONTIERS
Award-Winning Authors & Original Voices

Flame Tree Press is the trade fiction imprint of Flame Tree Publishing, focusing on excellent writing in horror and the supernatural, crime and mystery, science fiction and fantasy. Our aim is to explore beyond the boundaries of the everyday, with tales from both award-winning authors and original voices.

.

Other titles in this series:
After Sundown
Beyond the Veil
Close to Midnight
Darkness Beckons

Flame Tree Press novels by Mark Morris:
That Which Stands Outside

Other horror and suspense titles available include:
October by Gregory Bastianelli
Sebastian by P.D. Cacek
Fellstones by Ramsey Campbell
The Lonely Lands by Ramsey Campbell
The Queen of the Cicadas by V. Castro
The After-Death of Caroline Rand by Catherine Cavendish
Five Deaths for Seven Songbirds by John Everson
The Wakening by JG Faherty
Dead Ends by Marc E. Fitch
One by One by D.W. Gillespie
Stoker's Wilde by Steven Hopstaken & Melissa Prusi
Demon Dagger by Russell James
The Raven by Jonathan Janz
We Are Monsters by Brian Kirk
Hearthstone Cottage by Frazer Lee
Those Who Came Before by J.H. Moncrieff
They Stalk the Night by Brian Moreland
The Intruders by Brian Pinkerton
August's Eyes by Glenn Rolfe
Misfits by Hunter Shea
Lord of the Feast by Tim Waggoner

.

Join our mailing list for free short stories, new release details, news about our authors and special promotions:

flametreepress.com